T0283541

NECROBANE

ALSO BY DANIEL M. FORD

The Warden

NECROBANE

DANIEL M. FORD

TOR

TOR PUBLISHING GROUP
NEW YORK

NECROBANE

Copyright © 2024 by Daniel M. Ford

Map by Jennifer Hanover

A Tor Book
Published by Tom Doherty Associates / Tor Publishing Group
120 Broadway
New York, NY 10271

www.tor-forge.com

Tor® is a registered trademark of Macmillan Publishing Group, LLC.

The Library of Congress Cataloging-in-Publication Data is available upon request.

ISBN 978-1-250-81568-2 (hardcover)
ISBN 978-1-250-81569-9 (ebook)

Our books may be purchased in bulk for promotional, educational, or business use. Please contact your local bookseller or the Macmillan Corporate and Premium Sales Department at 1-800-221-7945, extension 5442, or by email at MacmillanSpecialMarkets@macmillan.com.

First Edition: 2024

Printed in the United States of America

0 9 8 7 6 5 4 3 2 1

To Zach, Bobby, and Joey

Listen as carefully as Tun; be as curious as Maurenia;
be as bold as Timmuk. Unlike Aelis, when you're hurt, *rest*.

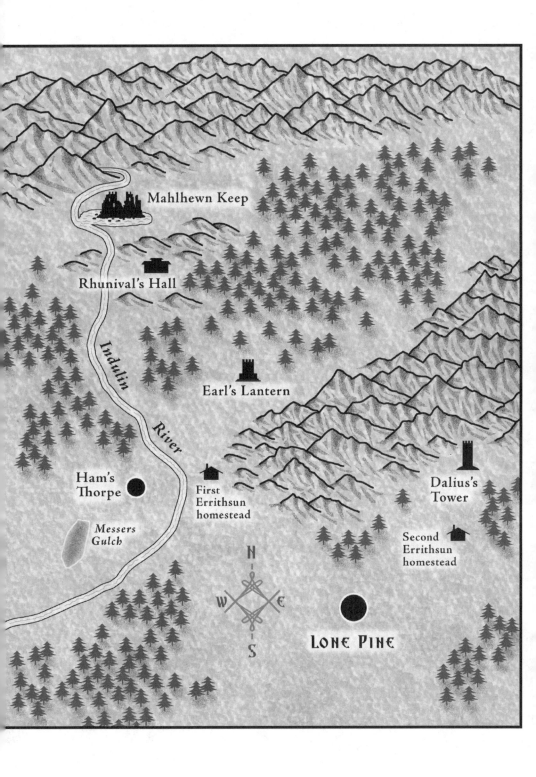

Mahlhewn Keep

Rhunival's Hall

Indulin River

Earl's Lantern

Ham's Thorpe

Messers Gulch

First Errithsun homestead

Dalius's Tower

Second Errithsun homestead

LONE PINE

N
W E
S

NECROBANE

1

THE FLIGHT

"Crypts?"

Aelis's own voice rebounded against the stone walls of the crumbling watchtower. It echoed even more loudly in her mind. Hurriedly, she threw her gear into her rucksack as she tried to process what that might mean. Doors all over Mahlgren like the one before her, with its blood bowl fastened into a skull with the jaw wide open, swinging open to reveal row after row of animated skeleton soldiers. Barracks-crypts emptying, releasing who knew what kind of spectral or corporeal undead mayhem into the wilderness, and more importantly, onto the farms, villages, and orc bands scattered throughout it.

These thoughts gave Aelis a burst of energy that could only be born of fear. She tightened her belt, lashed her stick to her pack, and ran.

In retrospect, she should've rested and then set off at a vigorous but manageable pace.

Aelis quashed her growing panic. She did not let herself try to count how many sites Duvhalin had marked for her on the map that led her here. She set out exactly on the trail she'd left, pumping her legs. For the first hour, she maintained a good pace. Certainly she'd eaten up a few miles at least.

But the exertions of the day had been the equal of many of her hardest days training at the Lyceum. And while Lavanalla and Bardun Jacques were perfectly capable of making a student feel like the threat of imminent death was real, it never truly had been.

Aelis was learning, quickly, that the heat of combat was a very different thing from any kind of training. The energy that had bloomed in her when the crypt's watch-spells had delivered their chilling message quickly dissolved.

The result was that an hour or so after setting out, her legs growing increasingly leaden, Aelis kicked one foot into the back of the other with a misstep and catapulted herself forward onto the muddy, foul-smelling ground.

"Onoma's frigid tits, I'm glad no one was around to see that," Aelis said around a mouthful of cold, brittle grass.

She pulled herself into a sitting position, yanked the walking stick Tun had made her from its lashings, and used it to lever herself to her feet. Aelis sighed as her feet took her weight; her right ankle protested. It wasn't badly hurt, but she'd kicked it hard when she went down, and an ache was settling in. She had a lingering suspicion that walking on it all the way back to Lone Pine wasn't going to do her any favors.

There also isn't any other way to get there, so start walking. Make a brace tonight.

So, shifting her stick to her right hand and matching every swing to her left foot, Aelis began walking—much more sensibly—south by southeast.

She made it another hour before the combination of the cold, the oncoming dark, and the ache settling into her ankle forced her to a halt.

A rising wind whipped her hair across her face, and she found herself wondering, not for the first time, why anyone lived this far north. *And it's not even properly winter yet*, she reminded herself. She was able to crest a small hill, thick with pine trees, and secure herself some shelter from the worst of the wind. With teeth gritted, Aelis remained on her feet as she dug a firepit and cleared it of needles.

"Setting the entire forest ablaze *might* slow down any oncoming dead," she murmured. "But thinking like an Invoker is not going to get me anywhere."

When she had a small and properly contained fire lit, she dug out her lantern and anatomist's bag and set them on her lap. Gingerly, she eased her right foot up into her lap and began probing the ankle.

"Not broken," she muttered. But it hurt, and it had stiffened, and it was going to hurt more after a few hours' rest.

"Nothing for it but a brace." Other options floated across the surface of her thoughts, half formed. She shoved them away before they turned coherent. There wasn't time, not here: not for alchemy, not for a serious crafting of a brace, not for any more significant Necromantic interventions. She briefly wondered if she could Enchant herself into simply not feeling the pain, but the anatomist in her knew that would lead to far worse damage in the long run. Pain was a warning, and a teacher.

Aelis pulled some cloth strips and some pieces of flat, stiff steel from her travel medical case. With the cloth she quickly bound the steel splints to either side of the sore parts of her ankle, her trained anatomist's fingers tying quick, secure knots. Then she wound more cloth around the initial strips, till her ankle was tightly bound and the steel pressed cold against her skin through her stockings.

"It'll do." Aelis dug deep into whatever reserves of energy she had left for one final ward; Bayard's Wakefulness. She was only able to extend it in a ring that barely went beyond herself and her fire, but if anything larger than a small dog crossed the space as she slept, it would wake her.

A bear would probably have the time to eat me before I woke, she thought, but before she could summon the will to argue with herself, she had already drifted off.

♦ ♦ ♦

Aelis's dreams were troubled. There were skeletons with points of all-too-bright fire in their eyes wielding swords that hadn't rusted away. There was Maurenia fighting them with her until the half-elf's own enormous green eyes had turned to ice-blue flame and the flesh over her cheeks sloughed away.

There were other animated corpses, driven by more than magical power, but by some inner force, like the one Aelis had put down at her Necromancer's test. She imagined she saw Archmagister Duvhalin looming over the shapeless battlefield, as if she were a game piece and he the player.

There were others in the battle, if that is what it was; the Dobrusz brothers, Otto, Elmo, even Pips. It wasn't quite a nightmare. Aelis had never been given to those; even in her dreams her power exerted control over her surroundings. But this treaded close.

Aelis woke startled. She had felt nothing and seen nothing to indicate that her Wakefulness had tripped. The sky was lightening, but only just.

With half a mind to look around her camp for tracks—animal or otherwise—she levered herself to her feet. Then Aelis imagined Tun's disapproving glare if she voiced such a thought.

"As if I'd know what to look for anyway," she muttered as she gathered her gear and shoveled dirt over her already-dead fire. When it came to the heavens, however, she did know. The sun wasn't visible over the treeline, but the green moon was a sliver high in the sky. *Still probably an hour till dawn,* she thought. *Nothing for it but to get walking.*

♦ ♦ ♦

The next three days were much the same, only colder. Though Aelis already wore the heaviest garments she had—and had slipped on what extra she had packed—she wished she had at least one more coat or another scarf to wrap over her ears and head. Or a horn of fire, or a brick set before a fire wrapped in a blanket and slipped into her pocket.

Wish in one hand, shit in the other, Bardun Jacques's voice sounded in her head. *And a handful of shit is the last thing I need,* she thought, as she pushed on. She was forced to stop more often than she would've liked to adjust the brace on her ankle. It had swollen considerably with all the work she'd put it to.

"This is going to require a week of light duty and careful healing, with pain management achieved via regular ingestion of fermented grape analgesic. Perhaps even *distilled* grape analgesic," she said. *As if I can even get drinkable brandy in Lone Pine,* she chided herself. "Not that it's going to matter," she added, going back to voicing her thoughts out loud, if only to hear something spoken. Aelis didn't much like silence, and there'd been almost nothing but for days now. "Because there's not going to be any light duty."

On the prior two days of her walk, Aelis had avoided running through the treatments she had for her ankle. As was typical with that kind of injury, the only true treatment was immobilization and rest, and neither of those was going to be possible. She knew that she could make a more effective brace with some of the tools in her tower. She could distill some potions and refine them effectively now that her calcination oven was operable.

The problem there, of course, was that she'd need a steady stream of painkillers, strong enough to keep her on her feet yet not dull her senses or her power. And such action was likely to compound the original injury.

"Can't perform surgery on myself, unless it comes to something really desperate," she muttered. Another option did occur to her. *An extremely short-term solution, at best.* But she was already trying to recall which chapter in *Advanced Necromancy* covered the deadening of flesh. She shoved the thought away as quickly as it came, or tried to.

With gritted teeth and a firm grip on her walking stick, she trudged on, feeling every patch of frozen mud and every cold, hard rock in the heel and up the back of her complaining foot.

She caught sight of the dim lights and chimney smoke of Lone Pine as the sun was setting on that third full day of walking. She had approached from the northwest and skirted her tower. As much as she wanted to head immediately for its familiarity—and the full range of medical options at her disposal there—she decided the inn was more warranted.

While she most wanted to tell Maurenia and Tun—in what order she couldn't quite decide—Martin and Rus had the pulse of the town and the measure of the folk in it.

"I can't tell them the whole thing, so I'd better start thinking about what I can tell them."

It was, of course, entirely possible that Lone Pine would face no threat. "But it's entirely possible that any further animated corpses, hybrids, constructs, or bound spirits will have some method of tracking an incursion or an enemy, and Onoma knows I did sweet fuck all to hide or disguise myself. Not that there was much I could do."

Bardun Jacques's words came to her in a flash. *Never stop in the middle of a fight or an investigation to start doubting yourself or second-guessing the action you've already taken.* "Don't be impulsive. But once you act, don't stop to think what you could've or should've done differently until your action is over. Dedicate your mind to what remains in front of you, not distracting it with what lies behind." Aelis muttered the words as she hobbled down the hill and prepared to dance lightly around the truth of where she'd been and what she'd been doing.

She tried to minimize her limp as she slowly made her way. It was late enough at night that only travelers and serious drinkers and layabouts, of which Lone Pine had few, would be up and about.

And she was right. As she swung open the inn's door, most of the lamps and rushlights had been doused. A few shapes huddled near the hearth, where even now another one—Rus, she was sure—was smooring the fire. As one, everyone silhouetted before the dim flames turned toward her, and their relative heights made it clear that she was looking at the Dobrusz brothers and two taller folks. *Unless other dwarves have come to town*, she thought.

"Warden?" Rus came forward, wiping his hands on his apron. "I'm afraid we've not got any hot food. Martin's already off to bed, but . . ."

"That's quite all right, Rus," Aelis answered, conscious of the constant ache in her ankle and the way it made her whole leg feel wooden. Rather than come forward, she stood in place. *Let them come to me. Command the room.* "I'm not hungry." A bald-faced lie; she was starving for something other than the dried rations she'd survived on for the past six days. "But I do have some news to pass on."

The Dobruszes—it was them, she could tell by the rumbling from Andresh, the dwarfish words she could never make out—came rolling up toward her. Maurenia, the tallest shape in the dim taproom, stayed a few paces distant.

"Something bad?" Rus's face came into focus. A bit sad, a bit worried, as it always was, but it was a determined face, too. A lived-in face.

"Well, it's not a parade of fairies farting gold and pissing ale into every pot that's held for them," Aelis said. "I don't want to get anyone too alarmed, but if the folk have got procedures for threats, they should start engaging them."

"You don't want folks to get alarmed, but you are telling them there's a threat? That'll alarm them a hell of a lot more than if you just tell us what's what, Warden," Rus said, rubbing a hand against his forehead.

"These folk aren't children," Timmuk said, while Andresh muttered behind him.

They're right, Aelis thought. *I'm going to have to tell them something.* "Rus, what I mean is, I'll lay out some steps folk should take. It's probably nothing to worry too much about. But if I could, I'd like to stay in the village tonight."

Behind him, Maurenia stirred. Rus made as if to speak, paused, and simply nodded.

"Of course, Warden, of course. No problem at all. I don't know that you'll be able to address the whole village at once, different folk going all about the place, but Martin and I'll try to gather what ears we can to listen to what you have to say."

"That would be a help," Aelis said. *And it allows me time to think of just how I'm going to lie to them, which is nice.*

"I'm off to bed then, unless anyone needs aught else?" Rus looked down at the dwarves and back over his shoulder at Maurenia, and when no answers were forthcoming, darted off to the dark kitchen and beyond.

"I'm going to assume," Timmuk began, "that you bear ill news that we will all be loath to hear. Is it best to save it for the morning? Will it keep, or must it be whispered in the dark around cold coals?"

"I think I need sleep if I'm to tell it correctly, Timmuk. But I am glad to find you here. I may have work for you."

"We are warranted to return south before too much longer, but exceptions could be made, at need. The morning, then."

And with the heavy footfalls of the dwarves receding, Aelis was left alone in the dark taproom with Maurenia, who moved to her side and took her hand. "How bad? Don't try to distract me with nonsense, either."

"Bad," Aelis whispered. "I think."

"On a scale from 'someone could get hurt' to 'it's the end of all things, so let's get drunk in bed'?"

Aelis chuckled ruefully. "Bad border skirmish," she said, after some thought, resisting the urge to lean against Maurenia's shoulder.

"A bad border skirmish might as well be the apocalypse to this village," Maurenia said. "Are there troops nearby that can be sent for?"

"Might be," Aelis said. "And if there are, I'll look for volunteers to go get them." She shifted her weight, and Maurenia's elfish eyes read her wince too well.

"You're hurt," she said, frowning.

"Nothing a bit of rest won't cure," Aelis said. Fatigue and hunger clashed in her, and with a different kind of hunger as Maurenia slipped an arm around her waist.

Going up the stairs was more of a chore than it should've been, and she found herself leaning on Maurenia despite her determination not to. Standing still had given her ankle time to stiffen and swell and generally become a bastard thing, and Aelis was keeping her foot clear of the floor by the time they made it into Maurenia's room.

Her impulse was to dump her stick, her pack, and all her other gear in a heap in a corner, as she would've done in her tower if no one was near. But Maurenia kept her spaces tidy as a rule; Aelis knew that much for certain. So, leaning against the wall, she set her stick in the corner, unslung her pack, and began fumbling at her swordbelt.

Before she got it off, Maurenia was behind her, encircling Aelis's waist with her arms. She dealt with the swordbelt first, laid the tooled calfskin with sword and dagger carefully on her small footlocker, then she was behind Aelis again, her hands strong and careful, urgent without being demanding or forceful. Before Aelis knew it, she was down to her chemise and her stockings and socks, and Maurenia was leading her to the bed. She sat down, quiet and unprotesting. Her skin felt warm despite the cold drafts in the room. Maurenia's hands lingered in places. Aelis's breath caught in her throat. She felt Maurenia's fingers stop at the strips of cloth bound over a brace around her ankle.

"I suppose prolonged bed rest is out of the question for this?"

"Afraid so," Aelis answered, her voice turning distant.

Maurenia made quick work of the brace. Aelis exhaled sharply as the half-elf's fingers probed the swollen skin. "This looks bad."

"I'll examine it in the morning. A few hours of sleep in a bed will set me right," Aelis murmured.

Maurenia prodded the ankle again. It was all Aelis could do not to yank her leg away from her touch. "Please let the medical professional deal with that."

Maurenia stood, her nose wrinkling, and leaned in close, her face inches from Aelis's. "I don't suppose there's any chance of getting a tub dragged out and water heated before you sleep tonight."

"Rus and Martin will hop if I call, but I won't," Aelis said. "Because I don't want to abuse their trust, and because if I sit in a tub with more than three inches of water in it right now, I will certainly drown."

"Drown?" Maurenia tilted her head to one side.

"I am going to fall asleep in a very short while whether I'm in a bath or otherwise."

"Fine. Into the bed with you then."

Maurenia gently pressed Aelis back upon the bedclothes. The rough mattress and homespun blankets felt as soft and luxurious as the finest sheets in her father's best palace. For a moment, she was dimly aware of Maurenia sliding in beside her, and then she was asleep.

2

PLANS, COUNCILS, AND BAD ANKLES

Aelis swam toward morning through a sea of half-remembered classes where the lecturers and her fellow students turned into animated corpses, their skin sloughing away, or malevolent spirits tearing out of their flesh like a bather shedding a robe. Over them all, the voice of Archmagister Duvhalin urged her on, berated her, criticized her form, her perceptions, her mastery of the Orders.

When she finally did wake, she was surprised not to find herself tangled in sweat-soaked blankets. Somehow, she expected her nightmarish dreams to have awoken Maurenia, who would be shaking her shoulder, worried, anxious to console her.

Instead, the half-elf was sleeping soundly, noiselessly.

The sun was only just up, a kind of barely discernible gray glow. She would've expected Maurenia to be the kind to be up before the sunrise, but in the time they'd spent together, she'd come to realize that the half-elf and the Dobrusz brothers viewed their jaunt as post-wagon drivers as a kind of holiday, a break from a hard lifestyle.

Aelis felt she couldn't afford to do the same. She sat up, trying to do so with a minimum of jostle. She made it out of the bed carefully enough, but then put her weight on her injured foot. Her ankle bent inward, collapsing under her. She caught herself against the wall with a sharply bitten-off "Fuck!"

Maurenia sat bolt upright in the bed and rolled off it with a knife in her hand. Aelis had no idea where the blade had come from. But instantly, the half-elf's eyes focused on Aelis, and she lowered the knife.

Aelis turned to her, raising a hand and beginning to murmur an apology. Maurenia caught the hand, waved away the apology, and leaned in as if to kiss her.

Maurenia broke away, waving a hand in the air. "Gods, your breath could stun an ox. None of that business till we've both bathed and scrubbed our teeth."

Aelis laughed, though largely to cover a sudden burst of shame. She tried to push herself off the wall, but her ankle was too tender to take her weight; she was forced to lean back against it.

Maurenia's strong arm slid around her back. Before she could stop herself, Aelis shrugged the arm away and hopped to the only chair.

Maurenia stepped away and went to the pile of Aelis's gear atop the room's single chest. She reached into the rucksack and pulled out the medical bag, then grabbed a roll of bandage and the metal strips—all neatly folded and piled—and brought them to Aelis, who hadn't done a great deal more than curse and fume at herself.

"I'll go and have a bath made ready," Maurenia said.

"There's no time. Not for a proper soak, anyway," Aelis said.

"Just what did you find out there, then? If you're going to be cryptic and dance around it, I'll go get that tub up here anyway. And I won't let you in it." Maurenia tried a smile. "You'll have to watch."

Aelis cut her mind off before it could run too far in that particular direction. "A high-ranking wizard sent me maps showing the locations of old barracks-crypts all over Old Ystain and directed me to neutralize them. I found one. A small one. I destroyed the animated corpses inside it."

"Sounds like victory to me. What's the problem?"

Aelis took a deep breath. "If I'm reading the signs right, when I opened one barracks-crypt, I opened them all."

Maurenia was not—and this was one reason Aelis found her so alluring—one to gawp or to waste time. She grasped a situation quickly, and had a gift for zeroing in on the information she needed.

"Define *all*. All in Mahlgren? All in Old Ystain? All on the entire continent?"

"I think somewhere between the first and the second. Certainly, *several* crypts were linked in one system. I had to . . ." Aelis hesitated. "To demonstrate my competence to gain entry to the first. Once I did that, I think the system assumed a catastrophe was imminent, or that I possessed a control device of some kind. It referred to *crypts*. The *crypts* were opened."

"Does the door swing both ways?" Maurenia held out the materials for Aelis's makeshift brace.

"That's the first thing I tried. No luck, again, not without some kind of control device. A rod, a stone, a scepter, who knows? Typically one of those, though." Aelis placed the first piece of steel against her ankle, wincing not only at the cold metal but at the pressure. Sucking in her breath to keep from gasping, she bound it quickly, then the second piece on the other side, and soon had her ankle tightly wrapped.

"So how many crypts opened, then? We're still not any closer to an answer."

"Frankly, two is too gods-damned many." Aelis stood, testing her ankle. It hurt enough that she bit the inside of her lip to keep from yelping, and tried to let the pain wash over her as she dressed. "All of those on the maps I have has to be my working assumption."

"And what are they going to do?"

"Some of them—perhaps as many as a quarter, a third if we are lucky— are going to crumble apart after years of disuse. It'll depend on the materials, what kind of animations or bindings we're dealing with. The rest? Spill forth and look for enemies."

"And what'll they find?"

"My tracks, for one. Possibly some roving orc hunters. A hibernating bear or two?" Aelis swallowed as she cinched her robes closed over her leggings and chemise. "And, much as I hate to say it, possibly Lone Pine."

"Aelis. If they find your tracks *and* orc bands, then orc bands will probably *also* find your tracks. If we take these numbers and add them together . . ."

"We get a gods-damned diplomatic breach, a border flare, a restart of hostilities." *Fuck. How did I not think of that? I was too focused on my first ring of consequences. I ignored the second and the third.*

"So, what do we do?"

Aelis sighed. "Let the town know so they can prepare a defense. I can send a message if need be, but no aid is going to arrive in time to matter."

"You've got mine. And Tun's, I wager."

"That's a start. The Dobrusz brothers?"

"I can talk them into it. Money would talk them into it faster."

"Then we'd better get started. I'll talk to Martin and Rus, ask them to gather the most reliable folk of the village, the veterans."

"And then?"

"I tell them what I need to tell them. Then . . . I don't know. But I need to gather resources, consult a book or two." Aelis heard Bardun Jacques's voice echoing in her mind. *Don't go running for the fucking books when there's a problem that needs* action. *Reading is not* acting.

Maurenia nodded. She gathered up the rest of Aelis's gear—swordbelt, rucksack—and helped her put it on, then went for her own clothes.

"We're not going to get on the road tonight," Aelis said as she headed for the door. "So don't pack everything."

"What are we going to do today, then?"

"Talk to the folk. Make a plan, get ready, pack. And, if you're still interested in a bath, the calcination oven in my tower can boil water in two minutes."

+ + +

Aelis asked Martin to spread the word to have Tun, Elmo, Otto, and Emilie come to the inn to speak with her. "And anyone else who is a veteran or can be trusted to keep their head in a crisis," she'd added.

"I can get the bulk of the village, or I can get Tun, but probably not both, or it'll take all day. They're too far apart," Martin had said, then Maurenia volunteered to go find the trapper.

Martin put on a heavy fleece coat and a shapeless hat, and set off into the cold morning. Maurenia, similarly bundled, left Aelis alone in the inn.

Aelis wandered outside, testing her ankle, hoping the morning wind might blow some of the stink off her skin. The ankle didn't feel any better, but it didn't seem worse, either. She could slowly hobble about without too much pain, but she'd never make it all the way to her tower.

She breathed in the frigid air, trying to find something beautiful in it, found it nearly intolerable if she wasn't generating some warmth by trying to walk swiftly through it. She wondered how the folk of Lone Pine, farmers and shepherds, would take to hearing that animated skeletons and assorted other undead horrors might be bearing down on their crofts and flocks.

"Warden."

Aelis turned, hissing as she pivoted on her bad ankle, to see Martin having snuck out of his kitchen, holding a mug in both hands, trailing fragrant steam. The mug teased her with a scent she'd almost forgotten.

"Martin," she said, "is that . . ."

He held out the mug to her, and as she took it, Aelis nearly forgot the pain in her ankle.

"This is the first cup of coffee I have seen since I left the last post-house," she muttered, holding it almost reverently.

"Didn't know we had any, but I was pokin' about and came across a small sack of the stuff that still smelled right. I think it was left here by a traveler last year. Seemed like the morning might call for it. I hope it suffices; I only ever drank the stuff when I had to, back in . . ." Here, Martin's narrow face fell and his eyes briefly darkened. "I hope it's good."

Aelis closed her eyes as she sipped the hot liquid. A hundred memories and past tastes flashed through her mind. The way coffee had been a mystery when she was very young, a morning ritual her older siblings had all been inducted into, but not her, until she finally choked down a half cup with as much sugar as she could spoon into it. How that had been the beginning of a lifelong reliance on the stuff, reaching for it at any hour, in all weather, hot or cold, black or with cream, with brandy or whiskey or one of dozens of liqueurs on offer at Tindayr's in Lascenice, with sugar and without. She liked it every way she'd ever had it.

On its own merits, this cup of thin brown coffee matched that available in Lyceum refectories at two in the morning. But here, on a windswept day on a village green months after her last cup of any coffee, it was perfect.

"It's delicious, Martin. Thank you." Aelis said the words and meant them more fully than she had probably meant any thanks she'd given anyone in Lone Pine since she'd come to take up her office there.

"Come back inside," he said. "There's fresh butter for the oats and I made a half pot of this . . ."

"I think I'd like to sip on this first cup out here, if I might," she said, bending for a second sip. She kept an eye on Martin, though, gauging his reaction. He shot a nervous look at the back door that led to his kitchen but then looked back to her.

"Didn't pick you for the kind to greet the morning in the cold air," he said, watching her, at least for a moment, the way a deer might watch a hunter who hadn't made any sudden moves yet.

"Oh, I've seen my share of sunrises," Aelis said. "Just usually from the wrong side." Martin chuckled and some of the wariness left his eyes, some tension slipped out of his shoulders.

"Have to be early risers here if we want to feed farmers."

"How'd you learn to cook?" Aelis took another careful sip from her mug. Her instinct was to gulp, heedless of scalding her tongue. In general, she was not inclined to small bites or dainty nips, but she was going to make her first cup in months *last*. There was also the fact that this was the longest she'd seen Martin out of his kitchen, much less out of doors, in the months she'd lived here, and she wanted to see how far she could draw him out.

"Self-defense after I took up with Rus," he said, slipping into a grin. "I love that man, and he has many fine qualities, but I learned fast never to let him touch a pan. He could burn salt."

Aelis laughed, and so did Martin, and she decided to venture on to a more significant question.

"Martin, how honest can I be with the folk here?"

"Completely, I hope." He looked around, then leaned close. "Warden, what is it? Something bad?" he whispered.

Who does he think is listening on a morning as cold and dark as Onoma's heart? "Yes. But I can't see how to say it without spreading panic."

"Warden . . ."

"Aelis," she said.

Martin licked his lips and tried out her name, drawing out both sylla-bles slowly. "Aelis." He swallowed. "We're not, as a rule, folk who are much given to panic. You can say what you need to say, straight on, and we'll find our way of dealing with it. After all, if there's some threat—some *new* threat—it's our lives and livelihoods in its way."

"I don't know, Martin, we're talking about something very dangerous . . ."

"Aelis. We may not be Abjurers, but we're not as fragile as you think."

Aelis nodded and decided then and there she'd be as open with these people as she possibly could. *They probably don't need the history of Dalius or to see Duvhalin's maps, but I can tell them what might be coming. And that it's my fault.*

He nodded in turn. "You can count on me, at need. I don't want to pick up a weapon again. But I know how."

"I hope it won't come to that. I'll do everything in my power to see that it doesn't."

He gave a longing look at the door to his kitchen. "Come on, Aelis. Eat some breakfast. Get off that foot you're favoring. D'you need a hand?"

"I'm fine," Aelis said, waving Martin away. Once his back was turned, she took cautious, pained steps back into the inn, careful to keep her mug steady.

♦　♦　♦

An hour later, full of Martin's boiled oats and butter that he'd promised, she'd had a bit more of a wash in what heated water his kitchen could spare. Nothing like a proper bath, but she didn't feel quite so grimy. She tightened her brace and practiced gritting her teeth against the pain so that no one else would notice.

For once, Aelis was grateful for what had always been one of the more annoying parts of her noble upbringing, that stiff-lipped carriage nonsense that said you couldn't ever show the world, especially not *other* classes, how you were feeling. Pain, hunger, fatigue, despair, lust, anger, and sorrow were all meant to be carefully examined *internally*, measured and dosed out in solitude.

"Was never any good at it," she muttered as she took a step here and there, practicing that vaunted de Lenti control with every muscle of her face as static as she could keep them.

There was a rap at the door and Maurenia, her cheeks flush with cold and exertion, looked in. "Full house downstairs. Martin didn't stop at Otto, Elmo, and Emilie."

"You find Tun?"

"More like he found me." Maurenia's face twisted sourly. "How does anyone that size move that quietly?"

"I haven't ruled out magic." Aelis looked for a moment at the walking stick Tun had made her propped against the wall in the corner. It'd make taking the stairs easier, but the people of Lone Pine knew well she wasn't an Invoker, and leaning on it would make her appear weaker in their eyes.

"Help me down the hall and the first couple of stairs, would you?"

"You're never making it to your tower, Aelis," Maurenia muttered as she got her arm around Aelis's shoulder.

Down the stairs they went, though, with Aelis disentangling herself before they were in view of the common room, which was more crowded than Aelis had expected, even with Maurenia's warning. Otto, Elmo, and Emilie sat at a table together, but she also saw Bruce and his wife, Ada, Matthias, several other farmers she knew by sight whose names she could come up with if she thought hard.

The Dobruszes were holding court before the hearth. Timmuk was, anyway, with Andresh mimicking the tale his brother told, girning his features behind his beard, flexing his arms, stomping forward at the gaggle of children gathered before him, scattering them with squeals of delighted terror. Pips, Otto and Elmo's niece, was so absorbed by whatever tale Timmuk was spinning that she didn't even look to see Aelis come in. During the winter, she'd let her hair grow from its short rough crop and she now had a fine head of tight black curls. She looked happier, healthier, cleaner than when Aelis had first met her, her dark skin, a contrast to her uncles, practically glowing in the light of the nearby fire.

Tun took up a corner of the room entirely on his own, prompting Aelis to wonder if she'd ever seen him inside any village building besides her tower and his own home.

As always, he was—on the surface, at least—a model of stillness so complete a painter would have had no cause for complaint while attempting a portrait. And yet there was a tightness in the way he sat, with his arms drawn up, his feet firmly upon the floor, that gave Aelis pause.

He's actually nervous, she thought. *I've never seen him nervous before. What could possibly make him nervous?* Then it came to her that she'd never seen him in a crowd before, and hardly indoors, and that had to be difficult. *I'm sorry, Tun,* she thought, *but I'm probably going to ask worse of you before this is over.*

Whatever tale Timmuk was telling had the audience so enthralled that no one paid much mind to their entry. Aelis took the opportunity to glide as quietly as she could around the edges of the crowd, working her way to the back to sit with Tun while Andresh roared and flexed his massive arms.

"You can barely walk, Warden," Tun whispered, his lips barely moving around his protruding teeth. "How are you going to manage the wilds?"

"Better than you're managing civilization, such as it is," Aelis hissed, half in pain and half in frustration, as she sat down. "What's the matter?"

Tun was silent for a moment. Aelis could overhear a snatch of Timmuk's story, something about fighting tentacled monstrosities on the frontier, with Andresh appearing to be both tentacled monstrosity and bold Dobrusz warrior facing off against it. Finally, in a voice so low she could barely hear, Tun spoke.

"Have you told the others about me?"

For once her tongue did not outrace her brain, and instead of blurting out *Told who what?* she thought through his words, biting her lower lip all the while.

"No," she said, as softly as she could manage. "Not my secret."

"Well, it seems like something they may soon need to know," Tun murmured.

"You'd know that best."

Tun made a small, noncommittal sound, and they were both silent as Timmuk finished his tale. With a final flourish and a bow, he cleared his throat and held one hand out to where Aelis sat.

"But, ladies and gentlemen of Lone Pine, please do turn your attention to your lovely Warden, who has called you here today." Andresh said something to his brother in their native tongue, and Timmuk responded, then added, "Our fine mime here has offered to provide wrestling lessons, free of charge, for any of the children who have the courage to face him on the green."

Andresh lifted his left arm and flexed it once more, the muscles bulging through his sleeves, then trotted off behind a crowd of children who looked like they wanted to begin the wrestling *immediately*. He paid about as much mind to their attempts to slow him down as an ox would a kitten.

Aelis cleared her throat while the village folk stood up and carried their chairs or stools closer to her or moved to the long benches beside the main tables that took up the middle of the taproom.

"I'm not going to lie to you, folk. Look around. Like as not, you have realized that everyone I asked to be here has military experience, and knows one end of a weapon from another."

"You're not here to draft us, are you?" Matthias said. Aelis hadn't known the older farmer, possibly the oldest man in Lone Pine, would be here. But if Rus had called on him, he must have had experience, or been considered trustworthy in a crisis.

"No. Just to warn you. And prepare you." She took another deep breath. "There's a chance—a slim chance, but a chance—that Lone Pine could be threatened in the coming days. By animated corpses."

Silence. Nobody reacted. No one batted an eye.

"By what now?" That was Otto, scratching at his stubbly neck. He was better dressed now than he'd been just two months ago, his clothes patched but the patches new and holding. Like his niece, both he and his brother looked better.

Aelis sighed. "Undead." *Onoma's Black Mercy, I hate imprecise terminology.*

That word set them jittering. Voices, some scared, some excited, some a mixture, all competing, shouting questions in one unintelligible mass until Aelis raised a hand to still them.

"As I said, it is a slim chance. Tomorrow, or the day after, I will leave with a few volunteers and try to intercept them before they come anywhere near this village or any other. This does not mean I'm leaving you to fend for yourself. My hope is that none of you are ever going to see a single skeleton."

"Saw enough of 'em the early days in the war," Otto said. "Was happy enough lettin' 'em go into battle ahead of us. Provided we didn't think too closely about who they were the week before."

"Regardless, I want those of you who have the experience to set up a watch. If this is going to distract from regular chores, I'm sorry. I can remunerate you for any losses incurred."

More blank stares. Maurenia, looming behind them all, didn't bother to hide her smirk.

"I'll pay you," Aelis said, "if you lose money, goods, animals, or crops because you do what I'm asking you to do. And I can provide you with a few helpful oddments before I go, I think."

"Weapons?" That was Emilie.

"Something like that," Aelis said. "If you have an organization or a plan for this kind of thing, for a crisis, now's the time to put it into practice. If you don't, it's time to make one."

"We'll figure that out," Rus said. He snapped a cloth against the wood of his bar. "But where might these undead be coming from, Warden?"

"And how many?" Emilie added.

"Hidden barracks-crypts remaining up in Old Ystain, around Mahlgren. My hope is they'll come looking for me, and by going off into the wilderness I'll keep them away." She took a deep breath. "How many? I can't say. One is too many, but there'll be a lot more than one. Animated skeletons are most likely, but there could be other things, worse things." Aelis took another deep breath and said the words she dreaded.

"I loosed them, unknowingly, while I was up north on Warden business." She forced herself to look up and meet faces that had turned stony. "But as *your* Warden, I promise you, I am going to fix this."

She looked around, hoping someone might say something, anything, but they stared at her with a mix of disbelief or, in Emilie's case, distrust written openly on a scowling face. Her eyes flicked over Elmo, whose face was drawn as if he was warring with something in himself.

Then he stood up. "I believe you, Warden." He looked around at the room, his throat working as he sought words. "If she wasn't here, Otto and I'd both be in the ground now, and the raising of Pips left to the rest of you." He looked back to Aelis. "You need a guide or a scout out there, I'm your man."

It took a great deal of de Lenti control to keep Aelis from smiling. She wasn't entirely sure she succeeded either, but she had control of her voice when she spoke.

"I thank you, deeply, Elmo, for volunteering. I think I already have a guide, and I believe everyone will need you here."

In the back corner, Tun may have barely inclined his head. Aelis couldn't be certain she hadn't imagined it, but she let the notion that Tun would come with her—wherever it was she was going—fill her with confidence.

"Now you know what might be coming," she said. "I have work to do, and so do you. Let's all be about it, eh?"

The meeting broke up in a clatter of benches and tables. Aelis, teeth still secretly gritted, stood and shook hands or slapped shoulders with everyone on their way out. Even Rus, who was bundled up again, slipped out, whether for some chore or just to give them privacy.

Once it was only her, Maurenia, Tun, and Timmuk, Aelis finally let out a heavy breath and slumped against the wall, lifting her throbbing foot clear of the floor.

Maurenia and Tun both took steps toward her, but Aelis waved them off.

"Aelis, should you really be . . ." Tun began, but Aelis stopped him with a pleading look.

"I'm the surgeon here, Tun. Once I get to my tower, I can fix this."

"You won't make it there," Maurenia said.

"I will," Aelis said, gritting her teeth once more and taking determined steps.

3

A BATH

Outside, Andresh was covered in shrieking children, at least one to each limb, who could not move him, much less drag him to the ground.

When he saw Aelis and the others emerge, though, he shook the children off none too gently into a convenient pile of snow, setting off a fresh round of shrieking, and joined them.

"Can I count on the four of you?" Aelis asked once Andresh had come within earshot.

"Of course," Tun rumbled. Maurenia answered by putting her hand on Aelis's back. Andresh spoke low and fast to Timmuk, who replied, then shrugged.

"I'm coming," Timmuk said, "though we'll have to talk terms. Andresh is going to stay. Peace of mind if the walking dead get this far."

Aelis decided to skip over her indignation at the words "walking dead" and looked to Andresh. "But nobody in Lone Pine speaks dwarfish, do they?"

"I do." An unexpected voice from a few yards behind her; Otto, leading a horse. His words didn't sink in at first, and she stared at him.

"I mean, I speak and understand his tongue. His accent's a bit off from the fella what taught it me, during the war," Otto said. "Thought I'd forgotten most of it, but havin' the pair of them around in the inn of an evening has brought it back."

"He's a regular scholar, this one," Timmuk agreed. "Still can't make a proper dwarf joke, but he'll come along. Any rate, Andresh isn't as much for traipsing about in the woods as I am, so he'll hang about here and clobber the last dried-up turd out of any corpse that shows itself. A little peace of mind while you're out of touch, Warden."

Andresh gave her a small salute, then patted the balled-up bicep of his right arm. Aelis laughed, then focused again on Otto and the horse he was leading, which she recognized as the docile Pansy, owned by Rus and Martin.

"Rus asks that I see you t'the tower on horseback. And then bring the horse back myself because he doesn't want her standin' out in the cold all night." Otto suddenly grimaced. "Not sure I was meant t'say that last part."

Aelis felt her cheeks color at the memory of her embarrassing lapse on her first night in Lone Pine, but she mounted the horse by leaning on Maurenia's shoulder, and bit her lip as her ankle throbbed. Maurenia and Tun walked behind, lapsing into quiet talk she forced herself not to eavesdrop on. She hoped the ride and the cold would dull the pain.

✦   ✦   ✦

It didn't.

She saw few people, the occasional child—bundled up under fleece, hide, and whatever scraps of fur they could afford—driving a flock of sheep or goats, who all looked as miserable as their herders.

By the time she reached the door to her tower and was helped out of the saddle by Tun, every movement was a stab of agony.

She fumbled with her purse and pressed some coins on Otto, who looked at her blankly.

"I'm not lookin' for coins, Warden," he muttered, a little insulted.

"I know," Aelis said, although she hadn't until he'd said as much. "Do me a favor and take them, please. Keep one yourself, against all the time and trouble you're going to, and try to slip the others to Rus. He's too quick to let me do it."

Otto didn't reach for the coins. "Warden, I know y'already paid for the repairs t'mine and Elmo's cottage, so if anything, I owe you. Maybe . . ." Here he bit his tongue and lowered his eyes; Aelis thought he was about to tug at a nonexistent forelock.

"What is it, Otto? You can say what you need to say to me."

"You could try saying thank you with words, instead of coin." With that, he took the horse's bridle and started off without looking back.

There was a lengthy silence, and Aelis hauled herself up the short ramp to her door, angry but not sure why or at whom. Tun and Maurenia followed at a distance of a few steps.

Her goat nemesis was standing before her new stout door, probably ready to piss on it, or on her. She didn't even have the strength to voice curses or threats, only to chase it away with the tip of her walking stick. Aelis leaned heavily against the door, still with the shine of new work about it. It was a long moment before she pushed into her tower, dispelling the simple ward she'd left on it with a murmured syllable.

She heard Maurenia and Tun muttering on the ramp outside and then the door closed, with only Maurenia following her in.

"Tun will be back later," Maurenia said as Aelis leaned against the wall and let her pack fall to the floor, her stick clattering after it. Maurenia frowned and picked them up, stopped to look at Aelis.

"Despite your best efforts, seems like some of these farmer folk are coming to like you. It's not going to hurt to try to like them back."

"I do," Aelis said in a tone that was both unconvincing and unconvinced. "But a Warden is supposed to be a little apart, a little distant."

"That might work other places. Not here."

"Let me focus on a problem I can solve." With one hand pressed against the wall, she hop-walked into the central room, going straight for her large medical kit.

"Fine," Maurenia said. "I'll put this rat's nest in some order for you, get fires lit." Maurenia squeezed Aelis's shoulder as she swung away.

Aelis took her case and dropped into the nearest chair.

She discarded the boot and stocking, and ripped her hasty brace free.

Aelis approached her ankle as she would if it were attached to someone else's leg. She hissed as she probed it with her fingers.

"Swollen," she muttered. "Painful to the touch. Tissue damage, not skeletal. Possible tendon damage. Going to examine with Anatomist's blade." She spoke aloud as she worked at a diagnosis, always, because she'd been taught to do so at the College of Necromancy. Had she been working as a surgeon and anatomist in some great city, or some noble's palace, as her father would have preferred, a scribe or apprentice would carefully note everything she said. As it was, it remained a matter of habit.

Aelis carefully rocked forward in the chair and unhooked her dagger from the back of her belt. She discarded the sheath and laid the blade carefully over the swollen ankle, tried to focus her attention through the hilt of the dagger to the magical tools built into it. Under ideal conditions—when she wasn't her own patient, when the temperature was precisely controlled by a nearby Evoker, when there were other Anatomists assisting and monitoring, with Onoma's moon full in the sky—she ought to be able to diagnose just by laying the dagger against the skin.

In her tower, grown cold with no fires lit, trying to block out the throbbing pain, trying to diagnose her own injury, and no moon in the sky, blade to skin contact wasn't going to be enough.

Aelis sucked in her breath and slipped the sharp point of the dagger into the skin of her leg, just above the swelling. The tip of the blade was so sharp that her skin parted like a folded-over sheet of fine paper and no blood welled up initially.

Still holding her breath, she delved through the blade into her leg.

No damage to the bones. Soft tissues are . . . She paused, searching for a word for the tears, contusions, and inflammation that suffused the muscles and connective tissues around her ankle.

"Fucked," she finally said, aloud, matter-of-fact. She was particularly afraid to check on the long tendon that was essential to the joint's function. It wasn't torn, thank Onoma.

But it was frayed.

This is not good. Can bind it up and dose myself for the pain for a day or two.

And by the time that's done the tendon will be good and torn, and you'll be hobbled.

Aelis considered her options. There wasn't a brace or splint or boot she knew how to make that was going to do a damned thing to stave off this injury. Rest and treatment. She cast her eyes over her bookshelves, lingering over Aldayim's *Advanced Necromancy.* A sudden thought struck her but was just as quickly driven out of her head when Maurenia looked up from the nearby fireplace. After carefully laying her kindling, she'd struck exactly one spark into it, and smoke was already curling up into the chimney.

"How bad?" Maurenia took a long step toward her, crouched in front of the chair.

"I've had worse," Aelis lied, casually, letting the hem of her robe fall over her ankle and setting the foot carefully down. She knew she didn't quite keep the wince off her features and saw Maurenia frowning at her. She ignored it, leaned forward to try to kiss Maurenia, who allowed it, but only for a moment before pulling away to seek Aelis's eyes with her own.

"You're trying to distract yourself from the problem."

"More like distract you from asking me about it. Is it working?" Aelis leaned forward again.

Maurenia pulled away and said, simply, "*Bath.*"

"Ah yes," Aelis said. "I believe I made some boasts about how quickly my calcination oven can heat water. We need to drag out the tub, scoop up some buckets of standing snow, and gather some stones—four or five about the size of your fist. I'll get the oven started."

"Why do you get the easy job?" Maurenia stood and Aelis stood with her, the half-elf's arm tightening about her back to both help her up and press their bodies close.

"Because I'm the walking wounded," Aelis said, trying to mingle sultry with a touch of vulnerable in her voice and the set of her eyes. It must have worked; Maurenia's arm tightened even more and she leaned close. For a moment, it seemed as if thoughts of a bath were forgotten. Then just as quickly, Maurenia disentangled herself.

"Fine. I'll get the snow and the rocks, but Tun will be back in two or three hours. This oven best not disappoint."

◆   ◆   ◆

It didn't. The tub Aelis's tower had come equipped with was certainly no luxury affair, with barely enough space for either of them at a time. But the oven heated enough rocks to keep the water hot for a long while, and kept the towels warm. They bathed separately, but with each other's keen assistance. Some time later, they sat against the thin headboard of Aelis's bed with a bottle of wine, their skin flushed and glowing still.

Silence reigned, but it didn't feel awkward. The seriousness of the coming tasks felt safely put off. Aelis took a swig from her bottle, letting the heavy luxury of the dry red fill her mouth before swallowing in a trickle. Impulsively, she sought out Maurenia's hand. Their fingers entwined. The half-elf's hand was calloused with years of soldiering, of adventuring, of work. Aelis was no stranger to working with her hands, but the rough strength of Maurenia's fingers surprised her.

And delighted you earlier, she told herself. Somehow, she found she could still blush.

"How will your ankle be?"

"Give it a day to rest, it'll be fine," Aelis said, with a conviction she did not at all feel.

"You are not as good a liar as you imagine."

She snorted. "Let me get my wand and I can *make* you believe it."

Maurenia laughed, but let go of Aelis's hand to take her chin and turn her face so that they were eye to eye. The half-elf's auburn hair shone in the light the tower let in, and Aelis felt herself staring at it. The firm grasp of Maurenia's fingers turned into a softer caress down the side of her neck.

"Do not do yourself lasting damage to satisfy the political whims of the soft and coddled living eight hundred warm miles from here."

Aelis captured Maurenia's hand again. "Duvhalin is too powerful for me to ignore. But it's gone further than simple political machination by an Archmagister," she said. "I am responsible for these people. I volunteered for this, believe it or not. *Fought* for it through five years at the Lyceum. I can't abandon it because my foot hurts."

"I think it's worse than your foot hurting. I don't think you would've stuck that dagger into your own skin if it was a simple matter of bracing it right." Maurenia turned and lay back against the pillow doubled up behind her. "Did you really volunteer to come to *Lone Pine?*"

Aelis laughed, had another swig of wine, then set the nearly empty bottle on the table beside the bed.

"No. I most definitely did not. But newly minted Wardens have no choice of assignment. We go where we are sent."

"Where do you want to be?"

"Right here." Aelis was a little surprised herself at the suddenness and earnestness of that reply.

"Flatterer." Maurenia's voice was arch but she scootched closer to Aelis in the bed. "Where did you want to be posted, then?"

"Antraval. Montistyr. Lascenise."

"City girl."

"Proud of it."

"Why? Luxuries? Warmth?"

"*People,*" Aelis said. "I like crowds."

Maurenia shook her head. "Crowds are dangerous."

"Thrilling," Aelis countered. "The mixing of bodies and ideas, the movement of trade, the music, the fashion, the artists . . ."

"The grifters. The cutpurses. The murderers. The gangs."

"See, at least there a Warden keeps busy." Aelis reached for her bottle again, draining about half of what was left. "Frankly, I'd happily go up against a ring of kidnappers or smugglers or even an assassins' guild compared to whatever it is that's going on out here."

"What *is* going on out here?"

"I don't know. I don't even know that it's an 'it,' really. But there are secrets in Old Ystain, in Mahlgren, that I think I'm only just starting to peek at. I'm not sure I'll ever see the full painting, or that I even want to."

"This related to the gold we found, then? The hidden storehouses of undead?"

"I don't know, but I can't rule it out. The hedge-wizard who said she made those coins was vastly more powerful than she had any right to be, and Dalius had something to do with her."

Just saying the name caused a twinge of pain in her stomach. Self-consciously, she felt for the scar his attack had left.

"Dalius?"

Aelis found herself telling Maurenia all of it; the apparent old hedge-wizard who'd accosted her with what she'd taken for weak illusion. How *something* had interfered with her thought process, her ability to remember him and tell anyone. How a stronger Dalius had attacked her, making grandiose claims, and nearly killed her. How, when alive, Dalius had split his very soul into pieces with a Sundering, and how the pieces of him coming back together into one had almost killed her.

She left out Ephraze's Withering, the semi-forbidden spell she'd used on him, but not that Dalius's body had disappeared by the time she and Tun had gone to look for it. That only reminded her that her orrery was sitting idle and she'd need to calibrate and set it that night.

"I wrote to the Lyceum asking for information on Mahlgren's history and on Dalius in particular. What I got back was the map with all these barracks-crypts. Yet Dalius was not a Necromancer. He said as much when he attacked me; that he had not 'known Necromancy' before."

"This Sundering you mentioned. Wouldn't that take Necromancy?"

"It would take a Necromancer, I'd think. However it was actually done, they don't teach us now. But the Necromancer wouldn't have to be the Sundered."

Maurenia was silent for a moment. "Has it occurred to you that the maps and the letter *were* the Lyceum's way of answering your query for information?"

"Archmagister Duvhalin always did enjoy setting a puzzle to a student or an underling."

"Good teacher, then?"

"Brilliant teacher. Terrible man."

"Why?"

"He's a scheming wretch with an eye for his own comfort and hidebound ideas about his college. In fact, I have a strong suspicion that he's responsible for my posting here. He lacks the conviction to clean up after schemes he may well have been involved in. Because he clings to outmoded ideas."

"Outmoded ideas?"

"Traditionally, women were not accepted into the College of Necromancy. The other colleges never had or rarely enforced such traditions, but Necromancy, the First Art, clung to them longer than anywhere else in the south. They couldn't deny me, but every single chance he got, Duvhalin reminded me that he didn't think I belonged. And I think he saw to it that I got posted here as one last dismissal."

"Didn't you just say that here's where you'd choose to be?"

"Here as in 'this bed,' yes. But if this bed could be relocated somewhere civilized . . ."

Maurenia chuckled and silence fell again. Aelis finished her wine and set the bottle aside with a final, wistful glance.

"Aelis," Maurenia said suddenly, "if this Duvhalin is responsible for posting you here, and he's also the one who sent you the maps to the crypts . . . has it occurred to you that he sent you here for something more than petty politics?"

"In the Lyceum, everything is politics. Where you sit in a lecture hall? Politics. Whose classes you sign up for? Politics. Who you drink with? Politics. Who you eat with? Politics. Who you fu . . ."

Maurenia cut her off by placing a finger lightly across her lips. "Aelis. You are undoubtedly brilliant. And you are also, sometimes, an idiot, and I think you should listen to what I'm suggesting."

"Listening," Aelis muttered, the word muffled by Maurenia's hand.

"Now. Since you've come here, you have uncovered some kind of ancient, mysterious wraith or revenant or sundered spirit of a legendary Warden, and defeated it using . . ."

"Necromancy," Aelis muttered. "But I don't think I killed him . . ."

"Shh." Maurenia took a breath. "And now you've uncovered a vast danger pointed straight at the frontier and the fragile peace with the orcs, consisting of the unquiet dead, which you are uniquely qualified to combat and destroy, yes?"

Aelis nodded.

"And yet you think that this Archmagister Duvhalin sent you here to serve a grudge? To punish you?" Maurenia removed her hand and rested her head upon one bent arm, shifting a pillow beneath her shoulder and looking expectantly down at Aelis.

"I . . . admit that you may be forcing me to reconsider my stance, a bit." Aelis sat up straighter. "But, if there was some reason for sending me here beyond the fact that he could, and he knew I'd hate it, then why not *tell* me that?"

"I can think of a dozen reasons. Plausible deniability, first. You aren't up to the task and die, no one can accuse him of sending a promising young Warden knowingly to their doom. Perhaps there's some aspect of all this he couldn't admit to knowing, which is, admittedly, a political reason, but more about him than about you. He might not have known, merely suspected, and hoped you would bird-dog it for him."

"Bird-dog?"

"Do exactly what you did. Seize on to the first glimpse you got of this mystery and run after it till you brought it down. Or were brought down by it." Maurenia went right back to her list. "Perhaps it's a part of a longer game against some political enemy, and he needs an independent third party to confirm something."

"Most of these possibilities still answer to the description of 'politics.'"

"That they do," Maurenia said. "But the thing you seem to be missing is that they all have one major difference from your petty revenge narrative." She looked at Aelis again. "They are not, in any special or particular way, about *you*, Aelis de Lenti."

"It's a bit difficult to think that it isn't."

"Is it? Isn't it possible that Duvhalin simply sent the best candidate he had? Or the only candidate? I'm simply saying this: The world and everyone in it are likely not out to get you, Aelis. Because, Wizard or not, Warden or not . . . the world, and most people in it, don't know or care that you exist."

"Well," Aelis said, feeling her cheeks flush, "this is a bit . . . humbling, I suppose."

"You," Maurenia said, "are not humble. And I didn't say you should be, either."

"You said that neither the world nor anyone in it knows or cares that I exist."

"No. I said most people didn't, because they don't." Maurenia leaned down close, till the ends of her hair—still slightly damp—ghosted across Aelis's face. "But I do. I noticed you the moment I rode into Lone Pine. And I have rarely stopped noticing you since."

Aelis pulled Maurenia to her, sliding one hand into her hair. Their mouths met, and for some time, conversation ceased. Before they could get too carried away, though, Maurenia pulled away. "We cannot simply lie abed the entire day."

"You are far too practical," Aelis groaned, but she rolled carefully to the edge of the bed and the medical kit she'd somehow had the forethought to set within reach and began preparing a much sturdier brace.

✦ ✦ ✦

Tun and Timmuk brought lunch to their planning session, fresh loaves and a kettle of stew with the top wired in place that the dwarf set easily over Aelis's fire to warm. The four of them ate, speaking of nothing much, till finally Tun cleared his throat.

"You did not ask us here just to have a pleasant meal and enjoy the fire."
Tun could always be counted on to be direct.

"No. I asked you here because we need to plan what we're going to do
about the undead—well, animated corpses anyway—I just loosed all over
Mahlgren."

Tun was the first to grasp the implications. His eyes widened, and he
stood up a little straighter.

"If any bands of hunters encounter roving undead, the consequences
would be . . ." He paused, searching for a word. "Dire."

"That they even exist is a violation of every peace agreement we made,"
Maurenia said. "That they're loosed in land ceded to them is to start the
war over again."

"It means orc longships raiding every river from the Archipelago
down to Mizanta. They will bring fire and axe like they never have before. Bad days. The *worst* days, because they'll come south out of the
land your kings ceded them, too, attacking from two sides. You think
Ystain is bad *now* . . ." Tun said, shaking his head as his voice rumbled
out of his chest.

"The existence of undead soldiers is also a violation of the laws of the
Crowns and the Estates House, though not technically in our lands anymore," Aelis said. "A good diplomat could make enough hay with this to
keep a war from starting for months, at least."

"That means nothing to the orc village or homestead or hunting band
these abominations destroy," Tun said. His voice was as slow and careful
as always, but there was something deep and implacable behind it, a note
Aelis rarely heard.

"I know that, Tun. I know. That is why I called you here. I'm a Warden.
The people of Lone Pine are my charges, not all three kingdoms; that's well
over my head. But I don't want to hole up here and pretend I don't know
something awful might happen somewhere else."

"I think you'd better go back to the start of this," Tun said.

Timmuk nodded his curled beard enthusiastically.

"Fine. With Tun's annotations on the maps, I went to what seemed the
nearest location I could reach," Aelis began. She told the story more or less
as it happened. When she glossed over destroying the eight skeletons she
found, Timmuk stopped her.

"Wait," Timmuk said, lifting a thick stub of a finger. "You kicked down
the door to a crypt of eight undead soldiers and did what?"

"Destroyed them." Aelis said simply. She watched the dwarf's face make plain his recalculations of her. She also couldn't help but spare a glance at Maurenia, who smiled faintly.

"Well, we've got the mighty wraith-slayer here," Timmuk suddenly said, slapping his knee. "How much trouble can a hundred of the things give you?"

The reputation was nice while it lasted, Aelis thought. "First, there were no wraiths—I'm not entirely sure what you mean by 'wraith,' but I've got a copy of *Taxonomy of Spirits* by Kiaw on my shelf if you want to narrow it down. What I fought were eight animated skeletons. And, to be quite honest," she went on, her cheeks coloring a bit, "two of them fell apart instantly, and I was able to destroy a third before it acted. There were some complexities to how they were created," she added, uncertain how to explain this to laymen. She held up a hand for pause as she thought.

"In small units, corpses animated the way these were will grow more dangerous as their barracks-mates are destroyed. That kind of feature *shouldn't* pass beyond small units. Ten is the largest reasonable number that could be applied to."

"Will they coordinate? Form units? Move coherently? Choose targets?" Maurenia shifted in her chair.

"I don't know. Simple animated corpses can only hold a few orders at a time. They'll ignore commands that are too complex, but a properly encoded command will stick until the corpse is destroyed."

"Are all the crypts likely to be full of the same sort of undead? Simple skeletons?" As always when he was concentrating, Tun was utterly still. His voice practically emanated from the air.

"If you were building an army," Aelis said, "would you fill it with spearmen only?"

Three voices suddenly filled the air, everyone asking her what else to expect. Aelis lifted an eyebrow, copying the mannerism from Urizen's response to a student speaking without being called upon. She was so delighted when they instantly silenced themselves that she had to work to keep from grinning.

"I do not know what other kinds of animations or undead or malevolent spirits might be populating Mahlgren's other barracks-crypts. I can consult some books and make educated guesses. Animated skeletons are the most likely, to be sure. Sandbags will have rotted away unless the climate they were stored in is very controlled. Exotics are always possible, and one has to hope that any spirit bound away for this long has surely abandoned its post."

"Stop," Tun said, and everyone turned to him. "Sandbags? Exotics?"

Aelis cleared her throat. "Sometimes, depending on the corpses available, a Necromancer could . . . animate the skin or musculature separately from the skeleton. If the skin is more or less intact, you fill it with sand or dirt or straw . . ."

That she could read the rising signs of anger in Tun—the way he sat up straighter, the tiny tightening of his lips over his tusks, the crinkling of the skin around his eyes—was worrisome.

"Explain *exotics*, please."

"Animal corpses. Horses. Oxen. Perhaps mixed with human parts to hold weapons, but my understanding is hybridization never worked well . . ."

By the time "hybridization" was out of her mouth, Aelis wanted to cram it back in. Tun stood up and bolted out the door, moving faster than her ability to correct herself.

Aelis shot to her feet to follow him and the pain that sliced through her ankle almost sent her tumbling to the floor; Maurenia caught her arm. She nodded her thanks, shrugged her arm away, and hopped after Tun.

By the time she got to the door, he was loping steadily away.

"Tun! Please!"

He turned toward her, his chest heaving rapidly as he took deep, fast breaths.

"Tun," she said again, "whatever I said, I'm sorry." *You know gods-damned well what you said.* "But I need your help. I need it more than anyone else's."

"I know you do," he said, cutting the distance between them in half with a few steps. "Hearing some of the terms . . . sandbag, exotic . . . it was driving me to an anger past the point of safety."

"Tun, I do not make undead. I do not animate corpses."

"But you know how."

Aelis nodded.

"Not all knowledge is worth having. That is something your wizards cannot seem to grasp. Some things are sacred. Do you understand that?"

"Tun," Aelis said, feeling the cold air stirring her hair, her robe, and cutting into her skin. "I understand that better than you think. You told me once that there is very little you hold sacred, but that destroying the Demon Tree, or dying in the attempt, was one such thing. *That* is how I feel about these animations. I did not make them. But I will destroy them. As a wizard, as a surgeon, as a swordswoman: at the bottom of everything, Tun, I don't pervert death to serve my own power. I *fight* it. I am a Necrobane."

She paused for a stinging breath. "Which is to say, if I have to try to do this without you, I will. I must. Don't make me."

Tun lifted his head. The wind stirred his long braids as his breathing slowed. He looked back at her.

"I will ask you—one day, not now—if you have ever done it."

"Done what?"

"Raised the dead."

Animated, Aelis almost corrected. For once, she swallowed ill-considered words rather than spitting them out.

"One day, I will ask. And you will tell me honestly."

She nodded. "What will happen if you don't like the answer?"

"I will be angry." There was a pause, filled with the rush of the wind. "You should hope that I will not also be hungry."

Aelis looked at him for any sign that he was joking. His face was as still as if it were carved from wood.

He took a step toward her and pinched her arm speculatively with two fingers. "Hardly enough fat on you to make the meal worth it," he sniffed.

Tun ushered her back in—they couldn't both fit through the doorway simultaneously—but did not resume his seat. He chose instead to loom over them.

Aelis sank gratefully back into her seat, extending her bare foot out in front of her.

"Does each animated construct need to be destroyed in detail?" This question from Timmuk, who tapped idly at the table with his spoon.

"That depends on whether Mahlgren had a control rod. It was standard practice for any fief raising undead troops to key their animation to one artifact. If they were feeling fanciful, perhaps an orb or a circlet, but a rod or a scepter was standard. But I have no way of knowing for certain that they made one, where it was stored, or if it still exists."

"So, to sum up," Maurenia said, "you loosed multiple undead forces across the former Earldom of Mahlgren. If they encounter any orcs, they'll almost certainly attack them. If they come across any non-orc settlements—ignoring the fact that there aren't supposed to be any—the folk will probably panic and attack them. And if they do manage to track you back to Lone Pine, they'll attack."

"That's . . . fairly comprehensive," Aelis admitted.

"Well," Maurenia said, "there's only one thing to do." All eyes turned to her. "Go on the offensive."

"We're not an army," Timmuk said. "That's not a plan."

"We don't need to be an army," Maurenia said. "And perhaps *offensive* was the wrong word. You said there's a control rod, one device that can stop them all. We need to find that, end this all in one moment."

"We don't know where it is," Aelis said.

"At the very least, we need to make a fallback position in the pass and take them on as they try to come through it," Timmuk added.

"You dwarves and your desire to turn everything into a siege just so you don't have to move." Maurenia waved away the suggestion with one hand.

"It's not entirely without merit," Tun carefully put in. "But I think you are right, Maurenia. Our advantages, such as they are, are speed and stealth." He looked at Aelis. "Where would that control rod be?" Tun's voice was the quietest among them, but everyone—including Aelis— focused their attention when he spoke.

"A strong military position," Timmuk said. "A command post, wherever the lines stood when the tri-crowns were forced to give up their undead armies."

"No," Aelis said. "Somewhere near the channels of power. Somewhere Dalius and any wizards or wardens serving under him could get their hands on it if they needed to."

"Mahlhewn Keep, then. It has to be. Get out the maps." Maurenia sat down next to Aelis and wiped some imaginary dust off the table, making space for the map fragments Aelis carried.

"If a control rod is there, likely some of the animations will be drawn to it, expecting more orders." Aelis felt apprehension growing in her stomach as she unfolded the fragments and laid them on the table.

"All the more reason for us to go there," Tun said. "We can put more of them down even if we don't find the device."

"I suppose." Aelis looked at the map, sliding the fragments together and thinking of old history lessons, trying not to dwell too much on why she *didn't* want to travel to Mahlhewn. She wasn't sure she knew herself, but the flare of pain beneath the scars on her stomach told her she just didn't want to *admit* that she knew.

"Have you got a better idea?" Maurenia fixed her eyes on Aelis, who for once did not find herself distracted by them.

"I don't. Just an awful lot of uncertainty in the choice. If we go that far and find nothing, we've left Lone Pine to its own defenses."

"Well," Tun drawled, "is there anything you can do to narrow the odds here?"

Aelis thought for a moment, holding up one hand for silence. *I've got silver wire, a calcination oven, and a few other things that might do.* "I think there might be," she said. "I can give the folk a bit of a difference maker."

"Andresh will build a wall of twice-killed corpses before any get past him," Timmuk said.

"That might be overstating it, but Andresh is something," Maurenia said. "And the Lone Pine folk won't give up what they're building without a fight."

"What are the chances the control device no longer exists?" asked Tun.

"Very slim," Aelis said. "An object enchanted with as much power as this is likely to persist well beyond mere decades."

"And there's nothing you can do to track it? It doesn't, I don't know, send out some kind of signature into the aether, like smoke from a meta-physical fire?"

Timmuk chuckled at Tun's question, and Maurenia's eyes lit on her again, but Aelis could only shake her head.

"I'm no Diviner. Even if I was, I don't know what I'm looking for. I don't know that any living wizard could uncover a secret like that from this dis-tance. The histories might suggest a few of the first ancient elven Diviners who could have." Aelis shrugged. "But those are merely stories."

"Then there's nothing for it but to set off in the morning and make our way straight for Mahlhewn Keep," Timmuk said.

"Straight is an overstatement," Tun said. "It involves too many moun-tain summits for this time of year. The passes should be navigable. More or less."

Aelis wrote off her own doubts, and the needles she felt in her stomach. "Right. Mahlhewn in the morning."

"Best dress warm," Timmuk said.

"I have some hides that might do," Tun said. "And some wool blankets I've gotten in trade. Cut a hole in the latter, belt it around yourself, layer hides over that. They're cured but not cut. You won't care much about fash-ion when we move north. Before sunrise?"

"At my tower," Aelis said. *If I have to get up that fucking early, at least I'm not going to walk a mile south only to turn back north again.* As if in warning, she felt pain throb up her ankle so that she was forced to grind her teeth to swallow a yelp.

If any of them noticed, they did her the courtesy of not mentioning it.

4

SOAP

Aelis leaned heavily on one of her worktables, an array of alchemical equipment spread out before her. The ring was lit, burning with a bright blue flame, and the calcination oven, working at its highest setting, was heating the entire bottom floor. Aelis wished she could use the alchemical equipment for its heat, but running it that much would chew through her winter's supply of firewood in a week, two at most. The noise of it was a steady background roar. Aelis watched the large jar clamped above her ring on an armature and willed it to boil. After an interminable wait, small bubbles began to pop on the surface.

Aelis rooted in a trunk beneath the table and pulled free a black cloth bundle wrapped shut with twine. She set it down carefully and unwrapped strands of pure silver that, all told, were probably worth more than the entire contents of the village of Lone Pine. She took two of them—wires about six inches long—rolled them tightly and stuffed them inside a stone crucible onto which she fitted a cap.

Then, donning a makeshift face shield she'd gotten Harlond, the village pot-mender, to hammer out for her, and a leather apron and large, heavy leather gloves, she picked up the crucible and went to her oven. She took a deep breath and swung open the door.

It was like taking a red-hot anvil to the face. While the oven itself was relatively large, the space inside it wasn't even the size of a small hearth and was walled off with tiles that glowed orange. Being careful not to so much as brush against them, Aelis deposited the crucible inside.

She slammed the door shut and slipped off the face shield—she thought it had once been a pot lid, and it smelled of fat and rust—then set it where she could reach it.

She kept a careful count in her head as she crossed back to the table and lifted the glass jar, now merrily bubbling, off the heat and set it down on a woven pad. *Ten.* She bent to the trunk and pulled out a rectangular block of bright copper and a jar of soft white flakes. She unthreaded the top, set it down. *Twenty.* She picked up a set of clamps and put the reeking face shield back on. At precisely the moment her internal countdown reached thirty, she opened the oven. With the clamps, she retrieved the crucible—now glowing similarly to the tiles—and shut the door with an elbow.

By the time she set the crucible down on the stone worktable and dispensed with clamps, shield, and gloves, it had ceased to glow and returned to its eggshell color.

She took a deep breath and seized it with one hand.

She never, ever quite got over how quickly alchemical stone cooled and always had to steel herself to use it.

Aelis carefully removed its cap and looked at what had become of her pure silver.

It was a pile of ash.

With a nod of satisfaction, she upended the calcinated silver ash into the jar of still bubbling active solution.

There was a visible and audible fizz. But more importantly, there was a tingle in the air, in her skin, a buzzing at the base of her skull. She added a pinch of flakes from the jar, coaxing them out with a careful shake.

She could see the thickening of the liquid. Immediately, she flipped open the copper block and poured her concoction into the mold built into it.

Once inside the copper mold in four more or less equal portions, the liquid began to visibly thicken and cool.

Aelis took a deep breath to admire the fruit of her labor, small though it was. She was threading the cap back onto the jar of flakes when her door swung open. She could already recognize Maurenia's footfalls on the stone floor. She looked toward the entrance to the central room just as Maurenia was about to cross the threshold, a basket under her arm.

"You've been busy," she said, taking a small step into the room.

Aelis held up a hand to stop her. "You don't want to get close until I've got all the materials put away. You don't want this," she said, giving the jar a gentle shake, "anywhere near food or exposed skin. Trust me."

"What is it?"

"Extremely caustic alchemical salts."

"And what'll it do?"

"Burn right through your clothing and into your skin. Well, technically, deliquesce all the moisture in your skin, but the effect is roughly the same and, I would assume, deeply unpleasant. And I prefer your skin exactly as it is."

Maurenia chuckled. "And what're you making with caustic alchemical salts?"

Aelis bent down to begin storing away her materials, snuffed out the flame of her alchemical ring, and set gloves, apron, and pincers down together along one edge of the table.

"Soap."

"Not that many of the folk of Lone Pine couldn't use rather more soap in their lives, but exactly what is its use if animated corpses attack them?"

Aelis chuckled as she began wiping her hands carefully on an absorbent cloth. "This isn't soap you'd want to bathe with. Well, bathe a wound maybe, especially one that had gone necrotic. Do you want to know why?"

Maurenia grimaced but didn't say a word.

"Because," Aelis said sweetly, "this 'soap' is laced with activated silver, which will erode any necrotic tissue it comes in contact with."

Maurenia's face perked up considerably. "Well. That's a fine undead corrective to have in your back pocket."

"Indeed it is," Aelis agreed. "However, we are going to be leaving three quarters of it here with them."

"They'll need it more," Maurenia said with a nod.

Aelis finished squaring her alchemical gear away and hop-limped over to Maurenia's side. Without waiting, without asking, she put an arm around the taller woman's waist and sought her lips.

"How in seven hells are you going to go forth after the undead on that ankle?"

"I have an idea."

"It's not Tun and Timmuk taking turns carrying you, is it?"

"No, no no. It's very boring and technical Anatomist nonsense. I can do it while you pack our gear."

"Why am I packing for both of us?"

"Because if I do it, you'll watch and criticize and then get frustrated and do it yourself *anyway*." Maurenia frowned hard at her but had no retort, and retreated from Aelis's worktable.

Once Maurenia was safely involved in her meticulous packing, a practice that meant ruthless selection of items based on their weight, necessity, and redundancy, Aelis hopped to her bookshelf.

Aldayim's *Advanced Necromancy* was right where she'd left it. It fit in her hand as easily as anything ever had; she knew the cracks in the spine, the feel of the leather of the cover, where the book was likely to fall open. She pulled shut one of the curtains used to divide the large round room that made up the bulk of her living quarters and sat down. She flipped the book open, scanning the table of contents, looking for a chapter she hadn't often read.

"Necromancy and Advanced Medical Intervention." In one of the slightly archaic literary flourishes of which Aldayim was fond, there was a subtitle: "Deathly Magic and Living Flesh."

Aelis flipped to the page.

+   +   +

As usual, Aelis got so immersed in her reading that she didn't hear Maurenia steal up on her. "Looking for treatment options or just passing the time?" Maurenia said, tapping the cover of the book.

Aelis was still in enough control that she didn't jump out of her seat, but she started and slapped the book down on her lap like she had something to hide. "Both. Aldayim has plenty to say to the anatomist and surgeon. And reading, even a book I know as well as this, always transports me."

"Hmph. Never had much use for it myself. Rather work with my hands. Give me a singer or a good pantomime if I must have a story."

"Aldayim is not a great storyteller by anyone's measure," Aelis said. "But he *was* the most important Necromancer who ever lived. He was among the first to realize that the magic of death could be turned to medicine, but he was *certainly* the first to systematize and codify how one might do so. He was a genius, and the world is a bit better for his efforts."

"He have an answer for your ankle?"

"Could be. Maybe a small procedure before morning," Aelis said, injecting a brightness she did not at all feel into her words.

"Well," Maurenia said, "best get to it. If I know Timmuk, he'll be telling stories of the walking dead before night is hard upon us. Too much showman in him."

"If he terrifies the people with stories of animations pouring down out of the frontier, I will turn him into a skeleton and a sandbag both."

"You know, it is a bit worrying how casually you throw around those words." There was a pause. "Do you actually know *how* to do that? Turn one body into two undead?"

"Three on a good day, with his help," Aelis said, tapping the book. "But before you ask your next question, I have no intention of making any animations of my own."

"I can see the temptation of it, in a crisis of manpower. Turn over manual labor—the digging, the hauling, the rowing—to soldiers who won't tire, don't eat, won't complain."

"In fact, repetitive manual labor is generally a poor use for animated bodies because the wear and tear will degrade them very quickly. Better to use them as shock troops, throw them right into the fight." She stopped as she could see the musing look on Maurenia's fine features disintegrating into worry. "I'm sorry," she said, almost plaintively. "The practice is banned, yes. But the knowledge of it still makes up a chunk of the curriculum in the college of Necromancy. That I know all this does not mean I'm eager to try raising my own servitors or soldiers."

Another pause. "Have you ever done it?"

Aelis thought for a moment of prevaricating, of saying that Maurenia needed to be more specific as to what *it* meant. Instead, she just said, "Yes. Once. In a laboratory, under controlled conditions. Everyone who graduates the college must." Before her inhaled breath could become yet another pause, she added, "The bodies used are only those donated to the college by those who understand what it will be used for."

"Why would someone give up a body, their own or a family member's, for that?"

"Probably felt a debt to the college. Maybe a college-trained surgeon oversaw a difficult birth for the family once. Maybe a man came to the butcher's tents during the war with a foot of arrow in his intestines and only lived because a Necromancer was there."

Maurenia nodded, placed a hand on Aelis's knee. "I'm sorry for the questions. I should know that's what you do. But . . . I went into battle alongside an undead company once. I didn't like it." Maurenia paused but let her hand linger. "I've taken on risks in my life as a sailor and a soldier both. Knew either one could kill me. But it felt important that it was my *choice*, you understand? That was always most important to me. My choice. If I had fallen and the Necromancers with the company had scooped up my remains, it'd no longer be that. Didn't seem right, thinking I might be turned into one of them."

"Maybe two of them," Aelis couldn't help jibing. Maurenia swatted playfully at her, and Aelis's impulse was to grab Maurenia and pull her to the chair, tangle up with her again. But the day and its duties awaited. So she settled for holding her hands out and said, "Help me up."

As Maurenia held her steady, Aelis went on. "You go see to Timmuk and warn him off getting too vivid with his tales. I'm going to spend just an hour or two with Aldayim. I'll meet you at the inn."

Maurenia narrowed her eyes. "You won't be able to walk down there alone."

"Care to wager?"

Maurenia's eyes flared dangerously. "A half dozen of your precious Tirravalan orange, going with me when I leave, or sent back here at my expense."

"Done," Aelis said, though her face must've fallen, for Maurenia leaned close.

"I can't stay in any one place too long, Aelis. It's not in my nature. Not even if you're in it. But I'll come back."

They kissed, lingered, though not nearly so long as Aelis wished.

Once Maurenia was gone and her footsteps had sounded down the ramp, Aelis picked up *Advanced Necromancy* and opened to the page marked with the black silk ribbon, glancing at the subheading she wanted.

Necrotization.

In an emergency, the temporary necrotization of living flesh into functional animated parts is possible, especially in the case of sinews and joints . . .

◆   ◆   ◆

It didn't take nearly as long as she expected, really. Not with her dagger pricking the back of her leg and Aldayim's words on the subject to guide her. She had time enough to dig out her calculation books and prepare to set her orrery to rights when she realized she was leaving again the next day and it was unlikely to matter whether it was running for the next two or three days. No one would be here to answer any message, and nobody but her would ever use it as a reservoir for a complicated ritual or casting.

Aelis still expected every step she took around the tower to hurt; learning to trust her newly healed ankle was going to take a little time.

Healed is an odd way to describe it, she thought. She also gathered her strongest-smelling liniment and applied it, and wrapped the brace back around it, not dwelling on what these small deceptions said about what she'd just done. It was one of a long list of things she was filing as *figure out later.*

◆   ◆   ◆

She surprised Timmuk, Andresh, and Maurenia at the inn, with only a small crowd lingering over an early dinner. They were expecting a Dobrusz brothers performance like the one in the morning, but everyone was subdued. Pointedly, she walked past them, making sure to demonstrate how easily she moved, and approached Rus at the bar, trying not to grimace as she found Emilie seated there.

She produced a bundle wrapped carefully in cloth, which she unfolded to reveal three of the cakes she'd made that morning. She held one aloft, admiring the tiny sparkling flakes of activated silver within the light brown block.

No one else was impressed, it seemed.

"Looks like soap." Emilie didn't quite sneer at her, but there was a willingness toward contempt in her voice and stance.

"It is, essentially. But you wouldn't want to bathe with it. Instead, if, IF, mind you, you have to come to blows with any animated corpses—any undead—you wipe this across your weapon. Your spear, your club, your arrow, whatever you've got to hand. Not a lot, just enough to coat the business end till you can just see it."

"And what'll that do to an undead?" Rus stopped his endless polishing and leaned forward, squinting at the cake of soap.

"Hurt them very badly. Sever limbs and tendons. Disrupt their ability to fight and function."

"How's soap do that?"

The activated silver interferes with the necromantic energy expended to hold them together, and soap is the best, most durable, most easily applied suspension I could come up with. It's essentially one of those happy moments where an old wives' tale is true; silver hurts the unquiet dead.

"Magic," she said. "It won't last too long and I can't make any more of it today, so mind that you keep it somewhere safe, accessible, and ready to be used by any who can make good use of it. I'll leave it up to you to decide the details of that, but if I may suggest, keep it right here and give carefully rationed slivers to anyone performing any sort of guard duty."

There was a murmuring among the crowd, a mix of assent and dissent, but Aelis had no interest in getting mixed up in the middle of that particular argument. She had already handed the two cakes to Rus.

In the meantime, Elmo and Otto had come in and Pips bounded up to her and, with no warning, threw her arms around Aelis's waist. Surprised, Aelis rocked back a bit, expecting a jolt of pain in her foot and pleased at not feeling it.

"Have you been keeping up with your writing lessons, Pips?"

The girl nodded solemnly. "Can I come up to the tower and read out another story tonight after dinner?"

It was all Aelis could do not to glance at Maurenia in despair. "I won't say no, Pips. But I might be awfully busy and need to sleep early, as we'll be on our way out of the village before the sun is well up."

The girl looked like she was ready to pout, but eventually she realized that it wasn't a complete no, and she recovered quickly. "I'll be there before moonrise then," she chirped.

"So, you're leaving us to fend for ourselves then?" Emilie stood up, the blond woman as tall as anyone in the room save Tun. Her jaw quivered, her arms crossed. *Looking for a fight*, Aelis thought.

"Quite the opposite. We're heading out to try to intercept anything that might come this way," Aelis said.

"And who's *we*?"

"Me, Timmuk, Maurenia, and Tunbridge," Aelis said, jutting her chin toward where the half-orc sat, stiff and nervous.

Emilie turned around to stare at Tun. His face was hidden in the shadow of his hood, but he shifted in his seat, which creaked dangerously.

"Well," the woman said, turning back to Aelis, then sitting down with a sniff. "Maybe you've a chance of surviving after all."

"Thanks," Aelis muttered. "Now, we've got a lot of preparations to make, and I don't wish to keep you from your own work any longer than necessary." She slapped some coins on the bar and said, "Rus, I'd be grateful for anything I could take to my tower for dinner tonight and breakfast tomorrow."

"Martin already has a basket packed, Aelis. And several packages of twice-baked bread and dried venison." Rus went back to polishing his bar, studiously ignoring the coins that sat there, his bit of cloth whipping past them with a conjurer's skill.

Aelis went to Elmo's side, settling her eyes on the slightly bent form of the former army scout.

His brother Otto, stopped a pace beyond her. Aelis reached to the back of her belt and tugged something out of it, held it out toward Elmo.

It was his scout's longknife with its serrated edge, that he'd stuck hilt-deep in Otto's stomach back in the summer.

"You might need this. I'm trusting you to know if you do. But I'm going to ask for it back when I return."

Elmo looked down at the leather sheath in her hand and swallowed hard. "Give it to Otto," he croaked. "He'll give it to me if I need it."

Aelis nodded, turned, and held the weapon out to the older brother. With distrust twisting his features, he took it and headed out.

5

TALES AND DISTRACTIONS

Maurenia waited till they were back in her tower to ask the question that Aelis had been anticipating.

"How? You could barely walk when I left you, and now . . ."

"Magic," Aelis said, waggling her fingers. Maurenia caught her hand and pulled her close.

"I'm not a superstitious farmer," she said. "You can explain."

"It's very boring and technical," Aelis said. She wriggled out of Maurenia's grip, making sure to brush her hips against the other woman's as she did, and hefted the pack Maurenia had filled for her.

"Feels too light."

"It'll feel plenty heavy after a full day of marching. If ten years at sea and ten of army life are good for anything, it's teaching you to pack *only* what you need to survive. But I suppose there's a list of things I have left out that you simply *must* have."

"Only my entire medical kit, half my library, and a portable alchemy set."

"Why not put the entire calcination oven on the wagon?"

"Don't tempt me. But we should at least find room for that." She pointed to the last cake of silver soap she'd made.

"And in a pinch, we could use it on a wound, yes?"

Aelis briefly thought of what it might do to Tun if it were applied by someone who didn't know what he was. "It would have to be diluted. Copper's better than silver for preventing infection. Besides, I have other astringents and analgesics. I only have the one thing that can hurt the undead. If it comes to it, leave the decision to me. If I'm the one hurt, don't use it without my say-so."

Maurenia shrugged. "You're the surgeon." She drifted over to Aelis's side and slipped an arm around her waist. "You know, privacy is going to be hard to find in the field."

Just as Aelis felt the brush of Maurenia's lips against the side of her neck, she heard a knock at the door, followed closely by the sharp voice of Pips.

"Warden," the girl called. "I've come for a lesson."

Maurenia and Aelis sighed as one, and the half-elf retreated a step just as the girl came bounding into the main room of the tower.

"Good evening, Pips," Aelis said. "It's been some time since we had a lesson. Where were we?"

"Tizana the Mad in *Lives of the Wardens*!" Pips shouted. "You were just about t'explain what disemboweling meant," she went on, screwing her face up in concentration as she chewed carefully through the unfamiliar word.

"I could demonstrate." Maurenia murmured this just loudly enough for Aelis to hear, though Pips looked to her quizzically, knowing that she missed something.

Aelis sighed. "Well, you see, when Tizana wanted someone to *suffer*, she'd take a knife and make a small incision *here*," she said, drawing a line with her hand at navel height as she went toward her chair. Pips skipped after her, snatching a book she had trouble lifting off a table as she passed.

+ + +

The tale of Tizana and the many beheadings, disembowelments, impalements, and general mayhem she was responsible for in an out-of-control war against a crime syndicate in ancient Antraval kept Pips occupied for some time. The girl's reading was improving, to the point where Aelis only had to help her with the longer, more unusual words. Questions still came forth in a torrent, though.

"What does 'hung, drawn, and quartered' mean?"

"What does 'defenestrated' mean?"

"Why d'ya put a head on a pike and how would it still be screamin'?"

Aelis explained all as patiently as she could. Darkness settled around them as Pips kept on reading. For a time, with the mundane lamps on her worktables softly glowing, Aelis could see the darkly shining pools of Maurenia's eyes watching them from the edge of the bed, but eventually, these disappeared and Aelis feared she'd simply gone to sleep.

Finally, another question from Pips—one that she couldn't answer mechanically—jogged Aelis out of her stupor.

"What's that?" she asked, stupidly.

"I said, how come the other Wardens came along and took Tizana t'prison if all the people she was killing were bad?"

"Because," Aelis said, "it is not enough for a Warden to simply decide who is bad and to kill them."

"Why not?"

"A Warden represents the law. And the law tells us that we have to be able to *prove* that someone is bad, and to bring them to account for it if possible. We should only kill in defense of ourselves or others, when there's no other choice."

"But you've killed," the girl said. "Right?"

Damn it, Elmo, know when to keep your mouth shut, Aelis thought, even as she simply nodded.

"Just the one time?"

"Yes, Pips, just the one time. No, I had no choice. And I don't want to answer any more questions about this, alright?"

The girl frowned. "But won't I need to know this if I'm to become a Warden?"

"Slow down, Pips. We don't know if you can even become a wizard— and not every wizard becomes a Warden."

"Of course I'll be one. Both. What's the point of bein' a wizard if not t'be a Warden?" The girl's tone was so satisfied and so not to be trifled with that Aelis couldn't help but laugh a little. Clearly that was the wrong reaction, because Pips immediately pouted.

Aelis shifted the girl off her lap and set both hands on her shoulders. "Pips, listen to me. We've got to figure out what sort of ability you have, but I'm not trained or equipped to do that in the proper way." She paused and chewed on her bottom lip as she thought. "But here's what I can do. Do you feel any different when any specific moon is waxing or waning?"

"How does a moon wax?"

"Waxing is growing bigger. Waning is growing smaller."

"I don't know."

"Well, do you have peculiar dreams sometimes?"

"Aye," Pips said. She opened her mouth as if to go on, but Aelis stopped her with an upraised hand.

"No. Don't tell me now. What I want you to do is this. The next time, the very next time you have a peculiar dream—one that you can remember—I want you to come to me and tell me all about it. It may mean nothing, but just knowing when it happened, I can check on where the moons were, and that would give me some information. Do you understand?"

"What if I forget?"

"That's why you must come to me the very same day."

"What if it happens while you're gone?"

"Then make some kind of mark to remember it. Tie a ribbon around your wrist or tell your uncles and remind them to tell me. For now, though, you must go home. It is growing dark and they're probably wondering where you are."

"Can't I just stay here?"

Aelis looked longingly at the bed where she imagined Maurenia lay slumbering. "I don't think so. I've got work to do."

"Fine." Pips stood up. Aelis came slowly to her feet, still expecting her ankle to protest and pleased when it didn't. From a chest, she pulled out a spare lamp with a candle in it for the girl to light her way home. "Go straight home," Aelis told her. "I've got some things to do before I can sleep, and you'll have chores in the morning."

She gave the girl a gentle hug around her shoulders, followed by an even gentler push, and waited till she heard the door shut firmly before stepping quietly over to her bed.

As she suspected, Maurenia was asleep. But she jolted awake as soon as Aelis sat down beside her.

"The girl finally gone?"

Aelis nodded. Maurenia's hand reached out and patted Aelis's for a moment. "Why do you put up with her? Not your job to raise her or teach her."

"You aren't wrong, but you're not right exactly, either. Phillipa is smart, smarter than her uncles know how to deal with. They mean well, but don't know how to provide the girl a better life than the one they've got."

"A lot shared by thousands of children like Pips all over the three countries and beyond. You can't educate and entertain them all."

"Does that mean I shouldn't try to do it for one of them?" Aelis sat up straighter. "Besides, the girl may be gifted."

"You don't mean magically, do you?"

"What else would I mean?"

"In a serious way?"

Aelis shrugged. "That's usually impossible to tell before puberty. But there's latent potential in her. That I know for sure. How much of it, or what kind, I don't know. I'm not equipped to say. But if I simply let *that* go on top of everything else, I'd be remiss in my duties."

"Is recruiting the next generation a secret Warden task, then?" Maurenia sat up, blinking sleep away.

"Not secret, and not for Wardens alone. *All* wizards are trained to know at least the obvious signs. There is a branch of Diviners with special training for knowing specifically what a person with latent power can do, and how much of it. Timing is tricky, though; too early and you're just treading water. Too late and a lifetime of habit will ruin their chances of doing anything useful. So, the least I can do for Pips right now is give her the tools she'll need if a delver finds something in her whenever I can get one up here."

"Tools?"

"Literacy. The joy, or at least the habit, of reading. She's already got the curiosity. If you haven't got that, no amount of latent ability will carry you through."

Maurenia nodded vaguely. "From the way you talk, I can't ever decide if magic is a science or an art."

"The way the Lyceum teaches and practices, it's a bit of both. We used to all be priests, after all. You get the systematized learning and teaching that way, but a lot of mystical nonsense, too."

Maurenia laughed. "Mystical nonsense is rich talk from a woman who can see in the dark when Onoma's black moon is in the sky."

Aelis laughed, but uncomfortably. "What do you mean?"

"What I mean is that you seem like you might *still* be a priestess after all, whether you want to be or not."

Aelis waved that away. "I've got to write a letter. Go back to sleep."

"Letter? Who to send it? The royal post carrier is Timmuk, and he's coming with you."

"True. But if we don't come back, I need to leave a record of where I went and why. And I want to make sure *someone* knows about Pips in the bargain."

"Who'll be here to read it?"

"If a Warden disappears, another Warden comes looking for them."

"Fair enough. Wake me up when you come to bed. However you choose." Maurenia, veteran soldier and traveler that she was, sank back down into the bedding and blankets and was instantly asleep again.

Aelis wrote quickly, trying not to let her thoughts of how to wake Maurenia creep onto the page.

6

RHUNIVAL'S HALL

By the time green and red moonlight was melting into the gray of an approaching sun, Aelis and Maurenia were up, dressed, and waiting for Tun and Timmuk to join them, packs slung over shoulders, swords belted on hips.

Maurenia moved slowly but purposefully in the mornings, awake but grudgingly, having learned, it seemed, to keep some piece of her mind at rest until the day dragged it completely into the light.

"Your foot," she finally said, slowly. "You're still not limping."

"Nope," Aelis said, taking a couple more steps before she stopped and looked back at Maurenia, who was still staring hard at her.

"You haven't drugged yourself, have you?"

Aelis snorted. "I told you: magic. And liniment, and a good brace." Her heartbeat quickened. She hoped the relative darkness was keeping anything from showing on her face.

"Are you sure?"

"Mostly," Aelis said. "Look. I'm not going to say it doesn't hurt. But I'm *not* going to slow us down. I made a supply of this liniment to take with us." She patted her belt pouch. That was partly true, in that she did have it in her pouch. It had already been in her medical kit, though. *Telling an awful lot of small lies now.*

"We're going to envy Tun and Timmuk whatever sleep they got last night," Maurenia said.

"Probably." In truth, Aelis already did. A fog hung over her thoughts and her limbs felt distant. "I've never been very good at sleeping the night before something important. A trip, an exam, a venture into the wilderness to recover a necromantic control rod and destroy possibly hundreds of hostile animated corpses—they all ruin my ability to sleep."

"All the more reason everyone should have to do two years in an army. Teach you to sleep when sleepin' is good."

"Almost everyone in my family did a bit, anyway. My father, my uncles, my aunts, both older brothers. My oldest sister commands the family regiment. By the time I was old enough, the war was over, and besides—magical ability meant I wouldn't have been allowed until I graduated from the Lyceum."

Maurenia grunted but seemed mollified—or at least distracted—by Aelis's statements. Soon enough, Tun and Timmuk came marching up, as mismatched a pair as Aelis could imagine. Timmuk carried an enormous pack that added half a foot to his height, and Tun only a slim bedroll over his fringed coat, though his pockets bulged, mostly with the hard corn biscuits he favored as traveling food.

Aelis could read the tension in Tun's shoulders. As the last time they'd gone north, he had a stout walking stick in hand and no other visible weapons, though she imagined his handblades were in the pockets of his coat. He did have, however, a big wicker basket stuffed with blankets and hides tucked under his free arm.

"Best if we rope these up now. We can work on adjusting the fit and turning them into proper coats as we travel. I've got the tools in my pack."

With Tun's help they all quickly slung the heavy, soft hides over their heads through crude holes cut in their center mass. With braided leather thongs from his basket, Tun quickly belted them close. "Can cut and trim and add fur as we travel, do a little sewing each night."

"Going to have trouble carrying those furs and all, or do we need to share the weight around?" Given the pack Timmuk was wearing, it seemed likely the dwarf was carrying more than his share already.

Tun looked down at him, unblinking. "Trouble carrying them? Me?"

The dwarf shrugged. "Fair enough, master woodsman. Are we off, then?"

Moved by something—perhaps Maurenia's words the night before, which had been nagging at her—Aelis spoke up. "Maybe a prayer. A statement of intent. Or just a quick pledge to one another."

"A prayer? Didn't take you for the religious sort, Warden," Timmuk rumbled.

"I'm not, usually. But . . . we set out to do something sacred to Onoma. Could it hurt? Nobody has to say anything, just . . . maybe spend a moment in thought."

More to humor her than anything else, Aelis felt, the others fell silent. She lowered her eyes to her boots and took a deep breath. She shut out the world, the cold, the fog of morning and the fatigue already creeping into her limbs.

Onoma, I don't speak to you much unless it is to invoke your name in a
curse. I don't know if you hear that, or this, and I don't know that you care. But
I do think you care about the perversion and elision of death that the animated
corpses represent. Grant us your favor as we destroy them.

Aelis was silent a moment longer, tried not to dwell on the fact that
Necromancers had gleefully made undead for much, much longer than
they had set out to destroy them.

She felt foolish, yet also proud, certain that she'd done something right.

"Come on then," she said. "We haven't got all day to stand here gawk-
ing."

✦ ✦ ✦

They walked for six days before they saw anything other than themselves,
snow drifts, pine trees, and winter birds.

The scenery would've been lovely, Aelis often thought, if there weren't
so *much* of it. Tun led them on a path that passed west of where they'd
confronted Nath and the would-be Earl of Mahlgren, so little of it was
familiar to her.

Just how Tun navigated past so much sameness—especially during
the day when no stars were visible—she couldn't fathom. But then, she
couldn't fathom how he did most of what he did in the woods: move as
quietly as a squirrel, tell them exactly what animals were nearby, accurately
relay the time, quickly trap game with whatever he had to hand, and point
to north anytime she asked without a moment's hesitation.

Tun kept them supplied with what meat or forage he could find, con-
stantly counseling them to save their dried and preserved supplies against
later need.

She'd thought to be worried about shelter when they set out only to
find, upon their first camping, that a great deal of Timmuk's oversized
pack was taken up by a marvelously engineered shelter. It assembled in
moments with a collection of hollow wood poles and metal connecting
tabs over which canvas was tied. It had enough space to fit all of them, and
if it wasn't entirely comfortable for everyone, it at least kept them warm,
especially with some of Tun's spare hides draped over the walls.

She'd commented on how marvelously it worked and Timmuk laughed,
nodded at Maurenia, and asked who she thought had designed it.

The first night, as thoroughly exhausted as she'd ever been, Aelis had
still found time to worry about the sleeping arrangement, even as they
began laying blankets down onto the base of the shelter. Maurenia had set-

tled that question by laying hers right next to Aelis's, and when she woke in the frigid morning, they were wrapped in each other's arms. If it was more for warmth than romance, Aelis didn't mind; it brought something normal, something she badly wanted, to this journey.

Aelis was finding herself bored by the monotony of it all when Tun raised a hand and pointed. "Smoke. A chimney, longhouse fire maybe. Don't think it's too large. Do we make for it?"

He turned to face Aelis with his question, and she felt Maurenia and Timmuk do the same. She hadn't expected to feel the weight of all those gazes quite so keenly and to be entrusted with making decisions that affected them all. *Why would so many competent people follow me?* she wondered. She let her breath plume into the air.

"Orcs?" she asked Tun.

"No."

"Best we skirt around it, then. Whoever's down there's likely to be a survivalist hard case or an Ystainan loyalist. They don't fall under my purview."

"That's a hard way to look at it, Warden," Timmuk said. Ice had gathered on his beard and tinkled softly whenever he spoke.

"Whoever they are, they've chosen to live beyond the bounds of the law, which means beyond the bounds of my service," Aelis said. "If we see animations headed for them, I'll do whatever I can. But the people in Lone Pine are my charge, and behind them, those who live under the auspices of the Tri-crowns and the Estates House."

And so, at Tun's direction, they altered course slightly to skirt that thin trail of smoke. It was a surprisingly long walk, but the sky was clear and the smoke stood out against it easily. Tun put it to their left, and Aelis realized they had descended into a valley. The fact that they'd been a bit above the level of the cottage had possibly been the only reason they'd spotted the smoke through the tree cover.

They made their way north, below the lip of the valley, so that they were not themselves outlined against it, though the pine forest was dense enough Aelis wasn't sure they needed to worry over it.

When Aelis thought they had begun to ascend out of the valley, Tun stopped them with a raised hand.

"I smell something *wrong.*" He turned and looked at Aelis. "Something made of bone."

Aelis let out a long breath. "Where?"

Tun pointed north. His voice was a bare whisper, just enough for the other three to hear. "More than that I cannot say. Not on top of us, but not far." He pointed to himself, then Timmuk, and to the west, then to Aelis and Maurenia and to the east, made a circling motion with his hands.

"Skeletons probably can't hear us, Tun. We can talk strategy." Aelis tried hard not to be smug, not to let seep into her voice that she had something on Tun even out here in the deep woods.

"Then how do they know an enemy is near?" His heavy brows beetled together as if he wasn't quite sure he was willing to accept that.

"They're often directed by human leaders. Failing that, they can sense life and move toward it. A powerful Necromancer could *give* a skeleton extra senses, but there's no point."

"Fine. What do we do, Necromancer?" Timmuk had unlimbered his pack, set it against a tree, and was now loosening his arms by swinging the axe he used as a walking stick in small arcs through the air.

"The first thing is to listen to me. It may well be that blind brute force will do the job. It may not. Likely enough, there will be details about them that I might understand and you will not. Second, and probably most important, you cannot aim to *wound* them. The damage that will take a man out of a fight will only slow a corpse down. Take an arm, they'll pick it up and swing the sharpest end at you. Hobble a leg, they'll hop or crawl to you and pin your foot to the ground the instant you take your eyes off them. Third," Aelis said, as she realized that she had their full attention, "is to remember what I told you back in my tower. They may get *more dangerous* as you reduce their numbers, like those I fought in the small barracks-crypt. The last one was eight times faster and smarter than all the individuals when they began. Whoever made these animations was clearly capable of power and subtlety; don't assume you're facing simple shambling corpses."

"How is that possible?" Timmuk was now shrugging out of his extra hide coat to the more luxurious fur he wore underneath and overtop of his studded leathers.

"The few I fought in the small barracks-crypt I entered were designed to dump their animating magic into one another as they were destroyed. The last one was eight times faster and smarter than all the individuals when they began. It's not a common kind of magic, but whoever made those animations was clearly capable of power and subtlety. We can't assume whatever we will face are mere shambling corpses."

"With that kind of option available, why not chain a thousand of them together and end with one unstoppable undead warrior?" Maurenia's eyes were narrowed and Aelis could see her calculating the potential.

"Long answer or short answer?"

"Short," Tun answered. "Time is rather pressing."

"It's impossible," Aelis said with a shrug.

"I'll want the long later," Maurenia said. "So, for now, do what you say, don't act as though our opponents are simply men . . . anything else?"

"That should be all for now," Aelis said. "But . . . keep an eye out. If you see something more than just a shambling corpse, call out for me."

Aelis slipped off her pack, lashed her walking stick to it, and loosened her dagger and sword in their sheaths. Maurenia loaded a bolt, fiddled with it, pulled it free, checked the fletchings. She licked her fingers, drew them along the red and gray feathers, and placed the bolt back into the bow.

Aelis glanced back at Tun. Among the four of them, only he had made no outward sign of readiness. He hadn't even checked his pockets for his handblades or adjusted the grip of his walking stick. He just kept walking, keeping his steps small to match them to the swung-from-the-hip strides of the dwarf.

Some of Tun's quiet, unshakable confidence rubbed off on Aelis.

I fought eight skeletons myself and came out with nary a scratch, she told herself. *Okay, it was really five, but that's still plenty. And look at the hard cases I've got on my side this time. Piece of piss.*

Still, she checked the draw of her dagger again.

They walked on their steady northward course for a few more minutes, the ground gradually rising. From the corner of her eye, Aelis saw Tun come to a dead halt. He pushed back his hood and lifted his nose to the air, sniffing at the wind that stirred his hair.

"Just past that stand of trees, beyond that little rise."

"Everyone else, stay close. If I can, I want to see what we're up against before we go charging in." Aelis was already moving forward, clambering, up the rise. She heard someone just a few steps behind her, glanced back, and found Maurenia close on her heels.

"I said I wanted to—"

"I know what you said. But I know which of us is more likely to get spotted by any foe, dead or alive. And I'm not letting you out of my sight if I can avoid it."

The half-elf loped easily past her. Two steps and past a stand of pine trees and she'd faded from Aelis's sight, hidden in her long, dark green cloak as night descended.

She took a few quick steps into the same trees and Maurenia's hand shot out to stop her. She had her back against a tree and pulled Aelis to her tightly.

"This doesn't seem like the time . . ." Aelis murmured.

"It's not," Maurenia breathed, her voice barely audible, the sound coming from her throat more than her lips. "Look to your left, thirty paces, between the dead tree and the split bole."

Aelis did as she was bid and eventually found what Maurenia had pointed out. At first she saw only a squat, dark shape. Then she saw the eyes.

Blue dots, small and hard like gems, and closer to the ground than they should've been. She wished for Onoma's moon or an Illusionist's ability to call light.

However, she waited a moment to let her vision grow accustomed to the darkness of the trees and let the shape resolve itself.

"Dog," she breathed out.

"I saw. Is that bad?"

"Requires an adjustment in tactics."

She tried to recall what she knew about animating animal corpses. A dog had more natural weapons than a person, and a smaller skeleton took less energy to animate and maintain. More could be generated by a less skilled or less powerful Necromancer. Some had claimed that something of their pack instincts remained inherent in them, and that they were fiercer and more cunning fighters in groups.

"There's probably a lot of them. Maybe ten or more. This is likely a scout." She whispered all this as closely as she could; a dog's hearing might have been worth preserving by a skilled enough caster. "And I'm going to unmake it."

She slid her dagger free and felt its weight comforting in her hand. Then she called a spell to her mind, a Second Order Necromantic she knew well.

She pivoted on one foot and spun away from the cover Maurenia had dragged her into, putting herself directly into the animated dog's eyeline.

The head swung up, the jaws opened in a soundless snarl, and the skeleton leapt into motion.

The anatomist in her couldn't help but marvel at the structure of the animal. It was a big-shouldered mastiff of some sort. It moved soundlessly and fluidly, and with a grace that would do any living hunter credit, launched straight for her throat.

Aelis crouched beneath it, muttering dark words. A cold, gray light sprang into being around her right hand. She twisted upward, and with that energy gathered, punched straight through the fleshless spine. The blue eyes winked out and the bones clattered, almost sadly, to the ground.

Maurenia spun out behind her. The gray light around Aelis's fist shone off the half-elf's large dark eyes before it winked out.

"That was . . ." Maurenia said, "impressive."

"Necrobane's Hand," Aelis muttered, hoping it was dark enough that Maurenia wouldn't see her cheeks flush. "Simple enough spell."

Maurenia stepped close, slipping her hood down. "Why do you get flustered at a compliment? And why hide it? I've seen every part of you that can flush . . ."

Aelis thought it was an odd time for Maurenia to be teasing her, and was about to say that, when something drew her eye.

Six pairs of cold blue eyes, all just over knee height, had come into view over Maurenia's shoulder.

Aelis took a quick step to put herself in front of Maurenia, slipped her dagger into her left hand, and drew her sword with her right.

"Stay tight," she spat, while she pulled up the biggest, most bite-resistant ward she could manage.

For her part, Maurenia calmly aimed over Aelis's shoulder. Just before her ward distorted the air before them, the first bolt tugged at Aelis's hair as it flew past. It took one of those many eyes straight on, and Aelis heard the snap of breaking bone.

The dogs came on. Maurenia loaded her bow. And she whistled twice, sharp and loud.

Aelis called up that globe of unbinding around her hand again. A tiny part of her mind reveled in the cold glory of the power she called on. The more analytical part was sounding alarm bells. *Single-use Second Orders are not a long-term strategy against multiple opponents. Especially not while holding wards.*

Two dog skeletons leapt at her, one high, one low. The top and bottom edges of her ward were just enough to deflect them. They skittered off, one flipping over her shoulder, claws swinging wildly at her and Maurenia, while the other bounced backward and popped immediately back to its feet.

Could be sharing information, feeling out the edges of my wards.

She felt Maurenia step back and away from her. She couldn't spare a glance back. The five dog skeletons she could see were circling, weaving between one another, a worryingly sophisticated tactic. The one Maurenia had partially blinded had to keep its one good eye focused on them. Maurenia loosed another bolt, aiming to disadvantage it further, but it smashed against the snout, chipping bone and doing little else.

Aelis took the initiative. "Stay back," she snapped, hoping Maurenia would listen. She called up another ward, a round plane of force angled down from the hilt of her sword. Through the vial of her own blood encased in the iron hilt of her dagger, she called to mind a more complex Necromantic Order, nearly a third.

She charged the dogs, adjusting her grip on the dagger so that the blade projected from the bottom of her fist and slashed upward at the air with it as she came.

A faint, nearly invisible line of power—no more than a distortion in the air to the naked and unknowing eye—cracked like a whip. It sent two of the animated dogs tumbling away, bones splintering. The other three bounded away, but turned to regroup almost immediately.

Aelis heard a bitten-off yell from behind her. She spun around to see the one she'd sent flying past them with her ward latched onto Maurenia's shoulder, its rear claws scrambling at her back. Its flailing legs weren't finding purchase, scrabbling hard against Maurenia's thick hide coat and studded leather jerkin. But its teeth had evidently found something to hold tight to.

The half-elf let go of her crossbow—no matter since it simply hung from the sling across her chest—and her hands reached back to grasp the animated dog by the front shoulder blades before Aelis could yell a warning.

Unprotected, unprepared flesh did not want to meet the naked bones of the unquiet dead if their animator had any elegance or spare power. Maurenia let loose a ragged scream, but—and at this, Aelis was astonished—she did not let go or relent. Her fingers curled tighter and she bent forward, hurling the skeleton to the ground with such force that bones shook and ribs snapped. Maurenia wasted no time, leaping upward and pulling her feet up behind her, then bringing both booted heels down into the thing's neck with admirable precision and vicious force. The head bent unnaturally, the lower jaw went awry, and the dead dog struggled less fiercely.

Aelis had little time to contemplate the spectacle or to worry over Maurenia's wounds. The dogs she'd scared off were coming back into the fight, the three of them all bearing down on her like missiles.

She called up the Lash again, knowing it was a choice between that and a ward of any utility. The three skeletons were spread widely enough that she'd need her best ward or her best attack to fend off any two of them.

She hoped for a moment that Bardun Jacques, at least, would be proud of her choice to arm herself.

But doing so meant waiting until two of them were near enough to do her real harm. Which she did, hearing only the rush of her own blood in her ears and the clicking and rattling of bones as they charged. She swept the Lash out, severing cleanly the spine of the dog to her left but only clipping the one coming at her front. She expected, feared the impact of the third on her right and was turning to face it, forming a desperate cross-guard with sword and dagger.

Just in time to see the metal-shod end of a stick the size of a small tree lance the dog out of the air. Like a squire taking a prize in ring-jousting, Tun had expertly intercepted the corpse, spearing through it and shattering ribs. He pivoted away from her, the dog at the end of his staff clawing and snapping wildly at the air. With a twist of his arms, he flung it with such force that it flew end over end and smashed into oblivion against a tree trunk ten yards or more away, stripping bark where it hit.

Aelis had intercepted the remaining attacker with her awkward guard, but teeth locked around her sword, and the unnatural power in the animation's neck was trying to pull it from her hand.

Then Timmuk stepped around her and grabbed the top and bottom of its jaws with his thickly gloved hands. He struggled against it a moment, but dwarf muscle overcame Necromancer's art, and the dog's jaws burst in a shower of teeth. He threw the ruined thing to the ground, stomped one hobnailed boot onto its neck to keep it flat, and squatted to grab its rear hips with both hands.

Then he bent the spine forward against the pressure of his boot until it snapped.

Aelis whirled to find a slightly staggered Maurenia, the crumpled remnants of the dog she'd been fighting at her feet.

Aelis released the form of the Lash in her mind. The world dimmed, got loud again, and reoriented itself. "Is anyone injured?"

"'Renia clearly is," Timmuk said.

"I can speak for myself, Timmuk. And I'm fine."

"If you don't need immediate attention, allow me a moment to examine the remnants of what we just fought."

Maurenia nodded. Aelis sheathed her sword, but not her dagger, and bent to look over the bones. She used the tip of her blade to turn them over, trying to catch what light remained.

As she thought: along a mostly intact femur and the inside of a hipbone, runes glittered, dark and metallic.

She slipped off her pack, dug into her medical kit, and pulled free a rag. Careful not to touch the bone itself, she wrapped the smaller of the two in it, carefully, and then stuffed it into a pocket of her coat.

"Timmuk," she said to the dwarf who'd come to her aid. "How'd you touch the one and suffer no pain? Plain wool shouldn't have done the job while this animation remained active."

Timmuk laughed and pulled one of his gray wool gloves free of his hand.

Beneath it, his hand was encased in chain mail gloves locked in place by thick bracers that continued up his forearms.

"Good answer," Aelis said as the dwarf began slipping his glove back on. "Could you carry this femur for me without harm, then?" She stood, nudging the long bone with a toe. "We'll need to make camp."

"What do you want the bones for?"

"So I know how best to treat Maurenia's wound."

Timmuk shrugged and grasped the bone in his mailed fist.

Aelis slung her pack and came to Maurenia's side. She took one of the half-elf's hands in both of her own and looked at it.

"A few blisters," Aelis said, her fingertips moving lightly over the raised and reddened skin. "Nothing I can't fix."

"A warning would've been nice." Maurenia's face was pinched and pale with pain, her hair slick with sweat. They were surrounded by quieted monstrosities, with Tun and Timmuk, none of them had bathed in days, and Aelis *still* had to fight down the urge to seize and kiss her fiercely.

"I know. I hadn't thought it a possibility until I saw we were dealing with dogs. Animals are easier to animate, but to have maintained them for so long *and* have added that sort of defense would've required a very powerful Necromancer . . ." She sighed. "No excuses. I should've covered the possibility regardless. Can you make it to shelter or do you want me to treat this here?"

Maurenia tried to talk but let out a sharp shiver instead, and a decision snapped into place in Aelis's mind.

"We have to go try that hall," Aelis said. "Warmth and shelter are worth the risk of some hardliners or partisans." She did not like the symptoms Maurenia was exhibiting, and she needed light, stability, and warmth to examine the wound in her shoulder and whatever had been done to her hands.

"I'll make it there. Especially if there's something warm and strong to drink at the end of the walk." Maurenia smiled through her pain. Aelis's heart lurched and she wanted, again, to pull Maurenia against her.

"Get some brandy in her now," Timmuk rumbled.

"Absolutely not," Aelis said. "Not until I've had a look."

Maurenia had recovered herself but her face was still set in a grimace as they retrieved their packs, Tun leading them back into the center of the little valley with quick steps as Elisima's moon rose, shedding a pale green light over the forest.

Eventually they found a copse of pine trees surrounding a surprisingly large, one-story, longhouse-style cottage with outbuildings scattered around it and a woodpile forming a windbreak along its north side.

Aelis took a look at the rest of the party and said, "Perhaps I ought to go knocking at the door first."

"And why's that?" Timmuk asked. "I'm twice as friendly as you are, Warden."

"Maybe three times," Aelis agreed. "But I'm also not using an axe my own height as a walking stick or cradling a loaded crossbow like a baby, and I don't look capable of picking the house up and carrying it off."

"The least threatening and most irreplaceable member of the party should not be the first to walk into potential danger," Tun said.

"Counterpoint: I'm the one of us most likely to be able to respond to a threat with nonlethal force. If the cottage's residents feel like starting a ruckus, I'll just put them to sleep." In truth, it didn't look like much more than one person could inhabit the place. A small family, perhaps. But Aelis no longer found herself worrying about a dozen desperate men.

As she walked toward the cottage, she pulled together one of her favorite Enchantments, the Catnap, running through the words in her head, summoning the form and the power of them into her mind and her hand and her mouth, ready to unleash it at a moment's need.

She found the door, a low-hanging round thing with a heavy antler knocker suspended in its middle. She leaned her walking stick against the log wall and raised her hand, but the door swung open before she could knock.

The first thing she noticed was the beard. It was hard not to, as it surrounded the man's face like a dark cloud and ran down his chest in thick braided ropes. Behind this great black and gray mane, the man's age was hard to guess. What little of his face she could see was tough with sun and weather, but she guessed him to be middle-aged, probably close to her father in years. He wore obviously home-made clothing, old hides that, from the smell of him, hadn't been cured too carefully.

Still, he smiled broadly and in a clear and powerful voice said, "Welcome, wizard. I have noted your approach for some hours now. Come in!" He stood back, swept an arm toward the interior of his cottage. "Never let it be said that the hospitality of Rhunival's hall is lacking, even in winter.

Please, tell your friends to come. There is no time or energy for worrying over the blood or parentage of guests in a place like this, eh?"

Aelis was so taken aback by the man's sudden appearance, his stream of words, and his companionable demeanor that she didn't know how to react. She let her hand hang in the air for a moment, only lowering it slowly back to her side while he spoke. Finally, a bit hesitantly, she spoke.

"How do you know I'm a wizard?"

"I know many things," he said, tapping the side of his head with one thick finger, protruding as it did from a glove from which most of the fingertips had worn away. "But the doorstep is not the place to speak of that! Call your friends. All are welcome."

Still a little stunned, Aelis took up her walking stick and lifted it above her head, then carefully swung it side to side, signaling for the others to join her.

Slowly, the other three hove into view, Maurenia leaning lightly on Tun as she walked. Rhunival's eyes, large and shrouded by heavy, bushy brows, watched them come with what Aelis suspected was a smile behind his whiskers.

"So many weapons. You came expecting trouble, hrm? Or made some? Too soon to say, but I suppose the tales will be told one way or another."

With that, he propped the door open with a small piece of wood and shuffled back into the dimness of his house. The others came trudging up, Tun in the lead, Maurenia trying not to visibly lean on him, Timmuk bringing up the rear.

Maurenia gave Aelis a disbelieving stare. Aelis shrugged and waved the half-elf inside. Something made her check Maurenia's weapon, and she found that, even though the half-elf was pale and sweating, her crossbow was loaded and ready to shoot. She laid a hand on Maurenia's arm.

"Maybe unload the bow?"

Maurenia frowned, but she slipped the bolt free with two fingers of one hand and slid it back into the sheaf on her hip, then uncocked the string and let the bow dangle from the leather strap looped over her shoulder.

There was no similar way to make Timmuk's long axe seem any less threatening, so Aelis simply waved him in. When Tun came to her, he stopped, eyeing the dark threshold of the door and then flitting his eyes to her.

"There is something here I do not like the feel of."

"What do you mean?"

"Not like the animated dead, I do not think. Something like you, only wild, not of a city."

"Magic?" She felt sure her whisper was overheard by anyone with ears.

"Maybe." Tun rolled his shoulders and walked in. Aelis followed him, closing the door behind her.

One thing she was immediately glad of was the warmth. Rhunival's hall was long and low roofed and dominated by an open fire pit in the middle, the smoke trailing up through a square hole in the thatch above. The fire was well banked and carefully tended and it heated the entire cottage, filling it with the smell of charred wood and warm stone.

Tools, bags of onions, and bundles of dried herbs lined the walls. Such furniture as there was appeared handmade from roughly hewn logs; one long, low table, several stumps serving as chairs. The only bed was a simple pallet of hides and blankets near the edge of the fire pit.

"Sit down, sit down. Lay down your arms," Rhunival muttered as he knelt by the fire pit, seized a long poker that lay near it, and began stirring the coals, sending cinders flaring wildly toward the hole in the ceiling. "No need for them here, no need for them now."

Timmuk stared at him and fingered his axe hesitantly. Maurenia rested her bent arm on the stock of her crossbow.

"Go on," he said, "put them up against the wall. It's not going to come alive and eat them. Not anymore. Been years since it did that." He made a shooing motion with his hands, and finally Timmuk hefted his axe, took two long—for him—strides, and rested his weapon delicately against the wall. Maurenia was the slowest to move, gingerly unslinging the bow and setting it down almost reverently.

Tun, meanwhile, knelt carefully and then sat down next to the fire pit, having been forced to stoop until he reached that far into the house. Rhunival turned his cavernously dark eyes on Aelis, who met his stare evenly.

"Do the wishes of one in his own home, inviting you as his guest, mean so little to young wizards now?"

She found herself just about to reach for the scabbard, intending to unhook it from her belt and set it against the wall with the axes, when Professor Urizen's final words of advice before she left for Lone Pine echoed in her mind.

Wear the sword. Always wear the sword. If they come for you at three hours past the turn of the day fearing a changeling in a cradle, wear the sword.

"I'm afraid not, Master Rhunival. You have my promise that I shan't draw it except at direst need. But I need it to hand, and as a Warden, vested with the authority of the Crowns and Estates House, I am not legally bound to surrender my weapons to anyone."

"Warden?" Rhunival's thick brows shot skyward. "Do they make Wardens of children now, then? Hrm? In my day you saw proper Wardens, not beautiful lasses hardly old enough to carry a sword." But as soon as he protested, he raised his hands in defeat. "As you will, Warden. As you will." He addressed the group more generally then. "Sit, sit. Take the cue of your tracker there and be comfortable."

Anger flashed in Aelis's mind. For a moment she was back in a Necromancy lecture hall, feeling Duvhalin's false avuncular smile pass over her as he called upon a lesser student. Instead of sinking onto one of the stump chairs, she straightened herself up, setting her mouth in a hard line.

"I'll stand," she said. Aelis felt less unsettled for having asserted herself, even on so small a point. Rhunival shrugged as he swept some coals onto a smooth stone spot alongside the main pit, set a metal grate over it, and then a kettle atop the grate.

Then he stood and looked over the four of them again. He was not tall, Aelis thought, and round-shouldered beneath his hides, but he gave an impression of size, of taking up more space than he did.

"So, is it up to me as host to make introductions, then? I am Rhunival and this is my home." He looked at Timmuk where he'd sunk onto a stump, broad short legs spread before him. "Banker is the muscle, aye?" He looked at Maurenia then. "Warrior there, and maker, too? I have already named you the tracker; do I guess wrong?"

"You do not, Master Rhunival," Timmuk said, standing up and offering the strange figure a vague bow. "Timmuk Dobrusz, lately of the Dobrusz and Children Bank of Lascenise, lately of the Thorns of the Counting House Company, and presently of the Royal Post."

Maurenia did not stand, or bow, or do anything but say, clearly, "Maurenia Angra. Thanks for your welcome."

"Tunbridge," the half-orc said from his spot on the floor, pronouncing the syllables of his name carefully around his protruding tusks.

"I am Rhunival. Not Master Rhunival. Rhunival, master of nothing, of no thing, of nowhere, not any longer, no more. There will be tea—or what passes for it—and food, though very poor to your refined tongues, I suppose. You may stay the night and the day and the night beyond if you wish, though I do not know what I can do beyond feed you and warm you."

"That is plenty indeed, Rhunival," Aelis said. "We will not impose on your hospitality, and we'll offer fair compensation, especially if you can grant us the use of a table by the fire. One of us is wounded and I must tend her." She glanced at Maurenia, who seemed better for her spot by a fire, though her hair was still plastered with an unhealthy-seeming sweat, and pain tightened her features.

"What is fair compensation for the space in a home amid desolation, Warden? For the warmth of a fire? For the food brought slow and hard from the earth by sweat and toil?"

"Gold?" Aelis felt like she had to offer that answer first, though something told her it was going to be insufficient.

"Not much call to spend it out here," Rhunival said, exactly as Aelis expected him to. He had gathered a pot and a battered, stained wooden strainer that fit inside it. Into this he began dumping pinches of herbs while his kettle heated on the little grate.

Aelis and her party shared a quick, silent conference, eyes searching one another for ideas.

"Perhaps you need some kind of labor done, now or in the spring," Tun said. "Something heavy and difficult."

"I am not so old that work with shovel and axe is beyond me, woodsman. Whatever I cannot do here on my own piece of the world needn't be done. Not yet."

Tun looked back to Aelis and offered her the smallest of shrugs. She wasn't sure anyone else would've seen it or been able to interpret it if they had, but she found his gestures, his expressions, often conveyed as much information as his voice.

"Tales, then," Timmuk said. "Tales of far-off places, of the exotic creatures I have seen? Tales of intrigue in the counting room and knife work in the back alley?"

That caused Rhunival to stop his puttering and lift his head. Beneath his wild gray brows, his eyes widened and gathered in the firelight.

"That, master of sums, is a bargain worth the making." At his feet, the water in the kettle began to rattle against its sides. "But for every two hours you stay, I would ask an hour of tales. You may not have so many."

"Timmuk Dobrusz could tell a day of tales for every hour he spent under a roof," the dwarf said, his beard suddenly bristling. "It is not the tales I do not have. It is the time."

"We carry furs. Hides. The means to work them. Surely it gets cold here," Aelis said. She leaned forward as if trying to read Rhunival's reaction.

He tilted his head to one side as the kettle began to ping softly. "I suppose that could be a bargain. I would prefer ten days of tales."

"Ten days would be ten more than we have, Rhunival." Aelis felt compelled to speak up. "If you would take the hides and furs and Tun's skill in working them and such tales as Timmuk has time to tell, then we can work a trade. If that is not sufficient, tell us plainly what would be."

"The dance, the talk, the circling around of what I might or might not want, what you will or will not give, is that not a gift and a trade in itself?" Rhunival smiled and then bent down to snatch up the kettle, emptying it over the strainer filled with herbs. Immediately, a piney, herbal scent wafted to mingle with the woodsmoke.

"Put aside bargaining for now," he said as he poured carefully, using his bare hand on the iron of the kettle. "Tell me plainly why you have come. Then I will go so far as to serve you tea, and you will officially be guests."

Aelis suddenly felt herself, and the rest of them, balanced on the edge of a knife. Something about Rhunival tickled her senses. He was more than he seemed. Of that she was certain. That was Tun's instinct and now her own, and she was disinclined to ignore them. Taken together, they seemed law.

And yet she did not feel as if she could lie to the man or that she should. In a moment of weighing up all the possibilities—and her certainty that any lie would be found out—she settled on something close to the truth.

"Our purpose is twofold. There may be a danger approaching people in more civilized lands south of here, many days' walk. We seek to intercept it. And farther north, in the ruins of this earldom, there may be a way to prevent this evil entirely. We would seek that if we could."

This admission seemed to roll off Rhunival to no effect as he went to a low chest, took out a stack of small bowls, and began pouring his decoction into them. Somehow he managed to grasp five of them across his two hands and made rounds. Tun first, then Timmuk, Maurenia, and finally Aelis, offering each of them a bowl.

Rhunival sipped out of his own bowl. Aelis held her bowl close and inhaled its aroma. It was tantalizing, inviting. The pine scent she'd noticed when the boiling water first hit the dried herbs was followed by lavender, a hint of resiny sweetness, something sharp, like rosemary. She lifted it toward her mouth and paused for another inhalation.

"You mean the unquiet dead you found shambling about along the northern edge of my valley, yes?" Rhunival said this so matter-of-factly that Aelis almost didn't truly hear what he said for a moment.

She paused, mouth open, bowl in hand, tilted just enough to slop a bit of hot liquid onto her lap. She stood. In her peripheral vision, she realized that all but Rhunival had set their bowls down and had tensed.

"The roving corpses are nothing to do with me," he protested, sounding stung. "What do you take me for?"

"But you have seen them," Aelis said. "You could point us toward more of them?"

"You destroyed all that wandered through my valley. I'm aware of what passes here, whether I clap eyes on it or not." His eyes somehow blazed for just a moment as he stared at Aelis. "I hope you shed no blood upon my earth."

A trick of the firelight and the shadows, Aelis told herself. All the same, she was somehow glad that she'd set her bowl down without drinking anything and had to resist the urge to make sure the rest of her party had done the same.

"May I see to my companion?" Aelis said carefully. "With the warmth of your fire and the stability of your table?"

"You may." Rhunival pointed to a dark corner of his hall. "You'll find a table there and may make such light as you would, though I find little use for any but the fire."

7

BARGAINS AND BLOOD

Aelis produced her alchemy lamp and brought it to life, turning it in the direction Rhunival had pointed. She saw a square table, solidly made, with a few stout chairs about it. She guided Maurenia there and sat her down, then retrieved her medical kit from her pack.

"Let me see your hands first, then your shoulders," Aelis said as she sat down. She adjusted the settings of her lamp for maximum brightness, set it on the rough boards. In the white light it threw, Maurenia looked pale, drawn. *Beautiful still*, Aelis thought, *just hurting*.

Behind them she could hear a quiet buzz of talk, mostly Timmuk's, perhaps already engaging their host in the tales he sought.

Maurenia held out her hands. Aelis took them lightly and bent low, briefly letting go to drag the alchemy lamp closer.

"Could've used a warning about touching them bare-skinned," Maurenia said.

"As you've already said," Aelis replied, "and I'm sorry. I hadn't anticipated something that complex." She pulled Maurenia's hands closer to her eyes.

"Largely superficial burns," she muttered. "Going to hurt, but the pain will recede, and the swelling will go down in a few days."

"Largely doesn't mean totally," Maurenia countered.

"I know. And there are some blisters popping up. Those worry me a bit. For now, I'll treat them and we'll bind your hands up."

"No," Maurenia said. "No binding."

"I'm not going to tie mittens to them. But you'll need some light bandaging to keep from abrading it. Otherwise there's every chance you'll rip the skin clean off before it gets a chance to heal, and *then* you're looking at several months of healing instead of a few days or weeks."

"I need to be able to wield a sword," Maurenia protested.

"And I need you to have functional hands past the next two or three days," Aelis answered. "I like the things you can do with them."

Maurenia shifted in her seat but didn't answer this time. Aelis opened her kit. She pulled free a wooden jar, its cap kept tight with a length of copper wire. She opened it and a pungent smell filled the room almost immediately.

"What is in that?"

"You're probably better off not knowing."

"It smells like concentrated piss."

"There *is* a certain concentrate derived from urine in it," Aelis answered calmly as she set the pot down. She called up another Necromantic First Order; Aldayim's Clean Fingers. She felt the fingertips of her right hand tingle as she released it. Even the tiny amount of energy nudged her further toward sleep, but it left her with clean fingers and a clear conscience as she dipped into the jar.

"Is it going to smell like piss all night?"

"If the wards meant to keep it fresh did their work, yes."

"That's going to make sleeping hard."

"I can put you to sleep."

Maurenia frowned. "Hardly the place for—"

"With an Enchantment, Maurenia."

"Well, if it comes to that." A pause. "How much of that can you do in a day, anyway?"

"Not a great deal more, I'll admit. But the green moon is up." Aelis focused on rubbing the unguent into Maurenia's burned fingers as gently as she could, trying to let the medicine do some of its work before she abraded the skin too much. "Makes Enchantment easier."

Maurenia made a quiet, noncommittal sound. Aelis felt the greasiness of the unguent gradually dissipate as Maurenia's skin absorbed it. "Now let me see that shoulder."

"It's nothing."

"I'm the surgeon, I'll decide what's nothing."

Maurenia made as if to start peeling back her gear and clothing, but Aelis grabbed her wrists and set them down. "Not until I've bandaged your hands. Let them rest."

It was a bit awkward to remove Maurenia's pack, the baldric holding her scabbarded sword and sheaf of bolts, and then help her off with her makeshift heavy coat. But the more that was revealed, the more stiffly the half-elf moved, and the more Aelis was certain that the wound in Maurenia's shoulder was serious enough to warrant the care she was taking.

"I wouldn't have thought a dog could bite through so many layers and even break the skin," Maurenia said.

"A dog couldn't. The animated skeleton of a dog, on the other hand, has none of the self-preservation instincts of a real dog. A real dog might find its teeth hitting a metal stud in your armor or decide that attacking you in the first place was too dangerous, and it will rarely exert all the force its jaws are capable of. An animated skeleton will pay heed to none of that. It will bite with unnatural force, and it will keep biting until something makes it stop."

"And it'll burn the fuck out of your fingers if you touch it too," Maurenia said.

"Well, it will if it was made using a complex animating ritual. Fourth Order, at *least*, with a built-in defense mechanism deploying its own animating energy as a kind of shield. I understand it in theory, but I don't think I could do it. At least not spread across that many animations and persistent for this long." While she spoke, Aelis had been gathering other things from her kit: a rag, a jar of astringent, a needle, fine silk thread, tweezers.

"So whoever built these things is more powerful than you?"

"A more powerful Necromancer, certainly," Aelis answered as she wetted a rag and began cleaning away the blood. There were three jagged puncture wounds; *two of them*, Aelis thought, *likely still had teeth in them.* And of course, the skin around them was blistered with the same burns as Maurenia's hands. "And he probably had help."

"Isn't Necromancy your primary school?"

"Indeed, it is. But we only learn the rudiments of animating corpses, raising the dead, and binding spirits these days. The theories. It isn't practical any longer."

"You know," Maurenia said, wincing, "I always wondered about that. Wizards aren't noted for their dedication to ethics. Neither are nations. So why give up a source of free labor like that in the middle of a war, where no one gives a shit about philosophical niceties?"

Aelis was too focused on cleaning the blood and preparing to debride Maurenia's wound to flinch or start at her words, but a part of her mind certainly took note of them. *It's got nothing to do with a moral choice*, she wanted to say, and was oath-bound not to. *It has to do with unknown forces yanking them out of our control at unpredictable intervals.*

"Try convincing everyone else of that," she muttered instead. "And we'll see about going back to the old ways." She rested her hands gently on Maurenia's now-clean skin. "This bit may hurt. Do you want something to bite on?"

Maurenia shook her head. Aelis took up her tweezers, adjusted the dial of her lamp to focus the beam more carefully. She made her best estimates of where the teeth might lie in Maurenia's skin and reached for them. She felt the tweezers close almost immediately around something hard. Maurenia tensed and the muscle in her shoulder spasmed. Aelis almost lost the tooth but managed to cling onto it. She quickly, smoothly tugged it free. It was the mere tip of something long and jagged. She lowered her hand to show it to the half-elf.

"You're lucky only this much broke off."

"Don't feel lucky."

"It means that not as much of the tooth got in as might otherwise have done. There're some fairly important muscles, bones, and vessels it could've reached with a little more length."

"Why didn't it keep burning?"

"Broken off, lost contact with its animating force."

"You'd think someone would try to weaponize fragments that way, like baskets of arrows launched from a siege piece or javelin heads that shatter."

"They did," Aelis said. "It's a Fifth Order. Ongoing Rupture. Could go a few different ways; shatter into dozens of splinters, dig further into the muscle fibers, seek out blood vessels."

"Anaerion's balls, is there anything you people couldn't make more awful?"

Aelis resisted the urge to shrug her shoulders; movements beyond the minute and delicate were not the surgeon's friend. "Let's just say it would've been rare. I wouldn't want to meet the bastard who could put a pack of animated dog skeletons into the world, keep them up and running for decades with Death's Cold Shield upon them *and* an Ongoing Rupture. That's . . . that's *Lives of the Wardens* stuff, there. That's a whole gods-damned chapter." After setting aside the first tooth, she took a deep breath and settled her tweezers over the second wound. She thought better of it, put the tweezers back down on the cloth she'd laid out, and pulled her dagger free of its sheath.

"This will be cold," she warned. As she laid the dagger on Maurenia's skin, she realized she should've done that *first*. She was getting tired, and tired surgeons were sloppy surgeons. She gave her head the tiniest shake to clear it.

With her Anatomist's blade in contact with Maurenia's skin, Aelis could investigate the various systems—muscles, blood vessels, bones—affected by the wounds she'd taken, gauge her pain, and determine the best ways to proceed. Two more teeth were broken off in her shoulder. She held the knife in place with her left hand, reached for the tweezers with her right, and extracted both teeth with smooth, even motions. The last was buried more deeply and had wreaked a little more havoc, leaving a wide divot in her flesh and nicking a bone.

Aelis set the tweezers and shards of teeth on the rag she'd placed on Rhunival's table.

"Instead of sewing this one shut, I'm going to pack it with sterile bandage and some astringent. In a day or two, it may be ready to close."

She worked to pack the wound and to sew shut the other, shallower cuts, conscious of the way Maurenia had begun to shiver once more; Rhunival's fire was guttering and hadn't been built up since they'd entered his hall, it seemed. That work was simple, second nature to her hand and eye. The stitches were tiny, her needlework quick and accurate, and the two wounds were closed and Maurenia was clothed again before she had time to get truly cold. Aelis carefully wrapped up her instruments and the bandage she'd used, packing it away in her kit, not trusting she had any way to dispose of it in Rhunival's hall.

"Careful of the blood," Maurenia whispered.

"Which one of us is the surgeon? Come on. Let's get the fire built up and you something to eat," Aelis said. "Something from our stores," she added in a whisper. Then, quickly, she slipped her wand out of her sleeve and laid it to Maurenia's forehead with a muttered syllable. "There," she said. "It won't put you to sleep, but once you lay down, nothing will keep you from it."

Beside them on the table where Aelis had set down her instruments, and the teeth she'd extracted from her lover's shoulder, a single drop of blood had soaked through the cloth and fallen between the boards of Rhunival's table to splash, unseen and unknown, against the dirt floor of his hall.

8

ANSWERS OWED

Rhunival had set two iron pots over his fire. One held some kind of pottage, Aelis was sure, and it only smelled appetizing when she realized how long it had been since she'd eaten. The other was smaller, and the bearded man was bent over it, sprinkling herbs from a bag that quickly disappeared up his sleeve. Though the scent of woodsmoke crowded out most other things, Aelis knew mulling spices when she smelled them.

"You're a clever one, Warden. Deft with your hands." He turned his sun-browned face toward Maurenia, who held her bandaged hands awkwardly, eyed her keenly. "So is she, engineer and crafter and warrior all in one. Will her hands heal, do you think?"

That attracted Timmuk's attention from the fire he'd been staring into.

Aelis did not like how Rhunival's voice sounded, how hungry the words seemed in his mouth.

"In mere days," Aelis said, forcing her voice to be calm, reaching for the smooth-cheeked demeanor of the court noble. She'd never been as good at it as her older sisters, though.

With little taste for the talking dance Rhunival relished, she had half a mind to reach out to him with Enchantment, to try to compel some kind of declaration of truth from him. But her encroaching exhaustion—she had done a fair amount of magical work against the animated dogs and a little with Maurenia—was wedded to a growing suspicion that nothing she could cast, even when fresh, would touch him.

Rhunival bent forward and stirred the pot with a ladle. "I assume you have cups in those overfull packs you all carry." He pulled up a ladleful; the aroma of it nearly made Aelis weak in the knees.

"What bargain must we make to drink of it?" Tun was the first to come to the obvious question.

"None. It is freely offered. I simply don't have enough wine cups for the lot of you."

Timmuk pulled his rucksack to his seat and rummaged within. He pulled free a bundle of well-turned wooden cups nested together and bound by a leather strap hooked at both ends. He unbound them and tossed them lightly to his companions. Aelis went first to Rhunival's side, an honor or a poisoner's test, that they accorded her.

She felt slightly comforted by the fact that Tun loomed over her shoulder, blocking out the green moonlight that had begun to fall through the smoke hole in the roof. *If he does poison me, at least he'll have a werebear to answer to*, she thought.

Rhunival filled her mug. Steam curled up from it, blown about by a sudden sharp, cold breeze. Sweat drying on her skin reminded her of the exertions of the day.

She lifted her mug and sipped from it without further hesitation.

Rhunival smiled, but from what she could see, she thought it an honest man's smile and not a predator's grin. *Trust your gut*, Bardun Jacques had always said, *until it gets itself filled with a foot of steel.*

Tun took his own cup, then Timmuk and Maurenia in turn. Aelis had another sip. Generally, she detested a warm drink that was not coffee. While the wine in it, as dark as the night surrounding them, was not anything as delicate or layered as the wines she knew from home, it had a satisfactory earthiness, enhanced by the herbs Rhunival had blended into it. She was too cold and too tired from the energy of a fight to spend much time worrying at just what those herbs were, but she was certain in her assessment of its safety.

"Have you a barn or an outbuilding we might sleep in? Or may we erect such shelter as we carry on your grounds, and borrow some fire from your hearth?"

"You could still sleep inside my hall, full-bellied and warm by the fire and as safe as your childhood beds, for simply the true and honest tale of why you have come."

"I would tell you that for the space you've already given us, and the work it allowed me to do. Seems like a bad bargain for a night's sleep and two meals."

He thought this over, one hand practically disappearing into his beard. "Then you must agree to answer all questions I may have."

"Sorry, but I've been trying to tutor a child for too long now to agree to answer *all* questions. You get three."

"Ten."

"Five."

"Seven."

"Five," Aelis repeated, "or we'll chance sleeping outside." She wasn't sure if the confidence in her voice came from certainty or exhaustion, but either way it seemed to work. Rhunival nodded and said, "Five."

Aelis resisted the urge to throw down the rest of her wine, but she relaxed. Rhunival shared out the pottage: oats, beans, herbs, plenty of salt, and a suspicion of butter, but not an ounce of meat that Aelis could detect. Timmuk began some tale or other, his voice a slow, distant rumble. But the exertions of the day, the delicious warmth of the fire, and the way the hall held that warmth with five bodies clustered around had her asleep before she knew it.

※　※　※

The next thing she knew she was awake, with gray dawn light filtering through the smoke hole in Rhunival's roof. Looking up, she could see stars fading as the sun rose and a faint hint of the green of Elisima's moon in retreat.

For a moment, the confusion of being awake in a strange place warred with the pull to go straight back to sleep. Confusion won and she sat up with a jerk.

Around her she saw the sleeping forms of her companions. Tun stirred in his sleep when she looked in his direction, but the rest slumbered blissfully on.

Aelis had the sensation of being watched. She turned her head side to side and caught a glimpse of Rhunival seated at his table, a stick of wood and a knife in his hands. He was clearly working at carving something, but she couldn't even guess at what form the work was taking.

"Good morning, Warden," he murmured. "You still owe me answers."

"So I do," Aelis said groggily. Though she longed to sink back into her blankets, she resigned herself to wakefulness, pushed them back, stood up, and went to the extra chair by the table.

"Your companions endeavored to explain what they could as you drifted to sleep. It became clear that none of them alone, and not all of them together, had as clear a picture of why they were here as you alone did. And it seemed rude to awaken you after the amount of effort you'd expended." He made a few quick, decisive cuts with the knife, then considered his work again.

An animal figure, she thought. *Maybe.*

"In fact, none of them seemed to have any clear knowledge except that you had told them of the hazards of various undead. Or," Rhunival said, "to soothe your professional pride, *animations*. The half-orc follows you out of loyalty and trust. The half-elf, well, there is little most of us will not do when it comes to matters of the heart. The dwarf may have the clearest and purest motive of all: the hope of wealth. There is friendship there, true; he and the half-elf are companions of long standing, who have ventured through fire and death together. Those bonds are not easily broken. But silver would bind him to you better."

"Who," Aelis said, "are you? And how do you know all this?"

"I am Rhunival," he answered. "And I have said nothing that is not easily apparent to one who knows how to watch and listen. It is also," he added, a bit of a scold in his voice, "not my turn to answer questions. It is yours to relate your tale."

"Very well," Aelis said. "The truth of it." *Or as little as I can manage without an outright lie.* "A superior of mine alerted me, in a letter, to the presence of these animations, apparently scattered throughout what was once Mahlgren."

"What was once Mahlgren remains Mahlgren," Rhunival said quietly, but with a certain unshakable conviction. He gripped the carving knife in his hand a little more tightly. "Lines and maps, the words of man or elf or dwarf, no matter the crown they were, do not change that."

"A Warden deals in political realities, I'm afraid. I have no other convenient term to refer to it."

Rhunival shrugged, gestured vaguely with the wood in his hand. "Go on."

"The letter alerted me to their presence and suggested, rather strongly, that I investigate them, destroy them if possible. I aim to do so. They—" she indicated her sleeping companions with the sweep of a hand—"elected to join me."

"This is not your first time north of the Tri-crowns' arbitrary border."

"No," Aelis said, then stopped. *Got to do better than leading not-question statements to get more out of me, old man.* She found that she was rather less confident in thinking of Rhunival as a *man*, exactly, than she would've liked.

Beneath his wild gray beard, he smiled. "It is a long time since I have had a partner worth the sparring, Warden."

Aelis didn't let herself smile.

"Very well. The superior who sent you looking; who is it?"

"Archmagister Ressus Duvhalin," she replied.

"That is an impressive name. How many *animations* do you expect to find?"

"That I truly cannot answer, for I don't know. Fifty, perhaps more? Even this is a poorly educated guess."

"Hrm." Rhunival went silent, twitched his knife around a knot in the wood he held. The blade's rasp filled the quiet for a few seconds. "Why do you carry the aura of the unquiet dead yourself, and what has it to do with your dealings with Dalius de Morgantis?" He did not look at her as he spoke.

The way Rhunival casually spoke that name set off alarm bells in Aelis's mind. She was halfway out of her seat, dagger in hand, before Rhunival looked up. He frowned and shook his head.

"You won't need that, Warden. I am no friend to that creature."

"That doesn't make you my friend, either."

"It does not. But we may freely exchange in ways that benefit each other without struggling for advantage. I have done you no harm. I have offered you house room for questions, and wine free of obligation. I have done nothing to threaten you or the bargain we made."

"True enough," Aelis said, slowly sinking back into her seat. She was even slower to slip her dagger back into its sheath. She rather liked having the solid weight of it in her hand. "But you asked two questions just now."

"True. And you answered one of them without speaking; you are an enemy of de Morgantis. Very well. But the other remains unspoken."

Aelis shrugged. "I am a Necromancer. It is my nature to have that aura."

"No," Rhunival said, pointing the wood accusingly at her. "You are a *Necrobane*, or so you tell yourself. You should not have the aura of which I speak."

Aelis willed herself to stillness, despite the urge to hide her wounded ankle. *Have I said that word aloud in his valley?*

"I was in combat with several animated skeletons just hours ago. Perhaps it rubbed off." She had to resist a strong urge to scratch a sudden itch on her ankle, but she knew better than to draw Rhunival's attention to it.

"You do yourself no credit by evading, Warden. But I cannot prove you a liar."

In a Warden's world, proof is one of the few things that truly matters. Bardun Jacques's voice, in one of its quieter moments, floated across Aelis's thoughts. She decided to take the initiative and try some questions of her own.

"What dealings have you had with Dalius?"

"I told you I am no friend of that creature."

"I thought you said that evasions don't do anyone any credit."

"Then you admit you were evading," Rhunival said. He leaned forward, a slightly wolfish cast to his features.

"I admit nothing."

"Warden, if you have called upon forbidden rituals to arm yourself, or to extend your life, or to sap that of others, I cannot feel it. But there is *something* in you that draws from Onoma. Subtly—but not so a Necromancer would not know it if it had been done to them."

"What would you tell me about Dalius in exchange?"

"My history with de Morgantis is not to be had without higher cost, Warden. And I think your companions will wake, soon, and look ill upon you making any further bargains."

As if cued by Rhunival's words, Tun sat up, then Timmuk, and finally Maurenia. The dwarf, ever practical, busied himself by building up the fire.

Tun stood as best he could manage given the low ceiling, and went outside to gather wood, Aelis assumed, and to stretch and take the air. Maurenia, meanwhile, blinked away sleep.

"Remind me," she said, "the next time there is a featherbed to hand and nothing I must do in the morning, to have you cast that spell upon me again."

"Noted," Aelis said. "But there are tasks aplenty facing us, I think."

Maurenia nodded, stood, tested her shoulder by rolling it this way and that until Aelis's sharp hiss brought her up short.

"Do not tear out my stitches. If you do, I'll bind that arm to your side and leave you here with Rhunival."

Maurenia shrugged, adopting a blank and casually indifferent look. "That wouldn't be so bad. It's warm. He's a gracious host and a fine enough cook."

"My evening pottage has nothing on my morning oats." Rhunival grinned as he sat back in his chair and resumed his carving.

"Where to then?" Maurenia said.

"Follow the plan, make for Mahlhewn Keep," Aelis said. "Picking off groups of animations one at a time is going to be death by attrition for us."

"Well, we learned a few things yesterday," Maurenia said. "One, don't touch them unless you've got steel gloves like Timmuk. Two, give us some of the damned activated silver soap."

Behind her Rhunival's rasping knife strokes came to a sudden halt.

"Did you say activated silver?" He leaned forward, the grin having leaked out of his face.

"I did," Maurenia answered.

"You're going to want to save that for Mahlhewn if you're intent on going there. I suppose, of course, that's what drew you to my valley in the first place, given that it's only a day's hard walk away in fine weather; faster if you run, of course." He seemed to relax a bit. "And if you are, you're going to need a few other things."

"Keys? Wardstones? Maps?" While Rhunival considered his answer, Aelis reached for Maurenia's hands and carefully unwrapped the gauze she'd bound around the burns.

"All of those if they were to be found. Though if any wards made there persist this long since its abandonment, I would be shocked. And it has been many years since I could say such a thing," Rhunival replied.

"Then what do we want?" Aelis directed Maurenia to sit and went to her pack, intending to retrieve the same pot of unguent she'd used the night before.

"Well, a key for certain. And while I have no map, I can direct you to ways you would not find without me."

"And what exactly will that cost us?"

Rhunival smiled again, and it was the same predatory smile Aelis had seen and mistrusted before.

"I will ask only that you retrieve something for me."

"And what'll that be?" Timmuk spoke up, having finally stirred the fire into roaring life, and dug through his pack to produce one of those hard, apparently imperishable corn muffins that he and Tun enjoyed and Aelis could barely stomach.

"Just a trinket. Nothing of great importance to you, and nothing that will hamper your task, whatever it may be."

"And how," Aelis said, smearing stinking but cooling unguent over Maurenia's burns, "do you know it'll still be there?"

"Because it will be sealed in Mahlhewn's vault. Which was designed by the firm of Calabris and Dolovkin in its early days. The locking doors were made by Diboricek Dolovkin himself."

Aelis glanced at Maurenia with a raised brow; she shrugged in answer. Aelis then turned toward Timmuk, whose eyes were wider than she'd known they could be.

"Are these names I should know?"

"If you've any interest in protecting valuables from the light-fingered and sharp-eyed, yes," Timmuk said. "They're the best; every bank, counting-house, lender, gambling hall, merchant, and every member of the Estates House who can afford them makes a point of hiring them. Diboricek

Dolovkin was the greatest designer of locks, vaults, traps, and security systems this world has ever seen."

"So, you're telling me if the Mahlhewn Vault was built by this firm, it's still there, and it's still locked?"

Timmuk and Rhunival both nodded solemnly.

"And are you further telling me that you, Timmuk Dobrusz, will not be able to break into it?"

"Let's not be hasty. Given time and tools, I can break into anything. But we have little of the former, almost none of the latter."

"What, you haven't got an auger with you?"

"Of course I have. Just not all of them."

"How many can there be?"

"The biggest one requires a wagon to carry, and a horse or two very pissed-off dwarves to fully operate," Maurenia put in. "So I thought it was best we left it behind. In Lascenise."

"Fine. I take it that you do know how to open it?" Aelis looked at Rhunival as she closed her pot, wired it shut, and pushed a tiny ward into the wire to keep it sealed.

"I know what one needs to know in order to figure out how to open it. And I also know that its magical defenses were designed by one Dalius Enthal de Morgantis un Mahlgren." Rhunival had gone back to his carving and did not look up from the careful work of his knife.

That name fell over the room like a shadow. Everyone stopped and waited until the door opened and Tun stepped back in. His presence seemed to fill the entire hall, even stooped as he was.

"What? Someone see a ghost?" Tun asked.

"Dalius Enthal de Morgantis un Mahlgren." Timmuk repeated the name. "You said that, and the Warden here flinched. I don't know her too well yet, but I don't think she's much of a flincher. But I do know Maurenia well—and I never thought I'd see her fearful over a name being spoken."

"Do not worry over saying the name of that creature here," Rhunival said. "He has no power in my hall. Or not enough for such trifles to matter. Beyond these walls and certainly beyond my valley? I would fear to say it. As should you."

"I destroyed him," Aelis said. "By the power of the First Art, I pulled whatever life was in him out. He was a pile of dust and bone when last I saw him."

"And what of the bones, Warden?" Rhunival suddenly stuck his knife point down in his table; it quivered for a moment. "What of the bones?

Think of the power in them. Think of what you could make with that. Then think of *that creature*, what he was capable of in his first life and how much more he might be now, and tell me again that you destroyed him when you did not find his body. *He lives still.* And if you bested him once, he will never stop hunting you."

Aelis flashed back to the moment in her tower. A shard of glass buried into her stomach, slipping on her own blood, landing hard on the stones face to face with the desiccated corpse. She shivered and found her hand lowered over the scar on her stomach, then snapped back to the present, finding Rhunival's eyes huge, boring into hers.

"What is he, then?" Tun took a half step forward. And a half step for Tun was a couple of paces for most men, so it put him in reach of Rhunival, and between their host and Aelis.

"That is a question your Warden will have to answer. There is naught that you could trade me for it."

Aelis pressed her hands down at her sides, dug her nails into the callous of her palms. "You know everything I know, Tun. He was a Warden, and the uncle of the Earl of Mahlgren. Tasked with overseeing the defense of the earldom, he became something worse, and I don't quite know what." For the benefit of Timmuk, she added, "He tried to kill me shortly after we met last summer. I thought I'd killed him."

"Apparently," Tun said, "he takes rather more than an ordinary amount of killing."

"Was he the architect of this network of barracks-crypts? All the undead?" That was Maurenia, tugging uncertainly at the fresh bandages Aelis had wrapped her hands with.

Rhunival ignored the question, went back to whittling silently.

"I think we can assume he was," Aelis muttered. "Insofar as he took charge of the defense of Mahlgren in his mortal life, and that was their purpose. I don't think he was a Necromancer."

I have not known Necromancy for some time. She remembered Dalius's words just before he slammed a glass shard from her broken alchemical flask into her stomach. She felt another twinge in the wound she'd sewn shut herself.

"Be sure of your answers, Warden," Rhunival said. By now he'd taken all the bark off and worked the knots out of his length of wood. He spun the knife in his hand so that three of his fingers were curled around the dull edge and began working the point into it. "Be very sure, for much may depend upon them." He blew some dust off the wood.

All grew silent again. Rhunival's knife dug into his wood. A log in the fire popped as heat reached a bubble of sap.

"And I am still waiting to hear that you accept my proposal. Or that you do not."

Aelis jerked her chin toward the door. "We'll be back after we confer."

Rhunival's only answer was the rasp of his knife.

Once outside, Aelis stalked a few angry steps away from the hall and stared at the morning sky, balling her hands into fists at her sides.

"Who're you angry at?" Tun asked. He'd crept up on her so lightly that she started and half jumped into the air.

"Everything," Aelis spat. "Stop sneaking up on me."

She thought she heard a faint chuckle.

"The proposal, as I understand it," Timmuk said, getting straight to business, "is that this Rhunival fellow gives us the means to defeat a Calabris and Dolovkin vault. And that all we need to do is carry something back to him."

"And what if that something is 'everything of value in the vault?'" Maurenia walked stiffly, with her right arm cradled awkwardly at her side. Each step, Aelis knew, probably was its own small pain, its own test.

"Even seeing a Calabris and Dolovkin vault up close—opening it, seeing how it was built, how it fits together—has inestimable value," Timmuk said. "That should not," he quickly added, "be understood to act as a statement that forfeits right to whatever of more conventional value is within it. But merely seeing the thing would be a great reason to have made this journey."

"If you had an important object," Tun began, "such as, say, a rod, or a wand, that could command legions of undead—sorry, *animations*," he corrected himself after seeing Aelis's expression, "and you had an uncrackable vault with supernatural defenses integrated into it by a powerful Warden, would you not be tempted to store the former inside the latter?"

Aelis felt a sudden pang, a leap in her gut that told her Tun almost certainly had to be right. She cautioned herself against giving in to it, but Bardun Jacques had taught her to trust that sort of thinking. They'd assumed all along that the rod would have been housed in Mahlhewn; now she knew, with unshakable certainty, that it was.

But there was one more wrinkle to work out.

"I do not think," she said, dropping her voice to a murmur that caused all three of the others to take a step closer to her, "we can bargain and deal with Rhunival as we would an ordinary man. Any bargain we make is one we are, perhaps, bound to regret to one degree or another."

"What *is* he?" Tun's lips turned down around his tusks.

"Looks like a man," Timmuk said.

"Smells like one," Tun added, with a shrug. "Mostly."

"If I were an Illusionist, or a Conjurer, or had ever taken any of the material I read on it seriously, I might have a better answer, but I'm not and I haven't. I am certain he is not a man, or not *merely* a man. He is something more."

"A captured spirit?" Maurenia leaned forward as she spoke. Auburn locks of hair angled over her sharp, high cheek.

"Not captive and not merely a spirit; a spirit cannot manifest into a physical form in quite the way he has. It might be able to fool us for a while, but it couldn't, for instance, pick up a knife and a piece of wood and carve it into something else in front of us. Not unless it was so powerful that it seems unlikely it could've been captured in the first place."

"Could be a spirit that *let* itself be captured," Timmuk mused.

"In which case we're in the midst of some longer game that has little to do with us, and that will likely go on after our deaths. In any case, here's what I do know," Aelis said. "We must be careful. We must be precise. But he can be trusted to hold to any bargain made provided we do the same."

"How do you know he's not just some old wizard? How do you know he's not another piece of Dalius?" Maurenia was slowly prodding her right shoulder with her left hand, testing for places where it hurt, ways she could move it.

"I don't," Aelis said. "But I think if he were Dalius, none of us would have survived the night."

"We do not seem to have much choice," Tun said. "Can we break into this vault without his help?"

"Given enough time, enough tools, and a big enough barrel of blasting powder, absolutely," Timmuk said.

"And do we have any of those things?"

"Not a fucking one," Timmuk confirmed. "But give me time to think on it. I'll come up with something. I'll pile enough rocks against a wall that it will collapse. I'll dig a tunnel that lets a natural spring into it . . ."

"We haven't got the time for any of that," Tun said.

"Tun's right," Aelis said.

"You'd do well to remember that," Tun muttered. "It would save time in future."

Aelis glared up at him for a moment. "If what we seek is in that vault— and I think we all agree it's at least a strong enough possibility to warrant investigation—then we need Rhunival's help to get into it. It's that simple."

One by one, they all muttered their agreement.

"Does anyone else want the burden of bargaining, or is that down to me?" Aelis looked around.

Timmuk stroked his beard. "If you could tell me surely what he was, Warden, I'd do it myself. But without that knowledge . . ." He stopped and spread his hands and Aelis nodded. She turned on her heels and marched back into Rhunival's hall.

9

FORAGING

She found him standing over his table, having set a simple wooden vise grip upon it. The length of wood he'd been carving was set in it, and he had a thin auger in his hands, which he was slowly, methodically working into the wood, hollowing out the center.

"Making a flute?"

Rhunival shrugged and adjusted his grip on the drill.

"Suppose music helps pass the time," she mused.

"Suppose it would, if passing time was what needed doing. This is something I'm making for you, should you choose to accept the bargain."

"Well, if we could, I'd like to hammer out the details. My friends are eager to move on."

"I think only one of the people out there is your friend. The woodsman, of course, is as true a friend as one could hope for, provided one is true in turn. The iron-handed master of sums, now—he's a friendly sort and full of great phrases on the subject. But his actual friendship is perhaps reserved for those of much longer acquaintance."

Aelis folded her arms and tried to find some store of patience by counting backward from one hundred in increasing intervals of three. She hadn't gotten past seventy when Rhunival's words brought her up short.

"The engineer—she is not your friend, either. She is much more, eh? Your lover. And yet, how much do you know about h—"

"Rhunival," Aelis snapped, "the terms of the bargain, please."

"It's very simple. I give you what you need to open the vault. You give me something from within it."

"What?"

"Do you accept the bargain?"

"I need to know what I'm bringing you."

"You don't, in point of fact. You can agree—and I think it likely you will—without knowing."

"Are we going to get anywhere unless I agree?"

"It seems remarkably unlikely."

"Fine," Aelis said, tiring of the nonsense, of this strange man and his roundabout words, of feeling beholden to him in his hall.

"Fine, you agree?" He turned to her for the first time since this discussion had begun. "You need to be more specific than that, Warden."

"Fine, I agree."

"Swear upon your power that, should you recover it, you will bring what I ask and not turn it to your own hand. Do that, and you shall have what you need of me."

Aelis did not like the sound of the words in his mouth, or the way his eyes suddenly gleamed in the firelight as he spoke.

But she was increasingly certain she had little choice.

"I swear," she murmured.

"Then do so," Rhunival said sharply. "Speak the words themselves. Do not think you can evade me on this, Warden."

Aelis was surprised at how she had to force herself to eye him directly as she spoke. "I swear, upon my power, to bring you the object you ask for, in exchange for the knowledge needed to retrieve it. I swear not to turn it to my own hand."

"Very well." Rhunival seemed to shrink, to recede into himself, and his eyes lost their shine. "I will need the rest of the day to finish this," he said, waving the carving vaguely at her. She saw now it was a fish of some kind. But its mouth was hollowed, and holes seemed to be destined to be drilled in other places, if the smaller hand drills Rhunival had set out were any indication.

"Why do we need to wait for that?"

Rhunival's smile was now less predatory spirit and more maddening imp.

"Had you not guessed, Warden? This is what you'll need to get into the vault."

♦　　♦　　♦

"A gods-damned flute? A flute in the shape of a fish?"

"He didn't say it was a flute. He didn't exactly say it wasn't a flute, either." Aelis and Maurenia were walking a wide circuit of Rhunival's hold. Occasionally, their hands would fall together and clasp for a moment, but between gloves and Maurenia's bandages, usually not for long. Still, Aelis found she enjoyed the way they continually found ways to touch each other lightly as they walked.

"You know, a musical lock sounds all to the good," Maurenia practically spat. "All whimsy and cleverness and beauty. And if they aren't tuned every month by someone who knows what the hell they're doing, they go straight to shit."

"There are musical-lock tuners?"

"There are musicians who also enjoy knowing about locks and vice versa," Maurenia said. "You're missing the point."

"Please do direct me to it, then."

"That if this thing's been sitting out here—how long since Mahlgren was officially abandoned?"

"Depends on who you ask, but Mahlhewn Keep fell six years before I was born, and that was Mahlgren's great bulwark. Very little lasted after that. It wasn't an earldom full of large settlements."

"Of course it wasn't," Maurenia said. "Small holds full of hardy, fiercely independent people, no doubt. But the weather too hard and the land too unforgiving to build proper cities even once everyone else figured out how. No wonder orc raiders rolled over them."

"The point?"

"The point is that after twenty-eight years without proper maintenance, tuning, and upkeep, not to mention possible exposure to the weather, damage from looters, or half the castle falling in on it, a vault with a musical lock is probably fucked."

"One problem at a time," Aelis said. "If we decide the next steps are impossible before we even see them, we're bound to screw up this one."

"Your teachers did a number on you," Maurenia grumbled.

"What's that mean?"

"It means you think every problem has a solution. That there's always a right answer."

"There is always a solution. Usually several of them. Doesn't mean any of them are *good* solutions. Sometimes being a Warden simply means knowing how to pull the lever that will drop the smallest bucket of shit on your head." *Bardun Jacques would be proud of that metaphor,* Aelis thought.

Maurenia laughed, the first real laughter Aelis had heard from her since the previous night. "That is one way to put it. You were never a soldier, so I always wonder where you find your more colorful language."

"I had at least one teacher who did a number on me."

"What, no siblings?"

"Oh, plenty of those," Aelis said.

"You don't talk about them."

"We weren't close, mostly. I was the youngest, and a bit doted on. I missed out on the war, on compulsory service, and had more tutors, more diversions than they did."

"Well, how many? What are their names, all that?"

"Oldest is Aleyan, my father's heir, not exactly a war hero but not shy about wearing his medals and exaggerating. He's almost twenty years my senior. Then there's Tarlin, who I haven't seen since I was a child because he became a Silent Son of Onoma, then Delphine, who commands the family regiment and downplays what she did in the war, but I strongly suspect that Aleyan is jealous of it. Yseult, a mere decade older, and probably the one I was closest with."

"Bit of a gap there. Parents went at it hammer and tongs and then decided to take a decade off?"

"There were twins between us. Jean and Mallory. I only know them as portraits."

"Ah," Maurenia said. "Lots of nieces and nephews, then?"

"Too many to keep an accurate tally. Why all this interrogation?"

"Because you never talk about your family, and if I'm too quiet, you'll start asking me questions."

Aelis paused to gather words. "We de Lentis are not an affectionate people."

"Could've fooled me." Maurenia emphasized her words by wrapping her arms around one of Aelis's and squeezing for a moment.

"Families in the Estates House live very formal lives. Expectations are clearly laid out, very early on. I only escaped the brunt of them because of my power."

"But you just said you were doted on."

"By the time I came along, Count Guillame and Countess Elena were too tired, I think, to trouble overmuch about me. Throwing tutors and distractions at me kept them from having to think on me much. Don't misunderstand me," Aelis said, leaning against Maurenia's shoulder. "I love my family. They love me. But being a Warden keeps me distant from them, which is best for all concerned."

"Do you wonder where you'd be if you hadn't become a Warden?"

"I don't dwell on whether I would've failed something I plainly succeeded at."

"Well, what if you hadn't had that drive?"

"I'd be a court wizard somewhere. Perhaps for my father, or some distant relation, some earl or duke with an eligible second or third son."

"Ah." Maurenia looked away from her then. "Was the Lyceum a welcome escape from . . ."

Aelis shrugged. "I can enjoy the company of men, if that's what you mean. Tirravalan families don't trouble themselves about that sort of thing anyway. You marry and produce an heir if you must; that's duty. Love does not interfere with it; nor does the opposite."

Maurenia pondered this. "I better keep close to you, then. When your time is up, you can go marry some old duke with a weak heart, make me your official mistress, and keep me in the style I deserve."

Aelis laughed, her breath turning to vapor in the cold midmorning air. "It's not the worst plan I've heard."

"Of course, there's the matter of this plague of undead to deal with first."

"Animations."

"Why do you insist on that difference?"

"An animated corpse—a skeleton, a fleshbag, what have you—is driven by a spell constructed by a Necromancer that draws on an extradimensional energy and sets it in motion. It follows a predetermined set of orders, and there isn't a great deal of modification that can be done once it's set. But as you've seen, that can last a long time."

"So what makes something undead?"

"That," Aelis said, "means raising someone—or something—with a certain degree of its memories, skills, and understanding intact. It means, in short, binding a piece of a departed soul back into its body."

"Elisima's round *ass*! How did you people ever come up with that kind of horror?"

"Maurenia," Aelis said, putting patience into her voice, "Necromancy, as an art and a science, has been practiced for over twelve hundred years. Probably longer, but that's how far the records extend. It's the oldest of the colleges of the Lyceum, the First Art. I have practiced it for *five* of those years. I didn't come up with any part of it. I only studied it."

"Does it bother you that you *could* do that?"

"It didn't bother me when I used that very technique to save Otto's life." She watched Maurenia blink and straighten up in surprise. "I bound Otto's life-force—his soul, if you accept the term—to his body while I waited for my medical kit to arrive so I could treat him in earnest. If I hadn't done that, he'd be dead. And then I probably would've had to kill Elmo, and Pips would have no family left in this world, no one who cares what happens to her in the way that only family can care. So no," Aelis said, shaking her head, "I'm not sorry I can bind a soul to the flesh it is trying to depart."

"Could you do that? Raise the dead? Truly, I mean," Maurenia asked. "Not as a horror."

"If Onoma's moon was high and full," Aelis began. "And I had done nothing else that day. And the patient had been dead for less than a quarter of an hour. And if I didn't care if I burned myself out or caused permanent physical damage to myself or the patient. Then, maybe. But I wouldn't like to bet on it."

"No might have sufficed," Maurenia said.

"Too much studying. Makes me run at the mouth," Aelis replied. "I notice you're asking an awful lot of questions without answering any."

"Mom owned a tavern in Mizanta. Father was an elf merchant passing through, and not her husband. Made life difficult for her when I showed up with these." Maurenia tapped her elongated ear with one gloved fingertip. "Her husband, Philoc, wasn't a bad man, as men go. He wasn't the sort to take his bitterness out on a child. But life there was not easy, or fun, and I escaped as soon as I could. Went to sea."

"Brothers? Sisters?"

Maurenia shrugged and Aelis, for once, had the good sense to let a matter drop rather than worry at it like a loose thread.

As if plucking the thought from Aelis's head, though, Maurenia said, "Not every story resolves. I made myself who I am free from my mother's failures and her husband's bitterness and whatever fears my half siblings harbored. I don't know if they still own that tavern, and I don't care to find out."

"I wasn't going to ask."

"Not today, maybe. But eventually you would have. It's what you do, who you are."

"It's a Warden's job to ask questions."

"I'm not your job," Maurenia said, and Aelis couldn't argue with that. They walked in silence for a while.

"What the fuck are we supposed to be doing, anyway?" Maurenia muttered. "Are we really meant to stay here an entire other day? Why can't he hand us that fish and let us go on our way?"

"Foraging," Aelis said as she suddenly remembered to look at the forest floor and not at her companion.

"For what? What grows here in winter?"

"Nettles. Onions. Mushrooms. Some herbs, I expect," Aelis answered. "Rhunival didn't give a lot of instruction. Timmuk seemed to have cutting and stacking wood down, and Tun was busy making the man a new robe, so he asked us to forage. We're foraging."

Maurenia grabbed Aelis's arm. "What *is* he?"

"I don't know," Aelis murmured. "I have guesses, but I don't have the firsthand knowledge or the books it might be concealed in."

"Then guess."

"Well, one guess I can make now is that it would be rude to have this discussion where he can hear us."

Maurenia looked around suspiciously, dropping her hand onto her sword. "What does that mean?"

"It means that I think, but lack proof, that he can at least guess at what we're doing and talking about while we're on his land."

"Then why'd you take us outside the hall to discuss his offer?"

"Because I didn't think that yet."

Maurenia looked around, brows knitting in worry. "How far does 'his land' extend?"

"He referred to 'my valley,' so I suppose as long as we're in one, we're on his territory."

"It's a slight valley," Maurenia said, "but it is one, I suppose."

"Geography, topography, and surveying are all Tun's department."

Maurenia peered at her and started to open her mouth, but Aelis stopped her with a lifted hand.

"Whatever you're about to ask about him, I'll say this: I trust him with my life; he's already saved it more than once."

Maurenia still looked like she wanted to ask more, and Aelis quickly said, "I stopped asking you about your life; you can stop asking me about this."

Maurenia seemed to accept that and nodded. Aelis's attention was drawn to a shelf of small, brown half circles growing from the trunk of a tree they passed. "Browncaps," she said. "I think."

"How does a city girl know what mushrooms to pick?"

"Alchemy," Aleis said as she took out a small, dull knife Rhunival had loaned her and carefully cut them from the bark.

"Do they taste good?"

"They're edible. My textbooks were never long on details of culinary usage."

"Then why take them?"

"Be suspicious if we come back with nothing."

"Suspicious? And what might we be doing to draw suspicion, hrm?" Maurenia gave Aelis a playful dig in the ribs. "To be honest, I'd half a mind to find a quiet little dry spot in the woods, build a little fire, and lay you down on the pine needles. But now that I know that old goat might be watching, we'll stay dressed, thanks."

"I'm not a bed-of-pine-needles kind of girl anyway," Aelis teased as they resumed a more careful foraging approach, eyes on the ground more than on each other. "More of a featherbeds and candlelight and cellar-cool Tirravalan Sceszin sort, to be honest."

Maurenia snorted. "More proof you were never in the army. You take your food, your drink, your sleep, and your sex wherever you can get it."

"Well," Aelis said, "if anyone *was* going to get me to roll in the winter grass, it'd probably be you."

She wanted to grab the words and stuff them back into her mouth, a feeling she'd become all too familiar with since coming to Lone Pine. Maurenia stiffened a little, went quiet, looked at her. Aelis sensed the half-elf was looking for words.

"Look, whatever it is you're about to say, let's just save it, alright? Put it away until we've dealt with the animations, however it is we're *going* to deal with them. And then, after I've stomped all the skeletons into nothingness with the Lash or the Fist and we're back home in my tower, you can say whatever it is you were thinking about how you can't stay in Lone Pine forever or how there are labels and definitions and things we haven't talked about and how some day we'll probably have to, and Onoma's Mercy, Maurenia, stop staring at me and say something so I'll feel like less of an idiot, alright?"

Maurenia stuck her hand awkwardly into Aelis's hair, pulled her forward, and kissed her on the mouth, urgently but softly. "You've heard Timmuk call me Renia. Why don't you?" Maurenia's lips moved against Aelis's as she spoke, and Aelis felt herself reconsidering her position on beds of pine needles.

Where in seventeen hells did that question come from? "Why . . . do you ask?"

"Because I like how you always say my full name, carefully. Like you pay attention to it. All of it."

Days of hard travel and dried food hadn't done their breath any favors, and the wind and cold had made their skin raw, but Aelis wanted to kiss Maurenia again anyway. So, she did, then murmured, "I'll remember that, Maurenia," against her lips. "But . . . we really should go back with more than a few mushrooms. Forage now, kiss later."

"Deal."

Even concentrating on their task, Aelis only found a few handfuls of mushrooms and one or two pinches of a hardier rosemary that had survived the wind and cold. Maurenia largely passed the time by complaining that shooting a deer would feed everyone a lot faster, until Aelis reminded her of the proscription on shedding blood.

By the time they came back, an hour or more after they set out, Rhunival was stomping around outside his hall in a new, warm-looking if crudely stitched together robe made of the spare hides Tun carried.

He appeared to be gathering things from his outbuildings, one of which, Aelis only just realized, was a chicken coop. Another appeared to be a mushroom shack, given the pungent air that wafted out when Rhunival opened the door. Another turned out to be a toolshed, into which he carried some of the woodworking tools he'd been using and brought out other, finer implements.

It seemed as though Timmuk and Tun had piled enough wood to last the old man through the winter and well into spring, and vapor rose off their sweat-soaked heads in great clouds.

"You're just in time to help get dinner on the boil," Rhunival called out as Aelis and Maurenia approached.

"It can hardly be past midday," Aelis answered.

"It isn't, but a proper boil takes a long time, and there's a lot of work between now and then. And there are things I have to tell you to temper our accord, and such things should be said as daylight falls but before the moons have risen."

But what about lunch? Aelis wanted to ask.

"What about lunch?" Maurenia muttered, just loud enough for Aelis to hear.

"I still have half a hard-rinded orange cheese in my rucksack," Aelis answered.

"There's water and a brush to clean the mushrooms, and a block and a knife to chop whatever herbs you found," Rhunival called as he puttered in his toolshed.

Aelis sighed and steeled herself for an afternoon of domesticity.

10

OLD LORE

Rhunival found ways to keep them all hopping while he continued to work on the now elegantly carved fish he had made out of the length of wood he'd started with. Mushrooms were scrubbed and chopped, then set in a pan with some wonderfully salty, bright yellow butter he produced from no animal Aelis could see. Between what Aelis found and what Rhunival pulled from his shack, at least four varieties wafted their scents into the air as Aelis found a moment to rest. A pot of oats was soaking—Rhunival was clear that it had to soak for hours before boiling, which took more hours—and soon enough Aelis had small green onions to chop.

In truth, any kind of fine work with her hands was easy enough to be pleasant, and she felt an odd thrill when Rhunival complimented the precision of her knife-work. Certainly, a part of her was wondering just why they weren't setting out immediately, but the simple work kept her from turning restless.

"You should see what I can do with a needle," she'd joked. But all the work with food and none of it to eat since breakfast had her starving when it was past lunchtime and no lunch was forthcoming. She found herself dreaming about the cheese in her pack, but every time she went for it, Rhunival found something else for her to do.

He, meanwhile, used ever finer knives to carve details in his fish: fins, a suggestion of scales, a fluted tail, an open mouth.

"What *is* that?" Aelis asked finally.

"A fish."

"And how will it get us into the vault?"

"It won't. It will give you what you need to get into the vault yourselves."

Aelis sighed. "Are you going to tell us more than that?"

"In due time."

"Let me guess," Aelis said. "The telling will take roughly as long as dinner will take to cook."

Rhunival smiled as he worked the smallest knife he'd laid out with two fingers. "Tell me, do they teach Wardens to be perceptive, or do they look for that when they draw you to the colleges?"

"Bit of both," Aelis answered. Finally, with the last onion chopped, he seemed to have no tasks left for her, and she sank gratefully onto a seat. Maurenia, ever practical, had sunk into a nap, while Tun and Timmuk entertained themselves out of doors.

"I notice that your companions have the knack of avoiding work more than you have. Why do you think that is?"

"Being a Warden means looking for extra work, not shirking what's in front of you."

"Hrm." He went back to his fish, blowing away a few grains of dust.

Aelis looked over at Maurenia, asleep against one wall, and weighed whether to wake her up to check her wounds. *Sleep is a great healer,* she thought. *Let it do what work it can.*

Suddenly, Rhunival stood, admired his fish in a ray of light through a parchment-covered window, and said, "It's done." He held it out toward Aelis, who came hesitantly forward.

"It's, what . . . musical?"

"I suppose one could play a tune on it," he said, "but such is not its purpose." He gestured with it for her to take it, and as she did, she almost felt it writhe under her hand. For a fleeting moment, instead of wood she thought she felt scales, a live wriggling thing. But the moment passed, and it was simply rough wood grain in her hand, albeit one with fabulous detail for but a few hours of work.

"Wake your lover. I will gather your friends. And then dinner on the fire. And a tale."

He glided outside. Still holding the fish, Aelis went and knelt by the sleeping Maurenia. Her hand was extended to the half-elf's cheek, not quite touching, when the deep green eyes opened.

"I was having a wonderful dream. Things came to me; things I could make, build. I wish I had brought parchment, some charcoal sticks, to sketch them . . ."

"I have some rough paper, pens, and ink with me," Aelis responded, "if you wanted to borrow them."

Maurenia shook her head. "They're all fading. It was only a dream, after all. Besides, how many better and bigger crossbows and siege engines does the world need?"

"Couldn't answer that," Aelis said. She took Maurenia's wrists and helped her to her feet. She heard the door open, and then Rhunival was directing Tun and Timmuk in the moving of pots and pans, draining the oats he'd been soaking, filling up a pot from a rain barrel, and finally getting it set on a grate over the hottest part of his fire.

"It will be some time as this cooks," Rhunival said. "Sit, sit and let the scents take you. Let hunger expand your stomach so that a humble but carefully made supper will fill it."

So far all Aelis saw in the pot was a giant pile of oats, and that in itself seemed less than appealing to her palate. Though she'd more or less gotten used to the plain food of the folk in Lone Pine, boiled oats tended to be something she *swallowed*, not something she *ate*.

Then, of course, she considered the array of other ingredients Rhunival had lined up: the mushrooms, herbs, a pile of thick salt crystals, a slab of butter, some dashes of cheese, half a dozen eggs, and she felt better about the prospects.

He went to his table and dug his hand into the salt, then opened it over the pot; the crystals lay heavy on the surface of the water that covered the oats. Rhunival whistled a snatch of song and stirred the tip of his finger into the water, and the salt dissolved.

"You are all," he began, "learned in some way or another. The Warden here holds warrants and degrees enough to staff an entire grammar school, no doubt. You, Master of Sums, undoubtedly there is great lore passed on in your various businesses. You, lady Engineer, know the movement of maths in the world and how to apply them to wood and steel, screw and lever, rope and chain, yes? And of course, Woodsman—you know how to read the signs of two worlds, perhaps three, depending on how we parse it.

"And yet, do any of you know of the Shapers?"

There was only silence. Rhunival turned to them as he asked the question, his dark eyes like slowly burning coals beneath his flyaway eyebrows.

A part of Aelis admired his showmanship, knowing as she did a handful of riveting speakers like Bardun Jacques, Urizen, and Vosghez. But still more of her was quickly won over, eagerly awaiting the answer she did not know.

"Before the world as you know it was given its moons, before the Seven Sibling Gods granted sapients the means of magic, before the Worldsoul began Her turning, before Onoma had welcomed a single elven soul, there were the Shapers."

Aelis shifted in her seat and felt the others similarly adjust as Rhunival's unsettling words draped over them. *Shapers? I have never come across that term.*

"Do not ask what race they were; they were all and none and in any form they chose, a hundred forms to a thought or one for a single day that would match the lifetime of the very oldest of elven folk. Do not ask where they came from, for even they did not say; they simply were, and the world moved in small ways to their will."

Rhunival paused here to take up a jug from his long table and took a slow, exaggerated drink from it.

"Some sang and some spoke, some declaimed verse and others wrote in smoke and sun- and starlight in the air itself. Some shaped earth and some wood and still others water, water as water, water as ice, water as steam. Matter was all much of a muchness to the Shapers.

"When I say some shaped earth, I speak of *mountains*," Rhunival said, drawing the word out for emphasis. "And yet, such a work could be made in an hour, while a Shaper might spend infinitely more time sculpting a crystal inside the mountain."

"Mountains are made by the forces of the earth," Timmuk said, "the flowing of its fiery blood, the shifting of its skin. I have been inside enough of them to know."

Rhunival smiled the indulgent smile of a teacher dealing with a too-precocious student. It was an expression, Aelis was forced to admit, she knew very well.

"There are many ways to understand the world, Master of Sums, though some would say it comes down to two; the way of tales, and the way of math: the marked string and the balance, the astrolabe and the compass, the ground glass lens. Though I can manage the tools of the latter, I know which I prefer." He paused to wet his throat with another pull at his jug.

"A Shaper might make a tree and the things of that tree down to the root and the seed and the veins in the leaf or the shades of color in the needles. The raw gem in its vein and the worked-in setting of gold. There are those— bolder than your poor host—who would say that the Shapers made you, Master of Sums, and you, Warden, and you, Engineer, and you, Woods-man. Who formed your limbs—or the idea of your limbs—in a time lost to any history but their own. And since the Shapers are long since lost but to the idle teller of tales, it is not a claim I would take to strict dialectic." He smiled once again like an indulgent teacher, but at Aelis this time.

"The fish of the seas and rivers and lakes, the fish of underground caverns that no eye has yet seen, the greatest leviathans of the deepest and darkest of oceans, to the bears of the caves and sheep and goats and long-haired kine of the meadow.

"Then, and only then, when the Shapers had made the world and all the things to inhabit it and all the valleys of it, did the Gods come. And the Gods, they wanted to take dominion of the things the Shapers had made. And it was not given to the Shapers to seek lordship or to own—that was a foreign concept, one the Seven Siblings taught, and well. By the time the Shapers had learned it, the Gods had learned their own kind of making, and they called it magic, and this the Shapers did not understand. It was not a war, no—had the Gods and the Shapers truly gone to war, then this world would not exist, the moons would have shattered, the very shroud of stars would have been rent asunder. But it was a contest all the same, one the Shapers were doomed to lose.

"Many tales I could tell then, of how a Shaper might have contended with Elisima, trying to win Her approval with rainbows that sprang in twelve bars of colors not before seen and never named, only to have Her *command* his acquiescence with but a wave of her hand. It was a Shaper who made the first wand, to her very hand, of rowan and willow and birch grown together in a plait, and the Shapers rued that day."

Aelis felt a jolt in her mind. There were schools within the College of Enchantment dedicated to the making of wands and the study of wood for them, and, as academics tended to do when left alone, they formed secret and semisecret honor societies. She had never been interested in them and never approached; the entire college of Necromancy tended to operate with that sort of theatrical ritual anyway, so she never felt the lack.

But she had once heard Urizen mutter something about being late for a meeting of the Sodality of the Plaited Wand, and she'd had no idea what he meant.

It was a small thing. An almost meaningless thing. But it struck a chord in her gut, in the way Bardun Jacques had taught her to trust herself, to allow that kind of leap and to fill in the details later.

Just how many fucking details do I need to get from here to there? she wondered.

Rhunival drained his jug and set it down. "So the Shapers retreated from the world. Perhaps to other worlds. But there are threads that bind them here, tenuous though they might be, and nets to snare their attention. Have you never passed a stand of trees every day and suddenly felt one was out of place? Have you not spent all your life looking at some sight—a mountain, say, or a range of hills—only to find some detail you had not seen before? Do not your natural philosophers find new fish, new fowl, new insects in places they have looked a hundred, a thousand times?

Do new stars appear in the sight of ever bigger lenses because you have built more keenly, or because the star itself is new? No, the Shapers do not walk the world as they once did. They do not make as much, or as widely, or as powerfully. But they are not gone. Nor are all the things they made."

Rhunival stood up and went to stir the pot. Aelis and the rest were so quiet they could hear his long iron ladle clanking against the inside of the cauldron.

"More salt," he muttered to himself, going to his long table to take a large pinch from a thick burlap sack, then sprinkling it over the oats.

"You may wonder," he said, as he stirred again, "why I do not speak of individual Shapers. Is it because to name one is to name everything they created, and this would take days? Is it because to tell one of their stories, every piece of it, is to beg to tell all their stories? Or is it because I simply do not know how to speak of them except as a whole?" He tapped the ladle against the side of the cauldron and sat back down, slowly, heavily.

"It is all of those, and more, and other things I do not know how to explain." He wet his lips, then suddenly eyed Aelis. "It is, after all, a poor storyteller who tells all he knows or who pauses for questions. And I am a storyteller, no more—not a scholar, not a lecturer, not a performer. How is it, then, that a mere storyteller, a barefooted and dirt-stained resident of a forgotten hall in a diminished wood in a fallen fief, knows this secret lore? How is this knowledge not debated by the great sages of Usir? Why is it not traded in the back alleys of Lascenise? Kept in warded rooms in the colleges of the Lyceum? And I say to these unasked questions, that it is in ways they do not understand. And that when they do understand, they hide it. From themselves, from one another, and from those who would learn from them. The mind will do anything to defend its coherence; the spirit that animates the body will do anything it can to preserve for itself the order its perceptions have been sharpened against.

"Those who do know, and do not hide it? They are mad. Or they are *called* mad, and that is too much to risk, too easy to lose what the fruits of long labor have won. But I? I have but this hall, a few acres of valley, my tools, my wood. Nothing anyone would care to take. No one about to call me mad."

Shafts of afternoon sunlight fell through the smoke hole in the roof, and Rhunival's eyes flashed, and he sat back, taking a deep breath and reaching for his jug. He gave it a shake and found it empty.

Somehow, Timmuk had already stood up to take it, going to the small barrel to one side of the table from which a smell of piney, slightly sour beer rose.

Is he mad? Aelis tried to distance herself from the story, noting the tricks he had used. *Stillness, followed by sudden movement. The cadence of his voice; slow enough to make us pay attention, fast enough to prod us past weak links. A pause to let us gather ourselves. Anticipating objections.* She could hear all her best teachers positively *howling* over the underlying metaphysical claim being made. That some intelligent, powerful race had made the world prior to the Worldsoul and the Six Siblings, only to have the Gods wrest control from them in some insidious plot.

Lavanalla would laugh him into shame. Urizen would try to draw out the failings in his logic by some maddening riddle. Vosghez would entertain debate through syllogism and dialectic. Bardun Jacques . . .

She trailed off, unable to picture the old Warden-professor arguing with anyone, much less this potent but laughable figure accepting his crude clay jug back from the dwarf.

Bardun Jacques would probably incinerate him. For being annoying. Or talking heathen nonsense.

And here you are, entertaining it.

"What," Tun asked, "does any of this have to do with us?"

Rhunival lifted a hand as he drank deeply from the jug. Foam danced in his beard as he answered.

"Why, everything. The only thing. Do you not wonder how you came to exist, Woodsman? Not simply the meeting of your parents, of course, but the thousand-thousand coincidences that have led you to this day, the thousand-thousand-thousand similar chances that have occurred for days and years unending—or near enough—to bring you here, now, a man of two cultures, of two sets of learning, of two . . ."

"Watch your next words," Tun said. His voice was very slow and very careful in a way that did not sound like the Tun she knew, and the hair on the back of Aelis's neck stood on end to hear it. He'd sat up a bit straighter, pulled his shoulders back, lifted his head.

Rhunival merely inclined his head. "I may read secrets in many places, Woodsman. In the scudding of clouds, in the pattern of mushrooms springing up after a rain, in the melting of snow, the curl of smoke and the gait of a man. But not all of them are mine to say, it is true. Let us return to the core of your question; what do origins have to do with you, now? Everything. And nothing."

"Nothing," Tun said, "because the evidence of my senses and the learning and language I have are the only tools with which I may make sense of the world. I must trust them, or I am lost. A wandering child of no account and no use."

"That's as may be. But there are more ways to understand the world than the one you have; that is all I mean to impart with this preamble."

"Preamble?" Maurenia sighed. "Going to need a drink for the real tale."

"The barrel is there, Engineer."

Maurenia stood, fetched down a mug from a hook on the wall and filled it.

Aelis felt a stirring of thirst in her own throat, but not one that was going to get her to drink beer that tasted the way that open barrel smelled.

"Preamble was the wrong word, perhaps, and it is all meaningless to you. But I have told you something—call it a tale, call it myth, call it metaphysics if you must—that none of you have heard before. And surely that is worth your continued attention."

Was "metaphysics" aimed at me? Aelis couldn't help but wonder as everyone resettled into their seats.

"Dalius Enthal de Morgantis un Mahlgren was a man of *many* secrets. Secrets of state, secret habits, secret knowledge, secret plots. If secrets are a kind of wealth, and many would say they are, he was among the richest men walking the world even before war blighted his beloved home.

"Do not be shocked when I say that de Morgantis loved this place and in his way, its people. He believed that Mahlgren represented an old kind of nobility, a kind won through hard sacrifice. Say this for him and his lineage: they were not afraid of the hard choices that demanded sacrifice *of themselves.* So many leaders are willing to ask their followers to go without, to walk the hard road. The Morgantis and Mahlgren lines were always first in the rank of those who paid and those who lost. If they were also first in the rank of those who won, then it seemed to many no more than they deserved.

"Secrets require places to keep them. And Dalius was a man of vision, of foresight. Some say he had a hidden talent for Divination, but that would have put four magics at his call, and the Warden here can tell you that no one has done that in living memory. And so he brought dwarves and men with the knowledge of iron and steel, of tumbler and key, to Mahlhewn Keep and he paid them well to build him a place to keep his greatest secrets. And he was, too, a man ever willing to pay for talent and the skill of the hands."

He paused for another pull at his jug. Aelis struggled to keep still and silent, fighting against her rising urge to beg Rhunival to reach a point.

"Dalius saw a war coming before many others did. He knew patterns and that the migrations of the orcs from their islands and archipelagos in the north and west were changing. Raiding was going to become invasion, plundering become farming. And he took steps to prepare for the inevitable conflict that would come. He researched old magics. Fell magics. Things that were forbidden; things that ought to have been. Dalius did not understand that making Mahlgren strong, that making himself powerful, would not be enough. There was no strength he could muster that would be enough. And so he lost. Mahlgren was lost."

"We all know the history," Maurenia said.

"Some of us were there," Tun murmured, almost too softly for Aelis to hear.

"But you do not *know*. You do not understand everything Dalius summoned. Everything he put into place, all the levers he pulled, all the careful ways he fit the pieces together."

Aelis was practically choking with impatience. *Just what in seven hells do you mean?* she wanted to scream at the strange man with the long gray beard. And yet some part of her knew that the odds of him answering were too long to count.

"All of you have seen at least one of these parts. Some of you have seen more. Some have come perilously close to Onoma's embrace in the seeing. Even I do not see all of it; I see only what bounds and binds my little valley, and that is so much less than I used to see. You do not know what was bound here, what was bound all over this country. You do not know what was *used* to do the binding. You will." He glared at Aelis and lifted a slightly trembling hand. "You will know, you will see it and know. You must."

Rhunival paused then, as if his strength was flagging. He looked at his little jar and set it down. "I have done what I can," he said. "I have told you of things you did not know. I have given you what tool I could; remember what I said. Dalius understood strength, and he tried to understand guile, but he did not understand so much more. It is time to eat. Someone, please, bring me a bowl of the oats. I need to restore my strength."

His mention of food snapped Aelis back to attention, and the big pot of boiled oats smelled better than it should have. The earthiness of the mushrooms, the eggs that had been boiled in it woke up her stomach from its long slumber. Suddenly, food was all she could think of.

But there was Rhunival's request, of course. And he seemed shrunken or shriveled somehow, receding into his dirty robe and folding up in his seat. Hungry as she was, Aelis found manners enough to fill a bowl for him first. She dropped a palmful of cheese on it, slid a spoon in, and brought it to him. He nodded his thanks, and she went to fetch her own.

By the time she was taking her first spoonful, Timmuk and Tun were on their way to a second bowl. All was silent but for the movement of spoons in bowls and the sounds of quiet chewing.

Aelis was shocked to find how strong all the flavors in her bowl were. Surely oats, salt, mushrooms, a bit of egg, and fresh cheese were not the kind of complex gastronomy the daughter of a count was used to. And yet something about it all tasted sharp; the cheese somehow brighter and stronger than the cheese she was accustomed to. The salt had the tang of the sea, though they were hundreds of miles from it. The mushrooms were so good, she wished she could identify them for the future.

The whole meal had a strangely dreamlike feel to it, though. She felt these things but could not have described them, communicated them to her companions, or asked any questions of Rhunival. While he seemed somewhat restored by the food, he showed no signs of continuing his tale. His bowl set aside, his chin sunk down onto his chest, he showed every indication of being asleep.

Aelis felt bone tired. *We haven't done so much work today, have we? Have I any reason to be this weary?* Yet she felt sleep sweeping her up like the tide.

Her Anatomist's mind, her medical training railed against it like a prisoner beating against the walls of his cell with bare fists. And had as much effect. She set aside her bowl, sought out her blankets by the fire pit, and lay down. Around her, the others did the same, with Maurenia lying close along her back.

She slept as deeply and peacefully as she could ever remember doing.

11

THE KEEP

She woke all at once, with a vague sense of dread that she recognized could become panic if left to its own devices.

Fear is a response to danger. The Abjurer does not know danger. The properly prepared and ever-vigilant Abjurer is the antithesis of danger. Thus, she cannot fear. Thus, her heart does not race. Her breath does not pant. Her palms do not sweat.

The familiar words instantly calmed her; by the last line of her Abjurer's mantra, she was whispering them aloud, and she felt Maurenia sitting up beside her.

Her first instinct once she was calm was to take a head count; Maurenia she could feel behind her, but she wanted to lay eyes on each of her companions to satisfy herself that none of them were hurt. Timmuk and Tun sat up from their blankets, struggling to wake from, apparently, the same kind of deep sleep she'd been in.

"Anyone hurt?"

She was met with an assortment of grunts, grumbles, and yawns, but none of them seemed to be hurt. Her next priority was gear.

She found it lying in a careful bundle right by her feet. Her swordbelt was wound around her sheathed abjurer's blade and her dagger, and her wand was carefully wrapped in a rag. When she took it out, the carved wooden length gleamed with polish and wax.

The wax she'd brought north with her was, she was fairly certain, still unopened in one of her chests of gear.

"Puzzling," she said to no one in particular.

Like her, the rest of them were absorbed in checking their gear. Timmuk made a great fuss over his axe, examining haft, blade, and counterbalancing spike with an eye for details Aelis didn't see.

"Might need to break this down, clean it, and reassemble it," Maurenia muttered as she fussed with her crossbow.

"Why?" Aelis looked at it over the half-elf's shoulder, but to her eye it appeared much the same as it always had.

"Because it's too clean. And it looks as if it's been waxed, and not with the kind I prefer. Too shiny."

"Too shiny?" Aelis's voice was deadpan.

"Well, I don't want it to gleam and give me away if I'm skulking somewhere, do I? Might have to rub some soot or some blacking on it to make sure," Maurenia added, though Aelis remained thoroughly unconvinced.

They busied themselves with strapping belts and weapons back into place. Tun had shed his long coat and carefully folded it. Aelis saw him fingering a spot that seemed freshly patched before he slid it back on. His handblades were already in his pockets, but he took them out to inspect them regardless. Unlike Timmuk and Maurenia, he found nothing to criticize and looked straight at Aelis.

"Where," he said carefully, "is our host?"

"I haven't the vaguest idea. Can you track him?"

The stare Tun leveled at her in answer was as good as an eyeroll from anyone else, and it was all the answer Aelis had wanted. *If we're laughing, we're not focused on how fucking weird this all is.*

"Nothing to do but look, then," Aelis said. She went outside the hall and saw their packs lined up in a row. Nagging thoughts instantly diverted her from looking for Rhunival, so she tore into her rucksack to check on her medical kit.

She found everything where it belonged. Aelis could countenance some messiness in her life. Clothes, papers, pens, coins, keys, food; all could go wherever they pleased. But when it came to books and to the tools of her calling—especially her surgeon's kit—she was meticulous with cleaning and replacing every piece in it the moment she could.

With her brief panic tamped back down, she pulled her rucksack onto her shoulders, loosened her sword in its sheath, and made a circuit of the grounds, walking widdershins to Maurenia's sunwise. Tun and Timmuk searched around the various toolsheds and outbuildings.

They met back at the entrance to the hall.

"There was fresh sawdust in the toolshed," Tun said, "and the tools we saw him use yesterday had the smell and feel of recent work. Everything was cared for, oiled. If he was some kind of sprite, he was a scrupulous one."

"I think he was no Illusion," Aelis said. "Not one of my colleges, but I'd know if I'd felt illusion *that* powerful." She shook her head. "And I'd rather not try and place him in any taxonomy of spirits I can call to mind."

"Why not?" Maurenia asked. "I'd like to know what we're dealing with."

Shows how much you know about spirits, Aelis thought. "Imagine if I suddenly start speculating on it and he takes that as a bad sign. Like we're looking for ways to fight or bind or even kill him. Does that sound like a good idea?"

"Best we assume, as Aelis tacitly suggests, that he can see and hear us," Tun said.

"In which case we thank him for the food and the fish and go about our business." Aelis suddenly unslung her pack again and found the wrapped oblong bundle of the carved fish ready to her hand. Even inside the cloth that shrouded it, she could feel the scales, the fins; it almost felt for a moment like it wriggled.

"So, it's on toward Mahlhewn Keep?" Timmuk slapped his hands together appreciatively. "Stregon's Balls, but I can't wait to clap my eyes on a genuine piece of early Dolovkin work."

"If it even exists," Maurenia said.

"I think," Aelis countered, "it is very likely that we were not told an entire truth this past evening. Or that we were told one view of a possible truth. But," she added, raising a finger, "I do *not* think we were lied to. I am certain of it."

"Shapers? All that creation myth bullshit? Doesn't fit any faith I've ever heard of." Maurenia couldn't stop fidgeting with her crossbow, rubbing at the stock with her sleeve, wetting her thumb and testing the string.

"The dwarves talk about Stregon—our Stregon, anyway—a little different from yours, less . . ." Timmuk paused, searching for a word, "less piffling, less puny, less wishy-washy," he finally said, "shaping our people by his own hand. But only to set them against one another in battles for his own entertainment," he added with a shrug.

"Aye, and that old coot just told us that these 'Shapers' were around before the gods and built the world only to have it snatched away from them. Surely we don't credit that?"

"What I credit," Aelis said, "is that there are still animations to be put down, and if we don't do it, no one else is going to. And, further, that based on what Rhunival said, it seems even likelier to me than before that any controlling device that can destroy the lot of them is going to be found in Mahlhewn in that vault."

Maurenia turned away, adjusting the strap of her crossbow angrily until she had it sitting back exactly where it had been.

"Nothing for it but to go on," Aelis said, "and we'll find out if we were . . ." She paused and fought down the urge to glance suspiciously around them, "misled. Tun, do you want to blaze our trail or take point or . . . whatever it is that you do?"

"Well," Tun said slowly, gathering himself in a way that let Aelis know she was about to be roundly, if fondly, mocked, "unless we are expecting an ambush or planning to set one ourselves, 'taking point' is out. And as far as blazing a trail, well, I did not bring any of the tools necessary for doing so, and I doubt we are expecting anyone to follow in our footsteps." He paused for a deep breath while everyone else had a chuckle. "Now," he said calmly, "if you'll show me on a map where this keep is meant to be, I'll happily walk first in line all the way there, and the rest of you can follow me. Provided you can keep up."

"Yes, Tun," Aelis said, keeping her voice deadpan. "Thank you, Tun. Why don't we head northwest a while—a long while, many dozens of miles—and when we see the broken ruins of a curtain wall, a barbican, and three huge towers, we'll know we're in the right spot."

"And if the wilderness has devoured these?"

"It's only been, what, twenty-three years since Mahlgren was officially abandoned?"

"Mahlhewn fell five years before the earldom was surrendered," Maurenia corrected, "so nearly thirty."

Timmuk spat in the grass. "If the earls built so poorly that the entirety of the place could be reclaimed in so few years, then it deserved to fall. And no doubt we'll find that beautiful Dolovkin vault sitting all by its lonesome in the wild, pop it open with your man's key, load up with the good bits, and stumble home in the snow."

"Key?" Aelis tugged at the straps of her pack and raised a bemused eyebrow at Timmuk. "You mean the fish?"

"Fish? What in seventeen hells are you talking about, fish? I mean the key we watched him carve."

Aelis felt her eyes slide shut and she pinched the bridge of her nose. A part of her, she admitted, wanted to fetch the thing out of her pack, carefully show it to everyone, ask them all to handle it, and dutifully record their impressions of it.

An interesting experiment with interesting results, no doubt, she told herself.

But daylight wanes, Rhunival is gone, and Dalius may await us. No time for academic curiosity.

"We'll settle this later," she muttered, more to herself than to her companions. "Tun, if you would, please lead us onward."

"Northwest?"

"If that is where the fucking keep is, yes."

"Well, in that case it's more like north *by* northwest but yes. Onward, to the keep."

◆ ◆ ◆

It was a long, slow, and increasingly cold trek northward. Snow had fallen deep already, and they had to wade through it in Tun's wake. The only pleasant moment of the first morning's walk was when they opened their packs to discover fresh food that had magically appeared. Largely cheese and dried fruit, it was still a welcome change from the jerky and Tun's dried corn muffins.

"Never imagined I'd find myself longing for boiled oats," Aelis said aloud as they ate some of those corn muffins early on the second day. She had found herself dreaming about their succulence, the soft cheese, the melting butter, the mushrooms.

"Boiled oats were a meal twice a week aboard the vessel I sailed on longest," Maurenia said. "Thought for sure I'd had my fill of them. But his were good."

"Dwarves have enough sense to turn all grains, corn, barley, oats, and wheat into something to drink. If Rhunival had a lick of sense to go with whatever secret sources of grain he has, he'd have a still set up in one of those shacks," Timmuk said.

"Who says he did not?" Tun asked. "And since when were you a sailor?" he said, pointing a finger at Maurenia. "I thought foot soldier, wagoneer, engineer, but sailor?"

Maurenia shook a shower of snowflakes off her shoulders. "First time I designed anything was when I looked at one of the large bows mounted on the ship and told them how they could brace more effectively without sacrificing traversal arc. I didn't know what to call any of it then, I just told the bosun, who—eventually—told the lieutenant."

"I sense 'eventually' covering up a story," Tun said. He was walking in the lead, leaving huge bootprints in the fresh snow. Aelis found herself aiming for them, despite needing to occasionally hop from one to the next, because even a child's game like that was more interesting than more endless pine woods, more snow, more dark, distant hills. Aelis followed him, occasionally switching off with Maurenia, and Timmuk walked drag-carrying the heaviest pack and the largest weapon and puffing like a steam iron.

"Well, bosuns and the like aren't any too well known for tolerating being told anything by a lowly mast-climber who hadn't got the letters or the math to back up her claim. But I was insistent."

"You don't say," Timmuk murmured, and Aelis stifled some laughter before Maurenia could glare at her.

"Once more, you make a single word do a great deal of work." Tun was still leading them forward at a hard pace, but Aelis thought she recognized what he was doing; draw everyone out a bit, keep their spirits up. It might make them feel more like a kind of unit, rather than just four individuals in the wilderness. She ought to have been doing it; she made a note, not for the first or the last time, to thank him for thinking of something she hadn't.

"I hid his illicit store of strong brandy and told him I'd tell an officer where it was if he didn't let me show him what I meant. An afternoon of woodwork later, and the bow was working better. Then it was our lieutenant, she . . ." Here Maurenia stopped and swallowed, and Aelis had to choke down a dozen more questions. "She saw what I'd done and asked how I knew to do it. Then she taught me to read, started loaning me books, the kind a tutor would use to teach a child basic math, then the real stuff, then how you navigate a ship, all that geometry . . ." Here she trailed off.

"Sounds like she might have been grooming you to make the jump to an officer's rate," Tun said casually. "They do not usually teach spherical geometry to . . . what were your words, a lowly mast-climber?"

"Might've been. She hadn't died, maybe I'd still be at sea."

"I'm sorry," Aelis said quickly, followed by Tun's apology, but Maurenia shook her head.

"It's a life of risk. All lives worth living are, you ask me. She knew what she was about; was her choice. That's what matters most in the end."

They were quiet in the snowfall a bit longer, then Maurenia spoke up.

"Now what about you, Tun? If I couldn't already see through the backwoodsman facade, you go talking about spherical geometry; where'd you learn it?"

"Tutors," Tun said simply.

"That's all? Tutors?"

"I have not always lived in Lone Pine."

Sensing that more questions were coming and knowing from the clipped tones of Tun's voice that he wasn't going to want to answer them, Aelis said, "I stabbed one of my tutors once."

Tun stopped walking to turn and look at her, as did Maurenia and Timmuk.

"He was my painting tutor—yes, painting, my parents thought they might make an artist of me once—and he decided he could punish me with a slap. So I pinned his hand to the table with a paint-knife." Seeing her companions' wide eyes, she added, "It was just through the loose skin between thumb and forefinger." She held up her own gloved hands and pointed to demonstrate. "It hurt, and there was a good deal of blood, but there wasn't any lasting damage."

"Already a surgeon's precision at a young age, eh?" Timmuk grinned at her like a proud uncle.

"Honestly, I think it probably wasn't sharp enough to get all the way through any other part of the hand. Lucky shot."

"And what became of his tutelage?" Tun asked.

"Well, the count had a long talk with him about how exactly one disciplines a young noblewoman and that what passed for a workshop apprentice did not pass in a de Lenti palace. Then he sent him on his way, and my guess is he's spent the past decade churning out make-work landscapes and portraits of rich merchants' wives."

"Palace," Maurenia repeated, slowly. "A palace. As in . . . more than one."

"I cannot help where I was born or to whom, Maurenia." Aelis knew she sounded more defensive than she wanted to, but she pressed on anyway. "But I'm here now and glad of it."

"Do not do us all the dishonor of *lying* to us," Tun said.

"Well, that's not what I meant," Aelis said. "Of course I hate this fucking weather, and I'm none too fond of sheep, and I'd condemn all goats to the seven hundred and seventy-seven hells, but look; I'm here with three fine, brave people, and I'm glad of that. I couldn't do this on my own."

Aelis held her breath in the silence that followed.

"Going it a little high," Timmuk said gently.

"Indeed," Tun agreed. "Much too high."

"Laying too much on," Maurenia said.

Aelis felt her shoulders hunching, then behind her, it was Timmuk who first burst out laughing, then the others followed, and she felt her shoulders rise and her heart unclench, just a little.

When the snow intensified, Tun risked an early stop and didn't argue against a fire, and Aelis thought all of them felt like she did: cold and miserable and hungry even for a pot of boiled oats, but less alone.

✦ ✦ ✦

At dawn on the next day, it was Maurenia who saw the spires of a keep in the distance. Aelis couldn't see much more than clouds and snow-capped mountains, but Maurenia lifted her hand to the horizon and called, "Towers!" with total confidence.

"Last time we were out here," Timmuk said, "it was Renia who saw the Gigants coming and got that big bow on the wagon ready for them. Without her warning, it would've been a nearer-run thing than it turned out. Doesn't pay to question her eyes."

"It accords with Mahlhewn on the maps," Tun said. "What's our approach?"

"I doubt the walls are ready to repel an assault," Aelis said. "In fact, they failed rather spectacularly to do that the last time anyone tried."

"Could be squatters, pioneers, or wandering horrors setting up in there," Maurenia warned. "Not our best bet to simply swan up to the front gate and knock."

"We've another several hours' march," Tun said. The others had come to recognize him as the voice of authority in the wilderness, as Aelis had long ago, and no one dissented. "Once we're close enough, give me a chance to go reconnoiter. If I'm not back in two hours, I'm not coming back."

"Fine. Then let's walk," Timmuk said, and they did. When Tun had decided they were close enough, he called a halt. Even Aelis could now make out the curving stone wall of the outer curtain. Mahlhewn sat wedged against foothills that rose toward the snowcapped Mahlhir Mountains, quarried from the same stone that made up the giant shelflike peaks. She told herself that the matching shades of gray were why she hadn't seen it, and not some failure of eyesight or lapse in attention.

According to the maps, the Indulin River should wend around behind it, with an offshoot leading right up to a cistern gate in the curtain wall. In the flat gray of the winter, Aelis didn't even let herself imagine she saw its distant sparkle.

Tun directed them to a small stand of pine trees and set down his walking stick. "Two hours," he said. "Or not at all."

"Tun," Aelis said, "you know if you're not back in time we're going to come looking for you, right?"

"How? You alley-bashers couldn't find me on a plain under the noonday sun if I didn't want you to."

"I may have a little more woodcraft than you expect," Maurenia said. "These are the only things I inherited from my father, but they work." She tapped a finger under her eyes.

"I'll learn Divination if I have to," Aelis said.

"Fine, fine. If I don't come back, you can all die in the wilderness looking for me."

Then he turned and lumbered off. He didn't seem to hurry, but then, he never did. All the same, with his long, determined strides, he quickly melted into the landscape and disappeared.

"Is he always like this?" Maurenia said. She slipped off her pack and slowly lowered herself onto it.

"Like what?" Aelis asked. She didn't want to risk sitting on her own pack or on the wet snow, so she dug her walking stick firmly into the ground and leaned against it.

"Disagreeable."

Aelis laughed. "No. Tun is, I think, unused to so much company, but he longs for it all the same. So he jokes, though . . . it can be hard to tell when he is joking until you spend enough time with him."

"Is he as good as he says?"

"How would I know? I'm just a foolish, spoiled city girl completely lost in the wilderness." Aelis, moved to mischief by Tun, opened her eyes as wide and still as she could, willing her face to an expression of innocence she hadn't felt for as long as she could remember. Maurenia turned to stare at her and they locked eyes until the both of them snorted with laughter, leaning against each other. Aelis laid a hand on Maurenia's shoulder, and the other woman winced.

"If your shoulder hurts," Aelis murmured, "let me have a look at it."

"It's fine," Maurenia said, losing most traces of the laughter they had just shared. She popped back to her feet, pacing and fiddling with her crossbow.

Timmuk had settled happily into what Aelis had come to think of as professional inactivity. He sat down with his back against a pine trunk, laid his axe over his legs, and appeared for all the world as if he might be falling asleep. And yet he never actually *did* fall asleep. She felt certain that if a threat showed itself, he'd meet it, axe at the ready, faster than she would. *Well*, she thought, with a note of pride in her draw and first step, *maybe half a step behind.*

Aelis wasn't sure what else to do with herself, so she dug out a scrap of paper and a writing stick, a thin nib of charcoal held in a wooden frame. As was her habit when her thoughts were disordered, she made a list. Her handwriting was dreadful while she leaned once more against her stick, and she wasn't sure she'd be able to read it later, but she went about it all the same.

She wrote *Rhunival*, then drew a short line and put *Dalius* next to it and *enemies* next to them both.

My enemy's enemy is probably still my enemy, she thought in a voice she was sure came from Bardun Jacques.

Dalius told me something about Necromancy when he thought I was defeated, she thought, without being able to come up with the words exactly. She wrote the following words next, one under the other.

Animations.
Demon Tree.
Nath/Mahlgren men
Rhunival some sort of summoned/bound spirit?
Other defenses?
Rhunival wants what? Rod? Orb? Amulet? Weapon?
Dalius: Conjurer surely. Illusionist. Enchanter. But the animations point to Necromancy. Not possible to master all four.

While nothing she wrote offered her anything approaching clarity, she'd always found that simply putting her thoughts on paper helped her order them, often setting her subconscious in motion in ways that might help later. In the meantime, she put the paper and the writing stick away and got her gloves back on, wishing that they could start a fire, which she knew Tun wouldn't want them to do unless he oversaw the sheltering of it. Failing that, she'd take a full alchemical lab so she could put together a little white Manganar into a suspension of powdered bone and stuff the whole thing into a leather pouch, warded on the inside and sewn shut. *A couple of those in my boots, my gloves, or inside my robes, I'd hardly feel the cold.*

She was still pondering this when, behind her, Timmuk popped to his feet. Maurenia was slotting a bolt in her crossbow when she heard a faint, angry snort come from outside their copse.

"I haven't made it back to get bludgeoned and shot," Tun's voice rumbled from out of sight. "So put all that away and listen well; we've got a problem."

Only then did he emerge out of the falling darkness, and Aelis once again marveled at how silent and certain his movements were. If the others shared her shock and admiration, they didn't show it.

"What's the problem?" Maurenia, as usual, was the first to focus. "Hordes of skeletons on the walls? An Orc warband? A mountain fell on the place?"

"All of those could be dealt with," Tun replied. "What we have is much less manageable. The river has adjusted its course."

"Oh gods-damn it," Aelis said, as the boring details of Old Ystain history she studied many a year ago came flooding back. "The people who built the keep diverted the natural course of the river with some kind of brute force engineering project."

"What do you mean? Locks, dikes, pumps?" Maurenia was suddenly interested, and Timmuk perked up as well. "If there's some kind of machine involved, perhaps it could be restarted. How bad is it?"

"The remains of the rear curtain wall are barely visible," Tun said. "The bottom levels of the keep are submerged. The courtyard is practically a lake. If the vault was built anywhere but the top floors of the inner keep, it's lost to us."

"I can swim," Timmuk proclaimed.

"If the vault hasn't collapsed due to the water pressure," Maurenia said, "you'll never get the door open. Unless you can lift the river so you can open the door."

"We'll dig a drainage trench?" Timmuk's voice sounded more pleading than hopeful.

"We'd need a couple hundred of you with shovels working day and night for a month," Tun said.

"There's too much we don't know," Aelis said, but she did think immediately of the exquisitely carved fish in her pack with a surge of dread and excitement that she decided to keep to herself. "We have no idea where in the place this vault would be located. Were there any visible threats, Tun?"

"None that I could see. The swollen river seems to have kept any major threats at bay."

"That is," Aelis said slowly, "without doubt, the worst pun I have ever heard."

"I have to amuse myself here in the benighted wilderness with only the three of you for company," Tun replied.

"Right. So we're free to move in and look more closely at the place then?"

"If anything is there to see us, my senses couldn't detect it."

Aelis nodded, but she took the hint in Tun's words. *If there are any threats, it's up to me to find them.*

"Let's go have a look then," Aelis said.

12

FIRESIDE ALCHEMY

"Well, that doesn't seem so bad," Aelis muttered when the gray stone walls rose before them. "Sure, it's right up against a lake, but we can walk right in."

Timmuk rubbed his hands together. "Remember, loose gems and jewelry first, followed by deeds, letters of credit and the like. High-value artwork is good too, but only if you've the eye. Paintings don't have to move in their frames if you've got a good, sharp knife. Clothing and weapons only if they catch your eye, and if you want the bars and coins, *you* carry them," he said with zeal.

All heads swiveled toward him, and he grinned widely beneath his beard.

"You've been rehearsing that," Maurenia said.

"Maybe a bit. Had to do something to stay warm while stomping through all this snow."

"What you're all failing to appreciate," Tun said, "is that we're looking at the barbican, not the main keep. This place was built on a massive scale, over generations. It was well on its way to becoming a fortress city before the first raids came along. This is not as easy as it looks."

Indeed, even as he said it, Aelis could see he was right. What had once been the gatehouse was the most prominent feature still left above the water.

"Did the ground collapse somehow? Surely no one ever built a castle on the bottom of a slope like this," Maurenia said.

"When the river took back its natural course, it collapsed many of the sublevels and foundations. Then years of it soaking the ground underneath the rest of the place, the keep slid downward. That'd be my guess," Tun said.

"Holds up," Maurenia agreed. "What are the odds this vault could survive that, Timmuk?"

"It'd hold. But it might be surrounded by collapsed foundation stones and then we've no chance."

"We have to proceed as if it'll be there," Aelis said. She tried hard for a tone that brooked no dissent, reaching mostly for Lavanalla's quiet assurance, with just a drop or two of Bardun Jacques's furious determination.

"We'd need a couple hundred workers and seventy hells worth of equipment we don't have," Maurenia said. Aelis turned to her, and Maurenia shrugged. "Look, I don't know anything about Necromancy, or magic. Obviously." She held up her bandaged hands and grimaced. "But I know impossible engineering projects when I see them."

Guess I've got to work on that assured voice some more. "We don't really have a choice. Timmuk, where would the vault be if the castle was intact?"

"If it's built to the same standards as their later work, it would have to be on a ground floor or below. Higher floors wouldn't support its weight," Timmuk said.

"Anything about orientation? Directions it might have to face? Superstitions of the builders? Sun or moonlight it might need to catch? *Anything?*"

"Word was, they had a design for a lock that would only open when all seven moons were aligned and the light passed through a lens, but nobody would pay for it."

Aelis's concentration was brought up short. "I'm not going to do the calculations, but that can't happen more than once every four hundred years. Why would anyone want a lock they'd never see open in their lifetime?"

"Diboricek Dolovkin was an *artist*," Timmuk said, as if that explained everything.

"Fine. What I wouldn't give for a diviner just now," Aelis muttered.

"If I still had the hides we left with Rhunival, I could build a little boat," Tun suddenly said. "It would at least give us a closer look; there could easily be air pockets or features we can't see from here. At the least, we might be able to take some soundings, see what buildings are left behind."

"How many hides would you need of those we still have?" Aelis asked, running her hand over the one she was wearing.

"How many of us need to fit in the boat?" Tun considered. "For me, probably all of them. For just you with one other . . . I could get by with two. But it'll be a cramped boat, and it won't last long. This is academic, of course, because we need—"

Aelis slung off her pack, dropped her swordbelt to the ground. She took a deep breath and stripped off her outer robe, her gloves, boots, socks, her top shirt, skirt, and the tanned hide under-robe Tun had made, leaving only a shirt and short breeches. The cold, which she'd come to accept as simply a fact of life after so many days of marching in it, came roaring in like a bastard. It seized her lungs in an angry fist, battered her skin.

"Aelis, you will want that hide," Tun began to say, though she was already shimmying back into the clothing she had left, though it wasn't nearly as warm.

"Let's make camp," she said. "You make your boat. I need someone to gather firewood and build up a fire. I can solve the warmth problem for two of us, at least for a while, but I won't try to order anyone else to give up their hide."

"Solve how, exactly?" Maurenia asked, though she had already unbuckled her swordbelt and her crossbow's strap, preparing to shed her own hide.

"Magic," Aelis said. "Well . . . actually alchemy, which is close enough."

Tun shook his head but seemed to accept that answer. "Let's find a suitable camp and get after some wood, then. I'll need some, too."

✦   ✦   ✦

Tun and Timmuk set out to gather wood while Aelis and Maurenia put their camp in order. With the shelter set up and the sounds of young pine trees cracking and snapping as they were felled along the wood line, Aelis unhitched a pair of spades from Timmuk's pack and tossed one toward Maurenia. The half-elf calmly watched it sail past her in the air and land on the ground a pace beyond her. Then she turned to Aelis and held up her hands.

"Still bandaged. Not doing any unnecessary physical labor. Doctor's orders."

"Fair enough," Aelis said. To hide her flush of embarrassment she paced out a firepit, then bent low to crunch the sharp spade through the winter-hardened turf.

"That's a bigger firepit than usual. Tun will grumble about it." Behind them, another tree thudded to the earth, Tun's voice calling above it for them to be careful.

"Tun is not the one who is going to attempt alchemy over a fire on the open heath of Old Ystain," Aelis answered, her breath puffing around in huge clouds as she worked her spade, first roughing out a circle, then shoveling out the clods of earth she turned over. "So, for once, he can be quiet about it."

"This isn't a heath," Maurenia countered. "Not exactly. Just meadow gone a bit wild."

"Well, then I don't ever care to see one."

By the time Aelis had the pit dug out, Tun and Timmuk returned. Tun had two saplings slung over one shoulder and a bundle of branches under the other arm, while Timmuk dragged what looked like half a dozen small trees behind him.

"If you would be so kind as to build up a fire as hot as you can get it," Aelis said to the dwarf as he dropped his burden, "I will owe you a bottle of wine of your choosing from either my stores or Rus and Martin's cellar."

"You get me a sight of a Calabris and Dolovkin vault built by the master himself, and that will be payment enough," Timmuk said. Then, as he picked up a log and began trimming it, he added, "You get me inside it, and that will be payment to *retire* on."

Aelis nodded absently while she dug out her traveling medical kit. Inside it were a few small, silken bags, and she had to pull them into the light to read the symbols on them. Finding the one for Manganar, she rubbed the bag between her fingers; she needed just a few hard grains of the precious stuff. She set it aside, then rummaged in her rucksack for the spare reagent vials for her alchemy lamp. She found them in a small wooden box, three cylinders of magically hardened glass, each about as long as her thumb. She selected two and slid the remaining one back into its padded box.

Odds were, she'd want these for her lamp before all was said and done; these prepared vials were costly to replace, time-consuming to make, and she had nothing like an inexhaustible supply. But the cold would kill her a lot faster and more certainly than darkness might. And she needed to see whatever could be seen out on the lagoon that Malhewn Keep had become.

Aelis considered the vial, full of a viscous yellow liquid, and the tiny silken bag tied closed with thin brass wires. She was working mostly on instinct. *No surprise there*, she thought, but she wanted to take a moment to consider her idea, so she turned to watch Tun.

With a woodaxe that looked like a toy in his hands, Tun had stripped and was now splitting one of the saplings he had brought. Timmuk and Maurenia were building up the fire as Aelis had asked.

"How exactly is he going to build a boat with hides?" Aelis muttered to herself.

"Build a frame, stretch wet hide over it, let it dry," Tun called out. He didn't even look up from trimming the trunk with his axe.

"I should've known you would hear me. How long will that take and how well will it work?"

"It'll take me most of the night, and it will be ready to float as soon as the hides dry. It will work for a turn or two around that lagoon, but I wouldn't take it out to sea." Aelis had known Tun was a gifted woodworker; the staff she carried and the others she'd seen him carve had been proof of that. But she'd never seen him work before.

The wood shaped itself under his hands. Massive though they were, they didn't miss a stroke or make a misstep; he bent over the sapling, holding it as lightly as she would a stick of firewood. He'd already stripped its branches, and long shavings of bark joined them, gently curled, gray on one side and yellow on the other. Timmuk was no slouch in woodcraft, but his work was done with more brute force and far less grace than Tun's.

"Orcs can make a boat out of anything," Maurenia said, keeping a log steady with her foot for Timmuk to chop into manageable sections for the firepit. "Their clinker-built coastal runners can play merry hells with larger Antravalan cogs if they feel like it. Lighter and faster than anything else, and they can make any manner of riverboat. Only Tyridice can make anything that can catch or fight them."

"You really do know your boats," Tun said appreciatively as he worked.

"Did you think I was lying about going to sea?"

"No, I just haven't met too many Tyridician sailors who *did* know much about boats."

Maurenia snorted in reply.

Aelis put all the chatter out of her mind and focused on her ingredients and her half-formed plan. Perhaps sensing her need to concentrate, the rest of them quieted down and attended to their own tasks.

+ + +

By the time they'd lost the last trace of daylight, Timmuk had a roaring fire going that kept the cold mostly at arm's length.

Aelis had set her vials and the Manganar on a flat rock and tried to gather her thoughts. Something distracted her, and she looked up to see Maurenia, moving her wounded shoulder freely, picking up a fresh log and tossing it into the fire.

"Your shoulder's that much better already?" Aelis narrowed her eyes.

Maurenia looked up, puzzled. "Suppose it is," she said, rotating her arm in its socket. "Seems well enough." In the firelight, Aelis could see the half-elf smile and wink. "Guess I have a good doctor."

"Not *that* good," Aelis muttered, hoping Maurenia didn't hear. It was true that some bodies simply healed faster than others. But that was remarkably fast.

She felt the cold drawing in and decided it was time to make some commitment. She looked at her glass reagent vials, her tiny bag, two strips of bandage cut from a roll, and some leather thongs.

"What I'm about to do," Aelis said, "is going to look *very* dangerous. It will only become so if any of you do anything to disrupt my concentration. Do you understand?"

There was a general nodding of assent. Aelis unwound the brass wire from the bag and slipped the tiny grains of metal into her hand. They glinted like iron in the wavering firelight. She closed her fist around them and cleared her mind.

There was nothing, absolutely nothing in the world, but the metal in her loosely held fist, the fire in front of her, and her other hand wrapped around the hilt of her sword. She drew her will through her sword, through the magical reagents at its core, the drops of her blood in the hilt, and felt the power she drew from the world gather in her hand, then stretch up and down her nerves, then suffuse her entire body. She gathered all of it into a ball and, repeating a whispered litany of words even she did not hear, wrapped it around her fist in an all-encompassing ward.

The Firewalker's Prayer. The Smith's Glove. Mazhanar's Crucible. This ward had many names; it was powerful, though of narrow utility. She felt a bead of sweat slide down her forehead.

Then she thrust her hand into the hottest part of the fire, into the coals that glowed orange-yellow, nearly white.

The heat was not as concentrated as her calcination oven, and the results wouldn't be as powerful, if results she got. But it should work for at least a few days.

Distantly, Aelis heard gasps, shouts. Heavy thumping footsteps as someone came close to the fire. A voice, quiet but firm, saying, "Let her work."

She could feel the heat around her fist, the way it pressed against her ward, hungry to consume her flesh. Academically, she knew that flames had no hunger, exactly, but try being sure of that when the only thing protecting your hand from the hottest flame an engineer and a dwarf could make was a barrier of will and power that had no material existence.

The ward protected her flesh, of course, but not what she held. And of course, under these less than ideal circumstances, it wasn't only heat that mattered, but *pressure*. The early calcination ovens of three centuries ago were room-sized things with heavy weights on pulley systems or screws that bore down on the ingredients they were reducing. Heat and magical refinement had obviated the need for that.

But she had only so much heat, and some pressure was going to have to be applied. She could not feel the metal in her hand—wards blocked nerve response, otherwise what was the point? But she could spare a glance. It was heating up nicely, beginning to soften, but it wasn't going to get to the state she needed it in without some extra encouragement.

Exerting the minutest control on her muscles, still deep within her cleared mind, she began to tighten her fist.

The effect was to press the metal between the indestructible edges of her ward. She closed her fist as tight as she dared and began to count slowly backward from thirty.

At twenty, she heard distracting, nervous tittering from behind her, and the ward came perilously close to retreating and exposing part of her hand. She forced her will back into it. The arm extended into the fire trembled; her sweat-slick swordhand clung to the pommel so tightly that she felt it digging into the callus on her palm.

At fifteen, she felt her whole body begin to shake, her muscles screaming to move, to give in.

At ten, darkness clouded the edges of her perception.

At five, she could feel herself swaying.

At zero, she fell back from the fire. A yawning darkness threatened, but she forced it back, biting the inside of her cheek to feel something, some pain that would keep her centered, aware, and hunted out the flat rock upon which she'd placed her other ingredients. She found it, cautiously opened her still warded hand over the strip of clean bandage she'd laid out.

A dust of irregular white-gray flakes fell from her hand onto the bandage. Truly calcinated, they would've been a silver powder. But this grayish dust would do for what she had in mind.

Finally, she dropped the ward and drew a great shuddering breath, then collapsed onto her side.

She was only out a few moments, then woke to Tun holding her up with one arm and Maurenia searching her face and rubbing her wrists.

"I'm fine," she insisted. "Fine. Just . . . a lot of exertion goes into that ward."

"You could've told *someone* what you were about to do," Tun said, his tone only slightly scolding.

"I could've," Aelis said, sitting up with a groan. "But someone would've tried to stop me or talk me out of it or at the least, make me pause and explain, and vital time would've been lost."

"What time would've been lost?" Maurenia asked. "The whole process didn't take more than a few minutes."

"If I stopped to explain it, doubt might've crept it," Aelis said, standing up and stretching. "If I doubted that I could do it, if I gave myself time to weigh the risk of using a Fourth Order Ward to stop from dealing a grievous injury to myself, I might not have been able to do it. Now let me finish what I'm about. Give me some light, but don't crowd me."

She bent over her flat rock while the rest of them got lanterns lit and undid the clasps of her medical kit. She selected a nearly flat metal dosing spoon and used it to divide the flakes of Manganar into two piles on two separate strips of the softest bandage she had. A finger held over one of the piles showed they were cool enough to handle, so she wrapped them up in the wool.

Aelis moved to the two cartridges for her lantern and wrapped the finest copper wire she had, meant for sewing closed a putrefying wound, around the top of each, leaving about three inches of it free. Then, with the leather thongs, she bound the wool to the cartridges, slipped both into the empty silken bags, one of which had held the Manganar in the first place, and pulled the loose copper thread through the top of each bag.

"Here," she said, holding it to Maurenia. "I don't know how long these will work. Days, at best, probably. The wind comes on, the cold is too much, you give the bag a gentle squeeze—gentle, mind!—and hold it and the copper wire against your skin. It will flood you with warmth. Now, don't squeeze it yet . . ."

Maurenia took the bag and immediately squeezed it, then held it against her neck, trailing the copper wire beneath her studded leather jerkin. Her eyes widened.

"I just told you not to do it yet," Aelis said.

"I needed to see if it worked."

"Thanks for the confidence," Aelis said flatly. "However, if you'd let me finish, I would've told you that until the Manganar calcinate has settled into a stable matrix, pressing it against the excited alchemical glass of the reagent vial could make the whole concern explode with rather more force than you'd expect."

There was silence at the campsite as Tun and Timmuk both took quiet but conspicuous steps away from Aelis.

"You handed me a bomb?" Maurenia paused with her hand half-cocked to throw the bag away from her.

"No," Aelis said. "I'm lying. At worst it'll fizzle, start smoking, burn the bag . . . you'd have plenty of time to get rid of it."

Maurenia's eyes narrowed and Aelis heard someone snort while trying to hold back laughter.

"The point, Maurenia, is, you *listen to the alchemist*." Aelis slipped her own warming bag into a pocket in her robe. "And that you should save the limited use it's going to have for moments when the cold might otherwise harm you."

Maurenia turned away without replying, and Aelis did the same, wandering out of the circle of firelight toward the shadowed bulk of Tun and the timber frame he was busy fitting together.

"It'll be ready in the morning," he said flatly as he measured a length of rope against his arm. He found the length acceptable, cut it, dropped the coil back to his feet, and quickly used the rope to lash two long pieces of sapling tightly together.

Aelis looked at his boat frame; it looked awfully small to her eye, but she was no kind of sailor.

"It'll be big enough for two, provided one of them is you and neither are me," Tun said, pulling the thought from her head as he seemed to often do. "You'll be able to pole it, but it won't be watertight. Someone will have to bail as you move about. But it will float, and it will serve our purposes."

"Knew you were a woodsman, but a waterman too?"

"Among my mother's people, we are both," Tun said. "Most orcs are. Even if the bands that roam Old Ystain aren't quite as bound to their boats as they once were, it's still in the blood and in the hands, as it were."

Aelis was bursting with questions, but she knew from long experience that, when it came to discussing his Orcish self, Tun would say what he wanted and not one word more.

"You can come take a rest, you know," Aelis said. "Finish in the morning. Mahlhewn Keep isn't going anywhere."

Tun grunted and, with the same knife he'd sliced the rope with, made some quick cuts to the wooden frame. "I like to finish something once I've started it. These sorts of boats are meant to be made at speed, used, and disposed of. Besides," he added, gesturing to the hides he had laid out on the ground right atop the snow, "I've got those good and wet now, and wrapped around this and left to dry before the waste of a fire you called for, they'll dry and shrink on the frame as nicely as I can hope."

Dropping her voice, Aelis said, "You don't . . . need the light?"

"They'll think all Orcs can see in the dark," he muttered with a sniff. "Let them wonder."

"Can I at least bring you food? Timmuk caught some hares and said something about using a sack of dried peas to make a soup." Even as she spoke, she could smell the first hint of a warm dinner, their first since leaving Rhunival's hall.

"That, I would appreciate," Tun said as he bent down to eye the side of the frame carefully. "Now get back to the fire's warmth and soak it up before it's your turn on watch."

13

NIGHT WATCH

"Why do you always take the first watch?"

Aelis was slightly surprised by the question. She was just beyond the edge of the fire's light, with the portable shelter open on the other side. She was awake and alert but focused outward, and freezing, minimizing use of her warming bag as much as she could. So she was startled, but not upset, when Maurenia suddenly sat down next to her, slipping a blanket over Aelis's shoulders.

"Easier to stay up later than to get up earlier, and I prefer the unbroken sleep."

"Necessary for casting spells?"

Aelis shook her head. "No, but focus and energy are. Too many days of poor or interrupted sleep will play merry hells with even the most powerful wizards. Shouldn't you be sleeping as well?"

"Old soldier habit. We're trying to take a castle in the morning. Don't much feel like sleeping."

"I think you'd want as much as you could get."

"Soldiers generally do. And most learn to sleep when and wherever they can. I knew soldiers who'd swear they could sleep inside a siege tower as it rolled into position, right up until the horn sounded or the thing took fire. And some would say they'd sleep through that, too. But I couldn't, not the night before action."

"Why not?"

"Wanted to live all the hours and moments I could, I suppose. When you expect to die in the morning, the stars and the passing of the jug and fires and the singing all take on more importance, eh? Don't want to miss any of it, no matter how small."

"We aren't going to die tomorrow. Seven Hells, we're just going for a boat ride. Maybe a swim if we're unlucky."

"This late in winter, that water will kill you. And it won't take long to do it. Nobody's swimming."

"There are wards for that," Aelis said.

"What, to regulate your body heat? Why aren't you using one now? I'd murder anything to be genuinely warm again."

"Well, keeping in body heat is a side effect of the wards I have in mind," Aelis said. "It's more a matter of keeping the water out. Now, if I were to work with an Invoker and we had a good Conjurer with us, I might be able to do something about body temperature. In laboratory conditions. Which are about as far from the here and now as it gets."

"I noticed," Maurenia said. "You don't hesitate—much—for an academic."

"I'm not an academic. I'm a Warden."

"Close enough," Maurenia said. "I guess I keep expecting you to act like a soldier. And you don't. Not quite." Slowly, Maurenia began to lean closer to Aelis until their shoulders were touching, and they leaned against each other.

"Wardens aren't soldiers," Aelis said. "They make that abundantly clear to us when we train. They served *with* armies, and might do so again, but always with an independent structure."

"What is a Warden, then? In your own words, not whatever the Lyceum calls them."

"Investigator. Magistrate. Guard. Wizard. Put all four of them in a mortar, pound them into a fine paste with a pestle, put it back together into a wizardly shape, you've got a Warden. With me, you get a bonus physician in the bargain."

"I suppose I knew you had the power of a magistrate," Maurenia said. "It's another thing entirely to hear you say it. Not sure how I feel about it."

"It's not one I'm eager to use. But how else would we enforce the law, especially in gods-forsaken postings like Lone Pine? Write to the nearest city and hope they send someone to hold an assize once every two years? What are we going to do in the meantime, keep everyone who's broken a law locked up until a civilian magistrate shows up? Only way the system can work."

"What happens when a Warden breaks the law, then?"

"We're not immune to any laws, if that's what you mean. But . . . there are procedures. Generally, if a Warden is suspected, other Wardens are expected to handle everything. Investigation, arrest, assize, accusation, defense, adjudication."

Maurenia made a noncommittal *hmmm* sound and grew silent.

"Your turn," Aelis said. "What leads a soldier into working with the Dobruszes?"

Maurenia sighed. "Running away to sea didn't get me what I wanted. I thought soldiering might, but it didn't either."

"And what was it you wanted?"

"To see things, be a part of something, make something. A sailor's life only gave me part of that. At sea, you live in a box maybe eighty, a hundred paces long, half that wide. Sure, you see some places . . . I saw most of the cities of Tyridice, for instance, but little more than the dockside taverns, and those all might have been the one I grew up in. Soldiering is much the same. Always someone telling you where to go, what to do, how to do it . . . I had enough of anybody telling me where to go, or when, or what to do when I got there. Working with Timmuk, I'm a partner in something, I have a say, and the moment I want to walk away, no one will try to stop me."

"And you think you'll do that some day? Just walk away?"

"You don't want to do that every day in Lone Pine?"

Aelis laughed softly. "I might not like Lone Pine, Maurenia . . . but I worked hard to be a Warden. I asked for this obligation, and by Onoma's Mercy, I'll fulfill it or die trying."

"That doesn't fit with the pampered city girl, the count's daughter."

"I told you, my family takes obligations seriously."

"But you didn't have any, did you? Why seek them out?" Maurenia's muffled question stretched over a yawn.

Aelis took a deep breath. "Because you cannot buy your way into the Wardens. Every teacher I ever had, save one, threw the words "rich girl" at me like a curse. I know it was just part of the training. They'll say anything to break you. But being a Warden belongs to *me*. Not my name, not my wealth. I had to win my sword in an Abjurer's test; I had to spend an extra year in the colleges for it. And if freezing in Lone Pine and birthing sheep for two years is what it takes to *stay* a Warden, I'll do it and smile."

A silence fell. Aelis felt Maurenia pressing more heavily against her side, and realized that the half-elf was beginning to fall asleep. *Am I that boring?*

Much as she wanted to let her stay there, Aelis could feel the warmth and gravity of Maurenia's body pulling her toward sleep as well.

"Maurenia," she murmured, turning her neck to brush her lips against her upturned cheek. "I can't fall asleep on watch."

"Nothing out here to kill us. Besides, we've got a Warden. And the biggest fucking half-orc I've ever seen."

Aelis laughed faintly. *And if only you knew exactly who Tun is*, she thought. "Yes, well, that half-orc will never let me hear the end of it if he wakes up for his watch and finds I've fallen down on mine. You'll stay warmer in the shelter."

Maurenia shook herself awake enough to stand and shuffle off, but not before saying, "When we get back, I want three days of nothing but baths, bed, and wine."

"Make it a week," Aelis said, then settled back into the meditative state she'd been seeking before Maurenia had come to her.

She found it, and the rest of her two hours passed without event. Among the first things prospective wizards learned to do was to clear the mind. Young Aelis had scoffed at the idea that it was necessary, but soon enough, it became essential. At the time, it had been seeing other students succeed, mastering simple cantrips and incantations when they stymied her, that had convinced her. There had been no formative teacher; in fact, teaching Meditation and the Clear Mind was a task foisted on advanced students rather than actual Magisters and professors.

There were theories about why it worked and arguments that first-year students carried on into the wee hours about whether it was spiritual or physiological. As a Necromancy student, Aelis had vigorously argued for the latter, saying that it freed the mind, allowing it to restore energy and heal like any other muscle.

Now, she might admit that she was less certain of her answers then. More to the point, she was less certain why she'd ever bothered to argue over it in the first place. *What matters*, she told herself, *is that it works, and allows one to focus the mind for the application of magic more effectively than without.*

She stood up as Tun approached from behind her; with the mind clear, her senses were sharper. As naturally quiet as Tun was, there was little chance that even he could throw off a pile of bedding and climb out of a shelter and walk to her without making *any* noise.

"You're getting better at timing these things," Tun said.

"No, I'm not," Aelis muttered, "just better at hearing you."

Tun patted her shoulder as they passed each other, and she slipped into an easy, if cold, sleep next to Maurenia.

14

SCOUTING

Aelis woke up cold, despite the presence of three other people crammed into the shelter and Maurenia pressed against her back. She found her warming bag in her pocket and gave it a tiny shake, then slipped it inside her robe, fiddling with the copper wire to get it against her skin. In no time, pulses of heat shot out from it, spreading throughout her limbs.

You know, Aelis thought, *I could manufacture these for the folk of Lone Pine to use when the weather gets dangerous.* She began totting up the costs in her head: the wire, the Manganar, the proper amulets, alchemically treated ceramics, the finest wool, and realized that a properly functioning device made of the most useful materials, not even accounting for aesthetic choices, would cost several gold tri-crowns, and she could not afford to outfit the entire village. *Perhaps I could make a few for folk in direst need,* she thought, unwilling to let go of the idea entirely.

She extricated herself from Maurenia, waking the half-elf up in the process, and crawled out of the shelter and into the campsite. A fresh slick of snow coated the grass they'd cleared, some settling on Tun's boat where it lay a foot or so from the firepit.

It was not a great deal more than a raft, but the hides were tight against it, and she and Maurenia could fit in it, though only just. It would have to do.

Behind her, she heard others waking up. Her instinct was to go stir up the fire, but Timmuk would kick up a fuss if anyone else did. Soon enough, he emerged from the tent, scratching at his beard. He picked up a long stick that rested against the firepit stones and stirred the coals to instant flames, sparks shooting into the air.

"How do you have the knack of keeping a fire ready to roar back to life after an entire night like that?" she asked, edging closer to its growing heat.

"There is nothing in this world that cannot be a craft, even an art, if it is practiced with due care," Timmuk said.

"And here I thought you were a city dwarf," Aelis teased.

Timmuk smiled beneath his brown cloud of beard. "You think there are not opportunities to practice making fires in cities, Warden? Let's say you want to burn down the house of a competitor. Or a creditor. Or a debtor. Hypothetically, of course."

"Of course," Aelis said flatly.

"You *don't* want that fire burning out of control and destroying an entire quarter. You don't really want it to kill anyone. But you *do* need it to smolder long enough and hot enough to make sure nobody gets back into the building to retrieve any documents or incriminating evidence of any kind . . ."

"Should you be telling this to a Warden, Timmuk?"

"Why, this is all hypothetical," he said, laying a hand on his chest. "I'm certain you don't mean to suggest otherwise. And even if you *do* mean it, I can provide documents proving my and Andresh's whereabouts the last time a dwarven Lending and Counting House went up in flames in Lascenise. We were hundreds of miles away leading a caravan in Antraval. Got the manifests and everything."

"I'm sure you do," Aelis muttered. By then everyone was up and moving, and the fire was hot enough to warm some bread and leftover soup to make a kind of porridge, and they sat down over breakfast to make a plan.

"We need to scout out the place on foot first," Maurenia offered. "Tun and Aelis, one direction around the place, Timmuk in the other. Look for a good approach to wet the boat, free of obstruction. And before anyone asks," she added, "I'm not scouting because someone has to stay behind and make a sounding line, and I don't trust any of the rest of you to do it."

"Make a what?" Aelis ran her spoon around the inside of her mostly empty bowl.

"A sounding line. It's how you measure depth. I'll take stock of whatever rope and cordage we've got, tie a knot every few feet. Standard is the six-foot fathom, of course, but I might make it three feet since we'd be in fairly shallow water, I expect. Stings wrong, though."

"Wait. Yesterday, you wouldn't touch a shovel. Can you handle the ropes? Let me see your hands."

Maurenia tugged off her gloves and held up her hands, free of their bandages, for inspection.

The burns were *gone*, and no tender new skin was in their place. Her hands bore no evidence of the damage that had been done to them by the Death's Cold Shield that had been active upon the dog skeletons.

"This is . . . remarkable," Aelis said, taking Maurenia's hands in her own and bending her head to peer closely at the skin. "It's like they weren't damaged at all."

"I had a good physician," Maurenia murmured.

"Do you normally heal fast?" Aelis was too invested in the examination to accept a compliment.

"Normally I try not to get hurt in the first place. Perhaps it's just a particularly strong batch of that unguent." She snatched her hands away and stuffed them back into the gloves. Aelis filed that tiny mystery away in the corner of her mind that could examine any given perplexity without occupying her waking thoughts. Likely enough, the magical burns hadn't been as bad as all that, anyway: poor light in Rhunival's hall, good elven skin, hands well protected by calluses. It would all add up.

"Let's be at it then," Tun said. "There won't be any great abundance of sunlight today. Let's not waste what we will get."

"Let me get my stick and swordbelt," Aelis said.

"So now what?" Tun leaned toward Aelis, murmuring just loud enough for her to hear.

"Get close enough to be inspired," she muttered.

"Why do I even ask?"

◆ ◆ ◆

They began at the spot where the barbican had stood, a gentle slope leading up to it, which Tun swore had been a road to the castle gate. Tun and Aelis walked north, Timmuk south, and both would end up at the place where the river poured into the sunken castle. Unless, of course, any of them spotted anything significant or a perfect launch site. If they did, Tun and Timmuk had arranged a call of barn owl or horned owl or some other kind of owl, Aelis was too cold and too preoccupied to pay all that much attention.

"We won't want to go in too close to the river," Tun pointed out as he and Aelis walked, she taking two or three strides to each of his ground-eating ones. "That poor excuse for a boat won't stand up to much of a current."

Aelis could see only the suggestion of shapes in the dark, still water. Her mind tried to organize them into towers and walls and gates, but she dismissed them as merely the search for order amid the chaotic unknown. Once or twice, something moved beneath them, small and quick. Fish, no doubt.

After they'd made it perhaps halfway around their appointed side, Tun stopped and, in as clear a fit of frustration as Aelis had ever seen him display, gnashed his teeth.

"Bah," he spat. "We waste time, danger grows. Let's just get the cursed, wallowing little hide boat in the water. Here's as good as anywhere."

Tun cupped his hands around his mouth and let out three great cries that echoed across the hard, frosty air.

"Barn owl? Horned owl? Great . . . spotted owl?" Aelis ventured a guess.

"Why," Tun said, slowly turning to face her, "would a *barn* owl be here in the great frozen north?"

"Tun. My education covered many topics. Sadly, bird calls were not one of them. My older brother Aleyan was a great one for hawking and tried to interest me in it when I was young. It didn't take."

"I despair of ever imparting any woodcraft to you. That was the call of a *barred* owl, so called for the stripes of its plumage, and it's much more likely to be seen hereabouts."

"What would've happened if some actual barred owl had called? What then?"

"They are active only at night," Tun said, "and they do not give three calls and then stop."

"I see," Aelis said, though she didn't, but it seemed best not to admit that. She dug out her warming bag, gave it the slightest of shakes, and for a moment the heat that spread outward from the little curl of copper chased away the edges of the cold.

"We might as well go to a closer shore, make the portage less onerous. Though . . . my boat can't weigh above a stone or two," Tun said. "Take only the gear you're sure to need, as any unnecessary weight will do you no good."

As they walked back, Aelis contemplated her gear. She *shouldn't* need her sword, but her old advisor's words echoed in her head again. Her walking stick, certainly not; she wasn't about to use it to pole them around. No pack, no medical bag, no food. Her belt with dagger and sword, her lantern, her warming bag, and her clothing. And Rhunival's key, or fish, or whatever it was.

They met Timmuk and Maurenia coming forward, the dwarf holding the boat easily aloft. Maurenia had a rope, now knotted regularly along its length, coiled over her shoulder, her crossbow and sword, but no pack. A long pine limb sat inside the boat, bobbing along.

"See what there is to see and report back," Tun said as he took Aelis's walking stick and a few extraneous pouches that weighed down her sword-belt. "Don't go doing anything foolish."

"Me?" Aelis widened her eyes in imitation of what she imagined an innocent maiden might look like.

Tun glared but said no more. He watched with concern as Timmuk carried his quickly made boat down to the edge of the lagoon and set it down. Maurenia hopped easily into it, holding it in place with the pole, and Aelis followed, making sure to tuck Rhunival's carving, wrapped in cloth, inside her robe.

She felt rather uneasy for the first few moments as the boat sank low against the waterline, and Maurenia poled them off the bank into the ice-flecked stillness of the water.

15

THE SUNKEN KEEP

Once they passed roughly thirty yards or so from shore, Maurenia paused in her poling to begin playing out the rope into the water. She let it fall section by section, the knots slipping from between her thumb and forefinger.

"Hrm. Not much more than two fathoms before I'm hitting something. Irregular surface, though, not a hard-packed bottom."

"Well," Aelis said, gesturing toward the looming skeletal remains of the walls they'd just floated past, "it was a big keep. Proud towers . . . can't be sunk *too* far."

Another few yards, and Aelis thought she felt Rhunival's fish tug against its wrappings, a faint buzz between her robes and her skin.

They paused again for Maurenia to take another sounding. The half-elf frowned as a fifth and then sixth knot slipped beneath the surface, calm but for the ripples of their passage. She started trying to pull the rope back in, but clearly it was obstructed, as she half stood, leaning backward, pulling on it as if she was landing a fish.

"Caught on something?" Aelis asked just moments before a skeletal hand, and then a skull, burst from the surface of the water, clinging onto Maurenia's sounding line, using the knots to drag itself upward.

Aelis swept her dagger from her sheath and plunged the heavy pommel straight through the top of the skull. She didn't even call on Necrobane's Fist this time, just let her weapon do the work, and the skeleton fell backward.

Maurenia, meanwhile, had been jerked forward, down toward the surface of the water, the rope she had coiled around her arm tightening. She was reaching for her sword, but off-balance as she was, trying not to be pulled into the water, she was having trouble finding the hilt, much less making use of the blade.

Aelis lunged forward and cut the rope free, saw at least one more animated skeleton sink into the water with it.

Maurenia lowered herself back into her squat in the boat and finally managed to claw her sword free, the tiny craft rocking perilously as she did.

In the excitement, Rhunival's fish had *certainly* begun buzzing and had, in fact, pulled itself half-free of the wrappings.

Aelis had a flash of insight.

"Get the boat back to shore," she said, slamming the dagger back into its sheath. "Get out of here."

"What? What are you doing?"

Aelis eyed the distance to the tower that stood above the now rippling black water. "Going for a swim," she said. "After I walk on water for a bit."

She slipped off her outer robe and let it drop into the boat, ignoring Maurenia's protests. She slipped her sword scabbard off the frog that kept it attached to her belt and thanked herself for being diligent about the maintenance of such things, since it gave easily and the weapon settled in the now water-logged bottom of the craft. She wriggled her boots off just as Rhunival's fish leapt free of its wrappings and darted for the water.

In the morning sunlight, there could be no doubt now it was a fish, and it looked as alive as any fish Aelis had ever seen, though its scales were shades of amber and brown rather than silver. It described a graceful arc, tail flapping, and Maurenia gasped.

"I'll draw them off!" Aelis shouted, cinching her belt, which now held only her dagger and her pouched alchemy lamp. She aimed a Lash at one of the animated skeletons flailing its way through the water, didn't even stop to see the result before leaping off the boat.

If Maurenia awaited a splash, she was surprised when none came. Aelis did not dive into the water head—or even feet—first. She bounded out, like a runner vaulting over a hurdle.

And instead of crashing into the water, she sprinted across it, taking long, loping strides.

What Aelis was doing with every step, was planting a series of tiny wards. Each was just big enough to stand on and lasted only long enough for her to push off. She began angling them and placing them higher as she neared the crumbling barbican tower. She launched herself toward a hole in the edifice, having seen a wet gleam of brown arc out of the water and through it. She tumbled in, but didn't have long to celebrate her triumph, having fallen right onto a carved stone staircase that wound up the inside of the tower. The fish, once more inert wood, tumbled alongside her.

And she would've kept falling had she not thrown one more ward, bigger and more solid than the small ones she'd summoned outside, and held it for long enough to get back on her feet.

"Only a couple of new bruises," she muttered as she righted herself and dropped the ward. "Could've been worse." She was worried about the amount of her will and her power she'd just spent. But none of the wards had been large and none held for very long. She wouldn't be caught defenseless, not yet. She thought about the sword she'd left in the boat. "Should've minded Urizen's words," she chided herself. "Wear the sword."

She took a moment to center herself and inhaled a deep breath. Almost immediately, she wished she hadn't. The whole place was suffused with the miasma of rot and mildew. She didn't gag, but it was a near thing.

Rotting flesh I could handle, she thought. *Stagnant water is so much worse.*

Aelis bent down to pick up the now inert fish and had a good look at it.

She turned it around in her hands, examining the startling detail of the scales, the fins, the pulsing gills, the moving eye.

To be an Anatomist, one needed sure, strong hands. Aelis was not clumsy. She did not drop things, she did not fumble them, and as a surgeon and swordswoman both, she had built strong wrists and a secure grip.

So had anyone been there to see, she would've told them in no uncertain terms that she did not drop the fish, but rather, that it wriggled away from her and flew into the water. Again.

"Onoma's tits," she cursed, before taking a deep breath, drawing Nieran's Sheath about her, and diving into the water after it. A ward of this size and intensity, drawn without her sword, was going to leave her with at least a dull headache for most of the next day. Probably longer.

Luckily for her, the thing glowed, a pulsing green radiance. Even more luckily, it was sitting in the water, unmoving.

Until she plunged in and caught sight of it. Then it turned and darted off, trailing green behind it in the murky depths.

Aelis was immediately faced with the problem of locomotion. Wrapped in the Sheath as she was—necessary to keep the cold of the water from killing her, she was sure—she couldn't propel herself forward.

This was, she would have admitted, not a problem she'd given a great deal of thought to. *A Warden adapts. A Warden acts. Is what I'm about to try even possible? A Warden does not run to consult the fucking library*, Bardun Jacques's voice screamed at her.

She pulled the Sheath up around her feet, locking it closed again at her knees. And with quick, choppy kicks, she began following the fish. It darted downward, down, down into a blackness in which Aelis could make out no details. She had the impression of more stairs, of rotting racks of weapons, of a barracks of some kind.

Her lungs were burning by the time the fish stopped and turned to face her again. Frantically, barely keeping her held breath—expelling it into the Sheath would do her no favors—she looked around for whatever could've stopped it. She had no sense that there was any obstacle. The gods-damned thing was just looking at a wall.

She thought of her lamp, tied to her belt. That was an even worse idea, and she wasn't certain there was enough air left in the Sheath to ignite the thing anyway, or what might happen if she did. Alchemical processes she could master, but theory, as usual, bored her too much to have given it real study.

As if in answer to her prayer, the fish opened its mouth, and a beam of green illuminated a bump on the wall just below a long-empty sconce.

A skull.

Aelis tried to pop her hand through the Sheath, but she couldn't maintain three exceptions to the ward's cohesion. It burst. She was instantly soaked, and the shock of it forced her mouth open. She swallowed horrid water, but only a mouthful.

Her hand reached out and grasped the skull. She felt it moving, heard the grinding of stone, and the wall parted. Water began rushing in, carrying her—and the fish—with it. But as soon as she was inside, the stone slammed shut. The torrent of inrushing water ceased. Aelis leaned forward and retched hard, twice, expelling the water she'd swallowed and about half of what she'd eaten that morning in the bargain. With her throat acid-raw, she heaved for several deep, sweet breaths, heedless of the rotting smell.

Which, she only just realized, was the smell of corpses, not mildew.

Fuck.

She took her dagger from her belt, clicked her lamp on, and turned. The tiny gap in the keep into which the fissure had admitted her was narrow indeed—just wide enough for her to stand in—but a few paces beyond, illuminated by her lamp, a path led directly into a barracks-crypt, one several times the size of the first she'd uncovered. Shadows beyond the feeble beam of her lamp moved sluggishly within.

Something flopped against her foot. Reflexively, she was about to stab downward when she saw Rhunival's fish. She bent and picked it up, wooden once more and inert as any carving, thrust it back through her belt.

Gripping her dagger more tightly, she plunged forward into the darkness.

16

THE VAULT

Time and moist air had done a great deal of Aelis's work for her here in the undercroft of Mahlhewn Keep. The animated skeletons—held together with leather and rope—had long ago frayed and fallen apart. The merest swipe of her dagger was enough to send them down to dust.

Just this first chamber had held thirty. Aelis fervently hoped that the conditions would persist the farther in she went.

Without the fish to guide her, she had very little idea of where to go, so she paused after swiping away the animating vestige of the last skeleton.

"Got to be under the courtyard somewhere. Did they hollow this whole damn place out? Fill it with undead?" She realized how preposterous the idea was as soon as she said it; the narrow passage went in only one direction, with small rooms to either side full of crumpled animations. A few of these were blocked by fallen rocks, and clearing obstructions didn't seem to be part of the animations' programming, if they were still functional.

Once or twice, Aelis thought she saw something, a shadow flitting at the edges of the beam of her lantern. She did not dismiss it, but neither did she reach for any of the spells at her command to probe it. *If it is something, no need to draw its attention.*

She decided that stealth—not generally part of her toolbox—was the best approach. She dimmed the lantern at her belt till she could see only a few steps ahead.

Aelis found herself taking small, careful steps, hunching her shoulders, walking on tiptoe, then stopped herself. She drew in a breath, held it.

I am an Abjurer. I am a Necrobane. If there is any spirit flitting about this place, it should be frightened of me.

With that thought held firmly in her mind, and her grip resettled on the dagger, she strode more confidently forward.

The main passage was wide enough for perhaps three of her—or one of Tun—to walk along. She continued to ignore the branching paths. Slowly, almost imperceptibly, the grade of the path inclined upward.

Aelis found herself face to face with a featureless metallic wall set flush with the stone, stray rivulets of water dripping down its face.

"Of course," she muttered. "Of course they'd surround the vault with animated soldiers." She could see nothing in the feeble white light of her lamp but the blank gray of its expanse. She thought at first it must be iron, but the trickles of water running down the surface would surely have left rust.

There was none.

She reached out to touch it, her fingers gliding along the preternaturally smooth surface.

"This," she murmured, "is not iron. Not as I know it." She was no metallurgist, but iron should've been rough, pitted. Even steel would've had a texture to it, something for her skin to graze against.

This didn't.

It was as if she couldn't *quite* touch it. Something was there, she could see it, and her fingers could sense it, but she could find nothing to push or grip.

Aelis dropped her hand to her side. It brushed the fish stuck through her belt, but nothing happened; it didn't come alive, or suddenly turn into a key in her hand.

If this is keyed to voice commands, she thought, *then I've already lost. So don't contemplate that.*

She closed her eyes, tried to will herself into an intuitive space. *If it is word-locked somehow, then the security it offered would become nonfunctional far too easily.*

"In the midst of a crisis," she whispered, "they'd need any average courtier or soldier to be able to open this and get to the control rod within."

So it must be a matter of touching the right spot, or in the right way.

"Or with the right tool," she said out loud to no one in particular as she slipped the fish from her belt. She held it close to the lantern, but with its beam dialed down, she couldn't make out much.

The carved wood felt different in her hand now. "At least it's not coming alive," she said. And yet, she felt it had shifted, grown longer.

She decided to search the wall of the vault methodically. Though the highest part of the wall she faced was well beyond her reach, she elected not to worry about it, reasoning that any entry point needed to be at eye level or lower. Taking small, shuffling steps, she worked her hand up and down the wall, searching for any hint, any depression, any suggestion of a keyhole, a doorway, or a lock.

Aelis lost track of how many steps she'd taken and had no sense of how far she'd walked when her fingers stumbled across something. The tiniest hint of an indentation in the smooth wall.

She felt the carving, held tightly in her now sweating hand, changing. The scales disappeared, the fins retreated, and for a moment, she had an impression of a key with half a dozen branching flanges and forks. Then the thing practically leapt into the wall.

Aelis expected an ear-splitting grinding of gears, something titanic, momentous.

But there was only a small click, a soft whisper of well-greased hinges, and a yawning blackness opened before her.

Her first instinct was to plunge straight into it, but she forced herself to breathe, to be calm, to focus and consider her steps.

Light first. She adjusted the dials on her lamp. It brightened considerably, but something about the open door swallowed the light, and she saw little more detail before her.

But there was enough to step inside, so she did.

Immediately, the door slid closed behind her, there was a great crack, and water began pouring through a broken metal panel in the roof.

She allowed herself but one instantaneous moment of panic, one quickly whispered *Fuck*, and then Aelis ignored the water splashing to the floor around her and tried to focus on what she had.

The inside of the vault was almost painfully bright after the darkness of the crypts and the increased output of her lamp. The metal on the inside of the walls, whatever it was, amplified and reflected that light back at her; some of the walls could've been used as mirrors.

And everywhere, weapons, tools, and wealth beckoned to her. Here a rack of swords, ranging from shorter than her willow-leaf Abjurer's blade to two-handed monsters longer than she was tall. One flamberge caught her eye. It was long for her, but something about the undulation of its edge called to her. A deadly light moved along its side and pulled her closer.

As she took a half step, water sloshed against her foot and shook her free.

"Not here for swords."

She saw at least two unlocked, iron-bound coffers spilling over with gems, fortunes available by the fistful.

"Not here to shop," she said, tearing her eyes away from daggers resting on velvet cushions, from a rack holding crystal-topped Invoker's staves.

The vault wasn't small, but it wasn't impossible to search in the time she had, if she had any time at all.

"Must act as though I do," she told herself, and so she began methodically searching the rooms *without* focusing on any one object. She let her senses drift and slide over the objects, waiting for a tingle of intuition.

And almost instantly, she had it.

In a corner, leaning on an end table that wouldn't have looked out of place in a lord's study, was a simple wooden rod. It hardly looked worked, but rather as if it had been plucked, living, from the end of a long bough. Leaves—wilting, turning to a faint rust color—still clung to the forked branches at its top.

That, she knew with dead certainty, *is what Rhunival wants*. Aelis walked over and took it from the table. It was heavier than she expected, as if made of stone and not wood. She tucked it under her belt and prayed she'd find a way to carry it.

"Now," she muttered, certain she'd solved at least one crisis, "if I were a magical implement made to control regiments of animated skeletons, where would I be?"

Water was swirling around her ankles now. More seemed to be pouring in from the crack, more still seeping in from fresh breaks.

As fast as she could take them in, she looked at and discarded other objects: a heavy black iron key; a glass knife with a trail of dark blue mist swirling inside the blade; a wooden rod so plain it had to be deceptively so; a bowl containing a black abyss; a jar full of glowing seeds.

Aelis's instincts guided her past all these things without a second thought. Panic threatened as the water was now nearly to her knees and moving around was growing more difficult.

Then she saw it: a wrought-iron candlestick, a single strand of metal wrapped in a kind of spiral that would, at its ends, hold two candles. Aelis didn't know how she'd recognized it or why. Perhaps the very fact that it wasn't given a place of importance, that it was left on the back corner of a table upon which more interesting objects—including a tiny coffret that sparkled a promising blue through its silver-lattice walls—caught her attention.

But when she leaned over it, the spiral and the base snapped into an unmistakable alignment.

A College of Necromancy Death's Head.

"You clever bastard," she said. "And I'll just fucking bet it requires candles to work; functions tied together." Aelis set down both candlestick and rod and used her dagger to cut strips of cloth from her sleeves, briefly and absurdly reflecting on how many of her best clothes she'd ruined since she came to Lone Pine. She tied the candlestick and the rod to her belt as securely as she could, then sloshed back to a table full of treasures. One handful was easy enough to stow, but the other thing she took—a small leather case with a silver buckle and runes embossed on the sides—she had to simply carry. The case clanked in her hand; for a compact thing, it was surprisingly heavy.

Then Aelis did the hardest thing she'd ever done.

She waited.

She was not, by nature, a patient woman. She had a need to *do* things, to fill her time with useful work, or fun, or some combination of both. Wardens were meant to be proactive, to work to achieve their aims, not wait. At times, patience would be required. But the difficulty of this specific call for patience was compounded by the fact that she was, in essence, waiting to drown.

She took deep breaths as the water pressed cold and heavy against her thighs and hips. Breaths came harder and shallower as the cold threatened, the weight of the water trying to drag her down. *No chance of putting on the Sheath. This could be far too long for that. I could do something to my lungs.*

Her thoughts flashed to the pages of Aldayim she'd consulted before they had left Lone Pine. *Deliberate Necrotization.* The ankle that was currently, in a very technical sense, *dead* felt none of the cold and pain of the rest of her leg.

"You idiot," she scolded herself aloud. "Can't do that to a lung the way you can to a ligament. You'll just fucking die."

Breathing was all but impossible now. Aelis wasn't entirely sure how water could be as cold as this was and yet not be ice. She kicked her legs to keep herself afloat as the water pushed toward the ceiling, her hands clutching the little kit, while Rhunival's rod and the iron candlestick threatened to drag her down, both heavier than they had any right to be.

She kicked off a wall, trying to direct herself toward the widening hole from which the water poured before it covered her head and obscured her vision. Then, as if a shroud had been pulled over her head, all was darkness.

It took only a moment for her eyes to adjust, though her vision was hardly clear. With powerful kicks, she propelled herself through the hole and into the water of the castle lagoon above her. Her lungs began to burn well before it was fair. The rod and the candlestick weighed her down, begging her to let them go. Even her small lamp and dagger felt like undue burdens. Her hand was frozen around the leather case; she began to lose the feeling in it.

When she felt as if her lungs surely must burst or face permanent damage, a spot of light appeared in her vision.

And she realized she was still a goodly distance from the surface.

An Abjurer does not know fear. An Abjurer is the antithesis of fear.

She tried to reach for a spell, the Sheath, for at least that would give her the chance to expel her held breath and take in some stale air. Not a longterm strategy, but perhaps enough to buy precious seconds.

But casting a spell without speaking words aloud was a task for masters of the school. Oh, it could be done; she knew the theory. Certainly she had seen Lavanalla, Urizen, and Duvhalin all do it in their disciplines.

But for her, under this stress, it was like trying to spark sopping-wet tinder to life by banging a rock against the edge of a dull knife. Every time there was even a spark of power as she summoned the forms of the ward, it instantly fizzled.

She had no choice; the breath rushed from her lungs, her mouth opened, tried to suck in air.

Aelis took in fetid, freezing cold water instead.

She gagged, tried in vain to keep it from her lungs, knew she couldn't succeed. She kicked furiously for the surface, and her face broke into frigid air. Almost immediately, she retched and very nearly sank back beneath the water. She kicked up, cast her head about looking for anything solid She saw the vague outline of a wall and made for it.

It wasn't far, a few yards at most. But the frantic, desperate moments of swimming were, Aelis thought, probably the most graceless and difficult moments of her life. She reached the wall, sticking one foot hard against the stone and scrabbling for purchase with her full hands. She clung to the stone and, finally feeling at least somewhat stable, took the opportunity to vomit.

She got most of it on her arm.

"At least this putrid water is here to wash it away," Aelis muttered through teeth that she only just now noticed were chattering.

You have moments, at best, a calm, detached voice that sounded like an anatomy professor told her, *before the cold starts to take over your body and kill organs.*

She looked this way and that, searching for shore, for any sign of her companions, when she heard a shout that sounded like her name, albeit stretched by distance and echo.

Aelis found both, and while Maurenia's voice carried, it appeared the rest of them were busy.

Fighting.

They weren't, from what she could tell from this distance, in danger of being immediately overwhelmed, but they were set upon on two sides by skeletons.

Aelis smiled and lifted the iron candlestick from the water, uttering a simple Necromantic first order as she did, imagining that's how it would open up its power to her.

Her spell immediately rebounded and dissipated. The iron stung her hand so hard she nearly dropped it.

"Fuck," she swore, the word tearing at her raw throat.

Aelis pushed off the wall, intending to swim to shore. She gathered most of the breath she had left and called out, "Tun! I'm coming!" She thought she saw the figures on the shore turn to her, but she was already shocking herself by diving back into the lagoon.

She hadn't gotten very far when she realized just how bad an idea that was. Her muscles began to cramp; the chattering of her teeth and the shaking of her limbs against the cold seeping into them were making it harder and harder to push in any one direction.

The shore, she soon realized, was not an option. Perhaps the barbican was, being about halfway between her and where her companions were demolishing skeletons on dry land.

But then her legs spasmed and she felt herself sinking.

As she tried to come up with motivating insults to growl at herself—a habit during Warden and Abjurer endurance training—she took in another mouthful of water. She felt it lap over her head.

She struggled against it, curled her arm tightly around the candlestick and the rod, and tried to push for the surface. Panic bloomed and died in her chest, and her body betrayed her in spasms and cramps. She sank.

17

RETREAT

Aelis woke with a cry and a great deal of pain.

She didn't dare open her eyes, but she could feel a hulking presence looming over her, smell the clean but powerful scent of smoke and wind and animal that lingered on him.

"Tun," she croaked. "Please tell me I'm dead this time."

"You're dead this time," he said, without a hint of laughter or jest in his voice.

"Oh good," she rasped. "I'm afraid that being alive is going to be even more painful than this death."

"Is this some kind of private joke for the two of you?" Maurenia's voice, above and behind Tun's.

"I'm touched by your concern, Maurenia," Aelis murmured.

"I *am* concerned," she protested, stung.

Aelis, eyes still closed, raised a hand, opening and closing her fingers. Maurenia took her meaning and clasped it with her own two hands, wrapping Aelis's hand with relief.

"I know," Aelis said. "You sounded angry, which you wouldn't be if you weren't interested in my survival. And no, it isn't the first time I've woken up in heroic amounts of pain and asked Tun if I was dead."

"Probably won't be the last," Tun said.

"Onoma's Bleak Mercy, I hope it is," Aelis said. She finally dragged her eyelids open—it felt like pulling a rasp over her eyes—then pulled herself into a sitting position using Maurenia's arm.

They were inside their traveling shelter, with Aelis wrapped in what seemed like every scrap of hide and fur they had to spare. A fire burned in a pit dug out of the cold earth, the smoke escaping through an opening where sections of the shelter met.

"How did you lot handle the animations without me?"

"Got a lot easier once we remembered we had that alchemical whatnot," Timmuk said.

"It's a kind of soap, technically," Aelis said, beginning to grow drowsy in the shelter's warmth. "At least, it's activated silver and . . ." She waved a hand vaguely in the air, "a few other things suspended in a soap."

"Right. Well. Soap. Killed them proper."

"My alchemy professors would be so proud," Aelis said.

"At the risk of ruining the dramatic tension," Maurenia said, "did you find what you went in there for?"

Aelis grunted and shrugged off the blankets they'd buried her in. Her eyes were adjusting to the semidarkness, and she saw her gear in a jumble nearby. She pawed at it frantically till she touched both the rough wood of the rod and the cold iron of the candlestick. "Yes," she said, trying for more certainty than she felt. She lifted the length of wood, caught for a moment in the way the firelight reflected off the faintly rust-colored leaves from the far end. "This is Rhunival's. I'm certain of it. And this," she said, struggling a bit to lift it, "is the command totem for the animations."

"It's a candleholder," Maurenia said. But then Aelis turned it so that the two upraised holders faced the half-elf, and Maurenia's eyes widened in alarm.

"What . . ." Maurenia said. "What am I seeing?"

"You look at this from the right angle, and it's the seal of the College of Necromancy," Aelis said. "Bit of a giveaway."

"Well, then, we've got it all sewn up," Timmuk said. "If we could just linger here a few days to give me a chance to scheme how to get into that vault again—after you draw me whatever you can remember, that is."

Aelis cut him short with a wave of her hand. "There're two problems. One is that the vault and everything that remained in it is now underwater. Two," Aelis said, setting the candleholder down, "is that I haven't yet figured out how to make this work."

"One ventures to suggest," Tun said, "that it may require candles."

"It almost certainly does. The trick is figuring out what kind of candles."

There was a moment of silence in the tent. Timmuk took the opportunity to put a few more small sticks on his carefully controlled fire.

"Please tell us that you mean tallow or beeswax or some other common candle," Maurenia said.

"Tallow or beeswax wouldn't matter nearly as much as the more esoteric ingredients. I can puzzle it out . . ." Aelis said, before trailing off.

"But . . ." Tun said, supplying the unspoken word for her.

"But I probably need to get back to Lone Pine to do it," Aelis said.

Timmuk sighed. "A Dolovkin vault and all its secrets lost," he murmured.

"I may," Aelis said weakly, "have a small answer to some of your concerns."

She rummaged in her gear till she found her alchemy lamp. A twist and a pinch, and one of the cylinders that held fuel reagents swung open. She dug her fingers into wet leather and tugged hard, pulling free a small bag. She tossed it to the dwarf, who fumbled for a few moments to undo the drawstrings.

Even in the dim firelight inside the shelter, the gems that fell into Timmuk's hand gleamed.

"Didn't want to make everyone come all this way without a souvenir," Aelis said. "Never let it be said that working for a Warden is entirely without profit. Should be enough for everyone who wants a share to split." Then she pawed around some more, looking for the leather case she'd gripped so hard, she felt the tools inside digging into her palm. When she couldn't find it, she let out an annoyed growl.

At least, she tried to growl. What came out was more of a whine that she couldn't believe had originated from inside her, which made her all the more angry at herself. It wasn't quite so bad that tears threatened; Aelis had never been much for crying. But she did shut her eyes and try not to voice her anger and disappointment.

"What?" That was Maurenia, as Tun had ducked out of the shelter to stretch and Timmuk was too entranced by his handful of gems.

"I had found something," Aelis whispered, shutting her eyes as she tried to remember what had happened, and berated herself for having lost something so valuable. "Something for you."

"I don't want a magic sword, Aelis," Maurenia murmured. "I prefer knowing the skill is in my hand and not a weapon."

"Wasn't that," Aelis said. "Artificer's toolkit. Alchemically treated steel tools, diamond-edged chisels the size of a pen that can lever open a coffin, tools for measurement and scale . . . I must've dropped it in the lagoon."

"You got what you went in there for," Maurenia said. Aelis kept her eyes closed rather than face the disappointment she thought she could hear in that voice. "That's what matters." Aelis felt her move away, and only then did she look up at the roof of the shelter, then to the dwarf peering at a few select stones in one gloved hand.

"I'll say," Timmuk said. "Quite an eye you've got, Warden. Enough to make a former banker think you might have been in the jewel trade. And there was more like this?"

"Enough to disrupt the gem market for a generation," Aelis said. "And I am sorry to tell you, but no one is ever getting into that vault again."

"How did you do it, then?"

"I followed the fish. The key. The thing that Rhunival carved," Aelis said in a rush. "It guided me through some of the drowned parts. And others, well . . . the vault was underneath the courtyard in the middle of a vast barracks-crypt. Most of which, I hasten to add, was destroyed or unusable." Tun, bent practically double, slipped back into the shelter as she spoke. She had no doubt he'd heard everything that had been said inside.

"Looks quiet out there. No more skeletons . . . pardon, *animations* that I can see. So . . . do we return to Lone Pine first or go to Rhunival?" Tun said. "Or do we do the unthinkable and split up?"

"We definitely do not do that," Aelis said, echoed closely by Maurenia. "I think we go to Rhunival first. I do not want him thinking we mean to do anything less than hold to our agreement with him."

"I do not want him for an enemy, but he seemed reasonable enough," Tun said.

"Trust a wizard's intuition. If this rod is what he wanted," she said, without even the tiniest doubt that it was, "if it looks even for a moment as if we intend to abscond with it, it could go poorly for us. And before anyone asks, yes, I do think he would know. I don't know what he would do. I don't intend to find out."

"Fine. Then we make for Rhunival in the morning and Lone Pine immediately after?"

"Yes. In the meantime, I can do some rudimentary examination of this thing and figure out what I need to make it work."

"What you need to do is rest," Maurenia insisted.

"I'll take the first watch," Aelis said. She tried to stand up only to find both Tun's and Maurenia's hands pushing her back down to the ground.

"You nearly drowned," Maurenia said. "If it weren't for Tun's boat, you would've. So, you're sleeping as well as you can, the rest of us are taking the watch, and we're moving in the morning."

"Fine. What happened to the bones of the animations you were fighting on the shore?"

Timmuk and Maurenia shared a look. "Still there, I suppose."

"Good," Aelis said. "Before turning in, someone is going to walk with me out there and help me collect some. May need it."

"Why?"

"Because the powdered bone of the previously unquiet dead could be a reagent that will help in the construction of candles that will make this device function. Once again, if I have to answer questions about every step of every magical and alchemical process I may need to engage in, this is going to take a lot longer than it needs to. When it comes to Necromancy and Alchemy, let's just assume I know better than any of you and let me get on with it." Her gratitude for being fished from the water, warmed up, and cared for should've lasted longer than it had, Aelis reflected. But she had never been one to take questions about that sort of thing lightly.

"Fair enough," Tun said. "I will go with you, as I am best equipped to carry you back when you collapse."

Aelis snorted and tried to hop lightly to her feet. The world swam around her, and she very nearly pitched over, but discipline—and her own desperate grasp on dignity in front of Maurenia—kept her upright. Her ankle twinged worryingly, and she resisted the urge to do some quick calculations on how much longer that particular Necromantic procedure should be kept in operation.

Well, it's not like I can turn it off now anyway, she thought, and tried not to favor that foot as she left the shelter behind the nearly crouching Tun. Once outside, the vastness of the night sky nearly overwhelmed her; the stars seemed oppressive in their number and closeness. She found herself reeling and very nearly called for Tun, only to find him turning around. He placed her walking stick firmly into her hand.

She nodded her thanks, confident he'd see it despite the dark, and began following his shaggy shape. After they'd gone only a few yards from the shelter, he abruptly stopped.

"You don't smell right. Your ankle."

"What do you mean?"

"It smells dead . . . What did you do to it?"

"Tun," Aelis said, not bothering to even try hiding the weariness in her voice, "I did do something. You're right. I couldn't have gotten out here otherwise."

"What did you do?"

"I cast a spell."

Tun sniffed. "That is not an answer."

"I used a complicated Necromantic Order to help restore function."

"Do not lie to me, Aelis. I won't abandon you out here in the wild if you do. But I will think less of you."

Aelis grimaced and folded in on herself as if she'd just taken a body blow. Then, between gritted teeth, she started thinking about how long it had been since she cast the spell. *At least twice as long as recommended.* "I did what I had to do with the tools at my command, Tun."

"And is it dangerous?"

"Can be."

"How?"

"If it goes on too long."

"How long is too long, Aelis?"

Tun sounded so much like a stern but well-meaning uncle that she had to stifle a laugh.

"I don't know. Too many factors: how much use and stress it is under, any other stresses to the body, the relative power and control of the Necromancer who did the work. And I don't have the book with me to make any calculations or even to repeat it or dispel it safely, so it's all a moot point till we're back at Lone Pine. If I promise you that I'm not about to turn into a half-dead abomination, will that do?"

"Is that possible?"

"I know you haven't met Dalius yet, Tun, but surely you remember what I've said about him."

"Yet?"

"My first year in Lone Pine doesn't end until he's dead for good." *Or I am*, Aelis thought but didn't say.

"How do you propose to kill him?"

"I have no idea yet, but I hope I can count on you when I get one. Maybe I can use what I found in the vault to command the dead part of him. Maybe it'll teach me the Starless Void—an eternal imprisonment of the soul that Dahja the Gray is said to have deliberately forgotten . . ." Tun was silent as he walked on, implacable as usual. Then, suddenly he said "You speak so freely of things that make very little sense. You possess the capacity to make wonders—and terrors—and treat them most casually. It is strange for us, who know nothing of these things, to hear."

"I'm sorry, Tun," she muttered. "I'm also cold, hurt, hungry, filthy, and wearier than I knew it was possible to be. I promise you, back in Lone Pine with a jug of wine and a hearty fire, I will answer absolutely any question you want to pose."

By now, they'd made it to the edge of the lake where the others had fought off the animations while Aelis had been in the vault.

"Here," Tun said, poking at the ground with the butt end of his walking stick. They heard the unmistakable rattle of bone.

Aelis knelt and began gathering up a few pieces, stacking them together in one hand. She was shivering in the air despite the blanket she wore, and so unsteady that she thought the very earth under her hand and knee felt unstable.

Suddenly, there was a crack and a crash. She looked up and saw pieces of the keep on the far shore of the lagoon shaking loose and crumbling into the fetid waters, which rippled and lapped noisily at the shoreline a few yards away.

She clutched her handful of bones to her chest and stood up. Too fast, and she wobbled, then was caught by Tun.

"Probably just a cave-in," he said. "Whatever was left of the structure giving way."

Aelis was not sure he believed what he was saying. He sniffed at the air, and so did she. There was a rotten, musty smell, too strong to be the small handful of bones. It came wafting across the lagoon that covered the keep, and Aelis felt a tingle along her spine and the back of her neck.

And then something—white where she could see it in the starlight, and twice the height of Tun from what she could make out—burst out of the water and attached itself to the barbican. It was sharp and irregular in its limbs. It moved in an ungainly way, scuttling up the side and then vanishing from sight entirely.

"I'm suddenly less tired," Aelis said as she and Tun turned and ran for the shelter. She was drawing breath to yell when Tun beat her to it.

"Fly! Something stirs!" he called out, just loud enough to carry to them without thundering in the night.

Maurenia spilled out first, followed by Timmuk, neither of them looking too ready to run.

"Fly?" Maurenia cocked her head to one side. "What kind of nonsense . . ."

"It's a monster. Some kind of monster. I didn't see enough of it to identify," Aelis said. "But we need to go *now* because I don't want to get close enough."

"Undead?"

"Maybe. What part of fly, let's go now, we need to run, is not being understood?" She brushed past the half-elf and dove into the shelter, gathering things and throwing them into her rucksack as fast as she could. Tun, a light packer whose pockets carried almost everything he needed, began collapsing the shelter, pulling the hides so that they fell outward, then rolling them up into bundles.

This seemed to spur the other two into action.

Across the lake, another, louder, crack of stone against stone sounded. Then a splash. Then continuous splashing—as of something, a large something, swimming.

They fled into the night, carrying what they could, leaving what they couldn't beside the reeking lagoon, with widening ripples splashing lightly against the shore.

18

THE MONSTER

Aelis wasn't the most naturally athletic of Wardens. Some had come to the colleges with military backgrounds, or from chivalric upbringings that stressed such things.

But one thing you do have, Vosghez had shouted at her as he rumbled along beside her while she paced one of the many warden training runs, *is the makings of a good runner. Do you know why that is, de Lenti?*

She did not, though she had struggled for breath to express that. Not that it mattered much to Vosghez, who was already bellowing his answer.

You're too gods-damned stubborn to know you should stop!

And she was. Once she started something, Aelis hated, *hated* not completing it. Hated even more if she did it poorly. So she had taken to running, and kept it up at Lone Pine when she could, and she knew that in their bulky hides and laden with packs, none of the others could catch her once she was a few strides away.

Well, Tun probably could if he had a mind.

Her exertions of the past day were certainly weighing on her, though, and she was glad of the fact that her hide coat was gone, neither restricting her limbs nor weighing her down. She did occasionally have to stop and give her warming bag a shake or a squeeze. Its output had already begun to wane, and she was going to be cold by the time they made it to Rhunival's.

She put those thoughts from her mind and concentrated on running. Tun was setting their pace at an easy lope, for him. She worked hard to keep up, still harboring a private hope that she could beat him at a sprint. Every time she felt she was approaching a wall, her lungs burning, he'd pull up and allow a moment's rest. Maurenia glided as if this was a normal morning's exercise. Timmuk puffed like a mad mechanist's engine. Tun was Tun; he showed no sign of strain or exertion.

Aelis felt very closely the possibility that she was doing lasting damage to her ankle and the necrotized ligament within. The rest of her body seemed to have moved beyond real pain into a kind of steadily burning numbness.

When the rising sun finally outshone the red moon, Tun raised his hand to call them to a halt.

"Think we put ten, maybe twelve miles behind us. We can probably risk a rest now."

It was only by sheer force of will that Aelis did not hurl herself to the ground and weep from exhaustion, but she certainly wanted to.

Timmuk didn't do any weeping, but he did immediately fall to the ground the way Aelis desperately wanted to. Even Tun leaned hard on his stick as he turned this way and that, sniffing at the air. Maurenia alone seemed unaffected, standing casually, fiddling with her crossbow.

Haltingly, Aelis went to Tun's side. "What?"

He shrugged almost imperceptibly beneath his fringed coat. "Smell something. Can't decide if it's just the smell of the dead things we fought clinging to us—and to you—or if it's something more than that."

"Do you think we're being followed?"

"I think you said you turned loose an entire army of undead soldiers scattered across Old Ystain. It is possible that there are other groups of them nearby, or the scent of them in the air, rather than that thing following us from the keep."

"Mahlhewn would likely be their rally point," Aelis muttered. "Or possibly they'd converge on the artifact I'm carrying. Stands to reason they'd be coming in this direction. If it were that thing, though . . ." She shuddered. "I don't know. I don't know what it was. If it was an animation, it was larger and more ungainly than any I've ever heard of."

"What else could it be?"

"Onoma knows, Tun. I've not got more than the most basic of theoretical groundings in summoning, in extradimensional creatures, in monstrous zoology. Wasn't something orcish, was it?"

"Fucked if I know," Tun said. He thought for a moment. "Could've been a Gigant, but . . . you never see those one at a time, and they don't make underwater nests."

"How long can we spare a rest?"

"An hour," Tun said. "And if I like the signs after that time has passed, a second. Go. Sleep. We need you more than any of the rest of us."

"What about you? You need rest."

He shook his head. "Part of . . ." Here his voice dropped till it was nearly inaudible, "what I am means that I can function on reserved energy for quite a long time, provided I can make up for it with a longer rest later."

Aelis's mind was suddenly flooded with a host of physiological and anatomical questions, but Tun could apparently read her well, and he raised an index finger to silence her before she could begin to ask. She sighed, said "Later," and wrapped herself up in such blankets as she'd managed to save, found a bed of pine needles, and dropped to sleep.

At least, sleep was the plan. In practice, her dreams were a nonstop horror of drowning, of being crushed beneath a collapsing Mahlhewn Keep, of being chased through its barracks-crypt by a huge, scuttling thing she could hear, could sense but never see. Occasionally, Dalius would suddenly loom over her, speaking threatening words and raising a bloodstained shard of glass.

It was a relief when Tun shook her awake. She sat bolt upright, tearing the blankets away, scrambling for a weapon.

"You were more miserable in sleep than you were awake," Tun commented. "What was it?"

Aelis didn't answer him. Instead, as her hands found her sword and closed around the hilt, she whispered the Abjurer's mantra to herself.

"Fear is a response to danger. The Abjurer does not know danger. The properly prepared and ever-vigilant Abjurer is the antithesis of danger. Thus, she cannot fear. Thus, her heart does not race. Her breath does not pant. Her palms do not sweat. An Abjurer does not know fear . . ."

She ran through the entirety of it twice, one hand wrapped around her warming bag, before her heart stopped racing and she got control of her breathing. Tun alternated between looming close and stepping back, but at least he was silent.

She popped to her feet and wrapped her swordbelt around her hips, cinched it tight, and checked the draw of sword and dagger. "Let's go," she said.

"It's not even been an hour and the others sleep well," Tun cautioned.

"Fine," she said. "Then you sleep. I won't."

Tun shook his head. "No. When next I sleep, it won't be for an hour or two. A day, perhaps."

"So, it's a process that can't be stopped once it starts, eh?"

Tun chuckled almost noiselessly. "You never stop collecting information, do you?"

"Nope. And you aren't going to answer me, are you?"

"Not at the moment, no."

"Well, sometime when we have a proper space, and I've got plenty of ink and paper."

"Why would you need to write it down?"

"Because all knowledge ought to be recorded. And because it sounds like what you're describing is magical physiology, which is, you may note, directly in my line."

"I told you once before that not all knowledge is worth having. Not all boundaries must be pushed. And even if I were to give you answers, I don't know that they could help you much. Most of this is simply known to me. Has always been. I didn't have to learn it."

"If I were to observe and record some of this, it might be of direct benefit to you," Aelis said, only just stopping herself from following up with a question about whether that meant that Tun had been able to transform himself for his entire life or if it was something that set in later, during adolescence perhaps. They were silent a moment.

"Thank you for coming with me on this frozen farce of an expedition, Tun. You didn't have to."

"No," he agreed, "I didn't. But as I told you once before, I think that you are trying to help. And, of course, you are my friend; I don't have so many of them that I can easily spare one."

Aelis went quiet, deeply enough and for long enough for Tun to clear his throat.

"Have I overstepped?"

"No, Tun. Not at all. I'm just bad at . . . feelings," she said, with an expansive shrug that turned into an outflung arm. "If it makes any sense, it's because you're my friend that I don't like having to ask you for help."

"It does and it doesn't." He paused. "I should have brought my pipe. Give me something to do now."

"Could borrow one from Timmuk," Aelis said.

"Borrowing another fellow's pipe is awkward at best," Tun began, when whatever he'd been about to say was interrupted by an echoing crack.

"That was a tree being snapped in two," Tun said, carefully, and then they heard it again. "Do we run or fight?"

"I think we don't stop to fight until we have no other choice," Aelis said, already moving to wake Maurenia and Timmuk.

✦   ✦   ✦

It turned out that the choice was made for them sooner than they wanted. They got moving again, but without the speed they'd had earlier, and the cracks kept chasing them, getting louder. Every so often, Aelis would look backward and catch a glimpse of something large shrouded within the pine forest and snow; a glimpse of long white limbs that looked too much like exposed bone for her to count out some kind of enormous animation.

She tried to think as she ran, to catalogue. *Clearly neither human nor animal. Some kind of exotic. A hybrid? But of what?*

The thing, whatever it was, was still too far behind them to present much of a threat. But it was gaining ground if they could judge by the sounds its passage made, and Tun finally pulled up.

"Let's find a defensible spot," he said, for once showing the slightest sign of weakness as he had to pause for breath.

"A hillock," Timmuk panted, "or a cave?"

"Not a cave," Aelis huffed as she leaned back, putting her arms behind her head to force her lungs to take in air. "If it can crush trees, it can collapse a cave. Come on, let's find high ground. Maybe that way we'll get a look at it."

The pine growth thinned out as they approached the line of hills that—many miles farther southwest—would diverge in its center and create Rhunival's valley. With a last burst of speed, they scrambled up a small rise. Maurenia pulled a small brass tube from her pack—a looking glass. She pressed it to an eye and looked back the way they'd come.

She lowered it, turned, dark-eyed, to Aelis, and handed it over.

Aelis hesitated, gripped her sword hilt for reassurance, and lifted the glass to her eye.

It was an exotic to be sure. Four long, rope-like limbs anchored to a central ball-like mass of bone that seemed hardly stable. If it had any sensory inputs, she couldn't find them. The central ball seemed almost to pulse as the limbs propelled it—working in no discernible order or pattern, merely swinging it wildly forward.

She leaned forward, strained, saw the sharp edges at the end of every limb, the loose mass of the central ball, and suppressed the bile that rose in her throat.

"It's a tooth-monster," she said, lowering the glass and handing it to Maurenia. Her training asserted itself. "A theoretical construct only. Until now. Some would call it a chimera, or a gestalt, as it's made from multiple creatures. Teeth are bone. You gather enough of them together and encode the commands properly, you can animate them like any other collection of bone."

"You people made some right fucking horrors," Timmuk growled as he shrugged out of his pack and unlimbered his axe. "How do you fight it?"

"At a distance, with blunt ballista bolts and other siege weapons if you've got them," Aelis said. "Or volleys from good slingers. Have you got a couple hundred of them in your pack?"

"I thought about bringing half a dozen but they're too hard to feed," Timmuk said, grimly deadpan.

Aelis swallowed hard, then dug into her memories of theoretical animation. "It doesn't have sensory inputs, so it isn't tracking us by sight or smell or memory. It's following a command."

"Someone alive is giving it orders, you mean? Or a spirit?" Maurenia had ceased nervously frittering with her bow. Now she was still and calm, a bolt slotted, the string cranked back.

"Undoubtedly, it's pursuing one of the artifacts I took from the vault," Aelis said. She knew it was a leap not supported by ironclad logic, but she *knew* it to be true, felt it come to her in that certain voice Bardun Jacques had taught all his would-be Wardens to recognize. "It was probably dormant until that condition was met: the item it was attuned to left its close proximity."

"So all we need to do is get close to it," Tun said. "I can cohabit with a monster made of teeth. I've lived with worse."

"Well, if by 'close' you mean inside that ball of grinding teeth at its center, yes," Aelis said, pointing to where the chimera had come clearly into view now. It was a hard thing to look at, its center writhing, its limbs shaking and quivering. A gust of wind brought the sound of chattering—of thousands of teeth striking against each other—as it walked and rattled.

"Why teeth? It seems impractical," Tun said.

"Waste not, want not. A skeleton doesn't need its teeth. People in a large enough settlement—a keep, a town—probably lose teeth every day in fights, to decay, in accidents. An industrious necromancer could collect them for years, and those of all the dead—people and animals. During the war, a College Necromancer had the right of first refusal of any corpse in the area he was assigned. Could gather quite a lot of them if you had a project."

The thing reared up on two of its limbs and lifted the others into the air, tentatively, pawing like a horse, or somehow like a dog, lifting its head to sniff at its surroundings. It was disconcerting—everyone save Tun took a half step back.

"How does one fight this thing up close, Warden?" Tun looked at the metal-shod end of the staff, then reached into his pocket, probably for one of his handblades.

"I didn't know it *existed* a moment ago," Aelis snapped, then took a deep breath as she drew her dagger. "I'd say the Necrobane's Fist, but—I don't like getting that close to it. I can try the Lash but . . . it's big."

"Can you put that spell on a crossbow bolt?" Maurenia didn't sound particularly optimistic.

Aelis shook her head. "Everybody behind me."

"What're you going to do?" Aelis liked to think that Maurenia's voice was tinged with just a bit of concern.

"Hit it as hard as I can from a safe distance," Aelis answered, even as she felt her voice and her perceptions distancing themselves from the immediate.

She drew her dagger, holding it pommel up, with the blade angling down along her wrist and forearm. In her mind, she formed the syllables of the spell she would cast, repeating them over and over again unceasingly, blocking out everything else. Color drained from the world. Sound—even the hideous scrabbling of the animated tooth nightmare pounding up the hill—receded. She felt herself alone on the single piece of solid ground that existed in any direction, and the pressure of what she was drawing on bearing down on her.

With the power gathered in her hand, time seemed to slow. The monster loomed over her, its foremost tendril of teeth just a few yards away. Details popped out at her; she could see the individual teeth making up the tendril extended toward her. Churning and spinning around one another, all jagged edges, white only from a distance—seen at the level of detail she did for that moment there seemed to be as much dirty yellow and rotting brown as white—it was a truly horrid thing.

She heard a snatch of the constant grinding of all the teeth against one another, an awful, nonstop hum.

Aelis poured more power into the resulting Lash than she had into any single Order before; when she finally spoke the words aloud and felt the power travel along her arm and through her dagger lighting silver runes on the dark blade as it went, she felt her hair standing on end and gooseflesh prickling up.

Aelis thought she knew what the commander of a siege weapon must feel like when their machine flung a rock or fired a bolt the size of a spear. She was rocked backward by the force, taking to one knee. A gray bolt filled the air between her and the chimera. The tendril extended toward her exploded in fragments—she felt a few pelt off her shoulders and arms, stinging where they struck, and others fall around like rain.

The monster itself was rocked back by the blow, clattering a few yards down the hill. For a brief moment, it looked like it might have been squashed into dormancy as it sank to the ground.

Aelis's triumphant yawp caught in her throat when the chimera reared back up, and teeth began racing forward from the central body and the other three limbs, almost crawling like ants, to even up the length of the limb she'd blown apart. It was shorter than it had been, all the limbs were, and down several hundred or even thousands of teeth, but it looked no less deadly as it gathered itself.

"How many more times can you do that?" Tun's voice was, for the first time she'd known him, slightly worried.

"Somewhere between zero and one."

"Well," Tun said, "this seems to be an extremity then. The rest of you, run. For Rhunival's valley. I will catch up."

He turned to Timmuk and tossed his walking stick at the dwarf, who caught it, puzzled. "Mightn't you need this . . . what's he . . ."

Aelis felt a cold ball growing in her stomach as Tun turned to face the beast and began taking deep, heaving breaths.

She knew what was coming. "Run! Save your questions!"

Aelis hoped her shouts would spur the other two into flight, but by then Tun had begun to grow taller, his shoulders widening, his back humping, his long braids beginning to cover his body in a thick layer of gray-flecked brown fur, and then the massive bear was standing in his place. On his hind legs, raising his forepaws into the air, he seemed almost equal in size and fearsomeness to the monster that bore down upon him.

She watched as Tun—the bear, she was unsure how to think of him in that form—lumbered two steps forward and hurled himself straight into the central ball of teeth with a roar.

Then Maurenia was tugging at her arm, and with Tun's final words ringing in her ears, ashamed, she ran.

+ + +

They ran until her lungs burned, until both of her legs felt as numb as the ankle she'd necrotized, until she thought she'd collapse. There were further roars behind them, some of them laced with pain.

Finally, after she did not know how long, her foot struck hard against a tree root, and she spilled to the ground. Maurenia was by her in a flash helping her to stand, but Timmuk had lost momentum and dropped his axe, puffing hard.

"How long," Maurenia said, through heavy, staccato breaths, the first sign of fatigue she'd shown, "have you known?"

"Since the summer, when he helped me track down Elmo."

"Didn't think t'share?" Timmuk's voice lacked its usual brio.

"Not my secret," Aelis answered hoarsely, still trying to master her own wind.

"Could've been useful for us to know, traveling with a cursed . . ."

"Stop," Aelis said, cutting the dwarf off and surprising them both with the force of her voice. "Stop talking. Not another word. There is no curse about it, and what all of us together don't know about the subject *might* just fill the Great Trench. Tun is a good man, and I expect he'll catch us up as he said, but he just put himself in harm's way to fight a monster that terrified us all. Alone. So not another word about curses or . . . or anything the fuck else about my friend."

Timmuk was shamed enough, at least, to turn away, nodding his head vaguely. Maurenia checked some minute detail of her crossbow again.

They stood panting for a few moments longer. A distant roar and a crash came to Aelis's ears, and she forced herself to run again.

✦ ✦ ✦

Rhunival's small homestead, with its ring of trees, scattering of outbuildings, and long central hall, was the most welcome sight Aelis had ever seen. She stumbled into it soaked in sweat and snowmelt, covered in dirt from numerous falls, and numb with pain and weariness. Timmuk seemed equally exhausted, the long pole of his axe dragging a furrow in the snow and dirt behind him. Maurenia appeared ready to walk another step, and even she stumbled here and there.

Coming down the slight rise toward Rhunival's door—which stood open, a hearthfire warm and inviting beyond—Aelis tried to slow herself down and couldn't. She stumbled and went facedown into the mud for what felt like the tenth time since they'd left Tun behind, alone.

She pushed that thought to the very back of her mind and forced herself back to her feet, Maurenia's arm once more at her elbow.

"Do your feet not work properly?"

I don't think they will for much longer, Aelis thought. She gritted her teeth, didn't bother to even try to wipe mud off her coat, and stumbled through the door.

Rhunival sat at his worktable with a small steaming pot before him.

The slightly oily smell of melted fat mingled with woodsmoke, and Aelis's heart leaped to see several thick tallow candles lying on the table.

"Are those . . ."

He lifted his eyes from where he carefully dipped a long length of wick into his pot. "If you would like to trade for them . . ."

Aelis unslung her pack and pulled the rod free from the knots that bound it to the frame. "If you want this, you'll give them to me."

"We have already struck an accord for that," Rhunival said. He stood slowly, reaching a height that seemed to Aelis taller than he had been before.

"And I'm changing it," Aelis said.

"This could end badly for you, Warden."

"This will end badly for all of us, Woodshade, if the tooth chimera bearing down on me reaches its target." Aelis tried to put a confidence in her voice that she didn't feel. Woodshades weren't her province, and she wasn't convinced that's what Rhunival was, but she spat out the name with force. She pulled her dagger free and laid the edge against the green shoot growing from near the end of the wooden rod.

"What did you call me?" Rhunival's voice came out as a rumble. Aelis heard Maurenia and Timmuk shuffling back toward the entrance to his hall. "You insult me with that word."

Distant alarm bells threatened Aelis's concentration; she didn't like being wrong on a good day, and this was far from that already. *Sometimes doing the wrong thing now is better than waiting for the right thing.*

"I swore not to try to turn this to my hand. I didn't say anything about jamming a Necromancer's blade through its green bits. So, give me the damned candles and pray if you've a god."

Rhunival seized a handful of the candles and hurled them to Aelis's feet.

"Maurenia. Come take this, and my blade. If he makes any move that you don't like, cut it into as many pieces as you can manage."

She kept her eyes locked on Rhunival as Maurenia came to her side and took both dagger and rod from her. Aelis finally broke her eye contact with Rhunival and bent for the candles, scrambling for the wrought-iron skull in her pack.

Without time to clear a proper place on a table, Aelis set the candlestick on the floor and jammed the candles in it, then sat down cross-legged before it. "Timmuk! Fire, if you would."

The dwarf stomped over to her, producing a coal from a horn he carried, handling it with the thickly calloused pads of his fingers without apparent pain. The wicks in the fresh tallow candles caught almost instantly and the smell of burning fat, underlaid with some pine scent, soon filled the hall.

Aelis wrapped her hand around the base of the iron and tried to clear her mind. She dug into the pocket of her jacket and pulled forth a handful of dirt, thick gray grains mixed in with the brown.

"What," Timmuk asked, still looming over her, "is that?"

"Bits of bone dust from a skeleton animated by a Necromancer and some dirt from the barracks-crypt it was in. I'm hoping that'll count as grave dirt. And I'd give anything for some refined cedar oil worked into the candles, but this'll have to do. Give me some space. If I pass out, just toss this thing into the woods and run."

She cleared her throat and her mind, then began forming the cold, harsh syllables of a First Order Necromantic spell, a simple diagnostic. After the powerful Lash she'd flung at the construction she'd decided to call a chimera, even finding the strength to do that much made her vision momentarily darken. But she did it, and then she dribbled the dust of a bone that had known undeath and the grains of grave dirt—more or less—over the flames of the candles. Her vision swirled, and suddenly her mind was untethered from her body.

19

ALDAYIM'S MATRIX

Aelis found her consciousness swimming, her vision a swirling haze of gray nothingness. It resolved into a weak view of a stone chamber with strong sunlight beaming through the arrow slits. Still her vision was blurry, as if she were looking at the events in a poor mirror or through thick glass.

Top of a tower, or near, she thought, based on the sunlight, the sound of the wind through the windows.

She—or the person whose vision she was sharing—was seated behind a heavy table strewn with papers and implements: fist-sized raw crystals, an oblong hunk of obsidian, a length of wood that looked suspiciously like the rod she'd threatened to destroy only moments ago.

There was a knock at a door. "Enter," said a voice that sent a chill through her.

In came a nondescript man in mud-spattered woodsman's clothes, an axe and a long knife on his belt and a heavy bag dangling from one hand. From it, he pulled the very wrought-iron skull Aelis knew her hand—if she concentrated, she could just feel it—was holding.

"Aldayim's Matrix," said another voice from behind the person whose vision Aelis was sharing. "I never thought I would see it. I wasn't sure it existed."

"Well, it wasn't easy to find," the woodsman said as he came forward and set it down on the table. "Good people died in the attempt. Now, before I'm burdened with any more secrets I don't want, I'd like to be paid and leave."

Casually, the man seated at the table picked up a stone in one hand—brilliant dark green, big enough to fill the palm of Aelis's hand—and tossed it to the woodsman, who caught it with surprise.

"I think any decent appraisal will show that to be more than fair. You are dismissed."

Aelis's vision was too obscured to know for sure whether the stone was emerald, but if it was, the woodsman had just been paid a fortune. It was a remarkable stone, of an unlikely color, dark and vivid at the same time, with notable luster. She tried to mark the woodsman's features, to burn them into her memory before he vanished, but he had no distinguishing features she could find. Brown hair, brown beard, plain clothes.

She watched as the man whose vision she shared picked up the candlestick in both hands, turning it so that the death's head the spirals formed became apparent.

"Can you use this?" He held it up to the man standing behind him, whose well-manicured hand came into view to take it. Aelis caught the edge of elegant, velvet-lined black robes.

"I may need some time to study it, unlock its secrets. It will not yield them easily. Some of what little has been passed down about it says it must capture some secrets of its own to give its power over. I've never been sure what that meant."

"You're the Necromancer here. Do as you must. You have an ample supply of material. You will, of course, share anything you learn with me." The man set the candlestick down and picked up some pieces of paper. Aelis's vision began to fade before she could read any words. An indistinct, black-robed form came raggedly into view and picked up the wrought-iron skull, then it, too, faded, and all went dark.

For a moment she had the sensation of floating. Was reminded of escaping the vault by nearly drowning and fought down a surge of panic. *An Abjurer does not know fear*, she began.

"How odd," came a voice, "that an Abjurer should be using my tool."

There was no figure or vision attached to the voice. It was a man's voice, rich, resonant, and powerful.

"I am a Necromancer first and foremost," she said in response, though she wasn't entirely sure how she spoke the words, formless in a dark void as she seemed to be.

"Then why the weakness of your connection?"

"My strength was nearly spent when I activated it. And the candles weren't made properly. No cedar oil."

"Tsk. Everyone thinks the grave dirt and animated dust will be enough and they don't bother to make the oil. No one takes the time to do a proper job of things. As if the forty hours of refinement in the alembic couldn't be productively filled."

Whoever this fellow was, he was clearly a professor, Aelis thought. "I didn't make the candles at all. They are plain tallow. I crumbled the dirt and dust over the flames once they were lit. It is something of an emergency."

"Everyone who comes to the Matrix assures me that it is an emergency. The kingdom they serve will fall. The banking house that hired them will fail. The king they advise is dying. Everyone thinks that the secrets of life and death must be rolled back for their particular need. Tell me then, what is yours?"

"People will die if I cannot figure out how to unlock this."

"Who?"

"Friends. One may have died already. And after them, people who depend on me."

"A disease, then? A plague?"

"No. Animations. Many of them. Loosed. Accidentally." She paused a moment. "By me. And all of them apparently keyed to this Matrix. And one very dangerous chimera in particular."

"What kind of animation can possibly threaten a Necromancer? Surely you have tools to unmake it. The Lash. The Fist. The Song of Unbinding."

"I hit it with the most powerful Lash I could manage. Fourth Order, at least. Did nothing but slow it momentarily. It's a loose-parts binding made of teeth. A tooth chimera. It remade the part I damaged almost instantly."

That gave the voice pause. "A tooth chimera, you say? Brilliant." Another pause. "Who are you?"

"I am Aelis Cairistiona de Lenti un Tirraval, Warden of Lone Pine. And I beg of you, Master," she said, trying not to let herself be overawed by whom she suddenly believed she was talking to, "innocent people will die, through no fault of their own, if I cannot help them."

"Why do you not simply create other constructs? Surely there must be beasts of the forest, or a graveyard nearby."

"Our college no longer does that if it can be helped. It has become too dangerous, too unstable. *Things* try to come through the parting. Spirits, demons, I don't know what they are, but they are dangerous. In this, I am not a Necromancer. I am a *Necrobane*."

"The fools," the voice muttered, "the fools. I warned them, or I tried. They did not listen." A sigh. "Very well, Necrobane. To impart knowledge of this Matrix, I will require secrets. Of your own, not kept on behalf of another."

Aelis wanted to ask *why*, less out of genuine curiosity than to buy time to weasel out of whatever this voice wanted her to do, but time was too precious. She sighed.

"I Necrotized my own ankle ligament before setting out on this journey—" she began.

"As if I could not tell that the instant you contacted me," the voice said. "Try again."

"When Onoma's moon is waxing and when it is full, I see in the dark as if it were bright daylight."

"That," the voice said, suddenly admiring, "is very interesting. But it is not a secret from those you travel with, is it?"

"I'm in love with one of my traveling companions," Aelis said suddenly, blurting the words out in a rush. "And even she does not know that."

"That is small beer in trade for what I offer," the voice said, "but . . . you have not uttered that aloud before, it is true. So, it counts."

✦ ✦ ✦

When Aelis's consciousness returned to her body and her surroundings, she expected to see the candles burned down and tallow dripping over the iron. She expected the tooth chimera to be upon them, to see a desperate rearguard action being fought.

She was startled to find that the candles had only just begun to melt. As if she hadn't been gone more than the span of a few breaths.

Well, I suppose a little time dilation is to be expected when dealing with a major magical artifact. She stood, gathering the candlestick up in one hand.

"The rod," Rhunival said, the first thing she heard as the world rushed back to her senses. Everything was sharper: the rough grain of the iron in her hand; the scents of earth and rain, mushrooms and ash in Rhunival's hall; the loud crackling of the small fire in the firepit. She looked to Maurenia and shook her head, could read the dilation in the pupils of the half-elf's bright green irises.

"Not. Yet."

She strode out of the hall, clutching the candlestick. She gathered her will, as little of it as she could, to form a First Order Necromantic spell and dropped it into the artifact in her fist.

It was like a drop of water falling onto a kettle drum, if that kettle drum was attended by an Illusionist especially skilled in auditory illusion who could make that tiny tap produce a massive, eardrum-splitting sound.

Her sense of the world suddenly expanded vastly, but only in one way.

She knew the location of every undead within miles. And there were dozens. But one bright presence stood out more than the rest; it was close and getting closer, within a mile now.

Aelis started walking toward it. She wasn't sure how, but she projected her thoughts to the chimera.

Come here. Fast. Rearrange your structure to move any blood internally and do not spill any on the ground you cross.

She stood at the very edge of Rhunival's cluster of buildings, waiting. Beyond, the trees rustled and the horrifying shape of the thing came into focus, galloping across the land. Its razor-edged tendrils tore up the ground as it ran, then skidded to a halt ten yards in front of Aelis.

"Down to two tendrils," Maurenia pointed out. "Tun gave it something to think about."

With her free hand she pointed one finger at the ground; the tooth-monster flattened itself as much as it could, leaving the central ball low enough for her to climb atop.

Aelis did not have a weak stomach. The flesh and bones and tissues that made up living things did not generally disturb her in any configuration. She was a surgeon, after all, an anatomist. Weak stomachs did not last long in the College of Necromancy.

But she still had to suppress a gag or two as she walked up the slick, chattering arm of teeth to kneel on the ball in the center. The teeth left some impressions on her knee but didn't cut it, or at least she didn't think they did.

Up. The thing stood. She rocked, steadied herself with one hand. When she felt the slippery, moving, *humming* teeth beneath her hand, she almost retched again.

Take me to the last thing you fought.

It lurched forward and began loping onward. In contact with the thing, Aelis's awareness of its construction and capabilities grew. She was right; it was keyed into the Matrix she carried, to hunt it down, retrieve it, and take it back to the vault if it left Mahlhewn Keep without the proper authorization.

It had taken quite a bit of skill and power to create. It could also have served as a hunter or assassin, provided you had some way to key it into the person you wanted found or killed.

Would probably move faster if, instead of running, it used its limbs to brachiate along the trees, she thought, and for a moment the monster acted as though it was about to attempt that. One limb reached out and wrapped around a nearby pine. *No!* Aelis's mind shouted, *keep running.*

Suddenly, it came to a stop. Aelis lowered it to the ground and leapt the last few feet to run toward an immobile lump she spotted in bloodstained snow a few yards away.

Tun, back in his half-orc shape, was breathing, and his heart was beating, though faintly. He was slumped forward, his face on the grass. He was alive—that much she could tell by initial examination. She couldn't tell much more because he could not be moved with her one free hand, and she couldn't locate his wounds without turning him over.

But she was holding one of the most powerful Necromantic objects in existence. She reached into it, but found herself stopped by a psychic barrier, and the voice returned.

A secret for my power, Warden.

Aelis winced. *I don't suppose you'd make an exception.*

I am but a programmed echo of a wizard who has been dead for hundreds of years. I cannot make revisions to the Matrix based on the urgency of your need.

Why the trade of secrets for secrets?

Think but a moment, Warden. Now—a secret.

I deliberately failed out of Basic Divination Theory. I could've passed it and progressed in that College. Maybe even passed a Diviner's Test.

Why in seventy-seven hells would any wizard pass up the chance to command another College?

It was boring.

She heard the professor's voice laugh. *Very well. Here.*

The knowledge came instantaneously. She anchored Tun's spirit in his flesh without the use of her Anatomist's blade, and immediately assessed his wounds. Many minor lacerations and one serious abdominal wound. She could fix it.

She also could read Tun's anatomy and sense its unusual elements, some of which she could only call magical. How his body displaced its mass, the unique structure of his bones, the incredible density of his muscle. The way his organs and tissues stored energy.

It took great force of will to stuff her curiosity back into a mental sack and stop short of exploring all the available details. *It would be a violation of his privacy*, she thought. *I'll only peek at anything absolutely necessary for treating him.* She set the Matrix down and struggled mightily to roll Tun over, but the power the artifact lent her remained strong enough to keep his soul bound and his wounds from getting any worse.

Aelis had her traveling kit pulled free of her rucksack and was digging in it for needles and thread and bundles of dried herbs before she'd even realized it. She found the silver needle she'd thought to bring along this time and carefully threaded it. Unlike the first time, she'd attempted her needlework on Tun's skin, it wasn't like trying to punch a dull awl through untreated hide. The silver slid through his skin so easily she worried about maintaining control, but eventually it came to her.

The abdominal wound was much more of a problem. With forceps she picked out fragments of bone, and bits of wood and plant matter that had accumulated in it, for quite some time. It took all the stores of pure spirit she'd brought with her to clean the wound, and she wasn't sure how long she spent kneeling at his side in the snowy grass before she finally had it loosely sewn and dressed to her satisfaction.

When she did finally come back to herself, letting go of his spirit tentatively, confident that it would hold in its own flesh, she found Maurenia and Timmuk standing to one side of her and the tooth-monster waiting patiently a few yards away. Surgery had always seemed to stop time for her, to focus her senses so completely that most things around her faded.

But she did not recall ever being so distant that Timmuk and Maurenia, huffing with the exertion of running, could arrive behind her without her knowing it.

The way Aelis lifted her head must've alerted them because Maurenia came to her side. "Will he live?"

"Yes," Aelis answered. "But there is the problem of transporting him."

"Can he ride on that thing?" Maurenia pointed uneasily to the humming, throbbing ball of teeth above their heads.

"I doubt we can lift him onto it," Aelis said.

"We can cut together a travois and can bear him back to Rhunival's hall. Who, by the by, is *frothing*. You best give him back that rod."

Aelis looked down at her bloodstained hands, and then her eyes found the wrought-iron Matrix at her feet. The candles were burned almost two-thirds of the way down, the iron covered in dried and drying wax.

She picked it up in one swift movement. "I don't think I care," she said suddenly, fiercely.

"What do you mean by that?" Aelis was dimly aware of Maurenia shifting a half step away from her, looked at the half-elf, and saw her dagger and the rod still clutched in her hands.

"I mean that I could order this construct to tear him apart and I don't think he could stop it. I could force it across any barriers or wards he erected."

As if it were responding to her thoughts and words, the massive construct suddenly stood up on its three limbs, the low-grade clicking it had been doing suddenly rising to a high-pitched, sharp-edged hum.

"That thing is like some horrid dog," she heard Timmuk mutter. "A giant murderous demon mutt that, wants flesh in its jaws and red on its muzzle."

"Nonsense," she shot back. "It has no feelings and does not need to feed." But through the Matrix, she could feel that it *was* eager to follow her commands, or at least *ready to.*

"Aelis," Maurenia said sharply, "you do not mean that. Rhunival dealt with us honestly. We owe him this thing."

Aelis lifted the Matrix up until the flickering tallow lights cast shadows on the half-elf's fine cheekbones. "Do we? Do you know what I can command with this?"

She reached into it, and through it, could sense the animations and undead that were keyed to it.

Hundreds of them. Tiny pinpricks of leashed Necromantic power. Skeletons in the main. Humanoid, dog, horse, ox, a few wild animals, and some exotics she couldn't immediately identify. There were others, too—a handful of spirits bound in phylacteries, awaiting the correct Orders of Binding and Unsealing.

"I could destroy Rhunival. I do not doubt that. I am not sure the world would miss him."

"Aelis . . ." Maurenia's voice sounded distant in her ears.

"I could loose the spirits still bound in some of the vaults upon Dalius, wherever he is. I know his name. That is all I'd have to tell them."

"Warden." That was Timmuk's voice. "This is not you talkin' now."

She turned on the dwarf, eyes wide. "I could command all the animations together to raise Mahlgren's vault out of the lake where the keep now sits. I could unseal all its treasures, and you could share in that, Master Dobrusz. Would you like to run a bank once more? I could give you the means."

Hands seized her shoulders and turned her sharply around. She locked onto Maurenia's large, crystal green eyes. "Aelis. This is not you. What are you? Every cliché about Necromancers that's ever been used to scare children?"

No, she wanted to snap back sharply. *I am a Necrobane.*

Then be one. She did not know if that voice was her own conscience, some figment of her imagination, some old teacher's voice. Certainly it was not Duvhalin's. It could have been Bardun Jacques's.

It could also have been the voice of the Professor contained in the artifact she held.

She closed her eyes, reached her will through the candleholder, and issued one command to all the skeletal animations.

Disband.

The consequences of her single command were immediate and devastating, best exemplified by the dissolution of the construct that stood only a few yards away. With a sound like a sudden rain, thousands of teeth gave up the bonds that kept them formed into a single entity and showered down upon the snowy pine forest floor.

Which meant that Aelis and Maurenia were suddenly up to their ankles in old teeth.

Aelis's eyes flew open and found Maurenia's again.

"Thank you," Aelis whispered. She leaned forward as if to kiss Maurenia, but the half-elf whirled away and retched noisily into the teeth that had pooled around her feet.

20

THE HIDDEN CLAUSE

They moved on from where the monster had dissipated its animation until they could not see the teeth, hear the wind set them chattering, or smell the miasma of decay that floated off them.

"When we get back to civilization," Maurenia said, struggling alongside Timmuk to draw the litter on which they pulled Tun, "I'm going to pay a surgeon to knock out all my teeth with a hammer and replace them with good, honest wood." Timmuk and Maurenia had lashed their packs into the middle branches of a pine tree, and Aelis carried only her magical implements and her medical kit. Timmuk's axe lay on the litter with Tun.

"As a surgeon myself, I can't recommend that," Aelis said. It was still an effort for her to move forward, so she was spared the work and leaned heavily on her walking stick just to propel herself forward. "First, no reputable physician'll do such a thing, so you'll have to find one in desperate need of the money. Second, a wound in the mouth is an invitation to infection, and you'd have so many broken stumps of tooth left, you'd be sure to get a handful. Third, wooden teeth splinter *terribly* into the gums, which brings us back to the second point. Fourth, wooden teeth would discourage kissing."

Maurenia stopped her with a waving hand. "Stop. Just . . . stop talking about mouths and teeth and kissing. Mouths and teeth are the sources of all nightmares and horrors."

Aelis fingered the heavy iron candleholder tied to her belt. She'd snuffed the wicks of the candle stubs and removed what remained of them to avoid the temptation of lighting them again. She felt diminished in a way she couldn't have explained to anyone except another wizard, as if some extra limb she had commanded was suddenly gone. Her thoughts were slow and leaden, her steps not much better.

It was a slow walk to Rhunival's hall. She paused every so often to check Tun's vital signs. He breathed, his heartbeat slow and steady, but he couldn't be roused, and after a vial of smelling salts waved under his nose had no effect, she didn't try again. By the time they could smell the smoke of Rhunival's firepit, the sun was setting and a sliver of blue moon lay on the horizon.

Rhunival waited for them outside the door to his hall.

"We had an accord, Warden. I had not known people with your title to treat an agreement so casually."

Aelis pulled the rod with its living green shoots from her rucksack and held it out as she slowly walked forward.

"I'm sorry. But I couldn't spare the time."

"You had given your word."

"And the life of my friend mattered more than my word," she said. "And it still does. Will your hall, its fire, persist after I hand you this rod?"

"Yes," Rhunival said and took a few quick, shuffling steps toward her, one hand reaching out, drawn to the rod. It seemed as his hand neared the rod, his fingers, browned by sun and wood, took on the appearance of wrinkled brown bark, and a shadow, as of a tree bent double in a wind, loomed over him. "It will. And you could have free use of it. I will not care."

"Good. Tun will need a place to heal."

With feigned casualness, she tossed the rod a few feet in the air. Rhunival snatched it greedily. His eyes seemed to glow, then they *did* glow, a bright and unsettling green. The shadow behind him stretched out to its full height, the limbs of the almost tree spreading wide to the air.

Then he turned the force of them on Maurenia and said, "I am sorry, elfling." He lifted a hand and spread his fingers, and a pinch of dirt—which Aelis would've sworn had not been in his hand before that moment—fell and was carried away by the wind, except for one tiny, dark red drop that fell straight to his feet. Aelis saw it, knew it for a drop of blood that should long since have dried, and tried to scream, to reach for her sword or her wand, but could do nothing.

There was a flash of light, a rush of wind, and he vanished so thoroughly that no prints were left where he stood.

Maurenia collapsed.

Aelis felt panic rise from her stomach.

✦   ✦   ✦

Aelis checked Maurenia's pulse for the fourth, perhaps the fifth time. It was steady, her breathing was even, but she showed no signs of awareness. Aelis had done everything short of rub fragrant salts under her nose to get a response.

The half-elf and Tun were both laid carefully by the fire, tended carefully by Timmuk, that smoldered in Rhunival's firepit.

"Why'd you ask if his hall was going to collapse?"

"Because I was afraid that it was built and sustained by magic, by his presence. That once he disappeared, it would as well."

"How would you know that?"

"I didn't, obviously," Aelis said, gesturing at the solid walls surrounding them. "But it was a fair question at the time. And if he was a woodshade, then frankly, it *should* have happened."

"Then what about all that nonsense about Makers?"

"What we call a woodshade might call itself something else entirely. I don't know; I'm not a Conjurer, and metaphysical naturalism never appealed to me much. I'm just guessing, and he's not here to ask."

"Thought something called a woodshade would be malevolent."

"They usually are," Aelis said. "Imagine a living tree that hates anything that walks about freely and wields iron and fire; humans, elves, orcs, dwarves, gnomes, all much the same. Now imagine a ghost made of a thousand of those trees."

She stood up, felt the iron candlestick's weight against her hip. She was seized with a sudden urge to take more of the tallow candles, find some grave dirt and bone dust, and seek answers from it.

As if it would even have them. Whatever's happened to Maurenia is not a Necromancer's problem.

"So, the walking dead are sorted?"

"In the main," Aelis said. "So long as all of them were made with this thing, then yes. I expect so."

"And if they weren't?"

"Whoever made these animations at Dalius's command used this to make and program so many. Perhaps past his own death."

"That candlestick is really so important?"

"I think this is Aldayim's Matrix, which . . ."

Her words were cut off as Maurenia suddenly sat bolt upright, her eyes wide.

Aelis was at the half-elf's side in a blink, trying to check her signs, preparing a diagnostic, the power coming more easily to her mind and hand than it should have, given all she'd expended. But Maurenia shook her off and launched herself to her feet, then out the door in a rush.

Even having just woken up, Maurenia was too fast for her. Aelis could only trail in her wake. She was certain that in a race on flat ground under even conditions, she would've more than kept up. But she ran haltingly in the darkness, fatigue filling her limbs, wondering just how much damage she was doing to her necrotized ankle. She had little time to ponder it before she heard a loud thud and a cry, and then she stumbled over Maurenia, who knelt in the muddy snow.

Aelis landed hard, the iron candleholder digging into her side and knocking the wind out of her.

"What did you *do?*" Maurenia's breath came in ragged gasps after her hoarse shout. "What bargain did you make? What happened to me?"

Aelis struggled to roll onto her back, much less to think of an answer, or to even understand why Maurenia was asking her these questions.

"What? What do you . . ." Aelis could barely get words out as she pushed herself up on one arm.

"I can't take another step farther than this. Not one. I am bound here. I know that, and I don't know *how* I know it. You gave Rhunival the rod, he told me he was sorry, and then . . . this." She stood and lowered her shoulder as if she was pushing against a cart stuck in mud, to no avail—she didn't move an inch, but strained until she screamed and then collapsed.

"But what, how?" Aelis still struggled for breath, the words coming out in a shocked rasp.

"You're the one who should know!" Maurenia shouted at her. For the first time she could remember, the half-elf's composure cracked, her voice grown shrill, the hint of a sob behind it. "You're the wizard. You're the one who knew what he was, or claimed you did. You're the one who made the fucking *bargains.*"

"Maurenia," Aelis said, "I don't . . . I don't know what happened. I didn't make any bargain over you. I never would. Come back to the hall and let me . . ." She reached out for Maurenia's hand, only to have hers slapped away. Her lover turned and ran hard into the dark and cold of the woods, too fast for Aelis to see where she went.

She trudged back to the hall, with a chill that had nothing to do with the season. She burst inside, startling Timmuk, who'd nodded off near the fire, tankard in hand.

"You didn't think to come after us," Aelis charged as she made for her pack. Anger joined with fear to give her energy.

"Didn't seem my place to get between you and Renia," Timmuk said. "And it's not like I match either of you in a footrace."

"That seems a weak excuse, dwarf." Aelis found what she wanted: her alchemy lamp. She knew it was low on reagents and hadn't the time to reload it, so she gave it a vigorous shake. She could just *hear* Urizen's voice in her head. *It's a sensitive piece of equipment. Shaking it will perhaps extract brief moments of life out of the reagents it is already loaded with, but it will damage the conversion filaments and eventually leave you with an expensive paperweight.*

She shook it once more, thought she heard something inside snap loose, but she tested it with the dial and it blazed to life.

"Sit here if you want," Aelis spat angrily as she stalked toward the door. "I'm going to go find her." She paused just outside the door to get her bearings, then set out.

✦   ✦   ✦

She searched till her feet and hands were numb with cold, till she stumbled through the snow. She searched till she wasn't even sure if she was still in the same valley or in what direction the hall lay. She searched till her eyelids grew so heavy that she found her eyes closing and her body pitching toward the ground before awakening with a sudden start.

Finally, her heart heavy, tear tracks frozen on her face, she looked to the sky. She found the curve of bright points that made the feather of the Quill and then down to the last star, the nib, and put it to her back. She'd set out west initially, so putting that at her back would take her, if not back within sight of the hall, at least to something she might recognize. By dawn, if not before.

Aelis was correct, though for once she took no joy in the small triumph of her competence. As light grew in the sky, she saw the long shadows of Rhunival's Hall and its outbuildings rise before her.

She could smell smoke from the firepit and see light flicker around the seams of the shuttered windows.

A tall, lean figure stood in the doorway.

Maurenia's face had once again assumed its typical reserve, her eyes free from any trace of tears, her mouth a thin line, skin drawn tight across her cheekbones.

Onoma, she is beautiful, Aelis couldn't help but think, even as her lantern quivered and died. She was glad it did, for she felt inadequate in front of her glimpse of Maurenia then, her face dirty, her braid unraveling, her clothes soaked with sweat and lake water and snowmelt.

She fumbled for Maurenia's hand and found it. This time she was not slapped away, but the half-elf's flesh felt colder, harder somehow.

"I know what happened," Maurenia said.

"What?"

"My blood. My blood touched the dirt of his hall, his home. If it were not for that, he would've had to seek a sacrifice to leave as completely as he did."

"How . . . how do you know that?"

"I just . . . do," Maurenia said. "The same way I know how far in any direction I can walk. The same way I know there is a fox just outside the shed over there that is hoping to get at the chickens, that I know there is a skunk fumbling about in the underbrush just outside my vision, that I could tell you how many birds are in the valley if I think about it. The same way I know there are no fewer than eight species of mushroom in the vicinity but that you should only eat three of them. The same way I know that you did *something* to your ankle before we left, and some sense I don't understand and can't explain is trying to tell me that *you* are the animated dead . . ."

"He bound you," Aelis said, in an exhausted whisper. "He bound you in his place. Maurenia, I don't . . . I am sorry. I don't know when or how . . ."

"You were tending my wounds after the animated dog skeleton had tried to tear my shoulder open. And you did a fine job of it, but one drop of blood was enough."

"That's all it took. That rotten, stump-fucking son of a bitch of a wood-shade. I will . . ."

"What you will do is *fix it*," Maurenia snapped. "Right?"

"I swear to you, Maurenia, by my power, may it be stricken from me if I fail. By Onoma, by Stregon, by Elisima and their moons, may they abandon me if I do aught but die in the attempt. May the Worldsoul end Her cycle and the world itself cease turning if I do not do this thing you have said." Aelis felt the words, the archaic forms, pour out of her. She felt something deep inside her respond, and knew that she had bound herself to this above all else, more deeply than she had bound herself to her oaths as a Warden, more deeply than she had bound herself to anything.

"Fuck's sake, I was hoping you could fix it *now*," Maurenia said. For a moment Aelis's heart sank, until the half-elf laughed. Aelis came forward to take her in her arms and felt Maurenia stiffen, but she did not pull away.

"If you can't do it now," Maurenia whispered into Aelis's hair, "you'd gods-damned well better get started."

Aelis herself laughed then, the mirth intermingled with tears of fatigue.

21

WORK TO DO

Aelis woke to an empty hall aside from Tun's sleeping form. She'd slept well into midmorning, but bread and boiled eggs were on the table, along with a pot of small beer. Seized with a hunger she hadn't anticipated, she'd cracked, peeled, and devoured three eggs and followed them with half a big, round loaf of brown bread before she even turned to the beer. She drained the pot in a couple of gulps and could still have had more, but duties called. She checked Tun's signs and found him perfectly healthy and totally asleep. She thought of the pungent salts in a tube in her traveling kit, then thought better of it.

She went outside and washed her hands and face with water from a rain barrel and was leaning over to wash her neck when a hand suddenly found the small of her back and a voice stage-whispered, "Morning!" behind her ear.

She jumped, banging a wrist against the barrel, and whirled, scrambling for a weapon that wasn't on her belt. Maurenia stood before her, laughing, green eyes beaming in the bright sunlight.

"Is it really that funny?"

"Yes," Maurenia said, "and as long as you're on my land I'm going to use every advantage I have to make you jump."

Aelis squeezed her hands into fists and took a deep breath, calming her mind and her racing heart on a slow count to five, a trick from her Abjurer's training. "Where's Timmuk?"

"On an errand for me. How long till Tun is back on his feet?"

"I think a day, at least. Not sure what kind of shape he'll be in. I expect he'll need a great deal to eat to regain the energy he used."

"Which is precisely what Timmuk is seeing to," Maurenia said with a small, self-satisfied nod. "Glad we came to the same conclusion."

"What, he's hunting? I can't see him bringing down a buck."

Maurenia snorted. "He'd never get close enough. Timmuk and his brother couldn't hunt a blind dog with a hangover. Above ground, at any rate. But they're cunning fishermen, and they'll take any excuse to sit on some ice and drink the day away. I found an auger in the toolshed and some strings, weights, and nets and sent Timmuk on his way." She then heaved a small sigh. "And it also solves the problem of getting him out of here, because he was absolutely furious when I told him what happened."

Aelis winced, gathered her breath to speak, but found Maurenia cutting her off.

"He has every right to be. I'm not just his friend, Aelis. I'm his partner. Together, we make money off the things I design and he and Andresh test. That's going to hurt the business, and the one part of a Dobrusz that you *can* hurt is his purse."

"That seems a little cold."

"How many family members do they support? How many people's wages do they pay?"

"I don't know," Aelis admitted.

"Because you haven't asked. They may have been lock breakers and strong-arm robbers once, but that's the world they came up in, and they're past that now. A lot of people in Lascenise eat well and sleep comfortably because of them. I was only a part of that, but a part."

"I will go to him and . . ."

"No," Maurenia said. "Wait for him to come back. Let him have a day of fishing, and drinking, and thinking about that pile of gems you handed him."

"I'm sorry, Maurenia," Aelis said slowly, sinking down to lean on the edge of the rain barrel. "I don't know why any of you followed me in the first place," she suddenly admitted. "I shouldn't have let you. I . . ."

"Stop," Maurenia said sharply. "First of all, that's not you. You don't whine, and you don't doubt yourself, and *that's* why we followed you. It's why I did, anyway. Timmuk?" She shrugged. "Ask him. Ask Tun, if you have to know. Second, if we hadn't, you'd be dead, and the undead would still be loose."

"Animations," Aelis muttered then immediately said, "I'm sorry. It's a bad habit. I'll work on it."

"Good. Now tell me what you did to your ankle. My . . . the land is telling me that you're the undead, or your ankle is, but . . ."

"I necrotized it," Aelis said, too tired to dissemble or distract or talk around it. "It was injured badly enough that I needed to rest it for a week or more. I couldn't afford that, and the brace wasn't doing the job I needed done."

"Necrotized? Killed it?"

"Temporarily deadened some of the flesh. The muscles and the connective tissue that were strained. Otherwise I wouldn't have been able to walk."

"How long is that supposed to last?"

"A day or two. Three at the most."

"And it's been . . . ?"

Aelis did some quick mental math. "Twelve days? And it'll be a solid fortnight before I get back to Lone Pine and undo it."

"That does not seem wise."

"Didn't have time for wise."

Maurenia snorted lightly and turned away, heading into the longhouse. Aelis followed, found her stalking around the walls of Rhunival's hall touching objects here and there, tools, crockery, furniture. "I'm still mad, you realize. Furious, even. You may not have done this on purpose, but you were, at best, sloppy."

"I know," Aelis said, and she felt the faint hope that had been blossoming inside her take a hard blow.

"But it is not in my nature to let anger direct my actions," Maurenia said. "I am looking at this as a *temporary* condition. You will fix it."

"I will do whatever needs doing," Aelis said, her voice a shamed whisper.

"And what will that be from Lone Pine? Got access to a great magical library there?"

"No," Aelis said. "But I can send emergency messages through my orrery, and I will. They'll send me any books or equipment it seems I might need . . ."

"So it's a matter of months, not days."

Aelis steeled herself to answer. "It's a matter of months . . . at best," she said.

"What do you mean?"

"I'm going to ask for information on woodshades, bindings, soul trades, other Conjurations and Enchantments I can't recall. I'll ask them for anything they have on that entity in particular . . ."

"And you're going to do that while continuing your duties as Warden of Lone Pine, following up on Dalius, deciding what to do about that lump of iron you're so reluctant to let go of, and gods know what else."

Aelis felt her resolve withering as Maurenia laid out her responsibilities. "Yes," she ventured, in a voice that didn't project confidence. *And also teaching Pips. And following up on what the Matrix showed me. And . . .*

"Stop that," Maurenia said. "Stop living in your own head. You've got work to do. Do it."

"Can't leave without Tun," Aelis said.

"He'll be fine, will awaken in a few days. You don't need to nurse him."

"In point of fact, I do. He's my friend *and* under my surgical care. I'll be here when he wakes up."

"Fine." Maurenia's hand settled on a heavy wooden rod with a rounded end set in a tall, narrow, wooden cylinder. "What the seven hells is this thing?"

"A kind of mortar and pestle," Aelis volunteered. "For pounding the leaves, flowers, and seeds of plants, I'd guess."

"I hope whatever is binding me here doesn't expect me to *use* any of this nonsense. I'm an engineer, an adventurer. I don't do . . . *house.*" The way she spat the word like a curse made Aelis chuckle despite the gravity of their situation. Maurenia saw and smiled faintly, if only for an instant.

Aelis swept close to her, laying a hand on Maurenia's arm. "Listen, I will do what I can. Whatever I can. I will fix this. I *will* free you. But you can help."

"How?" Maurenia didn't pull her arm away; Aelis counted that as a victory.

"You said yourself, you're a soldier, an engineer. Start figuring out some basics. How far can you walk in each direction? Can you push that boundary? Might it change with the time of day, the seasons, the moons? What exactly can you feel around you on this land, and what *can't* you feel?"

Maurenia's face scrunched up for a moment till she seized Aelis's hand. "Fine. I'll do that. But I'm not playing kind and gentle keeper of the land to birds and vermin."

"Wouldn't expect you to. If it'll help, while I'm here I'll start a list of questions worth answering, like those I just asked. And we can devise a system for recording the information and testing it against the variables."

"Only paper I ever liked working with had designs for siege weapons on it," Maurenia grumbled. "But fine. In the meantime, I need help with chores. Lot of work to do to prepare for Tun waking up. Need wood chopped to smoke the fish Timmuk is going to bring back. Get to it."

"Are you going to help?"

"I need to have a walk around, settle my mind." Maurenia looked at her for a moment, and Aelis was certain the half-elf was weighing whether to lean in and kiss her. Instead, she squeezed her hand and stalked off.

"Where's the woodpile?" Aelis called out after her, but got no answer.

◆   ◆   ◆

She found it, eventually, and the wide stump that served as a chopping block and the hatchet and wedge. Aelis set about the work, hoping that physical labor would help her do as Maurenia asked and stop living inside her mind.

It didn't, but nothing ever had. She kept turning back to the vision the Matrix had shown her when she'd first used it.

The wizard taking receipt of it was Dalius. Had to be, she told herself as she swung the hatchet sharply into the wedge, splitting a piece of wood. *But who was the Necromancer?*

Suddenly she longed for pen and ink and paper and the kind of work she was more familiar with. But this needed doing, and Maurenia didn't seem in a mood to argue overmuch.

It can't have been Duvhalin, she told herself. "I'd have recognized the voice," she murmured, giving up on the inner monologue for now.

"But it has to do with him somehow. Or maybe he knew that Dalius had found the Matrix and wanted to get hold of it himself."

And here, Aelis suddenly realized, was an extremely difficult and sticky question.

To whom did Aldayim's Matrix *belong?*

Her first instinct was to say, quite simply, the College of Necromancy, which Aldayim had founded. Second, she thought, was to say the Tri-Crowns and the Estates House, who probably technically did own it.

On the other hand, she could make her orders as a Warden stretch to hanging onto it a while. She, unlike a common adventurer, was not required to turn over loot or spoils—not even magical artifacts—if they assisted her in the course of her duties.

Aelis set another piece of wood before her. The work was becoming mechanical, but as usual, her mind was churning free of interference.

Holding onto it'll be a problem. She set a piece of wood, readied the axe. *Only if I tell Duvhalin I found it. Is this what he sent me here to do?*

"Not sure how long I can keep it buried." She split another log and then set the axe in the stump.

Nothing about the Matrix is going to help you with Maurenia's binding.

That's a problem for a Conjurer, or an Enchanter, only one of which you are, and even that only just.

She ran down a list of what books she'd ask for and what she might do with them. No question but she'd have to ask for whatever they'd send her on woodshades.

"Maybe I could call for experts. Have them send up a Diviner, an Enchanter, a Conjurer . . ." She selected another piece of wood, set it. "Sounds like the start of a bad joke."

She was so lost in thought, she didn't realize how much wood she'd chopped, how the glow of work had settled into her arms and would soon become an ache. The pile could've filled up the hall's firepit twice over, far more than they needed. What was more, the first half of what she'd cut was now lightly coated with fresh snow that she hadn't even noticed was falling. She started gathering the firewood, taking as big an armful as she could into the hall.

Timmuk had returned while she was gone. Strips of fish hung above a part of the fire where the coals were banked low and smoking heavily. Timmuk had much of his gear—axe, vambraces and gauntlets, some other oddments of lethal ironmongery she hadn't seen before—laid out on one of the long tables, rags and bottles of oil to hand.

"Might as well get your own sword and dagger out, Warden," the dwarf said. "Past time all our weapons got maintenance."

Aelis saw the sense in it and unhooked her swordbelt, laying it carefully on an empty spot on the table. "Didn't realize you carried so many knives," she said, gesturing at what was spread before them.

"Don't fancy dying for lack of ways to fight back," Timmuk said. "Besides, axes are no good for the closest kind of fighting, alleyways, someone tries to stab you in bed, that sort of thing. The right tool for every purpose. You don't use an axe to slit someone's throat while they sleep."

He nudged one of the rags toward her. Aelis decided to start with her sword, and they worked in silence but for the crackling of the fire and the soft swipe of rag against steel.

"She's bound here somehow, then?"

Aelis felt the air in the room change. She looked up to see Timmuk with a short, wickedly curved knife in one hand, rag limp in the other.

"I'll do whatever I have to do to get her free of it," Aelis said.

"Tell me this, and answer honestly," Timmuk said, tapping the hilt of the knife against the table. "Was it any part of a bargain you made?"

"No. A drop of her blood fell on the floor here as I tended her wounds."

"It is your fault, then."

"Yes," Aelis said, the word ash in her mouth. "I have already sworn the most powerful and binding oath I can that I will *fix it*."

"On your power?"

She merely nodded.

The dwarf seemed content for the moment. He tossed the knife in the air, caught the hilt, and drove the blade through the thick plank of the table with as much effort as if he'd been slicing cheese.

Aelis didn't let herself be startled or afraid. Her training asserted itself, and she had a trio of wards ready to put in place depending on what Timmuk did next. The hilt of her sword was already in her hand, and the pommel let out a faint glow as she drew her power through it. She tensed the muscles she'd need to spring out of her seat.

Timmuk took his hand off the hilt of the knife and stared at her, his dark eyes flat and calculating beneath shaggy brows. They flicked down to the glowing pommel of her sword and he let out a held breath, seemed to deflate.

Aelis didn't let go of the magic she'd called on, let the words and forms circulate in her mind as she watched the dwarf.

"Couldn't you just take her place?" he asked, after a moment's silence.

Only then did Aelis let her legs and stomach go slack. She shifted her sword off the table, careful not to show the blade to the dwarf opposite her, and touched it to the ground, dispelling her gathered power. Then she set it slowly back on the table and took her hand away from it, feeling the weight of Timmuk's eyes on her the entire time.

"Had I known that Rhunival would require someone in his stead, I would've tried," she began, before she was cut off by a sudden intrusion of light.

"No, you wouldn't have." Aelis was sure neither of them had heard Maurenia arrive, but there she was, her outline in the doorway. "Because your obligation is to Lone Pine, and you wouldn't throw that away."

The half-elf came over to the table and eyed the implements spread out upon it. She took a seat next to Aelis and lifted the strap of her crossbow off her shoulder.

"I don't suppose being magically bound as some kind of guardian to this land will have any side benefits pertaining to weapons maintenance, will it?"

"Depends on whether there are brownies or nixies who answer to you," Aelis said.

Maurenia sighed and began disassembling her weapon. "Probably not worth the trouble, then." She eyed Timmuk as she removed a bolt and dislodged the cocking mechanism from the stock. "It's flattering that you were ready to try to do violence to a Warden on my behalf, Tim," she said. "But I'd prefer her intact." She turned and looked Aelis over speculatively. "Perhaps a dueling scar or two wouldn't go amiss."

Aelis and the dwarf shared a laugh, but Maurenia only shrugged. "Everyone looks better with a dueling scar, provided it doesn't take an eye or peel back a lip."

She took a rag from Timmuk's pile. "In honest truth, Timmuk," Maurenia went on, "I'm not happy about this, but bloody vengeance against a somewhat negligent surgeon is hardly the answer. Especially when she's the person best suited to fixing it. And I'm certainly not *happy* about my condition, but I've learned to take my life on the terms I get, not go about wishing for better. Aelis will find a solution."

Aelis hardly felt as confident as Maurenia's words should indicate. *Best suited to fixing it, my soggy ass*, she thought.

"As you say, Renia," Timmuk answered, and the three of them lapsed into the silence of work they all knew.

* * *

Dinner was mostly awkward silences and slurping noises. Aelis had not been accounted a particularly graceful or mannered count's daughter before she'd gone to the Lyceum, but compared to the adventurers she shared beer, bread, and porridge with that night, she might as well have been the most talked-of debutante of a spring season, her every gesture demure and feminine. When they were finished, she went to check on Tun. Her Anatomist's blade, freshly cleaned, oiled, and sharpened, allowed her to Delve him by simply laying it against his skin.

Maurenia wandered over to stand near her in the flicker of the firelight. "Is he well? Does he need to be fed?"

"I think he'll need to eat when he wakes," Aelis said. "At the moment, I think his . . . other shape aids him. He will need to eat in quantity, but . . . you seemed to know that already," she added, gesturing toward the strips of fish that still hung over the low fire.

"I guessed," Maurenia said with a shrug. "Plus, it got an angry dwarf out of the house for a while." She put a hand under Aelis's arm and guided her up. "You need a bath. There's hot water, a tub, soap, and towels in the shed closest to the back of the hall."

Aelis hardly had time to answer before Maurenia was walking her toward the shed, arm in arm.

"Wash my back?"

"You're too filthy for it to be fun, and I've got to get a laundry tub sorted. I might come help you dry off, though."

Despite the cold air around them and the gravity of Maurenia's binding, Aelis felt a bright, hard hope flutter in her chest.

22

A CONVERSATION

Aelis felt renewed, in many ways, the next morning. She had slept next to Maurenia by the longhouse firepit, clean for the first time in weeks, with her clothes drying on a rack next to the fire.

They smelled like smoke, but they were warm and as close to freshly laundered as she was likely to get for some time, so she was dressed and pulling on her boots before she realized that Tun's slumbering form no longer rested on the other side of the fire.

She came to her feet and was halfway out the door, stumbling on the stone steps that led up to it, before she saw him sitting in a circle cleared of snow beneath a pine tree, head raised to the sunlight that filtered through the boughs.

"Tun," she called softly, as she came over to his side.

He grunted, then spoke hoarsely. "I'm not dead, then?"

"Afraid not."

"Everyone else?"

"Alive. But . . . complicated."

He nodded. She got a glimpse of his face, which seemed drawn, thinner, tired. He took a slow breath before speaking again.

"Is there any more fish?"

"I don't know how much Timmuk caught."

"Well," Tun said, "perhaps we can all go fishing. Are we wintering here?"

"I think only until you're strong enough to head back to Lone Pine."

"Then we definitely need to go fishing. No need to smoke them though," he added. "At least not on my account."

Aelis, realizing she was hovering over him, sat down beside him on folded legs. "Can I check your signs, Tun? Your pulse, your lungs . . ."

"They're fine. Weak, perhaps, but food will help with that. How'd you stop the . . . thing?"

"That candlestick I took from the vault turned out to be . . . well, I *think* it turned out to be . . . Aldayim's Matrix."

Tun turned slowly toward her and said, with deliberate enunciation, "And that should mean what to a poor, uneducated woodsman?"

"The only true part of that is 'woodsman.'" Aelis snorted. "As for the Matrix, it's a magical artifact. Kind of a library, instruction manual, and . . . power amplifier, all at once. I used it to shut down that chimera." Here Tun began to raise a brow, and Aelis quickly said, "The tooth monster . . . and the other animations I'd inadvertently activated."

"So, it's done then?"

"Onoma's rotting breath, I hope so."

"And Rhunival? Took his rod and vanished back into the nether realms of shadow and mystery, I take it?"

"I wish it were that simple." She took a deep breath. "He . . . bound Maurenia in his place. My fault," she added quickly. "When I treated her wound inside his hall, a drop of her blood fell to the ground. He would've tried something else, perhaps. Something violent, I expect. But with her blood, he didn't need to."

"Can you fix it?"

"Not yet. But I will."

"You sound confident."

"I figure if I sound confident long enough, I'll start to feel it."

"Good policy." He took a deep breath, closed his eyes. The wind stirred his braids, glinting on some of the amber and ivory ornaments woven into his hair. "You could," he said slowly, "stand to plan a deal more carefully. Blindly rushing forward worked this time. It won't always."

"I worked in the time I had," Aelis protested. It was weak, and she knew it.

Tun opened one eye and looked questioningly at her. "And you had no time with which to formulate a better plan? The barracks-crypts had to be investigated now and not in the spring when safer traveling would've been possible? You could not have written back to the Lyceum and asked for further clarification or a listing of the expected challenges?"

"To the latter, certainly not. Not without putting Archmagister Duvhalin in a terrible position. Which I don't care about in the abstract, but he can make my life, and many others, miserable by extension."

"Is he in the Warden chain of command?"

"Not exactly. But an Archmagister exerts an influence over their College nearly as powerfully as the Prince-Priests of Old Dalessia did their city-states."

"If he was covering outlawed activities, as you suggested, couldn't you have exposed him?"

"By now, I have to believe all the Archmagisters have whatever they need on one another to assure they can stay in power till they're gods-damned good and ready to relinquish it. The others would make him face no consequences. Perhaps some kind of secret Writ of Censure, no real teeth, no wards upon him, no checks on his power, arcane or otherwise. And what's more," she added, "I'm a lowly Warden posted out to the middle of the forest primeval."

"The *edge* of the forest primeval," Tun corrected.

"Fine, the edge. Point remains; to the Archmagisters, I'm no one of any real consequence. Maybe a bit more powerful than the average first-term Warden, some family connections that I don't intend to invoke . . . nothing to challenge Duvhalin on his own turf . . ." She suddenly trailed off.

"I can hear the 'yet' you aren't saying."

"The Matrix showed me . . . some kind of secret. A meeting between . . ." Here, her voice dropped into a conspiratorial whisper, "Dalius and some adventurer or artifact hunter who brought him the Matrix."

"The Matrix shows secrets? Why would it do that?"

"A defense mechanism, I suppose. To unlock any knowledge from it, I must give it my own. I suppose everyone who's ever possessed it has had to do the same."

"So, when it moves to the next wielder, they learn something about the previous. Something the other does not want known." Tun thought a while. "Was there anything distinct about that meeting?"

"There was a Necromancer there, but it did not show his face. It was not, regrettably, Ressus Duvhalin. Not unless he's shrunk a quarter of a foot since then."

"What about the hunter? Still alive?"

"Unlikely. Possible. Probably a resident of Mahlgren, one way or another."

"Anything distinct about him?"

Aelis sighed. "A woodsman. Carried a long knife and an axe. Spattered with mud, wearing green and rust-brown . . ."

"That could be thousands of Mahlgren men, I'm afraid," Tun rumbled. "Keep thinking of it. You had art tutors, no? Draw him. Anything might help."

"When am I going to find time to draw him, Tun?"

"I need at least one more day to eat and rest. Two would be better." After a brief pause, Tun added, "If you think Lone Pine is safe from the animations now."

"It ought to be," Aelis said. "With the Matrix, I can detect every animation for miles and miles. And I destroyed all of them."

"What of other things? You mentioned spirits, specters . . ."

Aelis swallowed hard. "There were perhaps one or two I might want to check on." Aelis patted Tun's shoulder as she stood. She took a step, then turned back to him. "Thank you, Tunbridge, for coming with me. I . . ."

Any more words she had been planning to say, she swallowed as Tun lifted a hand to stop her.

"Please," he rasped. "No declarations or professions. I'm in too fragile a state to deal with you trying to express emotions at the moment."

She took the hand he raised and squeezed it. It felt like squeezing a rock, albeit one that squeezed back.

23

ONE LAST SECRET BEFORE HOME

That day and the next, they spent in a sort of daze of domesticity. Snow fell and wind blew, though the worst of it didn't seem to reach inside the small valley that marked the limits of Rhunival's former territory. They fished, foraged, drank, shared stories by firelight, and slept far more than they had in the weeks prior. Aelis did take time, when the light was good, to use one of her finer writing sticks to try to sketch the man she'd seen in the Matrix's vision. It took a few tries to remember the old skills, and she warmed up by drawing Tun and Timmuk first, rendering them both quickly in only a few lines. She took a fresh sheet of paper and looked at Maurenia who, sensing eyes on her, turned and stared hard at her till she scrapped the idea.

She focused on what she could remember of the man. Not his clothing, but his face. He'd had a strong nose and jaw. That he'd had stubble but not a beard might be significant, or it might not. *What color were his eyes?* Brown, she thought, or maybe hazel. She glanced at her first sketch of him and found it worthless; it could've pictured almost any man with a hawk-like nose and stubbled cheeks.

Try again later. There were exercises she could do to tap into her memories of the vision; she supposed she could ask the Matrix to show it to her again, but she didn't want to do that unless she grew desperate enough to trade it more secrets. She inspected her dwindling stack of paper, folded a sheet, and tried again.

The next evening, Tun and Timmuk found reasons to make themselves scarce and Aelis found herself alone in the hall with Maurenia. They were silent with each other for a long time. Aelis kept looking within herself for the courage to speak, to say any of what she was thinking, but halfway through a large cup of resinous beer, words still had not come. Finally, Maurenia saved her the trouble by draining her own beer and slamming the cup down so that it rattled the other crockery on the table.

"For a woman possessed of reckless physical courage, you sure can be a coward sometimes, Aelis," the half-elf said, pouring herself a second drink.

"Sometimes words aren't adequate to the moment," Aelis responded, the words feeling entirely like the evasion they were. Maurenia snorted and turned a silent stare at her until she felt the weight of her lover's eyes force her to speak.

"I said I'm going to fix it. I admitted that it was my fault."

"Then what are you going to *do* to fix it?"

"Ask for information, maybe an expert. Someone with enough knowledge. A powerful Conjurer could probably handle this in an afternoon. I am not that person."

Maurenia took a deep breath. "Like I said earlier . . . I'm not one to go weeping after a better deal or something I wish I could have. But I'm not made to stay in one place. And my patience won't last forever. Or even very long."

"It's months at least," Aelis said. "This isn't a Necromancer's job, or an Enchanter's, or an Abjurer's."

"Would it have been if you had paid attention? If you'd had a thought for those around you instead of yourself?"

"I was doing this for the people of Lone Pine. The people I'm charged to protect."

"No," Maurenia said, heat creeping into her voice. "You did this because an Archmagister asked you to, because you hunger for approval and acclaim, and possibly because you thought it was fun."

"The animations were a threat to . . ."

"NOT until you woke them up," Maurenia said. "They'd slumbered for decades! They would've gone on doing so till you blundered in and screwed it up so badly we had to come to your gods-damned rescue. Stregon's blue balls, you're lucky you have the knack of making friends the way you do. You're lucky you're . . ." She waved a hand vaguely, and settled on, "you."

Aelis felt the heat of embarrassment and guilt creeping into her cheeks, the sense of realizing that Maurenia was right—that every step of what had happened, Tun's wounds, Maurenia's binding, all of it—was the fault of her own desire for the favor of an Archmagister. *Even one I already know hates me.*

"You're right," Aelis said, "about most of that. I . . . don't know what the last bit means."

Maurenia came and leaned down in front of her, resting one knee on the chair Aelis sat upon, draping an arm around her neck. "Tun trusts you because he's seen that you *do* take being a Warden seriously. That you were willing to go face to face with him in his bear form and go to every extremity *not* to kill him spoke volumes about how you approach your task."

"And you? Do you trust me?"

"I trust you to try to balance your many obligations in the way that seems likely to result in the best outcomes for the most people. And," she added, leaning more closely, "I think you're beautiful."

Aelis leaned forward to put her lips on Maurenia's but found only empty air. The half-elf had pushed off the chair and taken two steps back.

"And I think I could probably fall in love with you. But if I'm stuck here for the rest of my life, or unnaturally beyond it, I will never forgive you."

"I told you I'm going to . . ."

"You're going to *try* to fix it, Aelis," Maurenia said. "I don't know if you're going to, and neither do you."

Aelis had had enough. She pushed up off her chair, stalked over to Maurenia, and threw her arms around her. "If I don't fix it by the time my term at Lone Pine is done, I'll pack up, move here, and work on the problem until I die. I will have you free, Maurenia. To live whatever life you want. Whether that's with me, or not, or sometimes . . . I will."

"You won't throw away your career for it," Maurenia whispered.

"I will if I have to," Aelis said.

"I don't really . . ." Maurenia began, till Aelis silenced her with a finger on her lips. "We have a house to ourselves for who knows how much longer. Are we going to waste it?"

She could feel Maurenia weighing it in her stance, the way she held her body, the way her eyes searched. "When we leave, I'm probably gone for a month or more," Aelis whispered, her lips against Maurenia's. "Take that long for my ankle to heal." *If it does.*

Maurenia kissed her, and Aelis felt the doubt and hesitation start to melt away. "You'd better give me something that'll stay with me for a month then," she said, before turning and half-dragging Aelis toward a part of the hall hung with blankets.

+ + +

The next morning was gray and cold and threatened snow, according to Tun, who was looking fit and powerful again, if perhaps not quite as robust as before. Maurenia and Aelis said few words to each other.

Everything was said last night, I guess, Aelis thought. *Several times.*

She blushed at her own thoughts and busied herself with packing. Between all the fishing Timmuk had done and the plentiful food they kept finding stored all over Rhunival's grounds, they had little fear of short rations for themselves or Maurenia.

When it came time to leave, Aelis was working hard not to let her heart leap onto her face, even as it threatened to sink into her stomach.

They packed, hitched up bags. Timmuk took up his axe, Tun and Aelis their walking sticks, and the three of them were seen off by Maurenia not from the boundary of her land, but from the door of her hall.

Aelis stopped to kiss her. "Fix yourself. Then this," was all Maurenia said to her.

Aelis turned back just before the treeline. The doorway where she'd kissed the woman she thought she loved—and whom she had possibly doomed—was empty.

◆ ◆ ◆

"This walk has been so easy, one might imagine we were out for a health and pleasure hike," Timmuk said two days out from Maurenia's hall. The day was cold, but clear and beautiful, the snow was well packed and easy to walk in, and the dwarf's words jolted Aelis out of thinking how much she hated it.

"Health and pleasure hike?"

"Yes," Timmuk said. "It's something some of the gentry do now and then. Get out of the city and its crowds and ordure and foul air. Walk up a mountain and camp atop it for a night or two, commune with nature, expand the lungs, hurt the lower back by carrying too much, and feel proud of it. That sort of thing. Andresh and I thought about going into the business. Lot of coin in it."

"Is there treasure atop this mountain? Perhaps a library full of ancient knowledge? Or beautiful women and well-muscled, mute men waiting in a cabin atop piles of warm furs? Enough wine to swim in?"

"Ah, usually just 'rustic' feasts. You know, unsauced venison, birds without fruit in the stuffing, big flagons of ale."

"And people pay for this?"

"Yes."

"That's the dumbest fucking thing I've ever heard."

"Any openings in that business nearby?" Tun asked. "I'm looking for something less in the one-on-one-with-horrifying-tooth-monsters line."

"You'd make a killing at it, my friend," Timmuk boomed. "The authenticity you'd lend . . . if you're serious, we could dust off our plans . . ."

Tun shook his head. "I'm afraid I'd lose patience and eat someone who complained overmuch." They all shared a laugh, and Aelis snapped out of her reverie just enough to swing her rucksack around and pull out one of Duvhalin's maps she'd scribbled notes on.

"Wait," she said, pointing to a spur of hill to the west. "This was an old watchtower, yes? One of the Earl's Lanterns?"

Tun nodded in the affirmative.

"Take an hour's break. If I'm not back in three, leave me." She set off toward the structure.

"If you're not back in one and a half, we'll come looking," Timmuk called. "What're you doing?"

"Making sure of something," Aelis called back.

+ + +

With as much digging about in old ruins as Aelis had been doing the past few weeks, it was no work at all for her to find the foundations of the tower. She poked around at it with her walking stick for a long while until she heard it thunk against something that wasn't stone. Not for the last time, she wished for an Invoker's ability to call up fire to make the task of moving the snow easier, then settled for brushing it away with her hands.

She found the heavy iron ring set in the trapdoor and pulled. There was a great groan, and she got it halfway up before the weakened wood snapped. The trapdoor nearly slammed shut, but her walking stick was still looped around her wrist, and she managed to wedge it in before the door fell snugly closed again. Then she pried it open and spent a few moments with her lantern, flaring it to life.

Its light, after her rough treatment, was inconsistent, with missing bars in the middle range, and it had lost some of its ability to adjust width and height. But it worked.

She wasn't sure if the iron candlestick tied to her belt *actually* grew heavier and warmer or whether she had just convinced herself it did.

It wasn't large, as crypts went. It held few animations, and they hadn't been able to get out. But what interested Aelis most was not the piles of bones and iron wire scattered about the stairs she descended.

It was the nooks along the walls, about the size that might hold scrolls atop a desk or in a library. Not entirely out of place, as they might have held small remembrances—a personal dagger, a bit of jewelry, a prayer to Onoma or Stregon or the Worldsoul scribed at small cost or great, depending on the perspective of the bereaved. These were common anywhere soldiers lived and died; bodies could not always, or even often, be retrieved and interred. This gave the families and comrades *something*.

Aelis was drawn to one particular niche that held something that *looked* for all the world like a small wooden drum, the kind that might be a child's most annoying toy.

But it had a solid bottom, and the skin drawn tight across the top was not taut the way it should've been. Aelis set down her lantern and undid the knots in the thongs that bound it across the frame.

The drum was not hollow inside. Filling the round frame was a knot-work of silver inlaid over a stone disc. Even as Aelis watched, they began forming into runic patterns she could read, words that she would speak aloud simply by looking at them if she was not careful. The Beguilement that lay upon them was too powerful for even her to stare at for very long without giving in to it.

She pulled the hide back over the top of the drum, bound it with shaking fingers, and took several deep breaths. Then she carefully wrapped the entire artifact in spare clothing and slid it into the center of her rucksack. As she slung it over her shoulder, she thought she heard a faint buzzing sound, a suggestion of a note that would not quite resolve into music.

She almost walked straight into Tun on her way down the hill. He stood unmoving, leaning a little on his walking stick, waiting for her.

"I told you I would be back . . ."

"Aelis," Tun said, "secrecy and impulse is not how you retain your friends."

Aelis winced. "I'm sorry, Tun. It's . . . how we learn to work in the Lyceum. You don't share your notes, you don't tell anyone else what you're doing, you . . ."

"You may have noted already that this—" he indicated the wilderness around them with the wave of one hand—"is not a classroom or a library. And the grading system is rather more harsh."

"Does this count as a Pass with Distinction? Headed back to camp successful, unhurt, within the time . . ."

Tun cut her off. "There are only Pass and Fail out here. Pass is when everyone comes home."

Coming from Tun, Aelis felt that like a blow, but she settled a mask over her features, asserting the control her upbringing had taught. Tun put a hand on her shoulder.

"Come on," he said. "You will fix it by moving forward. I will be with you insofar as I can be. I think Timmuk will too, when it comes to that. He even has something for you."

◆   ◆   ◆

When they camped that night, once the shelter was up and the fire laid out and lit, Timmuk had called Aelis over with an insistent wave of his hand. Carefully, almost reverently, he opened a small box that contained a pipe and a few small, fragrant pouches. He lifted the pipe out and placed it in Aelis's hand. It was not one of the long-stemmed, elaborate pieces he regularly smoked, no silver mouthpiece or carved ivory bowl. It was of plain wood with a patina of long use. While Timmuk busied himself with the pouches, Aelis took a moment to cast a First Order Clean Fingers on the mouthpiece.

Timmuk began stuffing bits from the various bags into it, until the pipe's bowl was about half-full of loose shreds of dried, brown plant matter. He reached for another pinch, but Aelis stopped him with a smile. "I think that'll be enough," she said, "for my first time."

"If you say so, Warden," Timmuk rumbled. "It's about the same as a dwarf child might have in their first pipe."

Aelis knew when she was being baited, though that rarely stopped her from *taking* the bait. And had they been sitting in a tavern with soft landing spots to hand, she would've called Timmuk back and demanded he fill the bowl. But they were in the middle of nowhere, with snow and pine needles the only places to land, so she managed to rein herself in. Perhaps she should've wondered why Timmuk had wandered off into the woods chuckling into his beard as she lit the pipe with a twig from the fire, but she was not one to turn down a challenge.

A few minutes later, she very much wished she was the kind to turn down a challenge. She now lay on the ground beside the fire, groaning, too hot on one side and cold on the other, and absolutely unwilling to expend the effort to turn herself around.

"I bet you wish you hadn't taken him up on the offer," Tun said.

"Please," Aelis moaned, her voice muffled against the ground, "either make the world stop spinning or do me a kindness and murder me."

"Dwarven smoking leaf is often mixed in with more potent mind-altering substances. In this case, I'd say Greenstalk Mushrooms, a touch of some nightshade or other to put a bit of tingle in the limbs, and one or two other things I can't identify."

"I'd have thought if he wanted to kill me, he could do it more easily than this."

"I think it's perhaps his way of accepting you. An initiation, if you will."

Aelis gripped the twisted shanks of dead grass beneath the snow hard, her fingers twitching open and closed, as she searched for an answer. Tun must've noticed, because he chuckled.

"Trying to make sure you don't fall off? The effects shouldn't last too much longer."

"Do the effects end with my death?"

"No."

"More's the pity," Aelis muttered. In truth, though, she was already feeling better, so she rolled over onto her back. "I assume you didn't come over here just to check up on me."

"I did not," Tun said agreeably. "Since you can neither walk away nor distract me, I am going to ask a question. What were you doing in that watchtower you detoured to?"

"Checking on a barracks-crypt. Confirming that what I thought happened is definitely what happened."

Tun took a deep breath. "I will give you a second chance to tell me the truth, Aelis."

Her silence went on long enough to be as good as a confession, so she raised a hand to ask for time to compose a response and turned her head just enough to see Tun's outline in the starlight. He nodded.

"There were a couple of . . . intriguing points on the map of Necromantic defenses the Matrix showed me when I shut them all down. Most were just animations. There were three things that were definitively not."

"And you now have one of them in your pack. Why?"

"Because it's dangerous to leave it lying about. Because it's a powerful weapon, and I'd rather have it directly under my hand than loose in the wind."

"What is it?"

"A bound spirit. Of what kind, I cannot be sure until I have the time to examine it in my tower with tools and reagents to hand."

"So that you can dismantle it?"

"I don't know if I can do that safely. And . . . as I said, it's a powerful weapon."

"You have several of those."

"Not like this I don't," Aelis said. She dug hard for the ability to sit up, and managed to, leaning on her elbows. "And because if it's what I think it might be, it's better that I have it than anyone else find it."

"What do you think it is?"

"I think it's a Beguiling Blood Haunt, but there's a chance it could be an Eerie Sister or a Widow Grieving O'er the Waves."

Tun tilted his head oddly, fixing one eye upon her. "Those are not real names of actual classified spirits."

"*The Taxonomy of Spirits, Haunts, Specters, Ghosts, Apparitions, and Various Deadly Seemings and Vestiges* is a book nearly as full of itself as its author was," Aelis answered. "And it is also three hundred years old, with the prose to prove it. But it *is* the definitive text of the field, and the copy on my shelf at home is going to help me figure out what I'm looking at. If it's any of the above, it lures an unprepared target into releasing it and then does *terrible* things to them."

"How terrible?"

"An illustration of a wizard who came out on the wrong end of an attempted exchange with a Widow Grieving O'er the Waves featured rather prominently, his brains having melted through his ears and his nose."

"And you would take this thing home?"

"Better there than lying somewhere for an orc hunter to find it come spring. At my tower, I can bind it carefully, lock it in lead seals or silver if need be, or dispose of it entirely if I decide I must."

"Fine." Tun seemed to accept her answer for the moment, but she could tell simply from the way he sat that he had more to say.

"You called Lone Pine home," he at last pointed out.

"I never did," she protested, even as she ran the words back in her mind and found that indeed, she had.

"Neither did you object when I called it home on your behalf."

"Pfah," was all Aelis could think to say as she pushed herself up to her feet. She wobbled unsteadily and tilted forward till Tun caught her and pulled her upright.

"Admit to yourself that it isn't so bad as all that," he murmured.

"It's better than the wilderness. I'll give it that."

"What is there that you would not call better than the wilderness?"

"There's a tavern in Antraval called the Rat's Toe. To be allowed to drink there, you have to down a cup of the special barrel. It's where they dump all the dregs left on the tables night after night."

Tun blinked. "So, you . . . drank it?"

Aelis shrugged. "Of course I did."

"That," Tun said with a deep rumbling laugh, "is why I like you, Aelis. You cannot stand to see a challenge and not take it up." Then his laughter stilled and he fixed her with a serious look. "It is also why I fear for you. You barrel forward into things. One day, the thing you charge at is going to be too big for you."

"Well," she said, "lucky for me, I have friends."

Tun hmphed.

✦　✦　✦

The rest of the walk back to Lone Pine—aside from Aelis occasionally hearing faint musical notes coming from inside her rucksack—was as un-eventful as she could've hoped.

Until they got within about a mile of the village, when Tun stopped them with an outthrust hand.

Timmuk hefted his axe. Aelis dropped her hand to her sword and be-gan forming a ward in her mind, the Buckler, ready to bring it to life in her left hand.

"Come out," Tun said. "I know you're there!"

"Give the password, then!" a voice shouted back.

"The password is 'I am the Warden of Lone Pine and its surrounding area,'" Aelis called out. "'And detaining me while I am upon my appointed duties is a crime.'"

"Warden!" She thought she recognized the voice, a suspicion con-firmed when Elmo dropped heavily, though onto his feet, from the limbs of a large pine tree. He scrambled up to them, unstringing the short bow he carried.

"We'd begun to think you weren't coming back," he said. Aelis noted that the knife she'd given back to him before she set out was sitting prominently on his belt. "And . . . if you run into anyone else, the pass-word today is . . ." He searched his memory for a moment. "'Lemon cake.' I think."

"Lemon cake," Tun repeated carefully. "May we pass now?"

"Oh, of course, of course," Elmo said. He reached to the back of his belt, under the heavy homespun wool cloak he wore and removed a hunting horn. "Shall I blow to warn the village of your arrival?"

"I don't think that will be necessary," Aelis said. "Why are you out here?"

"Keeping watch, of course," Elmo said. "You told us to organize, warned us there might be undead. So, we set up a schedule . . . well, Martin set up a schedule, Emilie picked the guard posts . . ."

Aelis raised a hand to cut him off. "How many more posts are we going to run into on our way back?"

"Probably just the one, at the limits of the village. We've got wagons set in place blocking every major path."

"Why don't you walk with us and explain it all on the way?"

◆ ◆ ◆

Elmo was all too happy to explain, at length, what had gone on in her absence. Apparently, Martin had organized the guard schedules and assigned posts, Emilie had acted as a head scout, Rus had supplied weapons, and Elmo himself had taken as many turns on guard duty as they'd allow him. Other folks had manned the "wagon gates," as they called them—another one of Martin's ideas, apparently—or worked on supplying those on guard duty with food and warm clothes. They did wind up waiting a bit longer than Aelis wanted to get into town, with a farmer running to fetch a team to move the wagon gate. Either side of the road around it was piled high with stones and logs, and the way over the fields would've been a misery of snow to tramp through. Aelis found herself wishing they had let Elmo blow his horn.

When she got to the village proper, she sent Elmo home with praise for his sense of duty, then went to the inn. The heat of the place from the fire in the hearth and the press of many bodies struck her like a physical blow when she entered. There was a rack by the front door upon which rested a number of unstrung bows, rough quarterstaffs, spears, and sharpened farming implements. She didn't have time to process precisely how she felt about that because as soon as she walked in, there was a general cry of "Warden!" and she spent the next twenty minutes shaking hands and assuring a succession of villagers that she was fine and they were safe.

Timmuk was completing a noisy, back-slapping, rapid-fire-dwarfish reunion with Andresh that carried straight up the stairs to their room. Aelis glad-handed her way around the room greeting Bruce, Matthias, even Emilie, among many others. Aelis caught the innkeeper's eye as he descended the stairs with an empty tray after bringing food up to the Dobruszes. He clearly took pity on her and dispersed the crowd, some back to their tables and others to their homes.

With the crowd taken care of, Rus set her up at a small table in front of the hearth and brought her the first hot food she'd had since they set out from Rhunival's Hall. *Or is it Maurenia's Hall now?* she wondered. Thankfully, Rus asked her no questions until she came to find him at the bar.

"Seems like you folk kept busy while I was gone."

"It was the most excitement we've had around here in ages," Rus said.

"I understand that Martin organized most of it?"

Rus nodded, appearing reluctant to say more, so Aelis didn't press.

"Was there any sign of any undead anywhere near the borders?"

"Elmo reported strangers passing near him on a couple occasions. I think they were probably animals, perhaps orc hunters pursuing them. No threats to us."

"Good. What became of my alchemical soaps?"

Rus reached into a pouch on his belt and pulled forth a bit of wool. He unwound it to reveal a sliver of one of the cakes of soap. "Every volunteer carried a sliver, but they weren't to use it on their arms unless a warning was sounded by horn."

Aelis nodded approvingly, lapsing into silence for a moment. A moment became a long moment. A log in the fire snapped, and she sat up straight, realizing she'd been falling asleep.

"I'm sorry I made the people of this place go armed," Aelis said, slowly turning her face toward the rack of weapons that stood new and now half-filled by the front door. "I wish it hadn't come to that."

"We live on a frontier, Warden. It's dangerous. We all knew that."

"But folk weren't carrying staves and bows with them everywhere when I first arrived."

"Maybe they should have," Rus said. He cleared his throat and said, "Timmuk told me something of . . . Maurenia."

Aelis felt her lover's name like a cold knife laid against her throat. "And?"

"I have some of her things here in the room she let. Perhaps when the weather turns . . . you could take them to her?"

"That's . . . not the worst idea," Aelis said, even though she was uncertain she would have the courage to do any such thing. Some part of her did not want to face Maurenia till she came to her with a solution to her confinement. "I'll see to it that her room is paid for the time we were gone," she said suddenly, though Rus had not alluded to it.

"Timmuk already saw to that," Rus said. "You are clearly tired, Warden. You could stay in that room tonight if you wish. No charge, of course."

"No," Aelis answered before she'd even thought it over. "I have work to do back at my tower. The sooner I start it, the better."

"I understand. Let me pack up some food for you for tomorrow. Might get more snow and be hard walking between here and there."

While Rus disappeared into the kitchen, Aelis busied herself digging her alchemy lantern out of her pack. *At least I'll have its buzzing for company*, she thought.

24

HOME

It was a long, cold walk back to her tower. It was still locked tight and precisely as she'd left it, with no welcoming committee, no goat, and no fire. It was the last bit that bothered her the most, and so she set about building one as quickly as she could. Her breath puffed as she shuffled about, brushing dust off her inert orrery, setting down her pack, picking up her gloves again and putting them down in a second and then a third place until she was satisfied. Finally, she unwound her scarf and unbuckled her swordbelt and dropped them to the floor.

Then, thinking of Maurenia's voice chiding her, she picked them up, carried them to their pegs, and hung them neatly.

A range of possible ways to spend the rest of the afternoon into the evening occurred to her. Most of them involved a bottle of wine and lying in bed until various parts of her stopped hurting. Of course, there was that one part that *should* have been hurting, and did not, and the sooner she saw to that, the better. She flexed her ankle one way, then another, let it take most of her weight, and felt nothing. That was bad.

The quiet emptiness of the warming tower settled over her, and she decided she could justify ignoring her magically deadened ankle just that much longer. She had never been one to struggle with being alone. Far from it.

But the last time she'd been in her tower, Maurenia was with her, and the space felt unutterably forlorn without her.

"Can't go feeling sorry for myself," Aelis said aloud in a voice that was not as resolute as she wanted it to be. "Maurenia has it far worse. And it's my fault."

Two things happened in rapid succession. The first was that Aelis felt tears threaten to fill her eyes. The second was that she beat them back with fury.

"I am not," she said, clenching her jaw, "a cryer."

So, she set about furiously doing every task she could all at once. She unpacked her rucksack, putting everything back where it belonged. She assembled a pile of dirty clothing, which she would launder the next day. She took all the instruments out of her traveling medical kit, cleaned them with distilled spirits and soft rags, and replaced them in the larger kit. She cleaned and oiled her sword and dagger, then oiled their scabbards and her belt. She set her wand on her worktable and got out a small pot of beeswax, melted a tiny pinch in her hand, and treated the wood with it.

With all this fine handwork, Aelis hoped to clear her mind and master her thoughts. But as she worked, two things buzzed continually in the back of her mind.

First, of course, was Maurenia. Second, and nearly as insistent, was the song of nearly heard notes, of faint and disappearing tones, the almost-tangible tug of the spirit trap she'd taken from the ruined tower on their route back.

Since she could do nothing about Maurenia's condition yet, she dug the trap out of her rucksack, set it on her worktable, then looked through her equipment.

"Let's see," she muttered as she moved packages around, finally selecting three and going back to her table. From the first wooden box she'd taken from her trunk, she removed a pair of thin tongs and a pair of tightly fitting gloves and pulled them on before opening the second box, in which lay thin sheets of white lead. With the tongs, she slipped one out and began teasing it around the wooden drum holding the spirit trap, careful to keep it at arm's length. She put one longways, then two across the middle.

Already, the buzzing had receded. Tensed muscles in her neck and shoulders began to relax. But she was not done.

When dealing with *whatever* was in that trap, one could not be too thorough. So once the three lead strips were wrapped around it and pressed into place, she used a separate tool, this one from her medical kit, to draw out strands of silver wire from the third box. Careful not to touch the lead, she wrapped the silver wires around the drum in an X shape. She set it down, admired her handiwork, the sheets and wires drawn taut and smooth against the trap.

"Is that enough?" She chewed on her bottom lip as she pondered. "It isn't." Back to the trunk then, where she got a bulging sack that thunked heavily onto her table. Then she climbed up the stairs to where her alchemical supplies were stored, and came back down holding a jar.

Aelis untied the bag, set a bowl near to it, and poured about half its contents—pure white sand—into the bowl. Then she opened the jar, took

out a pinch of flakes that gleamed in the shadow-filled tower, and sprin-
kled them over the sand still in the bag, then stirred. Then, careful not to
disturb either the lead or the silver, she slipped the drum into the sack,
poured the rest of the sand over it, and carefully drew the sack's thongs
closed, tied it shut, and considered her work.

She was about to tuck the sack into her trunk when she selected one
more silver strip and wound it into a knot around the leather thongs holding the bag shut.

"Let's see how you like that, you noisy little shit," Aelis murmured as
she set the drum inside a trunk, covered it with a spare robe, and shut the
lid.

"Not a bad improvised Null Cage, if I do say so myself." Aelis took a
deep breath to center herself.

Dinner. Ankle. Oh, and get some light in this place.

Before she allowed herself to dig into the sack Rus had given her or
open a bottle of wine, Aelis dipped into her writing case and pulled free a
sheet of paper, a pen, and a bottle of ink. She uncorked the ink, dipped the
pen into it, and began quickly counting under her breath.

At the top, she quickly dashed out Maurenia's name. Then she made
one quick mark for every single day that Maurenia had been captured and
slipped an edge of the paper under her orrery.

Her inert orrery.

"Gods-dammit." Aelis sighed. She got out a bottle of wine and set it
down, then the tiny book full of orbit calculations and a scrap of paper and
a writing stick. She bent over the book and began flipping pages, looking
for the rows of figures and positions she wanted. The columns and rows
swam and danced before her eyes, and she suddenly felt a bone-deep weariness settle in her limbs.

"Tomorrow," she said. Without pausing to think if it was a good idea,
she snatched up her sword and the wine, swept the blade up the side, and
sent the cork flying into the hearth.

She held the bottle up to inspect it and sighed again.

"Of course. Not a single crack, and no one here to see it." Then she
brought the bottle to her lips and tilted her head back.

◆　◆　◆

The next morning, Aelis woke up to a warm tower, a pile of aches and
muscle pains, and the desire to sleep through the day. Warden and Abjurer
training forced her to sit upright and throw the covers off, alerting her to

the fact that while her *bed* was warm, the tower was less so. She took a deep breath, stood, and decided to indulge in a show of fanatical discipline by making the bed. By the time she'd snapped the corners of the blankets tight, a to-do list was taking shape in her mind, so she went to her desk, got out paper, pen, and ink, and wrote out the points.

  1. *Calculate the orrery's position and get it working again.*

With a fire laid, breakfast eaten from what was left of her trail rations, she got out the calculation book and walked outside to observe what she could of the early morning moons and stars. The yellow moon was high and nearly full; a slim crescent of blue was low on the horizon to the east. She marked their positions, looked up the possible conjunctions in the book, and stomped angrily back into her tower.

A boring and fiddly hour later, the orrery was once again in nearly soundless operation, though Aelis had granted it only enough magical energy to make it through the day.

It was time to deal with her ankle, and she could not afford to tax her power too much just yet.

  2. *Deal with your ankle.*

Then a space, and she hastily added *Medically.* For that, she would need to make preparations. She poked the fire and laid more wood in it as she contemplated the rest of her list.

  3. *Research the spirit and the conditions of its entrapment.*

She scooted over to her bookshelf and started to pull out her copy of the *Taxonomy*, the largest and heaviest volume in her library. The old wooden boards were bound with iron and a small lock. She was about to search for the key somewhere among her trunks, when she snapped at herself.

"The ankle is a bigger problem. Deal with that *first.*" She slid the *Taxonomy* back onto its shelf and retrieved her copy of Aldayim's *Advanced Necromancy.* The ribbon was still in place over "Necrotization of the Flesh," and she skimmed the text until she came to dismissal. She dragged a chair over to her worktable, placing it before another chair. She bent to read with a deep, apprehensive breath, tension gathering in her shoulders. She read silently for perhaps half an hour and let out a sigh.

It dissolved none of the tension in her shoulders. Her jaw was taut, and her whole mind was attuned to every sensation—really, the lack of any— from her ankle.

Aelis pulled her leg up onto the second chair and got out her Anatomist's Dagger. She was on the verge of Delving herself when she was startled by a mighty pounding at her door.

Aelis leapt to her feet, snatched her swordbelt off its peg, and ran to the entranceway, loosening her sword in the scabbard.

She threw the bar and opened the door, startled to find Pips and Otto. The former had a basket of bread that practically went flying as she rushed forward to throw her arms around Aelis, while the latter carried a heavy crock of something savory and fragrant wrapped in cloth.

Aelis was nearly bowled off her feet by the girl, but recovered in time.

"Don't go hurting her now, not when she's had a long chase off in the wilderness again, and in the snows of winter," Otto grumbled at his niece.

"It's fine, Otto, it's fine. I'm happy to see you too, Pips," Aelis grunted as she gently disengaged herself from the girl, taking the basket from her hand. "Come in, come in," she said. "Too much for me to eat alone and I'd feel wrong opening a bottle just for myself."

Otto stood stock-still in the doorway for a moment, and Aelis decided not to let him hesitate any longer. She grabbed his arm, ushered him inside, and shut the door behind him.

In fact, the farmer and former soldier refused to let himself relax inside the tower until Aelis had forced a cup of wine into his hand and had a few sips herself. He raised it, clutched it like a talisman in his big fist, and downed the liquid in one go. Aelis stifled a laugh as his eyes lit up with the flavor and warmth of the wine she'd poured.

"What *is* this?" he mumbled as he looked in wonderment at the cup she'd given him.

"It's one of my family's vintages; two grapes, the Michaelis and Torrinos," she said. "Named for some of my great-great-great-uncles, or something like that. They're only called that on paper, of course. The folk who tend the vines call the one bloodpearls and the other summerdusk, which I think are by far the more interesting names."

"Only vineyards I ever saw were burned, trampled at the edges of battlefields," Otto muttered. "Seemed a shame." He chuckled then and said, "Some of the lads got the idea to try to make wine, picked what grapes they could, smashed them up, and tried to keep them in sacks with moldy bread.

Sergeant got wind of it and made them throw it out, said men in another company had gone blind trying to make wine on the march."

"March wine," Aelis said with a grin. "I like the sound of that. Could be a song."

She caught a slight movement from the corner of her eye and turned to find Pips having poured herself a cup of the dark red wine and taken a full, unwatered sip. She watched the girl's face screw up in disgust and the way she forced herself to swallow it. Aelis gently pried the cup from her hand and set it down.

"Wine," she said, "is not small beer. And it's something you need to develop a taste for and take watered until you grow to appreciate it."

Pips only nodded, wiping her mouth with the back of her hand.

"Did you keep up with your reading? And practicing your hand at letters?"

"She did," Otto answered for his niece. "She's a better eye for the letters than I do now, though I can still out-sum her."

"Well, let's eat, and then I can put that to the test, eh?" Aelis was hungry, and while Otto and Pips both looked healthier than they'd been when she'd first met them, a hot meal wouldn't do either of them any harm.

The three of them working in concert put quite a dent into the huge crock of beef, onions, and turnips in gravy, and Aelis herself wrought ruin upon the bread by the time Otto finally spoke.

"In truth, Warden . . . I didn't come here only to bring dinner. We've got a bit of a problem down in the village."

"What kind of problem, Otto?"

"There's some new-come folk, arrived out o'the woods."

"Why's that a problem? Are they thieves?"

"Not as I know."

"Murderers?"

Otto shook his head.

"Are they corrupting the morals of innocent sheep, Otto?"

"No," he said, drawing the syllable out slowly.

"Then I'm struggling to see the problem, exactly."

"Well, they just . . . they're not very well liked."

"There was a time, not very long ago, where you could easily say the same of me."

"It's different," Otto burst out. "They're not well-liked people because they've always been a bit . . . above, you know? They always had it easier, lived apart from other folk, looked down their long noses at the rest of us.

And now they've had a bad winter of it and come here looking for help, and . . ."

"And they should get it," Aelis said. "If they're hungry, feed them. If they're cold, give them a spot by the fire, if—"

Otto stood up from his chair with a snort of disgust, and some heat crept into his voice. "That's easy for you t'say, Warden. When have you ever worried about hunger or cold? When have you ever had to work every hour of light and half of the dark to have just enough? And you'll tell *us* to share what we've barely got?"

Aelis felt anger flare white-hot inside her. She was so furious that she could not find her voice fast enough to stop Otto from growling, "Phillipa! Let's go," and loudly stalking toward the door.

Pips turned huge dark eyes from one adult to the other, clearly unsettled, even frightened.

That focused Aelis enough to stand up, and she said clearly and coldly, "I am not done with you, Otto." He was already halfway to the door, then turned around to face her.

"Where are these people now?"

"Down in Rus and Martin's stables." He must've seen the flash of surprise in Aelis's eyes and interpreted it as anger. "There's too many to give rooms to and they won't be separated. Weren't my doing."

"Are they warm, dry, healthy, fed?"

"I don't know. Rus prob'ly fed 'em."

Aelis frowned. *Probably isn't good enough for me to sit this out.* "Wait for me, then."

"Now, Warden, I—"

"Did I give the impression I was *asking?*" Aelis's voice cut the air like a bullwhip. From the corner of her eye, she saw Pips flinch and she felt a moment's regret, but she also wasn't about to back down from the line she'd taken.

She kept Otto waiting while she fetched her belt, scarf, gloves, and heaviest cloak. She saw Pips still staring at her and sighed. "Otto. Please wait outside."

"You just ordered me *not* to leave, what am I . . ."

"*Please,*" Aelis said, her teeth gritted.

Otto gave her still-new door, if not quite a slam, a harder pull than it needed, and Aelis decided not to hear the various curses he muttered.

"Phillipa," she said, looking down at the nearly crying girl, "dry your eyes, please." Her voice was probably colder than she wanted it to sound;

anger was interfering. When the girl didn't move, Aelis took up a clean rag from her worktable and handed it to Pips.

"Now, before I left, I believe I gave you a task. What was it?"

The girl, her eyes unsure and still liquid, held her hand up and pushed back her sleeve; there were three strips of plain cloth tied clumsily around her wrist.

"Three?" Aelis tilted her head. "You had three strange dreams?"

"Aye," Pips said. "An' it was at the end of the green moon-time and the start of the white," she added.

"What were the dreams?"

"One was in a book, but not any o'the ones you've read t'me or let me read. It was somethin' tellin' stories o'Wardens, and there was some sort o'iron skull involved," Pips said. "Not like a real skull made of iron but, just, sorta the shape made out of an iron bar all twisted round itself like."

Aelis held up a hand and went to a locked trunk beneath one of her worktables on the other side of the tower. She bent down and unlocked it, unwrapped the Matrix from its cloth, and brought it to the dining table to hold it under a lamp.

"Did it look like this?"

"Aye," Pips said excitedly. "Just like that." She reached out to touch it, but Aelis yanked it out of the girl's reach.

"Were all the dreams the same?"

"Well, just pictures out o'the book, like woodcuts, only better."

"I see." Aelis wrapped the iron candlestick back up and walked slowly to the trunk where she stored it, thinking. "That is very good, Pips. Thank you for doing as I asked and for remembering the dreams. Why don't you pack up the basket and the crock and the linens and go outside? Ask your uncle to come back in, please."

The girl frowned, confused, then popped up from her seat, gathered what she could, and made for the front door.

Aelis waited with her back turned until she heard the door close, then open and close again, and Otto's careful, reluctant steps come close, but not quite in, to the big central room. Only then did she turn toward him and beckon him closer. He took one step and sniffed.

"I don't much want to sit or come closer, Warden," he said stiffly, "lest you just order me to leave again."

"Otto, this isn't about that." *No way to cushion this.* "I've been teaching Pips to read and write not only as a hobby, or because it'll help her, but because she has latent magical ability." She tried to make the words as precise and clear as she could.

"She has what now?"

"Pips very likely has some ability to work magic. Divination, I'm almost certain, though there's no telling what other talents she might develop in time."

"Our Phillipa is a wizard?"

"No, but with schooling and training, she *might* be. One day. Many years from now."

"How'm I meant t'pay for that?"

"Don't worry too much about that," Aelis said.

"I'm not out for charity, Warden. I'm not one for handouts . . ."

"Wardens can sponsor students at the Lyceum. Once I've finished two years here, I can bring a student to the University. Provided they can do the work and wield the power, they'll not be charged a copper shaving."

"Surely there's other schoolin' needs doing before then."

"There is," Aelis admitted. "And that would not be cheap. But," she added quickly, "I have discretionary funds. And costs can be waived. Magical ability takes first seat over the rich dullards whose families can afford the price."

"Still probably calls for more coin from us than we're ever likely t'have," Otto said.

"It won't cost you anything," Aelis said. "And don't speak to me of charity. It's not a question of that. What Pips just told me was . . . well, it was something momentous."

"What, that piece of iron? Like as not she's seen it in your tower before and just dreamed of it," Otto said, waving a hand dismissively.

"Otto, that only just came into my tower yesterday. I guarantee you, Pips had never seen it before. Prophetic dreams, especially those that involve magical apparatus, events, people, or tomes, are a classic sign of the early stirrings of a Diviner's gift."

"So, where'll she have to go?"

"That's putting the cart before the horse a bit," Aelis said. "She has to want to go. You have to be willing to let her. One at a time. Speak of it with Elmo. Don't tell her what I've told you, not yet. I don't want her to start trying to come up with other dreams or saying what she thinks I want to hear. You understand? Talk it over with Elmo, and come to me when you're ready."

"I will do that, Warden." He thought for a moment, then added, "I don't understand everything you said. But I know that if Pips had a better life waiting for her somewhere, even the chance at one, a life not covered in sheep shit, not working every light hour that's in the day to break her fuckin' back, a life that ain't a bad month from hungry all the time . . ." He trailed off, then went on, his voice thickening. "Well, we'd miss her. But we'd want her to have it."

Aelis sought out Otto's eyes and held them, then took his hand and they shook twice, firmly. "I don't understand much about your life, Otto. But I know you love your niece. We'll figure out what she wants and needs, and how to give it to her. Now we're going to walk down to the village, and I'm going to look in on these newcomers and make sure they are healthy and not likely to do any criminal mischief."

✦   ✦   ✦

"The stables, Rus? Really?" Aelis had pried the innkeeper out of his warm taproom and neither of them was happy to be out trudging in the frozen mud behind the inn.

"I told Otto not to bother you with this till tomorrow," Rus grumbled. "And as to your question, I haven't enough indoor rooms for them all and they wouldn't be split up. Wouldn't even put the children upstairs. I did what I could."

Light leaked out from under the door to the stables. Rus knocked hard on the door before pushing it open. The Dobruszes' wagon team, Rus and Martin's own Pansy, and a few other draft horses were packed closely, into fewer stalls than usual. Two middle stalls had been turned into a straw-and-blanket-filled little den that seemed almost cozy. Blankets were hanging over ropes to grant some privacy. The murmur of voices and the shadows the lanterns cast suggested there were at least half a dozen people within, probably more.

"Warrun," Rus called out softly, "our warden's come to check on your people."

The discussion stilled instantly, replaced by the hum of whispers Aelis couldn't catch without getting much closer. A man's face, shrouded in darkness, slipped out from behind a blanket.

"Don't want to talk to any wizards . . ."

"*Want to* hasn't got anything to do with it," Aelis said. From the corner of her eye, she saw Rus wince. She softened her voice and added, "I need to make sure you're all healthy." She sparked her alchemy lamp to life on her belt and plucked at her black robes. "I'm a physician, anatomist, and surgeon. Rus is doing what he can for you; let me do what I can."

"We're all fine," the man said, before ducking behind the blanket again.

"Can try again in the morning," Rus muttered, but Aelis's spine was up now.

"Warrun," she called out, "this village is under my care and protection. That means you are now as well; it sounds like your people have been living rough. Let me make a quick examination of you tonight to make sure none of you are in any danger. If there's nothing worrying, we needn't talk again until the morning."

There was more murmuring behind the blanket, and Aelis decided she'd had enough of waiting. She stepped forward and yanked the blanket back.

The wide beam of her alchemy lamp revealed a half dozen adults and three children, ranging from roughly Pip's age to a child who likely hadn't walked to Lone Pine on his own feet.

"I'm going to insist on seeing all of you briefly." She turned her lamp on Warrun. "You first."

Grumbling, the folk lined up. Aelis didn't waste their time or hers. She put one hand on her dagger, one to each forehead in turn, and called on the lightest of Necromantic delves. She found sore feet, sore backs, sore shoulders, and signs of age, but none of the frostbite, agues, or fevers she feared among people who'd traveled in the Ystain winter. They could all have stood to eat better, but she had little doubt Rus would see to that.

One incongruous detail she couldn't quite understand was how all these folk were dressed both well *and* shabbily. Warrun, for instance, wore a fine shirt of blue and gray panels with gold and red threads chasing the collar, but it had been patched poorly and with plainer cloth. One of the children was wrapped in a fine fur coat, but the fur was flaking away. All of them had fine cloak pins and well-tooled leather goods that made them seem less like plain Ystainan farmer folk gone desperate and more like well-to-do merchants overcome by debt. But she didn't ask; her visit was purely medical.

When she'd given them each clean bills of health and bade them good night, she found Rus leaning against the stable wall speaking to Pansy, the horse he'd loaned her twice now, gently stroking her nose.

"Didn't take you for a horse man, Rus."

"I grew up on a horse farm. My father was a groom on a de Tarnis estate. Planned to follow him in that work until the war came along." He retrieved the lantern he'd set on a shelf and followed Aelis out into the night.

"I know you have the medical business well in hand, Warden . . ."

"Aelis."

". . . but have you considered that your manner with new folk could maybe stand a little . . . work?"

"How do you mean?"

"I mean that a horse surgeon talks to the animal to soothe it while he inspects its legs or its ears. You lined those folk up, did your magic, and walked away."

By now, they'd reached the back door to the inn.

"They don't teach that at the Lyceum," Aelis said.

"The Lone Pine folk are used to your ways now, or getting there. These new-come wanderers aren't."

"Tell me, Rus, why doesn't Otto want them here?"

The question took the man aback, his typically unblinking face registering shock for a moment. "He said that?"

"In as many words. Didn't seem keen on taking these people into the village."

"Aelis, that's a long story and I've not got the energy to tell it tonight."

"It seems unlike the people of Lone Pine, Rus. They looked askance at me because they saw black robes and thought I was here to make horrors from their bodies and bind their souls, but these are just common folk."

"No," Rus said, shaking his head. "They're not. They're Errithsuns, and they've always kept apart. Of their own choice, it's said."

"They're what?"

"Errithsuns. A family, big one, out of Old Ystain."

"Nobles?"

"Stregon's balls, Aelis, if you're going to pepper me with so many questions, let's at least do it inside where there's warmth and brandy."

25

LONG-DELAYED TREATMENT

Indeed, there was both fire and a full jug of fine brandy to pass. Aelis felt bad keeping Rus awake, so she limited what she asked of him and finally let him seek his bed when she saw Martin come creeping toward them in a nightshirt.

What she learned confused her even more. These Errithsuns must have once held some kind of warrant from the Earl of Mahlgren, given that they lived as woodsfolk without apparent occupation, without troubling themselves much about farming, and with a readier supply of venison than anyone not answering to the term *poacher* was likely to have. They'd apparently been more numerous in the past. She gathered there was some kind of catastrophe after the war that put a dent in them, but that might just have been the aftermath of many of their homes being overrun and then ceded away to conquering orc berserkers.

Aelis pondered all this as she moved about her tower the next morning, putting off the task she knew she had to face sooner rather than later. There was some mystery in these newcomers, but she couldn't let it divert her now.

Her copy of *Advanced Necromancy* lay open on her worktable. She bent over it, read a few lines, and stood up straight.

"Well, the theory's easy. Just like dispersing the various binding and quiescent spells used during surgery. Hmm." She set the ribbon back in place and closed the book. Aelis sat, took up her Anatomist's blade, swung her leg up on to the chair facing her, pulled back her robes, and laid the cold steel against her skin.

It was, on its face, a simple enough Second Order Necromantic dismissal. The spell wasn't unrelated to the Lash or the Necrobane's Fist, but less destructive. After all, she wanted to bring her ankle back to its natural state, not obliterate it. There were a few sentences in the text about preparing the patient and being ready for the aftermath, but she glossed over those as she readied the dismissal. She gathered herself, spoke the words simply and easily, and felt the tingle of magic moving and changing within her.

Then there was a spike of pain so intense that, as if trying to flee it, she pitched forward out of the chair, landing with a hard thump on the cold floor. She lay there a longer while than she wanted, till the cold of the stones seeped into her skin and her leg throbbed with a pain that began in her ankle and traveled up her calf to the back of her knee. She rolled onto her back and thought briefly about gaining her feet, but her ankle brushed against the floor as she turned and sent such waves of agony up her leg that she nearly bit through her bottom lip to keep from crying out.

Aelis took several deep breaths and tried to formulate a plan. She lifted her head to look for her dagger and found it glinting a few paces away. She took it up with a sweaty, shaking hand and pressed the blade against her cheek, mumbling a First Order Diagnostic.

The news that soon came to her through the enchantments on her blade was not heartening.

It took her a moment, given the pain she was in, to determine exactly what her Diagnostic was telling her, to sort through the colors that represented the different systems of the body and then the individual parts of each system.

The sinews that bound muscle and bone in her ankle were all but shredded. Without immediate intervention, she was about to be permanently injured.

"What are my options?" she said, trying to ignore how shaky and thin her voice had become. "Bind it up," she murmured, "well and carefully with wooden splints, and stay immobilized for weeks in the hopes it'll heal itself. Pray to Onoma for a miracle. Write to the Lyceum and beg for another Necromancer to show up and do surgery on my foot."

She considered the alchemical substances she had to hand and what she could make out of them. "Substrate of copper water in an astringent solution with comfrey, star bight, and a bit of wax—how I'd encourage the skin to grow back if burned or cut—that might do something." *But it would have to go on the sinew itself.*

"If I told the Lyceum I had Aldayim's Matrix, they'd send half the damned Archmagisters, and I could have my pick of surgeons."

Not worth it.

She took a deep breath and risked moving her foot a bit. She regretted that action immediately and acutely.

"Well, I do have Aldayim's Matrix," she said. "In a trunk. Across the room." Aelis closed her eyes and took another deep breath. She carefully bent her knee, lifting her calf and foot off the floor, and rolled onto her stomach once more. Then, slowly, painfully, with her ankle throbbing in the air, she began crawling across the floor. When she got to the trunk, she threw it open and stuck one arm in, digging blindly, at last pulling the cloth-wrapped wrought-iron artifact free and setting it down on the floor next to her.

She grasped it in both hands, and it was only then she realized she was going to need to get candles and other materials.

Aelis dragged herself to the chair she'd fallen out of and set the Matrix on it, then pulled herself to her knees, cursing and shivering with cold and pain. Then she moved the Matrix to the table and laboriously dragged herself into the chair.

"I could live here," she muttered through sharp breaths. "Just in this chair. Forever. Pay someone to bring me meals. Wouldn't be so bad. Get the occasional sponge bath, maybe."

There were a handful of candles in holders atop her table. She seized them and jammed them into the candlestick. Then she realized that the fire, small as it was, was all the way across the tower.

"Gods damn this nonsense," she spat, then forced herself onto one foot. Her balance was awkward, but the table held her up, and then the wall, as she went and seized the walking stick Tun had made her. She jammed it hard under her right armpit, angling it a bit for length, and found herself hobbling swiftly around to gather what she needed, finally stopping at the hearth to build up the fire in it and to light a long straw. With the candles lit, she sat down in her chair and reached for the Matrix, taking it in one hand.

The instant she felt contact, she thought, *I know there's no grave dirt or bone dust, but this is the third time I've used this device. It shouldn't be necessary. I should be attuned to it now.*

"Well, perhaps it's not necessary, but it might be cordial," came the Professor's voice.

"What are you suggesting? Is it like the stories of giving blood and mead to a spirit, to remind it of the life it had lived, and then to pepper it with questions?"

"I am not a spirit, merely an echo, a piece of the design of the Matrix. I have never had a life. But my creator believed a great deal in observing the form of things."

"I'll try to bear that in mind in the future."

"How long do you plan to use the Matrix?"

"As little as possible but as often as I need."

"That is a very flip answer. What do you ask today?"

"I, ah . . . may have necrotized some functional tissue for longer than is generally recommended."

"Tsk. What tissue, and how long?"

"An ankle. Specifically, the sinews of an ankle. And . . ." Here, Aelis hesitated. "For . . . two or three weeks? Maybe more. Not quite a month, though."

"Three weeks? The maximum recommended time is three *days*! What kind of Anatomist *are* you?"

"One who was desperate and had work to do that required a fully functional ankle."

"Onoma's rotting breath, you did this to yourself? Well, I hope you have no need of that foot. Your best bet is to have it amputated."

"Let me be a little more specific about my situation. I am a Warden, the only one for—I'd guess—a hundred miles in any direction. Possibly two hundred. I cannot afford to be incapacitated. I do not know if there is another Necromancer, much less a competent Anatomist and Surgeon, within twice that distance."

"There is no precedent for this. There is nothing I can tell you."

"There doesn't need to be precedent," Aelis said, or thought she said. Conversation with a wrought-iron candlestick quickly got metaphysically confusing, she'd found. "What I need is to know if something I plan to do is possible."

"If it has not been done and recorded, it . . ."

"Substrate of copper water in an astringent solution with star bight, comfrey, and wax to bind it."

"Well, my library indicates that yes, that could theoretically encourage and even hasten healing on badly frayed sinews and muscle tissue. Congratulations on devising a new medicament for topical application . . ."

"If the area is properly numbed and the alchemical mixture I described is applied internally, directly to the damaged tissue?"

"For which you'd need an Enchanter as well as an Anatomist."

"I am both of those."

There was a long, looming pause.

"You want to perform surgery on yourself?"

"I wouldn't say I *want* to. But is such a thing possible?"

"I have no record of it." Another pause. "And while it seems an indescribably stupid idea full of insurmountable obstacles, that does not mean it is impossible. Under ideal conditions, the correct room and diagnostic tools could make it possible."

"I have my Anatomist's blade. There'll be no sterile room, no Diviners or Illusionists mapping it for me."

"A Warden with one good foot is preferable to a dead one."

"They'll never let me stay a Warden."

"In the days when this device was constructed, Wardens were not demoted or discharged due to injury received in discharging their duty. There are Wychwood limbs . . ."

"The control of which is tightly regulated. I'll never get one. They will recall me from my post, stick me at a desk somewhere at an outpost or at Cabal Command, and when my time is up, they'll pat me on the head and discharge me with a minor pension and a letter of introduction to go tutor some noble children."

"That is not a bad life. It is one many wizards would covet."

"I am not many wizards. I am a Warden, and I intend to remain one. I also have obligations in the region where I am posted. Obligations that go beyond standard Warden tasks."

"If you are insistent on this foolish course, I have gathered the necessary procedures and Orders. But you must trade a secret for them."

"Fine," Aelis said. "At the Lyceum, I think I . . . once wrote a paper for someone."

"Most graduates of the Lyceum write papers for people. Provided those people are their professors or their tutors."

Aelis imagined her indrawn breath hissing over her teeth. "I wanted a friend of mine to succeed at this specific class very badly. I offered to help her with the paper. I helped more than I ought to have done."

"And what class was this?"

"First Year Abjurer's Theory. She couldn't quite wrap her head around explaining the warp and weft of raising Wards and was struggling to get her paper done."

"And your help consisted of what, precisely?"

Aelis imagined clearing her throat. "Taking the pen away from her and scribbling a couple of quick paragraphs."

"Collaboration is vital to the improvement and understanding of any magical theory."

"Which she then took whole, made into her thesis, and wrote the rest of the paper around."

"Ah." The Professor's voice was so dry in her mind, it sounded like frozen leaves shattering. She felt the weight of his judgment. "So your work was substituted for hers."

"Yes."

There was a short, heavy silence. "Technically, if you had given her permission to use this work, it is not entirely dishonest. I do not suppose your work was presented as, perhaps, a lecture or proposition and the rest of the work unspooled as a classic disputation?"

"No," Aelis said. "I helped her write the paper because I wanted her to be done with it so we could go out drinking."

"Is that all?"

"And . . . so that we could fall into bed after we came back from the wineshops."

"Ah." The voice fell silent, but Aelis felt less sting of judgment.

"Did you not have your own paper to write?"

"I already had. I never procrastinated."

"Because you wanted the time for drinking?"

"I don't rest well with an unsolved problem."

The Professor chuckled. "Very well. This moment clearly weighs on you, and it is a secret. Be prepared to write down this list when I am done . . ."

◆　◆　◆

Aelis looked over the list she'd hurriedly scribbled down.

Clean room certified by Invokers. Silver fixtures if possible.

A Diviner to confirm the probabilities.

An Illusionist to map the course of the surgery upon a mirror.

"Well," she said, papering over the sinking feeling in her stomach with mock brightness, "I can rule out those three." She drew careful lines straight through all of them.

An Enchanter to cast Zezum's Numbness and Iphegnum's Feel Not.

"That, at least, I can do. The first one, anyway," she said. "Try to do the second one and I'm likely to drop the tools halfway through."

The rest of the list described fairly basic surgical techniques; where and how to place Blood Bindings to stop blood flow to the area, where to make the first incisions, how to locate the impacted tissues, and so on.

"Going to be the rest of this day to make the compound anyway." Shoving her walking stick beneath her armpit, she levered herself to her feet and went to the trunk that held her alchemical supplies.

Pure water, Number 2 copper discs, dried comfrey and star bight, she had. She took an ordinary block of wax and left that and the herbs in place.

From another trunk, she took out a small sphere with a tube projecting from it, all made of strong cast iron.

She slung a small pack over her shoulder and put the water and copper discs into it, along with the sphere and fire-making supplies, and still using her stick as a crutch, made her way around the wall and furniture of her tower, sweating the entire time. When she got to the calcination oven, she was delighted to find a pile of wood in the basket.

She primed the oven appropriately, churning its magical heart into wakefulness with a single First Order Necromantic Delving that she dropped into it. Almost instantly, it began to warm. Before she did anything else, she took the sphere she'd selected from her tools and felt along the upper lefthand side of the oven. When she came to the switch she sought, she flipped it opening a small round porthole precisely the size of the sphere, which she screwed into place.

Then she began to build the woodpile the oven would need to work its alchemical process. She swung open one of the oven's many compartments—the one closest to the latch where she'd screwed in the sphere. Into that, she placed an open crucible full of two measures of water and three of the small copper discs. She shut and carefully latched closed the oven's door, double-checked the woodpile and the fit of the Substrate Sphere. Then she placed the tinder, struck sparks, and stepped back.

The heat of the oven instantly flared, filling her tower. The wood she'd placed in the fuel compartment roared brilliantly into bright white flame, the logs consumed as she watched.

♦   ♦   ♦

The rest of the day she passed by building a proper brace for her ankle, reading, and beginning to compose the first of the reports she'd have to send onward, tinkering with the exact wording of the draft and how much information it revealed.

The next day, having slept better than she'd anticipated, she woke up and collected the Substrate of Copper Water into her tightly stoppered sphere. She melted the wax over an alchemy burner, poured precise measures of dried comfrey and star bight into it, then uncapped the sphere.

She upended it, and tiny white flakes poured into the hot wax, which she stirred with a nearly flat silver spoon. The wax immediately took on a sort of shimmer with hints of green and gold in it, and a fresh, clean smell wafted up from the bowl.

"Well," she said. "At least step one is down."

She initially thought of climbing onto one of her tables, but she couldn't visualize how to make that work, so she settled on building a kind of brace on the edge of the table and testing what angle she could bend her leg to in order to work. It took some adjustments, and the work would hardly be comfortable, with her leg pushed quite high into the air so she could see the ankle clearly.

"At least it'll discourage blood flow if the Bindings don't hold," she said.

Then it was on to Zezum's Numbness, a long-lasting localized pain block that was relatively easy to maintain.

"At least so long as one isn't busy cutting open one's own flesh at the time, I suppose," she muttered. She checked, double-checked, and triple-checked her supplies; the jar of waxed medicament; the knives, three of varying sizes; two sets of small forceps; open jars of astringent and alchemical wound-clot; bandages and bindings; her wand; her Anatomist's blade. Then there was the mirror she'd, for lack of an armature to hook it to, hung off one of the swinging arms of her once again immobile orrery. It provided an imperfect and slightly quivering reflection of the site she intended to work on, but it was the best she could do. The orrery was still, not because it was completely drained—in the days since her return, she'd carefully built it back up. She hadn't turned it on, because she wanted the battery of magical power ready to hand if her finger slipped.

She checked everything once more, wondered if there was anything she was missing, and sucked in a quick breath. She swung her leg into place and made sure it felt secure.

Aelis took up her wand and laid the tip against the tenderest, most swollen part of her ankle, summoning a quick bright point of power and speaking the hushed words of the ward.

Immediately, the dull throb, the constant ache of her ankle receded. She tested it with probing fingers, then her thumb, then the heel of her hand with as much pressure as she could muster.

She felt nothing.

Aelis laid her Anatomist's blade against the bare skin of her other leg, then took up a knife. She drew in a small centering breath, held it, and cut into her own flesh.

✦ ✦ ✦

Last: Important to note have pioneered self-surgical technique for emergency repair of damaged tissue. Required use of Necromancy, Abjuration, and Enchantment in concert.

Aelis reread the notes she was composing for her orrery's transmission to its twin sitting in the Diviners' College in the Lyceum, looked over by an advanced student or even a newly fledged Wizard working his way to a coveted assistant professorship.

There was a heavy knock at the door. Through force of habit, she threw a handy blank sheet over the tiny letters she'd been carefully scratching into the tiny parchment before yelling, "Come in!"

A gust of cold air preceded Tun into the tower, but as he made his way into the main sitting room, he went straight to the hearth, seizing the poker and stirring the fire into roaring life.

He turned and looked at her then, pulling back his snow-crusted hood. "It smells of blood and wounds in this room. Not freshly so. But not so long ago as when you were attacked here."

"I performed some minor surgery on myself yesterday."

Tun thought over his response a moment. "Is there such a thing as minor surgery performed on *yourself*?"

"No, but I thought I'd try my hand at being humble."

"Doesn't suit you."

She snorted and took her walking stick in hand, rising gingerly to her feet. Her ankle was sore, carefully bound up in the tightest brace she could make. "I need a drink. You?"

"Why not," he said.

Aelis rummaged about a bit in one of the packing crates she'd gotten just a few short weeks ago, though it felt like a lifetime, and pulled out another bottle of Tirravalan red.

"Is your ankle well?"

"It'll be a few days before I can do much more than limp around my tower."

"Is it true," Tun said, as she began working at the cork with an auger, "that in Tirraval, they open wine bottles with a feather?"

"Only if they're feeling fancy. And it's not really the feather, but rather a combination of heat applied to the bottle followed by ice-cold water. It's a trick."

"To the uneducated, it must appear like magic."

The cork came free with a pop. "The wine is the only magic I'm interested in just now."

"Draining, then? The surgery?"

"Indeed," she said, filling two cups near to the brim and passing one to him. "A lot of small enchantments and abjurations. I had to invent miniature

Wards on the fly, coupling them with a Necromancer's sense of the body, in order to prevent the sinews I was repairing from snapping."

Tun took a sip of his wine and considered it thoughfully, his head tilted. "This is an excellent vintage. Lots of sun and not much rain that year, I take it."

"Why do you say that? Where did you learn about wine?"

"Same place I learned my vocabulary, inductive and deductive logic, mathematics, history, languages. But I *know* that because I can *smell* it."

"Is this your way of telling me you knew about my ankle?"

"I knew that something smelled wrong. Off. Not quite dead, not quite alive. A bit like the animations, to be honest. Though not as bad as the tooth-monster." Tun shivered, catching Aelis off guard. "Nothing," he said, "in this or any world, can smell as badly as that monstrosity did."

"Then why not say something?"

"You preserved my secret. It seemed only fair to do the same. But you also said that by the fire in your tower, with a bottle of wine to hand, you'd answer my questions." He sat forward, eyes narrowed. "What did you do?"

"I necrotized it. Made it dead, so that it would feel no pain and continue operating as I needed it to."

"You can make parts of yourself . . . dead?"

"In an emergency, yes." She raised her hand to gain time to wet her lips with wine. "It was developed as a way for a Necromancer to make herself or others deadlier in combat. But it has some life-saving potential as well."

"How does one technique do both of those things?"

"There are spells that summon weapons and implements that flesh is not meant to touch. It can also, apparently, put a wounded person back on their feet to do tasks that must be done, and I can see other uses; necrotize a wounded piece of flesh and a parasite might flee, allowing for easier rev-ifivication. It was another piece of sheer brilliance from Aldayim . . . and I can tell you don't want to hear about necromantic brilliance. I get *excited* about my primary discipline, Tun. I'm sorry it's unpleasant."

She drained her cup and reached for the bottle. "It was't a good idea, Tun. But I saw no alternatives."

"Because you did not look for any, like waiting till it was better traveling weather to begin the whole business in the first place . . ."

"I know, I know, I have to learn to plan." She shook her head as she set the bottle, already worryingly light, back down. "You want a plan, ask a Diviner. You want something to *happen*, point an Abjurer in the right direction."

"I am not suggesting that you change fundamental aspects of your identity, Aelis. Only that you consider less impulsive action. That is all."

"Well, I don't intend to engage in any actions, one way or another, till this storm blows over."

"It will be some time. But I think it likely this will be the last great storm of the winter. It will flurry, of course, drop an inch here and there. But not much more."

"Did you see the newcomers?"

"Heard," Tun said. "Avoided, lest they go blundering into the storm at the sight of me. But Rus did tell me to let you know he'd convinced them to come inside and take rooms, even if it meant being separated."

Aelis let out a relieved sigh. "That had been weighing on me a bit, Tun." *Now I can go back to just worrying about Maurenia all the time.* "Why was Otto so . . . hesitant about them?"

"Well—" Tun toyed with the wine cup she'd handed him; it looked like a child's teacup in his hands. "The Errithsuns are not well-liked folk in the main."

If she hadn't known Tun well, if she hadn't learned to watch him and his words carefully, she would never have seen how he stiffened when he said the name.

She leaned forward. "You know the name," she said. "Errithsun. You know the folk?"

"I knew a man who was related to them, though he had little to do with them. But he had family: brothers, sisters, cousins, children, nephews, nieces. A veritable backwoods empire of Errithsuns, before the end of the war, anyway."

"I gather they're a little more scarce now. Harder to live alone deep in the forest without the protection of the earl, I take it?"

"Something like that," Tun said with a bitter laugh that was entirely unlike him.

"What happened, then? Disease? Orcs? Bad harvests?"

"As to what happened to this current crop to bring them to Lone Pine? I couldn't tell you. Haven't seen any in years. The old days, though, when they practically ruled the woods out of the duke's or the king's view?" He pressed his lips together around his tusks. "I suspect orcs happened. There was a war, after all." He held out his wine cup and Aelis emptied the rest of the bottle into it. She couldn't quite shake the suspicion that he had more to say. She waited.

He took a long sip of the wine and held out a hand.

"I know your head is filled with questions, Aelis. I ask you, out of friendship, please do not ask them."

She forced words back down her throat by filling her mouth with wine, and they sat in silence and drank through that bottle and another, staring at the fire.

26

DEEP WINTER

Snow fell, proving true Otto's prediction that the roads would become impassable before Aelis could leave Lone Pine again. The wind rose and swirled and found its way into the tower even through the stone walls, occasionally scattering papers about the room.

The sheet with Maurenia's name at the top had grown crowded with rows and columns of short, angry slashes that now ran almost a quarter of the way down its length. It had been secured at each corner with heavy objects to prevent any stray gust from carrying it off.

Aelis's mornings were for sword-forms, spell meditations, and such exercise as she could get. At least once a week, three times if the weather allowed it, she walked down to the village proper to see to the medical needs of the people. Chilblains and other conditions of cold and moisture-damaged skin were the most common complaints. Her most common treatment was an admonition to stay dry and warm, but eventually she found herself making a topical treatment from animal fats, goat liver, and alchemical salts. Occasionally, there were sprains and even fractures from falls on the ice or the slippery conditions created by snow. When she saw cold-damaged skin for the third time on a member of one family, she organized a party of laborers to spend a day making repairs to their house and paid some of the better weavers and knitters to produce new stockings, gloves, and mittens quickly. Back in her tower, she tinkered with warded boxes that might keep outer garments dry, or dry them quickly, but realized that doing so would take expensive materials and a knowledge of Invocation she did not have.

She saw few people socially. Tun occasionally made it to her tower when the snows weren't too bad, and they talked, or he borrowed a book and read it by the fire. Sometimes when she was in the village, she came by his hut, ostensibly to check on his health, which was as unchanging as the cold.

Aelis saw little of the Errithsuns, but what she did see worried her.

Their boots were splitting, their few garments too fine and thin for this kind of weather, and they were too proud, apparently, to ask for more than they already had. She engaged in her usual battle of wills with Rus over money, then finally went around him and snuck to the back door with the idea of pressing a purse into Martin's hands.

She found him sitting on a stool next to his stove reading by a lantern on a hook over his head.

"What's that you're reading?"

Martin took a moment to answer, then closed the book around a fingertip to hold his place. "Oh, just some bits of silliness. *The Ballads of Gavelden the Graceful and Balendin the Bulwark*. I never could get enough of these chivalric romances."

Aelis smiled. "I never would have guessed that about you, Martin."

"You'd think going to war would have taken some of the music out of these silly poems and stories, but nothing quite does. To what do I owe the visit, Aelis?"

She took the purse out and held it out to him. "For putting up these Errithsun folk. I know Rus won't take it, but food and fuel and drink cost your silver and time." She made a motion to toss it to him underhanded. He nodded, she threw it, and he snatched it deftly out of the air.

"They've tried to pay in jewelry, but Rus won't take that either; says it's a bandit who takes a family heirloom to pay for a crust and a mug. To tell the truth, I don't know how they're going to fit in here."

"There's plenty of land available. Are they afraid they can't afford it?"

"Could be it. Could be they haven't been farmers before and don't want to be now."

"What are they then? Craftsfolk? I can give them a loan to buy tools and set up, and I won't charge any interest . . ."

Martin sighed and set his book down, marking the page with a ribbon. "I think you'd better talk to them. People hereabouts will forget the name Errithsun and why they don't like hearing it if Warrun and his family just get to the business of living. But they won't like the idea of supporting people who used to look down at them, or run them or their family out of their woods at arrowpoint. They held themselves apart so long . . ."

"I'll go talk to them," Aelis said.

Moments later she was just about to knock at one of the doors Rus had directed her to, when another opened.

Andresh, his beard and hair still wet from a bath, came out into the hall wearing only a sleeveless tunic over short pants. His cheeks were flushed, and he let out a rapid-fire array of dwarfish at her before pointing one finger at her, then at the floor. He disappeared back into his room, and Aelis, suspecting she'd been ordered to stay put, was too stunned to move.

When he came back out, his eyes still flared with anger. He held out one of the gems Aelis had taken from the vault in Mahlhewn Keep so that she could see it.

The muscles of his arms were as thick and corded as tree limbs, and the knuckles of his hands the size of walnuts, observations Aelis made while preparing a ward. He said not another word, just grasped the gem—a dazzlingly clear blue stone—in his fist and squeezed, staring hard into Aelis's face the entire time. He opened his hand and flung priceless dust at Aelis's feet, then stalked back into his room and shut the door.

Aelis felt her heartbeat slow and released the power of the ward she'd been gathering. A quick recitation of her Abjurer's litany restored her calm, at least physically, but she still didn't know what to make of what had just happened. She pushed the thought of Andresh away and knocked on the door.

It opened only slightly, with Warrun's sad, bleary eyes filling the crack.

"Come to talk," Aelis said. "About what brought you here and what to do now that you are here."

"What if I don't want to talk?" Warrun said, not opening the door any further. "We are none of us criminals, we're just unlucky folk who fled our home."

"I'm not here to accuse anyone of a crime, man," Aelis said. "But you came to this village in the middle of winter when people around here don't travel. Makes me think you might be the *victim* of a crime. If bandits or the like chased you out of your home, if that home was still inside the agreed-upon borders, then it's my *job* to find out. Do you want to tell me?"

Warrun opened the door, and Aelis saw that the room held three other people: Warrun's wife, Kellyn, and two children.

Warrun wiped at his eyes, and Aelis saw he wore on his pinky a ring, bright gold with a round, dark green stone. The fraying fur cloak she remembered from the night she'd met him was pinned around the neck of a boy maybe half Pips's age by similarly fine jewelry, three of the same dark stones set in it.

"This is Edder," Warrun said, introducing the boy, "and that's Margreth," he added, pointing to a girl a couple of years younger who looked shyly at Aelis and went to hide behind her mother.

"What brought you here, Warrun? Was it bandits? Orcs?"

"Was the ghost," Edder said from inside his too-big cloak.

"The what?"

27

GHOSTS

Warrun yelled at the boy; Kellyn hissed warnings at him. Aelis silenced them both with one of Urizen's favorite tricks: remaining absolutely still, unblinking, focused on the object of her attention, the boy, Edder.

When his parents at last quieted and turned to her, Edder clamped his mouth shut.

"Warden, we're . . ."

Aelis held her hand up to forestall Warrun's excuses. "I want to hear what the boy has to say."

"It's just nonsense . . ."

"If there's ghosts involved, I'll decide what's nonsense. Talk to me, if you would, Edder."

The boy looked from his father to his mother and then back to Aelis, then shook his head.

"It's no one's business," Kellyn said. Warrun opened the door, and his wife came to Aelis's side. When Kellyn's hand landed on her shoulder, Aelis turned her angry glare full-force on her.

"It is precisely my business. Now, you can explain to me on your own or I can enchant you one by one to drag it out of you. There's clearly some dangerous story behind your coming here, and I *will* have it."

Kellyn tried to match her stare but couldn't. Warrun looked at the floor, at his splitting boots, and said, "Please, Warden, no magic. We'll talk."

"Fine." Aelis wasn't sure she was up to Enchanting anyone, much less three or four people. Her ankle was letting her know that her analgesics were wearing off, and her odd encounter with Andresh had her off-balance. She gestured to the bed, and father and son both sat down on it; Kellyn picked up the younger child and carried her to the window.

"It was in the fall. Things started going . . . wrong. Bowstrings snapped. Tools broke. A shedful of grain went moldy . . ."

Aelis watched Warrun's face intently as he spoke, unfolding a tale of the kind of woes common to people hacking together a living in the wilderness without a wider support system. Individually, these were not necessarily too taxing, but taken together in rapid succession, they spelled doom for a family on their own. But if Aelis was hearing him right, they weren't exactly on their own.

"Warrun, forgive me," Aelis said, breaking in. "How many families lived on this property you describe?"

"Mine and both of my brothers'," he muttered.

"And your brother, his wife, they are two of the other adults here?"

"Aye, Gerrin, his wife, Mureal, our sister, Breda . . ."

"And your other brother?"

Warrun swallowed hard. "Finlo wouldn't leave."

"Not even with a ghost?"

"He didn't believe there was a ghost." He looked sidelong at Edder. "Not sure I do either."

"Tell me about the ghost then, Edder." Aelis softened her voice and turned to look at the boy huddling in his cloak as if he was suddenly cold. "I promise you, if there *is* a ghost and I can find it, I'll make sure it can't come back."

"It came on the night the big stone broke," the boy whispered.

"Big stone?" Aelis looked to Warrun.

"Part of the foundation of our house," Warrun explained. "It cracked."

"Snapped loud and woke me up," Edder said. "I looked out and saw something flitting around the house . . ." He got quiet and pulled the cloak tighter around himself.

"Do you often wake up at night?"

The boy shook his head.

"What did the thing look like?"

"It was hard to see, except for the eyes."

"What did they look like?"

"Blue. Bright blue. Blue in the middle o'nothin'."

"Did it say anything?"

"Not as I could understand . . ."

Warrun put his arm around his son protectively. "Warden! Must we . . ."

"Just a couple more questions, I promise," Aelis said softly. "It did speak, but not words you could understand?"

Huddled deep in his cloak, behind his father's arm, the boy nodded again.

"Did you get any kind of feeling when you were around the ghost?"

"I did. Like it wanted me to come outside," the boy said in a rush. "I ran away and hid, and in the morning, it was gone."

"Did it ever come back?"

The boy shook his head, and his father said, "Warden, I must insist . . ."

Aelis looked closely at Warrun, at the jewel on his finger and his ruined finery, and felt strongly that she did not trust this man, though she could not quite grasp why.

"Warrun, can you draw me a map to get to your house?"

"Why?"

"Because if there was a ghost, if you were haunted out of the place, it is very much my business. When the weather allows, I'd like to go have a look. Perhaps your brother is still there, and things have gotten better, no? If it were possible, would you want to move back?"

"I . . . why would you help us, Warden? We're not your people."

"You're sitting in Lone Pine, Warrun," Aelis said with a warmth she did not entirely feel. "That makes you my people."

Aelis left the Errithsuns' room on an increasingly painful ankle. She briefly considered asking Rus if there was a spare room for her, but decided she badly needed to get back to her tower and sort through her thoughts, see if she could figure out exactly which part of Warrun's family story she didn't fully believe. *It's not what I don't believe. It's what I don't see yet*, Aelis thought. *The fall. What happened in the fall? That's just after I arrived in Lone Pine.*

Down in the taproom, she found Timmuk smoking before the fire and dragged herself over to him, leaning heavily on her walking stick.

"Afternoon, Warden," the dwarf said.

"Timmuk." She paused. "Could you perhaps explain to me why your brother felt the need to crush a gem taken out of the vault and throw the dust at my boots?"

"Ah." Timmuk removed his pipe and considered the stem. "I believe he was telling you that you could not buy your way out of your obligation to our mutual friend."

"I wasn't trying to."

"I know. It was a warning, of a kind." Timmuk looked from his pipe to her. "I am Andresh's elder brother, and I can restrain him, to some degree. But he doesn't take oaths and intentions and feeling badly as seriously as he does *results*."

Aelis put a hand before her eyes. "Timmuk, if it seems like I'm not consumed by what happened to Maurenia, it's because I force myself not to be. I know I don't have the resources or the knowledge to win her freedom here . . ."

"Then what are you doing about *getting* it?"

"I sent a request for books and other gear I think I'll need via my orrery. I haven't received a response yet, but if it's approved, I'll still need someone to bring it here. Someone fast and reliable."

Timmuk turned the dottle out of his pipe into the hearth. "Have anyone in mind?"

"I might," Aelis said.

"And if your request from the Lyceum isn't approved at all?"

"Then I will have to spend a great deal of money buying what I need myself. Needing to hire a courier would still apply."

"I see," Timmuk said. "Well, the roads'll be passable any day now, and we'll be pulling out. Best have that list ready for us."

"I will," Aelis said. "In the meantime, I don't suppose I could borrow a horse."

Timmuk raised one bushy eyebrow in question.

"Just back to my tower," Aelis said. "My ankle won't make it there."

"Sure," Timmuk said. "The beasts could use some exercise anyway. Sit and have yourself a drink while I get a pair of them ready."

◆　◆　◆

Timmuk's wagon did more than carry her back to her tower; it brought her enough stores of bread, hard cheese, oats, wood, and beer to see out a couple of weeks. By the time she was inside, her ankle was no good for anything more strenuous than sitting and reading. Timmuk grumbled as he wrested the barrel of fresh beer against the wall.

"Where I come from, it's common to tip the porter. Generously."

"How about the porter consider himself free to enjoy the contents of the barrel?"

"That'll do," Timmuk agreed, and Aelis limped to one of her tables for a clean cup. Her eyes fell on a sheaf of papers, and she snatched them up as well. She carried them to Timmuk and handed him the cup, then said, "While you drink, I want you to look at this."

The papers she handed over included the sheet with "Maurenia" at the top, which had a mark on it for every day she was trapped. Each page beneath it was covered with script that started small and regular and eventually grew blurred and sloppy or trailed off to barely legible lines. Each had a different heading: *Woodshade bargain? Revive Rhunival? Swap or Trick Summons? Dispel Binding?*

Under those headings, Aelis had tried writing out different plans for freeing Maurenia. Much of that was obscure magical theory, mere supposition that she couldn't substantiate with the small library she had at her disposal. But as Timmuk riffled through the papers, his beer set forgotten on the hearth, she looked at her copy of Kiaw's *Taxonomy of Spirits*, with several extra ribbons strung throughout it highlighting various pages.

"There's one thing I can try from here, and I don't want to get hopes up. Mine or yours or hers."

"What's that?"

"Killing Dalius Enthal de Morgantis un Mahlgren," Aelis said. "For good this time."

"Why would that free Renia?"

"Because Dalius summoned and bound Rhunival to that place. I think it's possible that if he is truly destroyed, all his work will go with him, and whatever that woodshade did will likewise dissipate."

Timmuk considered this for a moment and set the papers slowly down. "Do you know how to do that?"

"I think I do," Aelis said. "I just have to find him. And now I think I know how to do that," and as she said the words, the pieces snapped into place in her mind.

◆　◆　◆

After Timmuk left, Aelis decided to get to work. She dipped a mug into the barrel the dwarf had tasted for her and found the beer too warm and too sour.

"I could do something about the first; get some snow, pack it in salt, concoct a tincture that would draw whatever heat remained out of it . . ." She had another sip as she pondered what ingredients she could use to make such an alchemical preparation. Then, in a sudden bolt of inspiration, she got out her largest pot, filled it full of beer, pulled open the door to her tower, and plopped the pot onto the ramp to let the cold night air and the flitting snow do their work.

She sat gingerly down in front of her copy of Kiaw and flipped it open to one of the ribbon-marked pages.

"Apparitions, Haunts, Specters, Spirits, and Vapors," she read aloud. "Understanding the differences." She settled in to read, and an hour or so passed before she came upon a classification that made her sit up straight up her chair.

"The Beguiling Blood Haunt" began with two woodcuts: in the first, a wizard, with the requisite tall hat and staff, drawn to a window by a spectral, loosely defined shape.

In the second, the wizard, having opened the window and been exsanguinated by the spirit's sudden intrusion into his body, sagged to the floor like a large wineskin that had been punctured. The spirit was a bright red shape, heavily inked with shadows, swirling over the drooping, limp corpse.

The Beguiling Blood Haunt is perhaps the source of legends of Vampires and other bloodsucking fiends (see Ursuela's monograph, Blood Beasts, Exsanguination Experiences, and Other Legends *for a full discussion of same). The Beguiling Blood Haunt is very definitely a spirit, however, and has no corporeal presence except that which it momentarily gains by interacting with the blood of victims."*

Aelis lowered the book, and the line of her gaze fell directly on one of her trunks. Before she even knew what was happening, she was opening it and pulling out a bag carefully buried under rags, equipment, and books. The bag was heavy in her hand, the sand shifting over the hard, round wood it covered. She looked closely at the silver wire wound around the leather thong that held the bag closed.

"Every time a Null Cage is opened, it is less effective," she said aloud, slowly and carefully. "Do I actually want to do this now, here?"

She glanced at the only two papers she'd left on her desk. One was titled "Killing Dalius?" The other was her latest drawing of the man she'd seen in the vision from Aldayim's Matrix.

"Onoma's breath, do I ever."

She immediately pried the silver wire off, untied the bag, and carried it to her table.

＋　＋　＋

Hours later, the time and her pot of cold beer at her front door forgotten, she had a candlestick at either elbow and her alchemy lamp propped on a pile of books, pointing a wide, bright beam at the trap she was holding.

Aelis had spent the first hour simply turning the thing over and over in her hands, wearing gloves to keep her skin from coming in contact with the soft lead sheets wrapped around it. She studied the designs on its face, sketching them carefully on sheets of paper. A part of her knew that she should've waited till full daylight to take on any part of this task.

But here she was, painstakingly unwinding the silver wires that bound the trap, then the lead strips. She put the lead and silver both back into the bag with the sand, closed the bag, tied it, and shoved it to the end of her table. Then she opened her medical kit, selected a delicate steel blade, and set it down on a clean scrap of paper. From her alchemical supplies, she got her thinnest sheet of silver foil, carefully pressed it around the edge of the blade until it was well covered, then tugged away the ragged edges of the foil. It wouldn't have done for surgery that way, with bits of foil curling along the edge of the scalpel, but for what she planned, it might just work. She was about to touch the blade to one of the symbols when she stopped, got one of her smaller silver needles out, and decided to use that, starting with the smallest rune.

She touched the very tip of the silver needle to it and immediately felt herself overwhelmed by craving. She had no words for it, not even concepts, nothing but a deep-seated and horrible *need* that had no starting point, no end, no bottom, no dimension. It was a fathomless hunger, vast and infinite yet also contained. The need, the craving, the want, the hunger, it strained at its bonds, it snapped and snarled and raged at them, soundless and wordless and towering in its rage against its captivity.

Stunned, Aelis pulled the needle away. "Well," she said. "I think we're dealing with a Beguiling Blood Haunt."

Her other candidates had been an Eerie Sister and a Widow Grieving O'er the Waves. She could safely rule out an Eerie Sister; nothing about its classification or behavior was quite that hideously hungry and violent in its basic nature. It would kill its victim, sure, but by draining them of their life slowly while posing as a family member, in a dream if it had to. There was nothing this directly confrontational.

"So how is a Beguiling Blood Haunt created?" She thought back over the entry she'd just read. *A violent murder is strictly necessary. The victim who becomes the Haunt most likely does not understand the reason or know the perpetrator. It seems most likely to occur if the victim's throat is slit or some other wound is delivered that causes death through exsanguination. The most likely configuration of the moons is . . .*

Even fresh in her memory, it trailed off at the boring math-and-calculations bit.

Aelis ruminated on the bit about not knowing the perpetrator. If the victim of a murder knew who had killed them and became a vengeful spirit, said vengeance was likely to be focused tightly on that person. Whereas a Blood Haunt would lure and kill absolutely anyone and anything it could get and would never stop until it was destroyed.

Which made what she was holding the most potent—and most unpredictable—weapon she had ever held. A sword was only as good as the hand that wielded it, and though Aelis knew herself more than merely competent, she could be easily overmatched by numbers.

A Beguiling Blood Haunt could probably destroy a small *army*.

On the one hand, she thought she should wrap it back up immediately, stow it away, and forget it existed.

"On the other hand, if someone breaks into my tower and seizes this, it could destroy the entire village of Lone Pine," she said out loud. Realizing she was halfway out of her chair, Aelis sat back down, then touched the needle to another, slightly larger rune.

This time the hate, the anger, the greed was more directed. Something had been *taken* from the spirit housed within this trap, something vital and strong and beautiful, and it wanted revenge. It wanted the life that had gushed out of it, to stuff itself full of what had been spilled, to kill and drink and kill again and drink more, drink until the world was empty.

Aelis sat back, wiping sweat from her brow. She set down the needle and the trap and went back to the book, tracing a finger down paragraphs till she got to Dispersal or Destruction.

Invokers have reported success with Fourth Order combinations of light and heat, with Mrzad's Sun Whip being particularly effective. Other swear by Fire Lances . . .

"Invokers think fire is the solution to everything," Aelis scoffed. She scanned the pages for any Necromantic destructions. The Necrobane's Hand and the Lash both made appearances, but since the Hand demanded actual physical contact, it was strongly interdicted; once a Blood Haunt had the scent, much less the taste, of someone's blood, it would frenzy until it had drunk them dry.

Aelis began pacing behind her table, thinking over her options. If Onoma's Moon had fully waxed, and she took this thing into a prepared space that she had Warded in advance, would she withstand its opening attacks?

"I could probably take it then," she allowed. "If I got a little lucky, and I brought my absolute best Lash, the biggest blow I could deliver. But then I'd have nothing left when the wards broke. And if I go down, it's a massacre." She sighed. "Destroying it is out."

She went back to the table, bent over the book again, and aimed the alchemy lamp to the paragraphs under the heading of Dispersal.

Some wizards have reported success in bargaining with the Blood Haunt. Presenting it with livestock to consume and then banishing it while it was dis-

tracted. *Warden Petrovintla reported Conjuring false shells for the Blood Haunt to consume and watching it disperse when it did not encounter the blood it expected, but this method has not been reliably replicated since Petrovintla's death in the year 426 SK.*

Aelis decided to ignore the ominous mention of Petrovintla's death and seized on the idea of fooling the Blood Haunt.

"I can't Conjure so much as a gust of wind or make an Illusion to fool it. But . . . maybe I can talk to it?"

Aelis was back in her chair and picking up her silver needle before she could think twice. She pressed it to one symbol, the largest rune square in the center of the trap, and pressed her scalpel to the first one she'd touched.

Then she sent a simple Necromantic Pulse down the scalpel. She was immediately assaulted by sensations. Blood spilling down her chest, wetting the robes she wore, cold and slick, and the world fading around her.

The trap grew hot against her hands and rattled on the table and threatened to break her connection; Aelis hunched over it and pressed the silver tighter against the symbols etched into the wood.

There was a silent scream that sounded only in her head. Light flashed behind her eyes and unconsciousness clawed at her; Aelis stamped her feet against the stone floor and gave her head a hard shake. Impressions formed from her connection to the spirit in the trap again. A face; a noble face with an aquiline nose, a close-cropped gray beard, and sad eyes. A face that she, Aelis, knew.

Dalius.

Then the sensation of blood falling down into her clothes again, of Dalius's sad eyes, watching her fall to the ground amid symbols drawn in chalk and silver powder, in a cold stone tower open to the night's wind, of her life leaving her body but being caught, held, forced to watch as she died, forced to see the stuff of life pour from her slit throat, a hand with a red dagger hovering at the edge of her fading vision.

I don't know who you were, but if Dalius is the cause of your death, I already killed him once. I mean to do it again. Aelis thought that vengeance might be a strong bargaining position.

BLOOD, screamed the spirit in the trap. MUST HAVE BLOOD. WHAT WAS TAKEN FROM ME. BLOOD FOR MY OWN BLOOD.

Yes, blood, Aelis thought. *I took his. All of his. Drained it right out of his body.* Technically she'd drained his vital energies, the invisible forces that made his heart beat and muscles contract and brain operate and so on, but this seemed a fairly mild lie, all things considered. His blood had dried into dust and blown away, and not for the last time, Aelis wished she'd been able to recover his body.

BLOOD. MY BLOOD. ALL MINE. MINE.

It's gone, Aelis thought. *Your blood is gone.*

ALL BLOOD IS MINE, MUST BE MINE, WILL BE MINE.

All blood is gone, Aelis thought. *All. You've drained it all. You drained the world. You are all that is left.* Given that it was locked in a trap that amounted to a tiny void with nothing but its own hunger, perhaps this lie could work. The thing had never been loosed upon the world; it had been trapped from the moment it came into being. She was counting on it not knowing that, on it knowing *only* a maddening hunger, its desire for vengeance against all.

LIES.

Do you sense any blood?

The trap rattled against the table and steamed against Aelis's hands. She dropped the needle and drew her dagger from the belt hung over the back of her chair, placed its razor-sharp point against the trap.

I can give you release, Aelis said. *The world is devoid of blood. The world is drained. But I can release you from the hunger for that which you can no longer drink.*

LIES.

The world is empty. Do you sense any blood?

THEN WHAT ARE YOU?

A construct. A piece of some long-dead god's power set to watch over this world. I can release you. This lie was certainly more audacious, and it made very little sense, but Aelis pressed on with it. The spirit was silent. *Do you sense any blood?*

No.

Do you wish for your hunger to end?

The trap rattled in her hand, so violently that she almost lost her hold on it, and the points of her dagger and scalpel slipped off the runes.

The two runes began to turn, slowly.

Panic rose to grip Aelis, but she pushed it away as any vigilant Abjurer would. Her heart did not race; her palms did not sweat. But that spike of fear sharpened her thinking, lent clarity and speed to the decisions she made in the next few seconds.

She clamped tiny wards—similar to those she'd used to stem the flow of her blood when she operated on her ankle—around each of the runes. The force that pushed back against them was enormous. But it was unfocused, and it could not bring all its might to bear against her. Sweat slicked her forehead. There was a boulder pounding against a door trying to knock it down, but the boulder had no room to gather its force. She needed only one good stick to lever it away, and with her wards, she had two.

The force receded and Aelis wasted no time locking the runes back into place. She left her wards atop them; they would not hold together long, but she would know if the Blood Haunt attempted to escape again.

"We're done talking, spirit," Aelis spat. She prepared a Banishment. These were not, according to the *Taxonomy*, meant to work on Beguiling Blood Haunts, because they were originally a piece of the world, merely trapped in it by their unjust, maddening death.

But the creature was not *in* the world, was it? It was in the distant void, the tiny piece of nothing that was inside a spirit trap. It had never been in the world and did not truly know what it was or where it belonged.

That should be enough, Aelis reasoned. She poured nearly everything she had left into the Banishment through her dagger. The hilt grew cold in her hand, and a dark line of black light traveled from the rune her point touched to all the others, slowly seeping through the metal that made up the face of the trap.

Once again, that boulder tried to push back. Her wards wavered and fell. The runes began to turn.

Aelis reached for that last reserve inside her, drawing energy out of the world through the drops of her own blood embedded in the pommel of her dagger. She drew so much power through it that the weapon turned hot in her hand; only the corded grip kept it from searing her skin. Her blood pounded in her ears and her vision dimmed.

There was a last, faint scream, and the trap was suddenly light in her hand. The runes all turned in their sockets, making only the faintest whisper of a noise, and an inert, empty, ready to use, well-crafted spirit trap sat in the palm of her hand. She fell into her chair, only just managing to hold on to both the trap and her dagger. She sagged and kept oblivion at bay by quickly levering an elbow onto her worktable.

With infinite care, Aelis set the trap down. She set her dagger next to it. Then she turned off her alchemy lamp, blew out all her candles, and fell into bed, still dressed, as the gray light of a dismal winter morning crept in through the windows.

Aelis's dreams were troubled. She relived the moment of the spirit's creation, or at least the moment *leading up* to it, several times. She was led through dark stone halls, pulled into a room lit by candles placed among precise magic diagrams, all for reasons she did not understand and that would never be explained to her. The dream disintegrated each time before it went any further, but Aelis tossed and turned to sensations of hunger, longing, and loss, all of which dissipated whenever she clawed herself back to consciousness.

"By Elisima," she spat, sitting upright in bed a few days after having banished the spirit. "Why couldn't I have found a spirit of lust instead of vengeance?" The *Taxonomy* listed some: the Ever-Stiff Wanderer, the Maddening Barb, the Many-Fingered Haunt. Succubi and incubi were more the province of Conjurers, but a Necromancer should be able to differentiate them, at the very least, and so they were listed as well: the Unslaked Rocking, the Root-Eaters, the Pinning Sitters.

She cleared her mind by arranging her seat in her bed, crossed her feet at the ankles, and drew in the deep, held breath of a meditation she'd use to prepare her mind for complicated casting. The dreams did not return.

28

LOCAL HISTORY

The world held out the barest promise of warmth to come and Aelis, on one of her trips around the village to tend to chilblains, minor injuries, and two new pregnancies, decided it was time. Her ankle still complained; it may always do so, now. But what was a warden's life without a few injuries? She was practically ready to whistle with good cheer when she walked into the inn.

Rus, in fact, caught her whistling. He looked up from his bar-polishing, surprise on his face.

"Why, Warden Aelis," he said, placing a hand dramatically against his chest. "One might think you don't quite hate living here anymore."

"Maybe I'm just an easy mark for the promise of spring," Aelis said.

"How are Ursla and Arbeth?"

"They'll be fine," Aelis said. "No reason to believe otherwise."

"Ursla's last was a difficult birth," Rus muttered.

"At the College, they taught us that they're *all* difficult. But I'll be here for this one; it'll be nothing I can't handle." Aelis leaned against the bar, grateful for the chance to get off her barking ankle. "How are our guests?"

"Keep to their rooms mostly," Rus said. "Go for walks now and then, but most folk don't want to speak to them."

"This can't go on," Aelis said. "I'm going out to their home tomorrow. Tell them that for me?" Rus nodded. "Got anything in the back Tun might like that I can bring him?"

"Martin's got some seedcakes cooling."

"I'll take two."

Rus eyed her for a moment. "Fine," she said, "four." She slipped a piece of silver from her purse, the innkeeper still watching her with a raptor's eye. She set it very deliberately down on the bar. "For the cakes, and only the cakes." Rus nodded and turned away.

Aelis counted to three, then leaned over and slipped a small handful of silver into one of the clay mugs stored on a shelf underneath the bar. Then she quickly took her seat again, looking as innocent as the new day.

Rus came back with a cloth-wrapped bundle from which rose a delicious, warm scent. With great ceremony, he picked up the silver double crown Aelis had laid down, then handed over the cakes.

"You know that when it comes to daily bread, your coin has no weight here, Aelis," Rus said. "Just for the seedcakes."

"Of course, of course," Aelis agreed. She slid off the stool, nodded Rus her thanks, and hurried out the door, hiding a small smirk. He'd find a way to get the money back to her; she'd found coins in a coat pocket, at the bottom of a flagon of ale, once, baked inside a pie—a big stack of them right in the center, so that her knife found them as she sliced into it and there was little chance of biting or swallowing one as she ate. Lone Pine was obligated to support her with food and material or allowance for clothing, but it seemed to her that too much of that responsibility fell on Rus and Martin, and she had started trying to pay them here and there. Rus was determined not to accept it, and so they had been trading a small pile of copper back and forth for a while now.

If she found them in her pocket again, she thought, she might take an afternoon to whip up the strongest glue she could with her alchemical tools and stick them to the bar.

"Like to see Rus work out how to return the coins *then*," she muttered. He'd never damage his precious bar to remove them.

◆　◆　◆

Aelis found Tun's cabin, still amazed at how small, tidy, and well hidden it was. If you didn't know it was there and hadn't approached from the right elevation to see the chimney smoke, you might not ever see it. She had her hand raised to knock at the door when she was startled by a throat being cleared a few feet behind her.

It took supreme control not to toss her walking stick and the cloth-wrapped cakes in the air and whirl around to face him, but she wasn't going to give him the satisfaction. Instead, without turning, she said, "I ought to know better than to think I can approach your home unseen, Tunbridge."

"Especially bearing a seedcake fresh from Martin's oven. I can smell *that* when he's baking it."

Slowly, Aelis turned to face him and held out the cakes. Tun waved them away. "Not till we're inside and seated. We'll do things properly."

Tun pushed his door open. It had neither lock nor bar, gliding open on silent hinges. He stirred up his fire, set down the bag he'd been carrying, hung his coat on a peg, and took Aelis's to hang next to it. He set his kettle over the fire and got down the box that Aelis knew he kept his tea-herbs in. Only when they were both seated did he unwrap the package Aelis had brought and bend low over the golden cakes, inhaling their aroma deeply.

"Ahh. To what do I owe this visit?"

Aelis knew better than to lie, or even prevaricate. "I wish it was just because I was nearby, Tun. But I need to ask you some questions."

"About?"

"I want to visit that Errithsun home. They've told a story I only half believe, but . . . I think it's worth looking into."

"Ah." Tun stood up again, returned with plates, a knife, and cloth napkins. He set down the plates, cut the first cake into halves, and slid one onto each plate, then set a plate before Aelis. "Why?"

"Because I think it will help me run Dalius to ground."

"That is quite a leap, Aelis."

"Is it? Because it sounds to me like their lives went to seven hells the moment I killed Dalius, or his husk, his human body, whatever he was, the *first* time."

"Why would you think that?"

"The foundation of their house cracked and the boy started seeing a ghost sometime in the fall. They weren't more specific than that. But I fought him in my tower in the fall."

"Could be a coincidence."

"Could be," Aelis said. "Could also explain how this family had an easy living for so long. And it fits some theories I'm developing about Dalius."

Tun raised a brow.

"It's guesswork, to be sure, and magical theory was never my strongest suit. But I think he tried to bind himself to Mahlgren, to become a spirit of the place. It was tied into his Sundering, splitting up his soul . . . and now he can't let go of it, or it can't let go of him."

"If all the above is true, and I'm not saying I agree that it is, are you sure you *want* to run him to ground?"

"He'll not take me unawares this time, Tun. I swear it, by . . ."

"You already have strong and binding oaths upon you, Aelis. Do not add to them lightly."

"Fair."

Tun took his half of the cake and bit as delicately from the edge as he could manage. Their scent, sweet but piquant, stirred Aelis's hunger, but she left hers untouched for the moment. Tun was a careful eater. She assumed it was something to do with his size and his appearance; people would imagine a half-orc to be a ravenous, slovenly eater. Tun was neither of those, but eating as delicately as he did took effort.

However, she also knew him well enough to know that he was being *extra* careful. He was delaying.

"What makes you think the Errithsuns are connected to Dalius in the first place?"

"It's fairly flimsy. So flimsy I don't even want to say it out loud."

"If a thing has *you*, Aelis de Lenti, at a loss for words, I have to hear it."

"In the vision, Dalius paid the woodsman with a green gemstone the size of my fist." She considered her cake for a moment. "Warrun and his family all wear jewelry with dark green stones. Finer than you'd think woodsfolk would have."

"The Errithsuns were always well-off that way."

"Without any apparent reason, right? They made their living easy. Because, if I'm right, they served a wizard, a warden, who tried to make himself more powerful than any one wizard should be, *and succeeded*. A bargain to serve him, was a bargain to serve the spirits of the land. It broke when I killed him the once. Help me find him, and I will make damned certain he doesn't make any more bargains."

"If I go looking for living Errithsuns and find any, they will not give me peace." Tun's voice was as low as Aelis had ever heard it. She reached across the table and laid her hand atop his wrist.

"I'm not out to force you to do anything that'll hurt you, Tun. Guide me there. If we find any people, disappear into the woods."

"Has it occurred to you that this might be a trap?"

"Oh," Aelis said, "I think it's more than half-likely it is."

Tun slowly broke another morsel off his cake and popped it into his mouth. He finally lifted his eyes from the table and looked at her intently.

"And you still want to go?"

"You have to get up pretty early in the morning to trap an Abjurer who *knows* you're trying to trap them."

"I will guide you there," Tun said.

"Thank you. Tomorrow?"

"Day after," Tun said. "I have chess with Emilie tomorrow. It is an engagement I do not break."

"Chess? Really?" Aelis tried not to let her distaste for the game into her voice, but she knew she'd failed when she saw Tun roll his eyes.

"Of course, a game of careful planning and strategic caution is lost on you."

"It's boring, Tun."

"Only if you don't know how to focus on it. Have you ever even played orcish chess?"

"Didn't know it existed."

Tun's face lit up and he fetched a case from under his bed. "Then allow me to teach you."

"Tun, I . . ."

"Do you want me to point out the flaw you've already made in your plan? If so, agree to play three games."

Aelis tried not to sigh too loudly. "Sure. Three games."

"Good. And the flaw is that if this is indeed a trap and you go haring off after it, you may have left something dangerous behind you in Warrun."

"I've been up close and personal with the man, Tun. I can't imagine him being a threat."

"Then what if he runs? If they were sent here to lure you . . ."

"That . . . that is a good point," Aelis said, feeling her spirits fall, then almost instantly lift as she saw a solution and snapped her fingers. "I'll hire Elmo to track them."

"Good. By all accounts, he did very well with the village under threat." Tun set his case down and opened it, set out a board Aelis didn't recognize and pieces that were carved similarly to familiar chess pieces, but with much less variation.

"Now," Tun said, "this is an asymmetrical game. Instead of two kings arrayed for war, one king is trying to escape the clutches of an army twice the size of his own. I'll let you be the larger army . . ."

29

TRAIL SIGN

"You know, you could be quite a chess player if you spent just a little time thinking about the game," Tun said. "I have a travel set—just cloth and flat tokens, not my good pieces—we could play when next we make camp." He was walking beside her, rather than in front of her for once, and they'd had an easy journey of it. She led a horse with most of their baggage and a saddle she'd taken advantage of for most of the first day, with her ankle still sore as it healed.

Aelis had been trying not to think about chess since Tun had handily drubbed her at it three times in a row two days before. She had been angry that he didn't take it easier on her and then *more* angry at herself for thinking that.

"Why, Tun? Why would I want to defend my king? Is he a *good* king? For all I know he's a shitty one, and the army trying to trap him has legitimate grievances."

"It's a game, Aelis, not a story."

"Then I'll stick with books."

Tun suddenly threw an arm out to stop her. She looked at him questioningly, and he pointed upward at a tree looming over the trail a few yards away.

Aelis didn't see anything noteworthy about the tree itself; as a specimen it was much like any other. Tall, needled, green, with a kind of silvery bark. Aelis could identify a tree, plant, or shrub that provided useful medicinal material; this wasn't one, so she couldn't.

"Look closer. Well up above the eyeline." Tun pointed and she tried to follow his finger.

It took her a moment, but then she saw it. Carved hard into the trunk of the tree, ten feet off the ground, was a face. Her eye would've passed over it on her own, but once she saw it, there was no mistaking it for some natural feature of the tree; it was the work of hands and tools. She walked closer and wished for a glass to study it for any notable marks. All she could tell besides the outline of a bearded face was that one eye was left to the mottled gray of the tree's bark and the other was carved out in detail, with an iris and a pupil inside it.

"Errithsun trail sign," Tun said. "I don't smell anyone nearby, so I suspect this place is abandoned."

Not for the first time since they'd set out a day ago, Aelis wondered about the younger brother's family that had supposedly stayed behind. Her neck itched with suspicion, and she wrapped her hand around her sword hilt to center herself. There'd been nothing unusual about following Tun out of Lone Pine, just that they went more west than north based on directions she'd badgered out of Warrun before leaving, and they weren't really in the wilderness. They'd passed a charcoal-burner's hut inhabited by a man named Gennady, whom Tun knew, and circled wide around a village Tun had named Ham's Thorpe. Now here they were, heading up a wooded trail on a slight rise.

Aelis looked closely at the trail sign again, uncertain of what it might signify. A thought rose, a name, and she quailed from it at first, then sneered and called it to mind with venom.

Dalius Enthal de Morgantis un Mahlgren. She forced herself to it, ignored the shiver it brought, resisted the urge to touch the scar on her belly through her robes. *I am hunting you, you bastard. If you can somehow hear this, I want you to know that. I will find you.*

✦ ✦ ✦

The houses they found were abandoned; that much was clear from a distance when they could see that the thatch was mostly fallen in.

Aelis was put immediately in mind of Rhunival's Hall; the main building was similarly constructed, a long single hall with an opening in the roof for its central hearth. Outbuildings were scattered about, but instead of just toolsheds and chicken coops, they appeared to be multiroom cabins. When they got close, the whole place smelled like rot, even to her.

Tun had reached for a rag and held it over his much more sensitive nose and mouth. Aelis reached into the medical kit slung over the back of her saddle to take out a small sachet of sweet-smelling herbs and tossed it to him. He held it gratefully under his nose as they approached. The timbers of the frame of the central hall were so sodden and weak as to flake apart when Aelis dragged two fingers across them. Sheds and outbuildings made of stone were fallen to pieces, whatever stores or tools they had once held rotted or vanished or scattered.

"This is unnatural," Tun said, his voice muffled. "This is decades worth of rot in a few months, at most."

"Perhaps they were just terrible householders. We're going to do our best to find out." There were many things a Conjurer or a Diviner might do with the mass of rotting timber and broken stone before her. If there was water gathered inside the house providing any kind of reflection, a powerful enough Diviner might have been able to use it to scry the events that had transpired in the place's years. If there were spirits about, if the place had been lived in long enough to have acquired some, the right kind of Conjurer could have called them up and asked.

Tun moved warily toward the door, its wooden frame askew, the door itself hanging on rotten leather straps for hinges. He used the end of his walking stick to cautiously push the door open, but the whole concern gave way and crashed outward, sending him jumping back.

"We ought to circle the place before we go inside," Aelis said. She looked to Tun and touched her nose, then her eyes, silently asking if he smelled anyone nearby or felt anyone watching. He shook his head, then went around the far side of the hall. Aelis took the near side.

Other than the tumbled sheds and a fallen-down cabin, she found nothing. No sign of animal tracks, not that she was any hand at the woodcraft that would've showed them to her, and no sign of people. She found one shed that had been used for storing tools and one that must've been a smokehouse, judging from the scent of charred wood still strong in it, and a third outbuilding whose lingering smell made its purpose all too clear. She met Tun behind the house.

"I'll have to go inside," she said.

He looked up at the roof, squinting. "Can't say I trust the timbers," he said. "Feel like it will come down around you. That would make a rather effective trap."

"Got to search for *something*," Aelis said. "Some sign."

Inside was every bit the rotting mess the outside was. Furniture, tables, chairs, beds had all fallen apart, broken to pieces. Aelis didn't see the marks of any weapons, nor of fire or other powerful magic. It was like the craftsmanship had all just given up, all at once.

There was the sludge of rotting food eating through a heavy iron pan on a cold, rusting stove. Aelis touched it with the tip of a gloved finger.

"These were prosperous people," she said, "to have a *stove* in this isolated place. And this house was . . . stout, well made."

"There's going to be no living with you once your theory proves true, is there?" Tun asked from where he stood just outside the doorway.

"I'm used to being right most of the time, Tun. I will keep the gloating to a tasteful minimum."

But a darker inspiration robbed her quip of its humor.

"Let's look for bones," she said.

They began a more methodical search of the place, and after the better part of an hour, Aelis had not found a single bit of mortal remains. Not in the bedrooms, the kitchen, around the hearth, the storage room where wood and coal and water had been hauled, not in the buttery or the pantry.

"Warden," came Tun's voice, strained. "The cellar."

Aelis followed his voice outside, and then down a short set of stairs dug into the earth.

He pointed silently, and Aelis followed his gesture to a pile of bones jumbled in a dark corner.

Her anatomist's eye told her, even from a distance, that these remains were human. But she was also instantly certain that they were not of a piece; there was not one or two skeletons there, but several, intermingled.

She drew closer, squatting down and drawing her dagger free, poking at the outer edges of the pile with the point. She saw long thigh bones, ribs, the thick knuckle-like bones of spines.

"This is . . . wrong," she whispered.

"How could it be right?" Tun asked.

"No, I mean . . ." She took a deep breath. "They shouldn't be so . . . clean. There should be tendons, muscle, they should be connected." The best way she knew to make a clean skeleton was to have a powerful Invoker blast it with a focused, quick flame. The second-best was to dip each individual bone into piles of ants, remove them a few days later, and reassemble them.

"These people did not die any kind of natural death."

"Can you talk to their spirits, ask them what occurred?"

"Can you read any sign in the cellar or around it?"

"It's been months; too far gone for any woodcraft to be of use."

"Same with their spirits," Aelis said. "But . . . there is something I can do."

She noted that the cellar was empty, its shelves clear of jars or sacks, no barrels or bins or crates on the floor that likely had once been stacked high with them. She didn't know what to make of it, but it struck her as odd.

Aelis shoved that thought away and took a crouched step closer to the bones, laying her dagger's blade against the nearest one, a bone from the forearm that she thought was not fully grown. She tried not to dwell on that observation.

She Delved it using one of the simplest Necromantic diagnostic Orders she knew. It would reveal whatever trauma the bone had undergone.

And as soon as she released the spell, she realized her mistake. The pile of bones rippled as if borne on an ocean's swell. Something in them, something that had been left behind, bound *into* them rather than binding them, something invisible but sleek and deadly, lunged for her.

She leapt to her feet, swiping her Anatomist's blade in the air before her while at the same time, drawing forth a Lash nearly as full of power as the one she'd leveled at the tooth-monster.

Rather than one punch, though, one huge blow, this was a sweeping, wild swing across the entire undulating pile of bones before her.

The bones shattered. Fragments smacked against her robe, nicked the flesh of her cheek. She heard Tun curse behind her.

From the pile of bone dust she heard the faint, breathy chuckle of an old man she'd once thought harmless.

"Piss-poor trap, Dalius," she said, and even as she spoke, the roof of the cellar groaned. Neither she nor Tun needed any urging; they ran for the stairs and bolted for the door as the eaves of the house collapsed around them. Aelis was almost clear when she tripped on the last step and went sprawling forward.

Then the side of the house came tumbling toward her. She scrambled on, trying to gain her feet but finding no purchase. A heavy beam closed in on her knee and was stopped at the very last moment when Tun lunged for it and caught it. Aelis scrambled forward and regained her feet, then thrust out one hand and stuck a ward beneath the beam.

"Release it," she whispered. "You'll be safe."

Tun, sweating and straining, let go of the heavy wood that had been holding up half of one wing of the house and looked on as it hovered in the air. Then he had the right sense to step back and clear his feet from under it. Aelis dismissed the ward and the beam fell to the ground with a crash that reminded Aelis it certainly would've broken her leg.

"Thank you," Aelis said, taking a deep breath.

"All I did was catch a beam. You appear to have destroyed a monster. Again."

"Mm, not a monster. Not exactly. Some kind of clever binding that I wouldn't feel . . . make no mistake." She exhaled hard.

"Go ahead and say it," Tun muttered.

"Say what?"

He lowered his head and stared at her, unblinking.

"I was right," she said.

"You were right," Tun's much deeper voice echoed.

They stood still for a moment.

"Now what?" Tun asked at last.

"Back to Lone Pine. If Warrun ran, we see if Elmo tracked him. Then I have a conversation with him."

"What kind of conversation?"

"I'll drag information out of him with enchantment if I have to," Aelis said. "But he's soft, and he's scared, and since I suspect that this trap was meant to remake the bargain with Dalius, I don't think I'll need it."

"What about the bones in there?"

"Oh, I'll have questions for Warrun about that."

"Can we give them anything like a proper burial?"

Aelis looked over the wreckage of the hall and stopped thinking about it as a trap set for her, focusing instead on the material that had baited it. The bones. The bones of people who had lived here, who'd likely taken as much benefit from the bargain as Warrun, but who'd been sacrificed once it fell apart. Whether that was by Dalius or by their brother, it was an ugly end, a crime in every ledger she could keep.

Aelis closed her eyes and let out a ragged breath. *Onoma, a terrible thing was done here. A perversion of the power you grant us over life and death. If it is needful and it is in your power, grant your bleak mercy to the people it was done to.*

She was startled out of her prayer by a loud crash and had her sword half-drawn only to find Tun leaning lightly on his walking stick and her borrowed horse trotting away.

"Shed collapsing," he said. "I think most of these buildings are going. We'd best be on our way."

"And here I thought Onoma might be answering a prayer," Aelis said.

30

THE HORSE THIEVES

On the trek back, having caught up to the horse Aelis had borrowed, they once more swung wide of Ham's Thorpe, and Tun pointed out a branching trail that he said led to another village known as Messers Gulch.

"You could always ride out to them to see if they could use a physician or a surgeon now and then," Tun offered.

"I could, but unless they send for me in an emergency, it's not a great idea."

Tun stopped in his tracks and turned to look at her, but she was ready for it.

"I am the warden of *Lone Pine*. That's where my efforts are to be directed. That's where I live. I'll help others as I can, of course, and finding Aldayim's Matrix was to the benefit of all the people on both sides of this frontier. But there are good reasons, beyond just what my warrants say, to stick to Lone Pine."

"Such as?"

"Short answer or long answer?"

Tun turned and started walking again, swinging his stick and his legs with easy assurance, forcing Aelis to hurry to keep up. "The long, since I know that your short answers will run that way regardless."

"The more a wizard inhabits a place, builds a routine, draws their strength from the ineffable forces that make a place *itself*, the more effective their work becomes."

"You get more powerful?"

"Not exactly. More efficient, let's say. It won't make a weak Invoker suddenly able to wipe out an emplacement of siege weapons with Moltke's Rain of Flames. It will just make the things you are capable of a bit easier, make drawing the energy faster, more secure, save and extend your strength across days, weeks, months. The effects are small in the moment, but stretched across years, they can make a difference. You move a wizard too much, you give up that advantage. There's also the fact of building trust and relations with the folk of a place, coming to know its contours and mysteries."

"This is what you think Dalius did, isn't it?"

"I think it's the *basis* of my suspicion about him becoming a spirit of Mahl-gren. But that would take decades and near-constant application of power, plus forbidden rituals I shouldn't even name."

"Is the fact that Mahlgren is cut in half relevant, do you think? To how he's acted since you arrived?"

"Could be. The lines on the map, not so much, but the fact that people don't inhabit the same places, live the same way. Perhaps he's more mad than sinister, but I don't care. Either way, he wants permanent killing."

"I suppose so," Tun agreed, and they lapsed into companionable silence once more.

+ + +

"Warrun and his family disappeared the first night you were gone." Rus was uncharacteristically animated. He'd met Tun and Aelis as soon as they came within sight of the inn, striding angrily out to meet them in his apron, towel snapping in his hand.

"That's more or less what we expected," Aelis said.

"Did you *expect* them to steal a pile of our best bedding and two horses, including Pansy?"

"I genuinely did not, Rus," Aelis said. She felt her own amusement at being right dissolve into anger and disbelief. "We'll go find Elmo and leave right away."

"You could've *told me* I was harboring a thief!" Rus shouted.

Upon being shouted at, Aelis's instinct was to insist on her power, her station, her authority, and *shout back*. She was about to do that when Tun leaned close.

"Rus," he murmured, "shouting at each other on the green will do no one any good. We did not tell you because we did not know, and you your-self know that plans shared widely are all the more likely to fail."

"Was I going to gossip about it, Tun?" Rus did not look like a man who was going to be talked down easily, but Tun's intervention had given Aelis time to reflect and not meet his anger with her own.

"Rus," she said softly, "it didn't occur to me that he would be that bold. I will not pause or rest; we will leave today, find him, and bring back your horses." She led her own borrowed horse forward. "Take care of this mount; I'll go on foot for this one." Her ankle twinged painfully as she said that, but she ground her teeth together and didn't let it show. She untied her pack from the horse's back and let it rest against her boots.

Packed heavy, she thought, and her composure almost broke as her next thought hit her like an Abjurer's Buckler. *Maurenia would've warned me.*

Only slightly deflated, Rus took the bridle of the horse and led it away.

Tun looked at her. "I'll go talk to Elmo. You go cadge whatever food you can get out of Martin."

"Should it maybe be the other way around?"

"Are you going to guide us to some new destination based on another scout's description?"

Aelis walked away toward the back of the inn without saying a word in her defense.

✦   ✦   ✦

Elmo did better than give Tun directions; he provided a map. Martin had a bundle of bread and cheese ready for them, and Aelis hitched up her pack as the sun set over Lone Pine, thankful, at least, that she'd have a couple of days before she had to start living off the hard corn biscuits in Tun's pockets.

"Looks like our man fled east. Stands to reason he'd go in the opposite direction, put as much distance between you and himself as possible." Tun was studying the map in the falling light. "Elmo's good at this," he rumbled. "Better than I would've thought."

"Is that professional respect I hear?"

"Might be. Never had much use for Ystainan scouts before." He folded the parchment and tucked it carefully away. "What's the plan?"

"We go straight there, drag whatever information we can out of him, and go for Dalius."

"And if we *do* find Dalius . . ."

"For that, I have a plan," Aelis said. "While we walk, let me tell you how a spirit trap works."

✦   ✦   ✦

They hadn't had far to go, but walking late into that night with her alchemy lamp lighting the way, and then up and at it again early the next day, Aelis started to feel like spring was a lie. True, the day had more than the bright but cheerless sun of Ystain's winter, but in her southern, sun-drenched blood, she harbored a suspicion that she might never know true warmth out-of-doors again.

"We are come, for the third time, to a small vale with a long hall in the middle of it," Tun rumbled around noon of that second day, pointing to a thin wisp of smoke far ahead. Aelis leaned against a convenient tree, resting her sore ankle. "It almost makes a pattern."

"Was this how Ystain was initially settled? Small freeholders in halls of this type?"

"More or less; my mother's people build this way. I suspect the Ystainan took us as their model."

"If we find Dalius down in that vale, tell him that. I think it might make him choke to death."

"Are you amending the plan you spent so much time explaining last night?"

"It was a joke, Tun."

"Until last night, so was the idea of you having a plan more complex than 'poke something and see what happens.'"

"Daylight's wasting. Let's go down there."

Talk lulled as they skirted the valley, Aelis shifting her pack and working her walking stick, her boots thumping against the turf. When they'd almost reached the north end, having gently climbed for an hour or more, Aelis saw the trail before Tun could point it out. A winding shepherd's path through the hills, hardly marked, but there to the eye that had a clue to look for it or knew how to read the country.

It led north, as they expected, switched back and then straightened once or twice and came to a clearing at the bottom of the vale grown wild with pine. They heard the sound of a tool against wood but saw no cluster of buildings.

Eventually, the trees parted to reveal the hall they'd seen from above. Poorly squared timber frames, the wood perhaps not seasoned, walled with flaking sod and poorly roofed with thatch. Edder, who was leading Pansy by a rope around her neck, saw them appear from behind the trees, let the rope drop, and ran into that long, low building that put her in mind of Rhunival's hall, if not half as well-built or homey. Smoke crept out of it, rather than streamed; there was no chimney, and the gap in the roof wasn't drawing well.

Aelis was wary, but she felt no tingle of magic or anxiety of danger here. Just a growing curiosity, and a kind of churning in her mind, a sure sign she was close to working out a puzzle, or that she already had worked it out and only needed others to play their parts to complete it, like a clockworks ticking its way slowly but inexorably to ringing the hour.

Warrun emerged from behind the low hall holding a woodaxe in both hands, like he meant to use it but didn't quite know how.

"You've no warrant here! We're not in Lone Pine anymore. We want naught to do with wizards!" He gestured with the axe, weakly.

"You've committed crimes in Lone Pine," Aelis said. "Horse theft is no minor thing."

"Then take the horses and go, but be off my family's land or . . ."

"Warrun." Tun's voice had a dangerous edge; Aelis could hear him breathing. "Another man . . . your brother, I expect? He is behind us, believing himself hidden, with a weapon. Tell him to put it down and come out where I can see him."

"Or . . . ?"

"Or people start *dying*."

"There's no need for that," Aelis said, taking a conciliatory tone and stepping between Tun and Warrun. "Warrun. I will need the horses back, and anything else you stole. But no blood needs to be shed here so long as you answer questions."

"Oh, you think that'll stop him?" Warrun pointed at Tun—not with the hand that held the axe. "How many of my people did you and yours slaughter? Come to finish the job, have you?"

Aelis had enough. With her hand around her sword hilt, she placed a ward just behind Warrun at ankle height. She came forward another step; Warrun backed away but tripped over her ward. Aelis ducked to grab the axe from his hands. His nerve gone, Warrun lay on the dirt and the pine needles and let out a choking sob.

"Gerrin," Aelis called, as she handed the woodaxe to Tun. "Come out. No one is here to hurt you."

She followed Tun's gaze to the treeline and saw a man in a ragged cloak that had once been dyed a fine bright green over a yellow tunic come out holding a coarsely made spear with a rusting head.

"Drop the spear!" Tun yelled. When Gerrin didn't comply fast enough, Tun hurled the woodaxe end-over-end. It flew straight past Gerrin and struck deep into a tree, the handle shivering and the tree's branches rattling and shedding needles.

Gerrin dropped the spear as if he'd suddenly found a live snake in his hands and circled wide around Tun and Aelis, toward his crying brother.

"Finlo's dead, isn't he? And his wife, and their children." Warrun didn't open his eyes but spoke through the tears he couldn't hold back.

"He is," Aelis said. "And their bodies defiled, all for your patron to make an ineffective trap for me."

"You knew," Warrun said, finally sitting up and opening his eyes. Gerrin remained a few awkward paces away. Like Warrun's, his trousers were half rags, stuffed into boots that were splitting at the calf, tied together with twine. "You knew it was a trap, and you went anyway?"

"I'm a warden," Aelis said. "Takes a lot to trap me if I even suspect it's coming." She knelt next to Warrun. Despite herself, she found some empathy growing for him. Here he was, sitting in the early spring mud in his too-fine clothes, trying to turn his soft hands to unfamiliar tools, the ways his family had always gotten by disappearing as he watched, helpless.

"Finlo wouldn't leave. We tried to talk him into it, but he wouldn't go," Gerrin suddenly said. He was clearer of eye than Warrun, straighter in bearing, younger, more able to take what had come on them, Aelis thought. "He was the truest believer of all of us."

"The truest believer in what?" Aelis thought she knew the answer. But she wanted one of them to say it.

"The old bargain," Gerrin said. "With Dalius. Our family served his, and then him, directly. For years."

"I know," Aelis said. She pointed to Gerrin's cloak pin. "I recognized the jewelry."

Warrun lifted his own ringed hand and stared at her. "How?"

"Magic," Aelis said, waggling her fingers at him. "But I knew . . . I guessed . . . about the bargain. I killed Dalius, or some form of him, last fall. And when I did, I think your house started falling apart around you. Whatever gardens you tended stopped fruiting. Animals came up lame, or sick, or sterile. Am I right?" She surveyed the shoddy house.

"Your folk hadn't known real hardship, and toil had always been a bit easier than it was for any other folk out here on the frontier, eh? The rain didn't come in through the walls. The cows didn't come down sick. The sheep were never lost. Am I right? You don't have to tell me. I know I am. I can read it in your face."

Warrun paled beneath his tear-stained cheeks, and Aelis knew she was right; she had made that leap from churning mind to absolute certainty. The picture in her mind was nearly complete.

"One morning, we awoke and our chimney had crumbled, blocked the airflow, and started pouring smoke into the house. Two cows were down, and half our turnips had turned to slime in their hampers," Warrun said. Suddenly he made a fist. "You! With foul magics, you . . ."

"Think very carefully before we add assaulting a warden to horse theft," Aelis said. She stood and extended a hand to the man. "I'm here to help. When I killed your patron, he was trying to kill me. I had no idea he had the kind of power to make these bargains, or that they would've been extant. I meant no harm to your family. I can help you now, and I can make you free of him."

Still, the man spurned her hand and pushed himself to his feet. "And what good does that do us, eh? Things got worse in early winter. House fell apart around us."

"When was that?" Aelis asked. "Be specific. What moons were in the sky?"

"What difference does that make?"

"You will find that it is best to answer my questions before I stop worrying about whether my friend gets angry," Aelis said.

Warrun's bleary eyes flicked upward and Tun obliged Aelis by letting out a faint growl.

"It . . . it was a blue moon. Alone in the sky. Just a sliver of it."

When Rhunival was freed, Aelis thought, and another stroke of the painting was revealed to her, the imaginary clockworks began banging the hour. Freeing him had dealt one more blow to Dalius's hold over Mahlgren. She was sure of that now, but not sure of why. *Puzzle later. Interrogate now.*

"That, on top of Edder talking about having seen a ghost . . . that's when we gave up and fled. Lone Pine was the only village we could walk to, but . . . Dalius came to me in a dream. He said it would all be well again if I just sent you to the old stead. I refused, but when you were so persistent, you demanded . . ."

"I think the chance of remaking the old pact has fled, Warrun. The best I can do is this; you help me find him, then you come to Lone Pine and make a life there. There's more work there than hands to do it, but you've a better chance surrounded by people, even people who don't particularly like you, than you do out here on your own."

"We'll do it," Gerrin said, much to Warrun's startlement. "It's our only chance," the younger brother spat. "Whatever lore we might still have, it's here somewhere. We have some old books, papers, a map or two. If they're what you need, take them."

"Bring them to me," Aelis said. "We'll wait."

She and Tun withdrew a bit from the door of the hall; Warrun and Gerrin vanished inside it.

"Aren't you worried they'll come out shooting?"

"If either of them has a crossbow and knows how to shoot it, I'll give up wine for a month," Aelis said.

"You'd die."

"No, I'd just wish it." She turned to look at him; he seemed his perfectly unruffled self, so unlike the open anger of a few minutes ago. "Are you well?"

"Oh, that? Was mostly an act," Tun said. "Worked, didn't it?"

"Did . . . did we just play soft and heavy with them? Did you make *me* play the soft one?"

Tun's lips drew into a tight smile around his tusks.

"I really thought you might kill one of them," Aelis said.

"I wanted *them* to think that. But these are beaten men. They want to save their families; I expect you'll give them that chance." Tun sounded certain, but Aelis wasn't. His hand was too tight around his walking stick, his lips too tight around his tusks, his eyes drawn too narrow. "They'll have to work off the value of what they stole with Rus and Martin, and I won't let Rus wave it off, either. You know . . ." She waved a hand at the hall. "They had two steads within a couple days' hard walk of Lone Pine. You'd think you would have known they were here."

"Don't think I haven't asked myself that," Tun said. "I've trapped out this way and near the other. Never saw them, never smelled them, never ran into one. I knew of some of their homesteads, of course, but not these two."

"Dalius's bargain probably hid them," Aelis said.

"It must've."

Aelis weighed ribbing Tun a bit more over this, but she wasn't certain his previous anger *was* just an act. He had been genuinely unsettled; she knew from experience that having a weapon pointed at him, even incompetently, tended to garner a reaction.

Soon enough, Gerrin and Warrun came out with a bundle wrapped in a hide in better shape than anything any of them were wearing. Aelis felt a tiny spring of hope come alive all at once, like an invoker's flame, but it died just as quickly when the bundle was unwrapped and she saw no familiar blue leather binding. There was a jumble of loose papers tied together with a string, a small book, and another folded hide.

"This'll be of most use, I suspect," Gerrin said, unfolding the hide to reveal a map, lovingly and beautifully drawn, but on a scale and of a place she did not recognize. Tun took it and held it out with both his hands for a long time, examining it intently.

"It's Mahlgren with all the Errithsun holdings marked, isn't it?" Tun said at last.

"Seems like," Gerrin said. "We're here," he added, pointing to one of the marks on the map.

"Tun," Aelis said in a sudden burst of inspiration, "do any of the marked places match any of the barracks-crypts on the maps of Old Ystain?"

Tun considered the question, then pointed to the hide. "Here."

Aelis followed his finger. She thought back to when she'd looked at all the animations spread across Mahlgren, and the three points where she'd felt something *else*.

That had been one of them; an old watchtower, she'd thought, one of the Earl's Lanterns like the one where she found the spirit trap.

"That's where the head of the family would go to make the pact," Gerrin said. "Finlo went ten years ago. One of us would've had to go and . . ."

"You don't have to finish that sentence," Aelis said as she remembered what the Blood Haunt had shown her, what she now believed *making the pact* meant. "If you do, I might retract your invitation to Lone Pine. Pack up and go now, today. Report to Rus and tell him what I said about working off what you took."

"And . . . and then what?" That was Warrun, talking for the first time since he and Gerrin had come out of the hall with the books.

"Then find work to do," Aelis said. "Someone'll always be mending a fence."

She turned to Tun and gestured at the map. "How long to get there?"

"Three days' hard walk," he said.

"Then let's get going."

"Sure you don't want to walk them back to Lone Pine and . . ."

"In three days, Onoma's moon will be high enough to make a difference for me. That's when I want to face him."

"We'll be eating corn biscuits and skinny game on the way home. If we're lucky."

"A woodsman I know once told me that most of the wilderness is edible."

Tun grinned again and picked up his stick.

31

THE TRAP

The night before they found the tower, Aelis wanted to go over the plan again, and as they sat by their small fire, something Tun had built more for the spirit of the thing than for its warmth, she tried to.

"Tell me again which runes . . ."

"Aelis," Tun said as he laid a small stick across his carefully built embers. "You have crafted a plan. You have taught me my part, which I can recite flawlessly. Let it go."

"Fine, fine." Later, fretful, unable to sleep, she dug out and unrolled the sheaf of papers the Errithsun brothers had given her. They weren't anything useful or interesting, so far as she could tell; they were inventory lists, troop movements, standing orders, the kind of thing a commanding warden of a region at war would have to worry about.

Stregon's Flail, I hope that's never mine to worry over. She turned these aside and came across a small book she hadn't seen before. It was no more than a dozen pages folded double and sewn together; the thread was coming loose, and so the whole thing had been tied shut with string. Onoma's moon was high enough in the sky that she could read as if it were daylight, and the cover struck her.

On it was a tree, a great towering pine, shaded in ink against a yellowing background. She flipped the page cautiously and was instantly bewildered.

Tun must have noticed something about her and stood up. "Find something interesting?" He took half a step toward her.

"If a language I can't even *recognize*, much less read, is interesting, then yes. I don't suppose these are orcish characters." She held the book out to him; he took it delicately and leaned in close, shook his head, and handed it back.

"Nothing I know."

"It's not Tirravalan, old, middle, or new; it's not elvish; it could be dwarfish, I suppose, but . . ." She flipped a few more pages, idly, and felt a cold thrill of hope run up from her chest.

"Tun. Tun, look. Look!" She thrust the book at him, and he bent low over it again.

"What am I looking at?"

She looked closely at him, at the way he squinted his eyes. *You don't see very well up close, do you, my friend?* Even at that moment, she was still a diagnosing physician.

"The drawing. It's the rod. Rhunival's rod."

"Then this book has something to do with that creature?"

"It was part of the papers given by Dalius to his servants. It *must have been.* I just need to figure out how to read it." She bent to it again, scanning the unfamiliar text, unable to make anything of it. There were no breaks between words and no paragraphs, just an endless run of characters filling the available space.

"You're not likely to decipher it tonight," Tun said. "And you need sleep."

"I never sleep well the night before something exciting." She remembered saying words like those to Maurenia the night before she entered Mahlhewn Keep all those weeks ago. Aelis felt another pang of guilt and loss, and anger flared within her. Her hands tightened on the book, and she had to force her fingers to relax so as not to tear the valuable pages. *Gods, I wish you were here, Maurenia. You'd probably see three things wrong with the plan we haven't even thought of.*

"Ambushing the unquiet spirit of a vastly powerful warden who has seemingly made himself immortal might require a bit of rest."

"I don't think it'll be an ambush; he'll know we're coming."

"He'll know *you're* coming. I am going to slip out before dawn and re-connoiter the place. I will leave signs in my wake, but I remind you that the *entire* plan depends on him not knowing I'm there. Which means *you* need to be fresh."

Aelis forced her shaky hands to tie up the unreadable book, to slip it back into the pile of parchment, and to wrap the entire thing back in the hide wrap.

"You're right, Tun. Will you have the first watch?"

"Of course."

Aelis reached for her swordbelt, coiled next to her, and pulled it into her lap. She wrapped both hands around the hilt of her sword, using introductory abjurer's training to clear her mind, to forget her surroundings, to calm her body.

Even she was surprised at how well these techniques worked and how easily she slept.

+ + +

Tun shook her awake before dawn.

"I'm off. You needed the rest more than I did. Wait two hours, then follow the trail I leave. It will be obvious, even for you. And if I think there's a danger there you haven't yet seen, listen for the call of a barred owl."

"Are there any barn owls about?" she asked, still groggy from sleep.

"*Barred* owl. Three times." Then he disappeared into the trees.

I could swear he's studied at least a little *illusion*, Aelis thought, not for the first time.

She ate the last of Martin's bread, unwilling to admit, as she let it soften in the back of her mouth, that by now Tun's corn biscuits were probably the better option. She cleaned up the campsite, buried the fire, packed and repacked her gear, oiled her sword and dagger, adjusted the fit of her belt, the hang of her pack, waxed her wand, and for lack of anything else to do, ran through her basic sword form exercises once, twice, then a third time. Then she settled for throwing rocks at a tree.

"If there's any woodshades here, I hope that pissed them off," she muttered before she finally judged that enough time had passed.

Tun was as good as his word as far as trail marking went; she found small scraps of ribbon tied at eye height wherever she needed to make a turn or a choice between two old deer paths.

She had enough sense of direction in the woods now to know she was approaching the tower, or what remained of it, in a winding circle; Tun was making her take her time rather than going directly at it.

Since her plan involved waiting for moonrise, that wasn't the worst thing.

It was noon by the time she thought she saw the structure and an hour after that when she *knew* she did.

Gods, that could be my tower. It really could've been, as it was built to nearly the same plan, out of the same riverbed stone. It had probably been taller, three interior floors rather than two, she judged, but now it was a tumbledown mess. Half of it had fallen down the slope it stood on, leaving whatever was left inside exposed to the elements.

"If that had been my tower, I would've turned right around and gone home," she muttered. Then she did the thing she hated more than anything.

She waited.

All the rest of the afternoon and into the evening, she nibbled on hard bread and the rind ends of cheese and sipped water. On the whole, this was an easier wait than when she'd been waiting to drown in the Mahlhewn vault, but it was also so gods-damned long.

Eventually Aelis felt the gentlest tug of Onoma's moon as it came over the horizon. She forced herself to wait an hour more, doing her abjurer's exercises, tensing and relaxing the muscles of her core, her arms, and her legs in sequence to keep any cramps from setting in.

Then, with the dark just falling, she gathered herself and began moving up the hill toward the open end of the ruined tower.

The way her stomach churned, and the way the hair stood on the back of her neck told her that she was right, that her instincts were dead on, and that she was nearing the end of her search for Dalius.

Aelis took a deep breath and, her spine itching, walked around the crest of the hill.

The hardest thing about it was keeping her hands away from her sword and dagger. She did it, though, let out a breath, then took another one, and held it.

She was three yards from the tower when she heard a loud screeching cry, then another, and another. She was puzzling over it when, a yard closer, she almost stepped into a bear trap, but some sense kept her foot hovering just above it.

Barred owl, she realized, and the trap shattered around Naeran's Greaves, the powerful ward Aelis had summoned. *Thank you, Tun*, she barely had time to think as broken, jagged pieces of iron flew like sling stones into the brush, pinging off the remaining stone walls of the tower. She called up the Buckler and lowered her face behind it, felt two pieces of the trap spring against it on ricochet.

Then, sword in hand, Aelis strode forward into the semicircle of fallen stones. There was a pile of bones heaped against the far wall and other, smaller bones scattered around. Aelis flexed her wrists and settled her right hand lightly around the hilt of her sword, drew it. The pommel let out a faint blue light from the wards she was summoning, holding ready.

"Come out, Dalius," she shouted. "You rotting coward. You ran from our last encounter somehow; I won't let you slink away from this one."

Then the pile of bones against the far wall stood up.

Aelis smiled and raised her wards.

Before her, the bones warped and cracked with hideous snapping sounds, till something vaguely man-shaped stood before her. It loomed even taller than Dalius had, easily touching seven feet. She tried not to focus on the individual bones; some, certainly, were those Dalius had left behind in her tower. Others were smaller, younger, but human all the same. She did not want to think about that.

Instead, Aelis focused on the face that emerged. Flesh wrapped itself around the construct, but raggedly, in the imitation of an older but still vigorous man; it hung off in patches, revealing bone and darkness beneath. Skin, or something like it, stretched around a skull that was supported by hipbones instead of shoulders, and features appeared in it; an aquiline nose, deep-set eyes, a high brow.

These features were recognizably Dalius as she had seen him, both in the vision of the Matrix and in her encounters with him, but horribly stretched, parodied.

Aelis seized her sword with both hands, fell into a closed guard stance with her left foot leading, blade held back by her right shoulder.

"The child Warden," the Dalius-monster said, the voice a grind of bone against bone. His eye sockets were empty blackness that slowly filled with hard blue dots of flame. "Come to die at my hand in truth?" The construct, or Dalius, or whatever it was, was still a couple of yards away from her, out of decent lunging range. "Did you manage to get all the glass out of your stomach? Or is some of it still *there*?"

Aelis said nothing; she had two Wards prepared: one large, one more directed. She was not going to be baited.

Then pain, white hot, flared in her stomach around her scar. She tried to push it away, to ignore it, but it was like molten glass suddenly loose in her gut. She staggered backward.

The Dalius-thing laughed, a guttural, awful sound.

"Ah, just the tiniest speck of it trapped in a muscle fiber is all it takes." The thing raised one of its awkward, bent limbs and made a small motion. A blast of pure force sent her sword spinning out of her hands and her staggering several steps backward. She saw the sword land far away, well out of her reach.

"Still too slow, still too clumsy, and with no reserve of power to fall back on." The Dalius-monster shuffled over the dirty pine needle-carpeted ground toward her and bent to wrap a bony hand—a hand made of the tarsals of a foot—around her neck. "Why did you think that sword would matter against such as me, child in the garb of a Warden?"

Aelis willed the pain in her gut into some faraway part of her mind, looked up at the hideous face before her, and smiled.

"I didn't."

Her left hand uncurled from behind her back, driving her dagger point forward into the mass of stretched, knobbled flesh and misconstructed bone before her. In the full light that Onoma's black moon cast for her, she could see the agony that crossed Dalius's distorted features in exquisite detail.

Instead of gloating or casting a spell through her dagger, she yelled, "NOW!"

And a form nearly as tall as and wider than the monster dropped almost noiselessly to the stones of the tower behind it.

Aelis had suspected, and now she knew, that the thing Dalius had become had only prepared for her as an Abjurer. It expected her to fight with sword and wards. That was the book that had been stolen; in their first fight, he'd immediately separated her from her sword, and she had thought it could be lured into doing so a second time.

She was right. And now, under the fullness of Onoma's moon—which made the world as bright as noon on a cloudless day to her—she saw Tun drop down behind him, the spirit trap in his hands. She poured as much Necromantic power as she could into a Binding, holding nothing back, feeling her power and will amplified by the moon and the light it cast for her. The world drew into sharp focus around her. Each needle of a pine tree rising above the crumbled wall stood out in sharp relief. She could read every dent, nick, and tooth mark on the bones—the tarsals, she could even identify—jutting through Dalius's face.

But she tried to ignore all of it, focused on the power flowing through her dagger, the power that Onoma's moon sent thrumming through her. Aelis used her strongest binding just to keep the spirit there, physically rooted in front of her.

Dalius, or the spirit wearing him, screamed and thrashed. It tried to bring its hand together to crush her throat, but the poor choice of materials meant it could not wrap tight enough, though certainly the edges of the bone could and did, dig into her skin. She felt it lacerate her neck, superficial cuts that grew slick with blood but didn't weaken her, wouldn't, not unless this went on longer than she meant it to.

With a sound of cracking bone, the monster rotated one arm back toward Tun; Aelis felt the powerful wave of Enchantment that rolled out from him. A Compulsion of a high order; it reminded her of the hammer-like power that Nathalie had wielded.

And she smiled as she saw it blast against Tun, wash over him, and dissipate against the charmed coins—Nath's coins, which she'd kept and repurposed once again—he wore around his neck.

"Ready for that one too," she spat as she twisted her dagger. She felt hot shards of bone and thick, viscous liquid fall against her skin.

Meanwhile, with exquisite precision and an elegance that belied his enormous size, Tun pressed the runes on the trap in the order she'd told him and held it out.

At first, nothing happened. Then the blue fires in Dalius's eye sockets flared wide, paled till they were nearly white as a bright light opened behind him in Tun's outstretched hand.

"You are *dead*, Dalius!" Aelis shouted into the monster's face as she felt its grip on her weakening. "You have been dead for years. Accept it."

"No," moaned the horrid, grating voice. "No. I have so much work to do to save Mahlgren."

"Mahlgren is gone, just like you. You have no organs, no blood, no brain; only a scrap of soul and flesh being ridden by a parasitic spirit. You are nothing but a gobbet of flesh nursing a worm. You cannot defend that which is gone!"

The form in front of her was shrinking, but she could feel its determination, the hatred of the riding spirit, the defiance of the scrap of human being it clung to.

"Dalius, listen to me! The spirit you invited in has deceived you. If you lived, I would feel your heartbeat, the coursing of your blood, the function of your body!" The hot glow inside her stomach had dimmed; a long line of blue-black smoke was flowing into the trap Tun held outstretched. The power of the creature before her diminished.

"I am a Warden like you once were," Aelis said, almost pleading. "It is *my* place to defend these people and their homes. Not yours. LET. GO."

Time stopped. The flash of light that was being drawn into the spirit trap became a solid beam. She felt like she was inside Aldayim's Matrix, in space that was not space, time that was not passing.

The hideously distorted face in front of her became something else entirely. The Dalius she'd seen outside her tower after first arriving. Old, pathetic, nearly powerless.

"I gave everything for this place. Everything. You have never loved anything so much, child."

Aelis thought for a moment of her home, of terraced vineyards in the huge Tirravalan sunset, the lights of the Lyceum, the feeling that somewhere in Lascenise something exciting, something that *mattered*, was happening.

"The people of Mahlgren, their halls filled with song, the way we could make a living from the forest and the rivers and never need to grub in the dirt. You cannot understand. You hate it here. You are no fit steward."

"The Mahlgren you're describing doesn't exist anymore. If it ever did."

"Liar!" His face went from defeated to furious, and a crackle of blue lit his dark eyes. "You don't belong here."

"I didn't think so either," Aelis said. "Just turns out, I was needed."

"I can give you secrets, Warden." His voice was no longer the old man's, but instead something vast and ancient, something that shaped each word with hard, cold angles. "So many secrets to feed to Aldayim's Matrix. You could be the greatest Necromancer since he who made it."

"Felt that power. Don't crave it again," Aelis said.

"Ah yes, so proud of yourself, *Necrobane*," that voice spat. Then Dalius smiled. "I can free your lover. One word of power will grant you that; my defeat will not. My power over the thing you think of as Rhunival was limited to binding it."

Aelis clamped her lips tightly together, summoned every bit of de Lenti control she could, but still felt the hope of what she might achieve quivering inside her like a dying flame.

"Ahhh, now I see. That, you might bargain for. All it would take is to allow a little piece of me to live in you. I'll not trouble you for decades yet. You'll have most of your natural life."

"The natural life is the only one I want," Aelis spat. "And that is your great sin, underneath all the others, Dalius Enthal de Morgantis un Mahlgren. You would give up the world to stave off death; you *cannot. You will not, not one second longer.*"

Aelis felt as though she was speaking in a voice greater, vaster by far than her own, something that made that voice of cold and distance recoil, and she snapped out of the space that was not space and back into a cool night in a ruined tower.

The creature turned its face back to look at the trap that was tugging tendrils of its soul-stuff into an extradimensional space, bounded by wards, enchanted wood, and silver. Then it turned back to her, and the face became featureless, all hint of Dalius lost, replaced by something alien, something that was only dimly acquainted with the *idea* of a face, and so the flesh and bone that made one up melted away.

"You. Are. Dead." She intoned the words through gritted teeth.

Above her, somewhere in a place vast and featureless, another voice, a more powerful voice, echoed hers, and the merest hint of it shook her knees.

YOU ARE DEAD, this Voice said. And though it was powerful, it was not without compassion and had no interest in Aelis's vengeance. That Voice only wanted a return to a more natural order for this thing that had once been human.

The ragged holes that the eyes had become closed and fell away. The paper-thin flesh sloughed from the falling pile of bones like wet paint. There was a scream that she felt more than she heard. The bones collected around her feet, the flesh disintegrated into the air, and she ran forward through the rubble to grab the trap from Tun's hand.

The runes of the Worldsoul and Onoma glowed with a heat that would scorch the skin that touched it. Quickly, Aelis wrapped a thick cord of silver wire around it thrice. Then Tun held out a bag, the same one filled with sand as before, and she shoved the trap inside.

There was a faint hiss and a spurt of smoke as the trap sank into her hasty secondhand Null Cage.

"Did we do it?" Tun wondered.

"I think we fucking did," Aelis said, fighting down the elation that threatened to derail her calm head. "We need to gather up these bones. All of them, I'm afraid. If you don't want to help, I understand."

"I agreed to help my friend with a great task," Tun said slowly, solemnly. "I don't recall saying anything about not helping with the unpleasant bits."

◆   ◆   ◆

It was an ugly and sorry task, but she felt it was important. Some bones were animal. Some were clearly those of a grown man, and tall. Tun was helping her sort them, identifying some as deer, beaver, and fox. Those she even suspected of not being animal went into the sack.

"I knew something about the Errithsuns," Tun said, during a pause. "I had no idea they were bound so tightly with Dalius. Had I known . . . perhaps I could've saved you some grief."

"If you had known anything important, you would have told me. I know that."

Tun looked as if he wanted to say more, then lowered his eyes to his hands.

Aelis stopped in her gruesome work and stood up. "Whatever it is you are struggling to say, you don't have to . . ." She raised her hands in an awkward offer of a hug.

"Aelis. You've been collecting bones with those hands."

"Right. How about I get back to that, and we get very drunk about this in my tower when we get home?"

"Deal." Tun sniffed. "You called it *home*. Again."

"Go find us a campsite."

"I . . . am going to wander the woods tonight. As my other self. You select a campsite, and I will find you in the morning. You will come to no danger. I promise."

"Before you go, can I ask a question?"

He paused, tilted his head expectantly.

"What did you see or hear while you held that trap open? Any words between me and Dalius?"

"Nothing. Should I have?"

"We . . . spoke. Somehow." She swallowed. "He offered to free Maurenia if I would let a piece of him live on."

"You didn't . . ."

"Of course I didn't. But I hoped that killing him *would* free her. He sensed that and taunted me with it. Said it wouldn't."

"Do you believe him?"

"I don't know what to believe. I know that I want to run all the way up there and find out . . ."

"But you can't, because you need to be back in Lone Pine." Tun came a few steps closer. "The gap between what we *want* and what we *must do* is where we learn who we are, Aelis."

There was nothing Aelis could or would say to that. He strode off into the darkness, quickly disappearing into the trees, and she finished her work.

Her initial impulse was that she did not want to make camp so near this crumbled tower, but a quick sweep aided by the dark moon above revealed nothing she should be frightened of, so she busied herself making a small fire, setting alarm wards, building the shelter, and preparing blankets.

Just before Aelis drifted off to sleep, as she ran through the events of her battle with Dalius, she suddenly remembered that Voice that had echoed her commands.

"You are dead," she had said, and something, she dared not imagine what, had agreed with her and exerted its power on her behalf. Her eyes shot open and looked up at the hide walls and wooden rods of the shelter.

"Onoma," she whispered, unaccustomed to prayer and not finding one rising from her memories. "Was that . . . was . . ."

The thought remained unformed as sleep overwhelmed her.

32

TREASURE

Tun found her an hour after sunrise. She was circling the tower sweeping away dirt and pine needles with the end of her walking stick. He deliberately crunched a few steps; she knew he could creep up on her silently if he chose.

"Looking for more bones?"

"No, I think we got them all."

"What are you going to do with them, anyway?"

"Feed them one by one into my calcination oven, breaking those that are too large to fit, and reduce them to dust."

"And then?"

"Wait for strong winds and toss the dust, by the handful, into the air, and pray to Onoma there won't be two specks of it touching two other specks anywhere."

"Good. Then . . . what are you doing *here*?"

"Poking around," Aelis said. "If this was the place the pact was kept, the place where Errithsuns came to meet their patron and make bargains, there might be treasure."

At that moment, her stick poked straight through something that gave in with a creak of rotted wood.

Tun and Aelis quickly swept away the dirt to reveal a wooden door cunningly camouflaged beneath dyed cloth, making it quite unlikely anyone who didn't know the door was there would find it.

Aelis's stick had punched right through the door, though there was still a small rusted lock holding it closed. Tun dealt with that by grasping it with one hand, giving it a good yank, and ripping the lock and handles clear off. Aelis pushed it open and looked down the narrow stairway into the musty darkness within.

"He had a cellar," she said. "Why don't I have a cellar?"

"Do you want a cellar? I'm sure the town could dig you one if you asked."

"It's the only place to store good wine," Aelis said. "Going to get started on one as soon as we get back." She took a step toward the stairs only to be stopped by Tun's gentle hand on her shoulder.

"Are you quite sure you want to go in there?"

"I'm an Abjurer, Tun. Show me a crumbling place that might be full of treasure and I *definitely* want to go into it." She patted his hand, then clipped her alchemy lamp to her belt, turned it on high, and went down below.

It was bigger than she expected, dug out well beyond the limits of the tower itself and walled in stone.

"It's here," she told herself. "It's the only place that makes sense."

There were piles of clothing, much of it well made, even luxurious, though now stained, reeking, and moldy. Fine fur robes and soft hide jackets lay strewn on the dirt floor.

There was junk in heaps and in crates: broken crockery of all sorts, tarnished cutlery, wood carvings half-finished and abandoned, rusting tools. There was also an odd assortment of musical instruments: a basket full of ouds and whistles, a lute with several broken strings, and at least a few sets of pipes, their bags rotting and falling away. She was put in mind of Mahlhewn's Vault, only far more pitiful.

"No books," she said as she swept the place. But she was only getting started. There were three beds rolled up against the wall. She slit the sacking of each one and was startled when she found them filled with what had once been fine down. "Be a terrible place to store books anyway."

Finally, the hope within her dying but not completely extinguished, she turned to the walls. Brackets for candles were set about the place, and she laid her stick against one to keep her place, then circled the entire cellar, pulling on each one. One did begin to give way, but her cackle of triumph died when it became clear she had just pulled a stone free with a hail of crumbled mortar.

She picked up her stick again and punched the wall in frustration. She'd been so certain.

Something about the sound of her fist thudding against the stone made her try it again, though more lightly.

"I wouldn't do too much violence to those stones if I were you," Tun said from the top of the stairs, his voice echoing. "This place doesn't look any sturdier than when you went down there."

Aelis ignored his warning and dug her fingers around the stone she'd struck, then tapped. Her fingertips found seams. Tamping down her rising excitement, she pulled the stone free.

Behind it were several closed bags, atop which rested a smaller burlap sack bulging with a hard rectangular shape. She peeled the sack away and there it was, the blue-dyed leather of the binding. She pulled it reverently free and looked at it with a deep sigh of relief.

Dwergoch's *Wards and Combat Abjurations for Sword or Axe*. She stroked the leather binding, its color matched perfectly to the blue slashes on the sleeves of all her robes. She opened it; here and there was a fingerprint or a smudge, but the book was intact. She hadn't seen it since she'd had her first interview with Dalius when she'd thought him a harmless, powerless hedge wizard.

The sacks it lay on clinked promisingly when she shifted them. "Although any coin in there is tainted by how he came by it," she said out loud.

That does not mean any of it is literally cursed. And if it's not, it could do a great deal of good for folk in Lone Pine. Or as restitution to the rest of his family.

"Fine. But I'm examining all of it, down to brass halves and glass beads, before I distribute any of it."

"Are you talking to yourself?" Tun called down.

"It's the only way I get intelligent answers out here in the forest primeval," Aelis called back.

She tucked the book under her arm and grabbed all the sacks, then hustled back up the stairs.

"Did you find what you were looking for?" Tun was inspecting one of his hard corn biscuits before biting off a piece.

She showed him the book. "Just felt like it must've gone somewhere."

"How'd it get here?"

"Dalius stole it," Aelis said, "back when I first arrived and he seemed just a harmless old hedge wizard. Probably stored it here as the safest place. But he also read it." She flipped the book open to a page of sword form illustrations, her own notations filling up the margins. "This is why he knew to get my sword out of my hand the first time he attacked me. Knew exactly what I'd do and how fast." She closed the book. "And that's why I came here to fight him as a Necromancer, not an Abjurer. I *told* you I could lure him into coming for my sword again, get him close enough to plant my dagger."

"Yes, yes," Tun said, "I know I am unlikely to hear the end of it."

"Of course," Aelis said, slipping the book carefully into her rucksack, then bending for the sacks of coin she had dropped onto the ground, "if my hired woodsman hadn't hooted three times like a barn owl, none of it would've worked."

"Barred owl," Tun said, with the weary end of not quite infinite patience. "Your *hired* woodsman? On what terms?"

"You're wearing quite a lot of gold around your neck . . ."

"And I recall that the wizard who gave it to me said that after three days of wearing it, I should get rid of it as quickly as possible, because the older and more powerful enchantments would realign."

In answer, Aelis hefted one of the sacks she'd hauled out of the cellar closer to him and let it fall open.

"You sure you want coin that came out of that place?" He tossed the rest of the corn biscuit into his mouth.

"I will look over it with every magical instrument and process at my disposal, and I don't intend to keep it. I'll use some of it to help get Warrun and Gerrin's families established. The rest could become a kind of . . . common fund for Lone Pine."

"Who would administer that fund?"

"Their Warden, obviously."

"Should there be a disinterested third party to make certain it does not go to buying wine?"

"If it did, it would be *public* wine," Aelis said.

Tun laughed, and they set off.

33

LETTER WRITING

At the start of their second day's walk from Dalius's tower, Tun suddenly pulled up and motioned Aelis to a stop. "You can find your way from here, yes?"

Aelis turned to him, too surprised at the question to answer it.

He looked away from her, then back. "If I leave you here, can you find your way back to Lone Pine?"

"Where are you going?"

"You want to know if Maurenia is free. Traveling alone, I can get there and back much faster than I can with you."

"I've always kept up . . ."

"As the bear, Aelis, I can make eighty, a hundred miles a *day*."

"Ah." She paused. "Give me five minutes to write a letter."

"Take ten."

Aelis unlimbered her rucksack and dug in it for paper and writing stick, two things she never traveled without. *If Maurenia had been here, she would've told me this was unnecessary,* she thought, then knelt and wrote quickly on her upraised knee.

> Maurenia
>
> *Have killed Dalius. Permanently, this time. Thought it might free you but I think I would know by now if it had. Have asked for relevant books and supplies. If there is anything you're short of, anything you need or want, tell Tun and I'll bring it as soon as I can.*

Aelis paused here and thought carefully over what to say next.

> *Don't give up on this. I won't rest until you're free.*

She wanted to write about how much paper she'd wasted, how many nights she had struggled against sleep while trying to find a new angle, that she'd trade herself if she could. Then she drew a line through *this* and wrote *me* above it. She signed the letter only with an *A*, folded it, and handed it to Tun, who slipped it into one of his capacious pockets.

"If you see Emilie, tell her I will only miss one chess engagement," he said. Before she could reply, he changed before her eyes into the gigantic brown bear, his hide flecked with gray. It was the first time she'd seen him do so without being under threat. There was no violence promised, no roar of challenge; a man had been standing before her, and now a bear did, and both were her friend. This time, no part of her quailed in fear, no remnant of ancient instinct sent her scrambling for a weapon. She reached out a hand toward him and he stood silently, watching her with those eyes that were still somehow Tun's, and she laid her hand against his coarse fur.

"Thank you, Tunbridge," she said. "I am glad to know you. I am lucky to have you as a friend."

The bear let out a huge snort, then turned and loped off into the woods. Aelis watched him go, grateful that at least in this form, he couldn't disappear so easily.

◆   ◆   ◆

The next morning, Aelis was somewhat shocked to find that Warrun and Gerrin had done exactly as she had asked and that they'd arrived in Lone Pine well before she did. Her first indication was seeing Warrun, wearing better boots but still his much-patched gray-and-blue-paneled, gold-threaded shirt, clumsily wielding a shovel under Martin's direction in a garden patch—or what was now clearly *becoming* a garden patch—behind the inn. Warrun looked miserable, but he had a sheen of honest sweat on his brow, and Martin worked alongside him, occasionally showing him how to use the tool better.

This might just work, she thought. Inside the inn, Rus was polishing his bar as usual, but Gerrin was also there pushing a whisk broom around the tables and benches. He still had on his once-fine yellow shirt under an apron, but like his brother outside, was wearing better, though obviously hand-me-down, boots.

"Warden," Gerrin muttered, tugging his forelock as she came in.

"We'll have none of that here, Gerrin," Aelis said firmly. "You can call me Warden or Aelis, as it please you, but there's no bowing, scraping, forelock tugging, m'lady-ing, heel-clicking, or saluting here in Lone Pine. The folk made that all pretty clear when I arrived, even if I'd been inclined to ask."

In the solitude of her tower and halfway into a bottle, Aelis might have admitted to herself that she had expected at least a *little* bowing and scraping. But now, as then, it seemed utterly wrong, even coming from a man working off a debt of theft.

"Understood, Ae . . . Warden," Gerrin said, smiling tentatively. "Don't know 'bout using your first name . . . yet."

Aelis set her too-heavy pack down against the bar. By the time she looked up, a small pile of silver coins had appeared in a neat stack in front of her. Rus was polishing a mug, his eyes focused on his work.

"The horses all well?" Aelis asked.

"Aye," Rus replied.

"Are you going to want an assize, all that formality?"

He flicked a look at Gerrin who was plying the broom with rather more skill than his brother showed with the shovel.

"Don't see that it'd be good for the town," Rus said. "No need to put any more attention on these folk than they'll already have."

"Good. You still want them to work it off, or do you just want some coin?"

"I'm not taking your coin, Aelis," Rus said. He still ignored the pile of silver on the bar. So did Aelis.

"Not mine. If it belongs to anyone, it belongs to them," she said, jerking her chin back at Gerrin. "And I'm not sure it's safe yet. But if it is, it'll be trivial to pay off whatever damages they did, get them houses built, and by this time next year, they won't be Errithsuns. Just Lone Pine folk."

"I'm not going to try to disagree," he said. "You'll just talk me into it." He placed the now-clean mug on the bar and set his rag over his shoulder, a sign, Aelis had learned, that he was moving on to new business. "The Dobruszes mean to leave tomorrow; only held out this long for your return because they thought you might want to place orders. They're out for a ramble, scouting the road, I think. Want to beat the rains."

"The rains?"

"Oh, the sun we've had the past few days is just a lie. Spring isn't really spring till we get a solid two weeks of rain."

Aelis let herself think for just one moment of the sun-drenched vineyards and cities of Tirraval without, she hoped, letting any yearning show on her face.

"Then I've got a lot of work to do." She was bone weary. Her ankle throbbed. Every tool she needed was in her tower.

"Rus, may I *please* borrow a horse to get to my tower? I'll bring it back later today."

"'Course, Aelis." He slid the pile of coins toward her. "But take these with you."

Aelis knew she'd lost some small battle of wills when she scooped the coins up, and gods but she hated *asking* for help.

But she rode a placid, easy-stepping horse the mile and change back to her tower, and on reflection, that might have been a kind of victory too.

✦ ✦ ✦

To feel more like herself again, the first thing Aelis did was make a list.

1. *Letters and orders to go south.*
2. *Deal with the bones.*
3. *Make rounds, esp for Arbeth's pregnancy.*
4. *Orrery.*

She put that list on the cleared top of her worktable, got out parchment, ink, pen, and paper, and spent three hand-cramping hours writing as fast and as neatly as she could manage. The first page she wrote on was the current one with Maurenia's name at the top. After she added the right number of slashes, she found her list of plans and crossed out *Kill Dalius*.

Then it was on to less important things, like her official letters to Cabal Command in Lascenise detailing how she had destroyed Dalius. She left out Tun's name, referring to him only as a hired man, but was otherwise truthful in every detail—the improvised spirit trap; the capture of whatever had animated Dalius; the planned destruction of his bones in her calcination oven. She also included detailed reports, including diagrams and a precise accounting of the orders she had cast, for her self-surgery on her ankle, as had been demanded by the terse return statements through her orrery.

Then she began a separate cover with shopping lists. From her initial tests done on the road, she determined that all the money recovered from Dalius's tower was clean, and she had ideas for things that might benefit the village. Tools, bows, extra seed corn, and the like; she left space on that page for anything she could add after checking in with people before the next morning.

For herself, she wrote out an order for six cases of wine, then made it eight. Aelis also set aside a pouch of tri-crowns with a note to buy as many stone of coffee beans as the gold could get at market rates, as well as a pot and a grinder. She might not have had the room to bring it on her initial journey to Lone Pine, but if she had friends carrying the post, by Elisima's Eyes, she wasn't going to go without any longer than she must.

With a smile, she set aside a similar amount to buy tea, a gift for Tun.

She gathered up all the letters and rode back into town, arriving in time to find a crowd gathering at the inn for evening beer and Martin's cooking.

She was pleased she'd had the foresight to bring a writing case with the supplies to write the letters she knew they were going to ask for.

Aelis exchanged greetings here and there, promising to write letters after she'd eaten, but sought out gray-bearded Matthias first, easing onto a bench next to him.

"How's Arbeth doing?"

"Time's comin' soon, Warden," he said, beaming. "I'll be a grandfather in the next month."

"I'll come out to your farm in the morning, make sure all is well."

"Emilie's been in to look in on her," Matthias said, then leaned closer. "She was none too happy to hear that Arbeth wants you to oversee the birth, though," he whispered in Aelis's ear.

Aelis was surprised at how happy she was to hear that, and not just because she still couldn't find it in her to *like* Emilie much.

The next hour was filled with more hand-cramping writing. As night fell and the fire was built up and the lamps lit, her list of what to buy for the village grew to include an anvil and some simple smithing tools; it happened that Harlond, Matthias's son-in-law, had learned something of the trade during his army service and was already the town's resident pot-mender and tool-sharpener and now thought he might be able to do more. She also amended her own list for new reagent cores and filaments for her alchemy lamp, which was flickering alarmingly.

Aelis was just about to tuck into a platter of cheese and sausage and a small cup of brandy when a voice shrieked her name and thin arms wrapped around her.

"Hello, Pips," she squeaked through the half-strangling embrace.

The girl clambered onto the bench next to her and began peppering her with questions, most of which Aelis did her best to answer.

"Yes, Pips," she said at last, wearily, eyeing her food longingly, "I did have a kind of magical battle, but I really don't want to talk about it. It wasn't very exciting."

"No Rains of Fire? No Shocking Coils?"

Aelis shook her head and finally took the chance to take a huge bite of cheese.

"Not even any pits opening in the ground or hurled stones?"

Aelis held up her hand while she chewed. "I'm not an invoker or a conjurer, Phillipa. You know that."

Aelis took advantage of the momentary silence of the disappointed girl to look over the crowd. Gerrin and Warrun and their wives sat alone on benches, silent, obviously snubbed.

"Pips," Aelis said, putting an arm on the girl's shoulder. "You see those folk?"

"Aye. Uncle Otto told me I shouldn't talk to 'em."

"Didn't he also tell you not to talk to me, once?"

The girl nodded.

"Did you listen to him then?"

"No."

"Then don't listen to him now. They have children. Younger than you, but they're going to need someone to show them around, get them used to life in Lone Pine . . ."

Aelis had barely finished the sentence before Pips had slipped off the bench and ran to the Errithsuns.

Aelis smiled, ate her dinner, got a pot of beer, and went up to the Dobruszes' room.

Timmuk and Andresh were engaged in last-minute packing of their gear, but they weren't so absorbed in it they couldn't stop for a drink.

When Aelis handed them her packets of letters, Timmuk took them with a frown.

"Provided the Crowns haven't revoked our Warrant for the Post," he grumbled.

Next to him, Andresh rumbled something in dwarfish, and Timmuk threw him a long stare, then looked back to Aelis.

"My brother reminds me that the probable value of certain gems recovered from the Mahlhewn Vault is likely to be worth . . . how many?" Andresh held up three fingers. "Three years of Royal Post Warrants. So even this late, we're doing well on this trip."

"I hope that means no more of them are going to be crushed and thrown at my feet."

It was hard to tell beneath so much beard, but she *thought* she saw Andresh flush.

"Andresh and I talked about that," Timmuk said. "And I spoke to him of the pages you showed me. We want our friend free, and we know you want the same thing; it's just that you're the only one of us who can do anything about it. We don't take well to that."

"To that end," Aelis said, digging out the small book from her writing case. "Please tell me this is some kind of ancient dwarf charactery." Timmuk took it gingerly and opened the first page, but was already shaking his head.

"Nothing I recognize." He held it toward Andresh, who shook his head after a glance as well.

"I was really hoping this was some old dwarfish," she said, flipping to the drawing of Rhunival's rod. "This book *must* have insight on whatever he was, whatever happened to Maurenia. But I can't even begin to guess what language it's written in." *Maybe if I stare at it long enough it'll start to make sense*, she thought as she tucked it away again.

There were no emotionally fraught goodbyes when she left that night. Those brothers weren't made for that, and neither was she. Both of them shook Aelis's hand, of course, and Timmuk promised that they'd see to all the goods she'd ordered and bring them back. He did give her hand a hard tug so that she was forced to lean close to his ear.

"Get our Renia free, Warden. Do that before next our wagon pulls up this road, and I'll put every coin back into your hand. You understand me?"

"Timmuk," Aelis said, steady and calm, "I would give every coin that's ever passed my palm for her freedom. There is no inducement anyone can offer me that will speed me faster than my own conscience." She almost said *heart* there at the last moment, but she didn't feel the need to reveal quite that much of herself to Timmuk Dobrusz.

34

PRIORITIES

Rus was waiting for her outside with the same horse she'd ridden that afternoon saddled and ready.

Gods bless him for not making me ask, Aelis thought as she rode away from the inn. She wanted nothing more than sleep; her ankle and her writing hand were competing to see which appendage could be more painful. But she had one more task which she could not put off, not for a whole night.

She lit up her tower; this was not work she wanted to do in darkness, though she didn't want to look too closely at what she did, either. She also made a note to thank whoever had built up her woodpile, which had her calcination oven flaring in no time.

For the first time since she'd bought them after her fourth year in the College of Necromancy, Aelis took out her bone saws. Finest dwarven steel, ebony handles, brass fittings; they were beautiful tools and a pleasure to hold, if one didn't think too much about what they were *for*. She improvised a clamp at the edge of a table, spread a drop cloth on the floor beneath it, and got to work.

◆　◆　◆

An hour before dawn, she was soaked in sweat. Her shoulder was sore and her hand could barely close. Her tower was sweltering from the heat of the calcination oven.

But outside, a strong wind was kicking up, and Aelis carried her largest bowl filled with a mound of dust. She made three circles around her tower, and at each cardinal point, she forced her cramping fingers to lift a handful of dust and let the wind carry it, intoning prayers to Onoma and Stregon the entire time.

Only when it was done did she sleep, dreamlessly, painlessly, well past the middle of the day.

◆　◆　◆

A month later, the packed snow had given way to brown grass and cold, hard mud. It rained as much as Rus promised it would, but Aelis still made her regular trips into the village, three times a week, to treat any and all afflictions and illnesses. The sheet with Maurenia's name was replaced with a second, with a running total written at the top, fresh marks made underneath it.

Eventually, the rain stopped, and her trips became more frequent and easier. While it was not what Aelis could bring herself to consider warm, spring didn't turn out to be a total lie. When the knock at her door came, she snatched up the kit she'd packed in preparation and opened the door on a breathless Harlond, stammering and wheezing.

"Let's go," she said, smiling at him.

He'd come running; Matthias and Harlond and Arbeth were not the kind of people to own riding horses, and likely enough whatever animal they did own was needed to do different work that day. Sensing that she could easily outpace the heavy-breathing farmer and would-be smith, she asked, "Do you want me to wait for you or . . ."

"Go!"

She took off. Running was never a pleasure for her, but she hated not being good at anything she had to do, so she ran easily beyond the village, then another mile to the farmhouse Matthias shared with his daughter and her husband, the kit bouncing on her back.

Aelis didn't sprint; she needed to arrive steady of wind and hand, and she did. Emilie was standing outside the house, her arms bare and her blond hair pulled back atop her freshly shaved sides.

There was a brief cry from inside the house, but Emilie didn't move, only stared into the house.

"She's been asking for you," Emilie said.

"And I'm here, like I said I would be." Aelis swallowed, gave up on trying to force Emilie to look down at her; she might never have Urizen's trick that way, and besides, it wasn't worth it just then. "I've never delivered a baby before. I take it you have."

Emilie nodded, *a little smugly*, Aelis thought.

"Then don't be shy about telling me what you think," Aelis said. "But don't try to get between me and my patient, alright?"

Emilie nodded her assent, and they went inside.

It was not, all things considered, a difficult birth. Aelis had a potion prepared to help block out some of the pain, and she'd been running over Enchantments she thought might be useful in the process. With her swordbelt laid aside—she still stuck to Urizen's maxim to always wear the sword—and her sleeves rolled up, she plied her dagger and her wand through motions she'd studied but never performed herself. Once or twice, Emilie ran her long fingers over Arbeth's taut belly and made suggestions about positioning or offered opinions on how much longer things might take. The only real complication came an hour in, with Arbeth clutching Emilie's arm and Aelis considering another Enchantment. Harlond's voice rang from the doorway, and it took him two or three tries to get through Aelis's concentration and make himself heard.

"Warden Aelis . . . there's men in the village. Other wardens, they say, asking for you."

One part of Aelis's mind couldn't imagine what other wardens were doing in Lone Pine, much less why they were asking for her. But she was in her physician's role right now, and nothing short of catastrophe would change that.

"Tell them to wait," she called absently.

"I told them you were seeing to a birth. Said they didn't care, that you were needed."

Emilie leaned over. "I can manage from here if . . ."

"No," Aelis said, startling herself with the force of her conviction and the burst of anger at being interrupted. "One moment, Arbeth. Just one."

She marched outside and eyed Harlond carefully.

"Tell them I'm with a patient who needs me more than they do. Tell them I don't care if they're Archmagisters, that I don't care if it's the entire fucking *council* of Archmagisters come to beg me on bended knee for some favor. They will *fucking wait.*"

"How long?" Harlond asked.

"As long as the baby wants them to," Aelis said and turned on a heel, going back into the house.

It was the better part of another hour until the baby arrived and was crying her first in Arbeth's bedroom, her voice loud and echoing out into the farmyard. Aelis had insisted on open windows, over Emilie's objections. Only with the baby swaddled and comfortable in her dazed mother's arms, and the even more dazed Harlond and Matthias by their side, did Aelis allow herself to think about the other wardens. She cleaned her hands twice, first with water and rag and then with a Necromantic order that left her hands tingling, and approached Emilie, standing just outside the bedroom.

"Emilie, can I clean your hands?"

The other woman held up her wet arms to show them already clean.

"I mean . . . magically. It's just called the Clean Fingers."

Emilie's mouth tightened. "Why?"

"Because there's a lot of dangerous substances left on them that water won't clean, that you and I can't see. I'm going to ask you to stay here and watch over them while I go into the village to spread the news and see to whoever these other wardens are. I would rest easier if you allowed it, and it would be better for Arbeth and her child."

Emilie twisted her lips but held out her hands. Aelis cast the spell and watched as Emilie shook her fingers.

"Thank you," Aelis said, and buckled on her swordbelt. She didn't run. Whoever these visitors were, they were going to wait for her time, by Onoma.

She noticed the carriage—not a wagon, but a carriage, on raised wheels over silver fenders that she knew were alchemically treated as soon as she saw them—from quite a distance. Aelis didn't have to look for the escutcheon on the side that she knew would be there; staff and sword crossed under a book done in silver against the red-painted doors. Gooseflesh rose all up and down her arms. The horses were still hitched, matched dappled white and gray, and the carriage seemed to sit more lightly than it should have on its springs. A red-coated driver still sat on the box and leapt down as she approached. Another, taller, blue-coated figure unfolded itself and stepped down into the mud. Even from afar, though, Aelis could see the slashes of red in the sleeves and breast of the long coat the figure wore. And as they advanced, Aelis realized the Invoker and Abjurer she was looking at was an elf, though not anyone she knew.

"Warden Aelis de Lenti un Tirraval," the elf called out. "You kept us waiting rather a long time. I thought I told your man that our business was *urgent*."

"Not as urgent as mine," Aelis answered flatly. "And he's not *my* man. Just a freeholder whose name you didn't bother to learn." Heads poked out of the inn's windows; the door creaked open. Rus, and to her shock, Martin, were at the head of the crowd coming out to watch.

"What urgent business could you *possibly* have in the midst of all this mud?" the elf said.

Aelis decided not to answer and met his eyes with a steady stare. She was not as calm as she looked; her heart was hammering, her mind racing. Whatever these wardens had to tell her, it couldn't be *good* news.

The elf sighed dismissively and strode toward her, pulling a scroll from inside his coat.

"I have recall orders for you, Warden de Lenti," he said. "I am Warden Amadin, and my companion is Warden Rhovel. He will be staying on in your place. I am to accompany you to Lascenise as immediately as you can ready yourself to travel."

"What?" Aelis reached for the scroll, a sick feeling in her stomach. "Why does the Lyceum recall me so soon into my appointment? Was it regarding the messages I sent . . ."

"Pardon me, Warden," Amadin said, his lips compressing quizzically. "I do not come from the Lyceum and neither do these orders. Rather, they are from Cabal Command. Your recall is temporary. The orders will have more detail."

No longer listening to him, Aelis thumbed open the seal on the scroll without even glancing at it for authenticity. She skipped over the verbiage at the beginning, the name of the Cabal Commander in Lascenise—technically her regional commander, but far enough away to be little more than a rumor. At last, several paragraphs in, she got to the root of the matter.

> . . . recall is effected and Warden Aelis de Lenti un Tirraval is required to stand as an Advocate for the Defense for a fellow Warden facing charges of Malfeasance, Misuse of Power, Assault by Magic, and Murder by Magic. You are forthwith commanded to present yourself to Cabal Command at Lascenise as soon as feasible upon receipt of these orders, which were magically sealed by Cabal Divination . . .

Aelis reeled. "Advocate for the Defense? Why?"

"They do not tell me, Warden. I am a messenger. These things are often assigned at random."

"Who am I to advocate for?" Aelis's mind rattled with the possibilities and came up with none.

Amadin leaned forward, whispering conspiratorially with a measure of fear on his face.

"Warden Emeritus Bardun Jacques."

THE END OF NECROBANE, BOOK II OF THE WARDEN
TO BE CONTINUED IN BOOK III: ADVOCATE

ACKNOWLEDGMENTS

Like its predecessor, this book has my name on it but many hands made it real.

Thanks remain due to Ren and Paul and everyone else at Janklow & Nesbit. Also to Oliver, Mal, Diana, Jeff, Rima, Rachel, Katy, Desirae, and everyone else at Tor/Macmillan, thank you for your hard work. To Lindsey for bringing Aelis, and everyone else, to life in audio.

Thanks to the beta readers: Yeager, Josh, Jason, Jacob, Ceejae, Stephanie.

To the editor cats who said goodbye before this book made it into the world; Hector, who was always happy just to be a part of things; Westley, who always made sure I knew it was time to go to bed, but would never go until I did. Both of them spent uncountable hours on my lap, at my side, or simply napping on the floor while I worked. And to Rose of Sharon Cassidy, who is still a little uncertain of her duties but still carries them out as best she can.

Thanks to my family.

Thanks to every reader who read, reviewed, or just talked about *The Warden* to their friends and family.

Though the word is far too small, thanks to L, who is the world and all six of its moons.